# Review

Stefan Vučak writes this intriguing novel using all of his imagination. Nothing is spared or left out of this Science Fiction thriller! I was on the edge of my seat with suspense wanting to know what was going to happen next, and not wanting to put this book down. This is a must read for any Science Fiction buff who craves action, adventure, mystery, suspense, politics, and a love for the unknown. Stefan is very descriptive in this novel and leaves no stone unturned, which is very satisfying for the reader to comprehend and imagine that they are there in the story, waiting to see what comes next!

Readers' Favorite

I0592569

# Books by Stefan Vučak

**General Fiction:**
*Cry of Eagles*
*All the Evils*
*Towers of Darkness*
*Strike for Honor*
*Proportional Response*
*Legitimate Power*
*Autumn Leaves*
*All My Sunsets*
*F/X-26*
*28th Amendment*
*Night Sirens*
*Broken Rose*

**Shadow Gods Saga:**
*In the Shadow of Death*
*Against the Gods of Shadow*
*A Whisper from Shadow*
*Shadow Masters*
*Immortal in Shadow*
*With Shadow and Thunder*
*Through the Valley of Shadow*
*Guardians of Shadow*

**Science Fiction:**
*Fulfillment*
*Lifeliners*

**Non-Fiction:**
*Writing Tips for Authors*

Contact at:
www.stefanvucak.com

# A WHISPER FROM SHADOW

by

**Stefan Vučak**

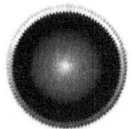

# Dedication

*To Jan ... a fellow traveler through life*

# Acknowledgments

Carina Nebula – Credit: NASA, ESA, and the Hubble SM4 ERO Team.

Comalcalco site map, courtesy of Claudia Espinoza, National Anthropology Museum, Mexico City.

My thanks to Professor Alan Walker, Penn State University, for information on fungal diseases.

Cover art by Laura Shinn.
http://laurashinn.yolasite.com

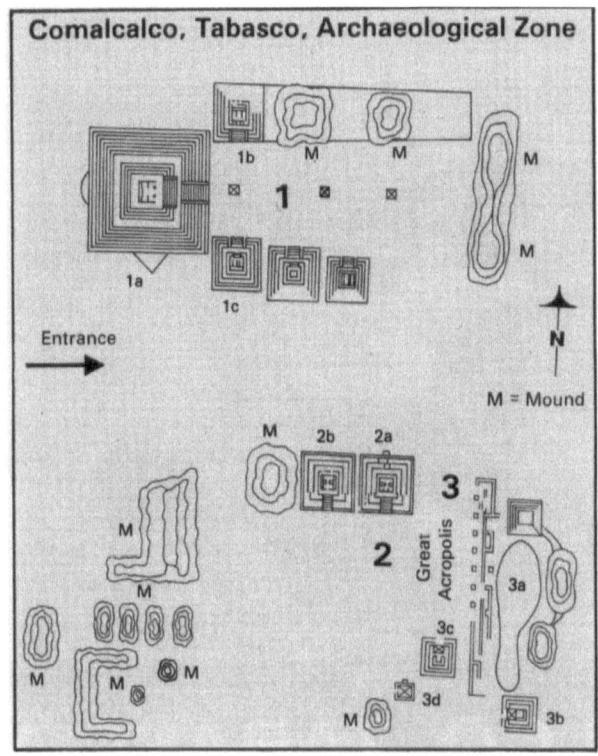

**Comalcalco, Tabasco, Archaeological Zone**

M = Mound

# Map of the Serrll Combine

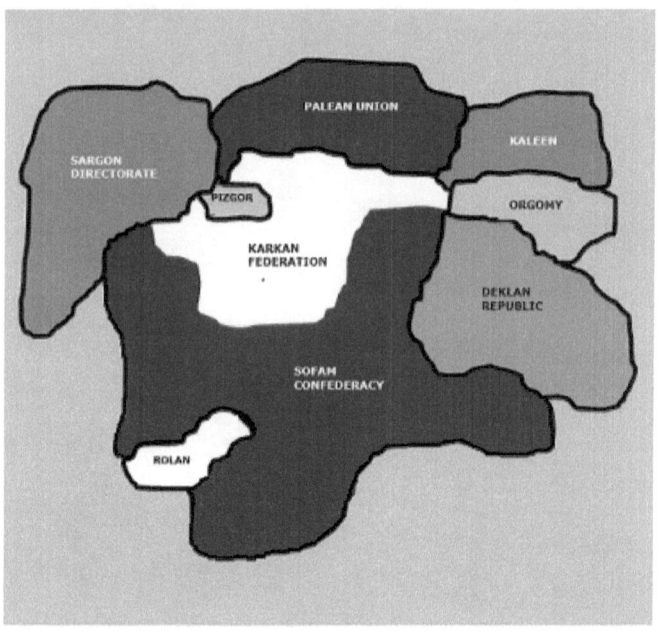

# Composition of the Serrll Combine

The 247 star systems that make up the Serrll Combine is an association of six interstellar power blocks, split between two rival camps—the Servatory Party and the Revisionists. Each star system has a single representative in Captal's General Assembly from which members are elected to the ruling ten-seat Executive Council. Seats are based on a percentage of systems occupied by each power block in relation to the total number of systems in the Serrll Combine.

| Name | No of Star Systems | Percentage of Total | Executive Council Seats |
|---|---|---|---|
| Sofam Confederacy | 83 | 34 | 4 |
| Deklan Republic | 19 | 8 | 1 |
| Palean Union | 28 | 11 | 1 |
| Karkan Federation | 46 | 19 | 2 |
| Sargon Directorate | 32 | 12 | 1 |
| Independents: | | 15 | 1 |
| - Kaleen | 8 | | |
| - Rolan | 5 | | |
| - Orgomy | 6 | | |
| - Pizgor | 3 | | |
| - Other systems | 17 | | |
| **General Assembly** | **247** | **100** | **10** |
| | | | |
| Outposts | 40 | | |
| Protectorates | 34 | | |

**Principal political blocks:**

| | |
|---|---|
| Revisionist Party: | Palean Union |
| | Deklan Republic |
| | Sofam Confederacy |
| Servatory Party: | Karkan Federation |
| | Sargon Directorate |
| | Nonaligned Independents |

**Composition of the Executive Council:**

| | |
|---|---|
| Security Council | Bureau of Colonial and Protectorate Affairs |
| | Bureau of Defense |
| | Bureau of Cultural Affairs |
| Administrative Council | Bureau of Administrative Affairs |
| | Bureau of Justice |
| Economics Council | Bureau of Economic Affairs |
| | Bureau of Technology and Development |
| Central Planning Council | Bureau of Central Planning and Development |

*"Here, then, is the beginning of when it was decided to make men, and when what must enter into the flesh of men was sought."*

Part III
Chapter I
Popol Vuh

# Prologue

In a burst of scintillation the ship emerged from subspace high above the planetary plane, beyond the gravity well of the small yellow star.

The ship's secondary shield grid flared in violet discharge, then stabilized. It paused, oriented itself and moved deliberately down into the inner system toward the bright points of a double world. It slowed as the twin horns began to resolve out of blackness: one gray and the other brilliant blue-white. The ship made one terminator orbit around the moon before moving toward the dark side to hang above a narrow valley of the north pole where it waited. Below, twisted masts reached up amid the radial pattern of the base. Shrouded in shadow, the base lay dark and silent, cold like the cliffs that surrounded it. After a time the ship rose and slowly moved away.

It climbed above the horizon to be greeted by a blue crescent of a sleeping world. The northern ice cap shrouded under untidy clouds stretching their twisted whorls into night. In a burst of speed, the ship vanished into the black shadow of the waiting world. It moved into a polar orbit as the planet shifted ponderously beneath it. It made a single circuit, looking for the sentinel cruiser, noting the scanning sensor probes coming up from the ground. It found the cruiser hanging above the equator. The ship maneuvered until both flew silently side by side in a locked orbit.

* * *

"Status?" Kukll-nn demanded with an impatient growl.
Oryana lifted her head gracefully and looked where he

stood before the high window, hands clasped tightly behind his back.

"They're sending down a landing boat," she said, her voice soft and musical, now slightly breathless. Her black eyebrows were arched and traced a thin line above large brown eyes. She pulled at her small pointed chin with a slim, delicate hand and turned back to the main display plate positioned above the sloping consoles. The tactical grid dissolved and the image reformed into a wide-angle pattern. She glanced absently at the small repeater plates and sighed dreamily.

"A ship from home! I wonder how much things have changed," she mused, eyes misty, lost in memory. Absently, she fondled the long, white tresses that spilled across her shoulders. Long hair cascaded down the middle of her head, streaked with twin bands of dark gray of a mature Deklan female.

Kukll-nn stood silent beside the window, his eyes far in another reality. The observatory gave him an excellent view of the city below. The lake, its black waters lapping softly against the massive stone walls, stretched north and west as far as the eye could see. Shrouded in blue haze the mountains arched toward a violet sky. Ice and snow capped the peaks, shouldering the lower slopes. How fragile, he thought, almost brittle in their stark and serene beauty. So much like his native Kaplan. He shook his head, surprised at the nostalgia that overcame him.

"Recall acknowledged?"

"All continental stations reported in two minutes ago," he heard Oryana say behind him. "The intruder has matched with our ship and is maintaining neutral status."

The Center quiet, waiting, the stillness interrupted by the whisper of computer reports and an occasional shuffling of feet from the watchstanders.

"Sachmm-nn?"

For a few seconds, more silence. Oryana stared at Kukll's back, then climbed out of her seat and walked slowly to the window to stand beside him. Following his gaze, she watched the natives busy at their work. Lord of this world, it would all now end. They expected this, and some probably even welcomed it. As the years marched, the waiting had not grown easier.

She looked at his reflection in the window and the face she saw was hard. A rough face full of slabs, chiseled with deep lines of power and determination. A face used to command. His hair rusty, shot through with patches of white. It had lost some of the gloss that used to make her breath catch. The years had been kind to all of them, she thought as she gazed at him with deep affection. And there have been so many years. Too many perhaps to face what they left behind.

"Do you really think that's necessary?" she asked gently and reached up with her hand, hesitating before touching his shoulder.

He tensed at her touch and turned to look at her, faintly amused. "Don't you? Yes...I can see it in your face. All the years we've spent here have not removed the longing. You still yearn for the worlds of Deklan. And me..." The fire in his black eyes waned and his jaw lifted with resolve. "Those worlds are no longer ours," he grated, each word a blow and she flinched. Slowly, he raised his hand and pointed a stubby finger at the ceiling. "That ship up there hasn't come to help us, remember that. You ask if Sachmm-nn is necessary. We shall see. Now, order it to power up and stand by."

Hurt, she turned to the operator behind one of the consoles. When he nodded to her, she looked at Kukll-nn.

"They have acknowledged," she said stiffly, torn with warring emotions.

They watched the city in silence. After a while, he turned to stare into the deep pools of her eyes and gently brushed her cheek.

"I am sorry, Oryana. I shouldn't have spoken to you like that. It's only—"

"Don't." She clasped his hand and held it. "I understand.

But…" She left it unsaid. Nothing left to say when the yester-days suddenly came crowding.

"We better go and meet them," he said at length and managed a faint smile that didn't touch his eyes.

* * *

The voice from the temple boomed and the people stopped their work and stood silent in the streets, markets, homes and farms. The gods were speaking. Leoichan, High Priest of Tiahunn-cc, heard the voice and listened. As he listened, his excitement grew. When the voice stopped, he ordered the priests to send a message to the king and gather the people to direct them to the star nest. The gods were coming!

Slowly, then with hurried fervor, chanting, the people moved down the broad avenues toward the star nest where the gods would come. The King, the High Priest, the Oracle and the multitude of peasantry waited at the gates of Tiahunn-cc. Black marble doors rumbled as they slid open. Clad in tight red coveralls, Kukll-nn emerged with Oryana at his side dressed in blue. The people held their arms high and sang the names of the two gods. With slow dignity the gods mounted an air chariot and it began to move. The populace shouted and danced and walked with them toward the star nest.

The valley walls fell away and the baked plain opened before them. Leoichan started the sixth chant of observance as he stared in awe at the two metal birds perched on their stone pads, surrounded by spidery towers. The minions of the gods moved about on flat air chariots and Leoichan watched it all and chanted.

Assembled, they murmured and waited, eyes fixed on the heavens from where the gods would come. A deep rumble shook the air and the ground trembled. The heavenly bird glittered in white light high above them. Leoichan began the eleventh chant and the priests around him held their arms high.

# A Whisper from Shadow

Clad with fire and light, it was like a star descending. With thunder that shook the heavens, white smoke billowing, the heavenly bird fell quickly. It slowed and hovered for an instant, roaring in tortured anger, then it touched the pad. The fires stopped and thunder echoed through the hills. Smoke drifted slowly down the valley. In the sudden silence, only the chanting could be heard.

The bird sat there breathing hot air, shimmering in the haze and everyone waited for the gods to emerge. Leoichan turned shyly and smiled at Kukll-nn and Oryana, proud to be near them. They smiled back and he felt warmed in his soul.

A hush fell over the crowd when one of the towers began to slowly move toward the bird. Kukll and Oryana mounted their air chariot and sped quickly down onto the baked plain.

Leoichan watched the chariot stop at the base of the tower. The gods climbed down and stood before the bird, waiting. A box descended within the tower. When it stopped, doors opened and he stood there, tall, his hair bright red and clothing silver. When Kukll-nn saluted, Leoichan gaped, his surprise complete. The other stared back a long time before returning the salute.

* * *

Kukll allowed his hand to fall to his side as his eyes raked over the thin form of his visitor. The man's long hands swayed and his fingers twitched in characteristic agitation. His small yellow eyes darted restlessly as they moved over everything. Hidden behind bushy orange eyebrows, they glinted with cold fire. The face pale white and pinched, fixed with a thin nose. Arrogance and hidden cruelty marked that face. The twin bands of thick red hair were rich and prominent. Kukll decided they weren't going to get along.

"Master Scout Kukll-nn, and my executive officer, First Scout Oryana," Kukll said evenly, trying to keep the distaste out of his voice. The man was a political busybody and the quicker

5

he dealt with him the better. "I see Prima Scout, that the Serrll Combine has not forgotten us after all."

"No, they have not forgotten, Master Scout," the other grated heavily and looked about him pointedly. "I am Virrchaa, on a special Executive Council Mission to look you over."

"Look me over or take me over? I suppose I should be flattered, but after nineteen years, taking into account four time dilation jumps, you'll have to forgive me if the excitement has kind of worn off."

"I should imagine." Virrchaa snorted and swept his hand before him. "Holy Master of Sin, man! What have you done to this world?"

Kukll glanced at the assembled multitude. "I have brought it life."

"I'm not in any mood for your worm shit!" Virr growled and led the way to the sled-pad. "Let's talk."

\* \* \*

"Is that all?" Virr said with icy politeness as his fingers drummed impatiently against the desk.

Kukll nodded and took a sip from a frosted tumbler. "I guess that's about the size of it, Prima Scout."

Virr glared at Oryana, but she became suddenly busy studying her nails. He pushed back his chair and started pacing. Kukll sat back and a faint smile creased his chiseled face. Whatever Virr expected, he certainly didn't like what he found.

With a growl of exasperation, Virr stopped before the wide window. The city below lay spread before him in neat patterns. It looked simple, belying the sophistication of its design.

"You were sent here on a follow-up survey mission," he hissed impatiently and turned to glare at Kukll. "And that was all!"

"That sounded okay nineteen years ago," Kukll pointed out.

# A Whisper from Shadow

Virr pursed his lips. "Look at it from my point of view. I break out of subspace and I think maybe I'm in the wrong system. There is no SC&C, no patrols, nothing. And the moon base? Abandoned. You were sent here to watch them, not mold them!"

Kukll shrugged and reached for the decanter. He filled the tumbler, stared at it for a moment, then looked up, his mouth hard.

"The bases on this world were set up for one reason and one reason only: genetic engineering experiments. Don't tell me you didn't know. So let's drop this indignant posturing nonsense, shall we? We don't need to pretend here."

Virr exhaled and bared his teeth. "I expect a measure of respect from you, Master Scout!"

Kukll laughed. "What are you going to do? Send me home?"

Virr glared, pursed his lips and turned to stare out the window. "They look happy down there. How much do they know?"

Kukll glanced at Oryana. "They know I teach and heal. When necessary, I punish. I leave it at that."

"How many other bases?"

"Two; one farther north and one on the western landmass across the ocean. We had a base on the southern island continent, but we had a reactor accident and were forced to abandon it."

"The natives?"

"They're developing. Not as fast as predicted, though. It's being looked into. The western continent is dry and getting worse. Here, we have a chance and the polar ice is receding."

Virr turned and looked directly at Kukll. "You will shut down all bases and terminate the experiments."

"Does that mean the natives as well?" Kukll asked calmly.

"This doesn't come from me."

"Tell me one thing. If the Executive Council intended to

close us down, why the regular resupply ships? In all my years here, there has never been even a hint of abandoning the project."

"I don't know—"

"Don't give me that! Not after coming all this way. What happened to make everyone suddenly want to salve their conscience? Look at them!" Kukll swept a hand at the window and stood up. "That's an indigenous population and this planet is a protectorate. You're sworn to defend what is here."

Virr smiled grimly. "You're right. The natives will be left alone. They can struggle on as best they can. But this," he said and looked about him, "this has to go and you will return to Captal for a well-deserved promotion and rest."

Kukll glanced at Oryana and chuckled. A mirthless laugh full of irony.

"What do you think of that, my dear?" He looked at Virr and shook his head. "No, Prima Scout. It won't be that easy. Our work here isn't finished yet. Too many things still need to be done to ensure the natives' survival."

"You like playing a god, Kukll?" Virr studied the other man, past the mask of a Serrll officer at the mantle of power radiating from him.

"A god?" Kukll lifted his head in genuine surprise. "You're a fool to think that, Virr. This, for what we left back home? I am prepared to return. We all are. Holy Master of Sin, who wouldn't be? Only if the Mission Plan is maintained and we're replaced. Only if the Mission Plan is maintained," he repeated, his voice flat and uncompromising.

Virr shook his head. "I cannot do that, and you know it. My orders are clear."

"And you don't have the guts to do the right thing."

"Even if I sent a message to the Executive Council pleading your case, my orders will not be rescinded. They don't have any reason to."

"Who the hell cares? By the time you get back, how many

months will have gone?"

"Seventy-three days. We can do two hundred times the speed of light now."

"At max boost perhaps, but you cannot push max for that long. Not all the way to Salina. Anyway, it's long enough for the Council to change its mind. Think, man! This goes beyond mere political expediency, or this experiment would never have been allowed to continue."

"There is nothing I can do," Virr said flatly. "Begin preparation for immediate evacuation, Master Scout."

"I have a ship up there and this place is defended," Kukll said softly.

Virr stared. "You mean that?"

Kukll's eyes were cold with resolve.

* * *

Leoichan watched the air chariot leave the gates of Tiahunn-cc and speed toward the star nest just as the summons arrived from Kukll-nn. He was torn, wanting to watch the air chariot, but the summons could not be ignored. Chewing his lip in frustration, he motioned to his retainers and the little group moved quickly toward the black marble gates.

When he reached the gates they opened with a low groan. With a feeling of religious awe and dread, he walked in. One of the minions greeted him and he indicated to his retainers to wait on him before following. He stood before Kukll-nn and the goddess Oryana many times, but each time he stood in their presence, he felt vulnerable and his soul naked before their gaze. His sins were many and it was never certain how the gods would judge him. He gave an involuntary shudder and hurried after the minion.

The door slid aside and his footsteps were loud in the quiet of the Great Hall. Light streamed in yellow shafts through tall windows and made warm pools through which he walked daintily. The god stood before one of the windows. Oryana, all in blue, sat on the reception dais and smiled at him. He sank to his knees and bowed.

"Your humble servant awaits your word, Lords," he whispered, not daring to breathe.

"Stand, our faithful Leoichan." Oryana's voice soft and clear and sent a tingle of excitement down his spine.

Slowly, he straightened and stood and waited.

Without turning, Kukll said, "Tell the King that all his people must leave Tiahunn-cc immediately. Tell him they must not stop until they've reached Tiukk-ll. Start now," he growled and waved his hand in dismissal.

Leoichan was stunned, hearing the words, not believing. Leave the city? Uproot their lives?

"Lord, have we offended thee that you should send us away?" he whispered, greatly daring.

Kukll didn't say anything. He merely stood there, his hands clasped tightly behind his back. Oryana got up and walked slowly toward Leoichan to stop before him.

"The gods are angry, my servant. Fire may fall from the sky, consuming all."

"The gods are angry with the people?"

"No, Leoichan," she said softly and placed a slim hand on his shoulder. "I am well pleased and so is Kukll-nn. My friend, a messenger from the stars brought us news of troubles. We must stay here and defend Tiahunn-cc, but you have to leave so that your people may be safe."

Leoichan did not understand. However, the gods have spoken and therefore it must be so.

"I shall stay here with you. All of us will stay and help you in your need," he said with sudden resolve and straightened. "Have you not cared for us?"

Oryana looked at him and he was awed to see a tear glisten

in her eye and slide down her cheek. "Thank you, faithful servant," she whispered. "The fire of the gods cannot be stopped. You must flee."

"To pack...there is so much..." He faltered and looked helplessly at her.

"Don't pack, just go!" Kukll snapped and Leoichan blanched, feeling himself tremble.

"Lord," he whispered and bowed low.

Relenting, Kukll walked up to him. "Don't be afraid, Leoichan. I didn't mean to be harsh, but time is limited. I shall not abandon you. Wait for me at Tiukk-ll. Don't forget the writings and the laws, my servant," he added, then abruptly turned and strode out of the Hall.

"Go quickly," Oryana whispered and followed.

Leoichan knew something terrible was about to happen if the gods were so troubled. Leave Tiahunn-cc?

* * *

The display plate cleared and Virrchaa glared at her.

"I want to speak to Kukll, First Scout," he said impatiently, his head held high and haughty.

"I speak for Kukll, Prima Scout," she said unflinchingly.

"Very well, then." He glanced at the chronometer readout. "Tell him he must evacuate all stations in fourteen hours. If he does not, I shall close them by force."

"I shall tell him, sir." Oryana nodded and his image faded. She turned to look at Kukll standing nearby and bit her lip.

"You heard?"

He barely nodded.

The black waters of the lake lapped below the walls of the fortress. Whitecaps curled and sent spray flying before the wind. About him, the city stood silent and empty. The last patrol reported all the natives evacuated. That was something at least, he mused wryly. After all the time and effort, it'll now

11

vanish in fire. What a waste. If the natives survived, it would still have been worth it.

Beneath him the floor shook slightly and he turned toward the command consoles.

"The last of the boats has taken off, sir," the technician said, his eyes wondering, asking the same questions Kukll was asking. "Low orbit in four point-seven minutes."

Kukll placed an arm over Oryana's shoulder. "Virr could be right," she said after a moment.

"Yes, I know." A cold smile tugged at the corner of his mouth. "If we leave, then *they* would have lost it all." He waved at the window. "He will wipe it all clean to remove a political embarrassment. He might not like it, but he'll follow orders. Who knows, in three or four thousand years the remnants might climb back to where they're now. The species will survive."

"And us?"

"We do what we must." He shrugged, turned and looked questioningly at the technician.

"Sachmm-nn is fully powered up and all stations have acknowledged. The local population has dispersed. All boats are in position. Target is in a low three-hour equatorial orbit. Our ship will shift to a geosynchronous position in twelve minutes from now."

Kukll nodded. "Open channel to Virr's ship."

When the plate cleared, the two men stared at each other, both resolved, determined to carry it to the end. Virr pursed his lips.

"Damn it, Kukll! This is madness."

"I agree, Prima Scout, but I cannot permit these people to be wiped out. Orders or not, that's murder."

"And I cannot permit Sachmm-nn and Tiahunn-cc to remain operational, Master Scout. You've made the population dependent on your technological and social infrastructure. You cannot be with them always."

"No, but without it, they'll revert to savagery, or worse."

Virr looked hard at Kukll and seemed to reach a decision. "I give you my word as an officer of the Serrll that I shall take no action against the natives. Provided all the bases are neutralized, with the exception of the moon base, of course."

"I might go as far as to believe you, Virr, but that doesn't bind the Executive Council."

"I meant the Council, damn it! I'll file a report with the General Assembly and the Council won't force the issue. As you said yourself, it's not worth it. You'll be free to return. I don't want to shed our blood for a cause I don't believe in and reasons that are expedient. Don't force my hand."

"On one condition."

"And that is?"

"The Serrll must send follow-up missions, to check up."

"That might not be so easy."

"Make it easy. Virr...you cannot afford to have your ship damaged. It's a hell of a long way to Captal."

"So it is."

When the screen faded, Kukll looked at Oryana. "What do you think?"

She tilted her head and frowned. "He appears sincere, but I don't trust him. He gave in too easily."

"Just so." He nodded and turned to the watch operator. "Maintain alert status and give me position of the primary target."

"They're maintaining neutral status, and their shield grid is up."

"Then we wait."

* * *

The comms alert beeped and Kukll turned as the image cleared.

"Sir, it's three hours plus," the operator said.

"Status?"

"All landing boats maintaining low orbit. The target has assumed a geosynchronous position above Sachmm-nn. All other bases—"

"I know," Kukll snapped and slammed his fist against the desk. "Is Virr's ship in line of sight?"

"Affirmative."

Kukll looked disgusted. "Get him for me, now!"

When the image cleared, Kukll stood straight, hands clasped tightly behind his back.

"You shifted orbit when I wasn't in a position to see. Why?"

"I don't make explanations, Kukll," Virr snarled, his eyes almost hidden by flared eyebrows. "I just want your compliance."

"You're not in any position to make demands, Prima Scout."

"A missile might change your mind, Master Scout!" Virr bellowed as he finally lost his temper. "I want your answer and I want it now. I'm tired of this whole mess. And I'm especially tired of you! Copy that, Mister?"

"Sachmm-nn has weapons capability, in case you have not been informed."

Virr turned abruptly, nodded and the image faded.

"Sir! Sachmm-nn reports they are under missile attack. Our defense screen has responded."

Oryana drew in her breath. Her eyes glistened as she looked at Kukll. "After all we have done…"

"He won't risk total confrontation," Kukll said flatly, thinking furiously. "He hasn't launched any scouts…yet. He wants to pull our teeth first. I cannot risk my ship and neither can he." He walked to the tactical plot and studied the plate. "Order Sachmm-nn to fire a burst at his ship. Rattle his shields a bit."

"Kukll!" Oryana cried. "This can only end in destruction for all of us. Then everything we've done will be a waste."

"It's already a waste. He'll either destroy us now or someone else will do it tomorrow. Unless the Executive Council intervenes, the politicians will erase everything we've done here."

She walked to him and looked gravely into his eyes. Her hands reached for him.

"You know, I have even forgotten what a Deklan sky looks like. Isn't that terrible?" she said tragically and her voice trembled. "I remember black sands washed by a warm ocean and the smell of flying spray, but it's only a memory now. Our reality is here. Understand me?"

He stared at her for a long time before squeezing her hands. "Are you sure this is what you want?" he whispered and she nodded. "Once committed, there is no going back. Not for a long time."

"I am sure, my love."

"Sir? Sachmm-nn received a near miss and our defense grid is holding. Prima Scout Virrchaa has shifted orbit."

"Open channel," Kukll commanded.

"The next attack will be on you, Master Scout," Virr spoke softly, but his eyes were hard and uncompromising.

"That will not be necessary, Prima Scout. I wouldn't want any stray missiles heading toward the natives."

"You don't trust me, do you?"

"What do you think?"

Virr's mouth twitched. "No, I guess you don't. You're wasted here, and when we get back—"

"We're not going back."

"What do you mean? If you are—"

"Don't worry. I'm not planning to throw away my life in some grand gesture. I have reconsidered our position. Particularly the follow-up missions."

"And?"

"We've been here a long time, Prima Scout. All of us have. Long enough to develop a certain affection for the natives and this planet. For me, Kaplan is a faded dream, albeit a fond one.

I intend to take volunteers and make a time dilation jump of fifteen years. It will buy the Council more than enough time to sort things out. Many of the people I know here will still be alive when I return. Enough for me to pick up the pieces, anyway."

Virr was silent, then shook his head. "Damnedest idea I ever heard of."

"But it will work. Besides, who do you have willing enough to exile themselves here?" Kukll asked, his voice full of irony. "About the Mission Plan. The General Assembly may pretend that this place doesn't exist, but they would still love to have it followed through. At least through Stage Two."

"I agree," Virr said.

"On one condition, Prima Scout."

"And that is?"

"Tiukk-ll and the other population centers must remain intact. This is not negotiable."

Virr sighed, then nodded. "Very well."

"And, Virr? My ship will remain in orbit and ready until you transit into subspace."

Virr didn't say anything as he cut contact.

* * *

It was hot.

Overhead, the sun a white furnace, too painful to look at. Few people were about and the temple grounds shimmered in the heat. Somewhere, a child wailed and there came a startled cackle from the poultry. A fly buzzed, then it was gone.

Leoichan hobbled slowly along the avenue, his stick tapping on polished stones. He was bent, his legs skinny, showing blue veins and tight, stringy muscles. Yet he enjoyed good health, even if he had trouble chewing with the few teeth that were left. Life had been harsh, but he did not complain. He had his sons and his family was powerful. He frowned as he recalled some of the practices at the temple and the loose interpretation of the laws. The king strong and the people prospered. Surely not as in the days of his youth, but obedient to the laws nonetheless.

He sat in the shade of the temple wall, lost in memory when shouting and the pounding of feet caused him to open his eyes. Squinting, he watched with amusement the running figures. In dismay, he realized they were coming toward him.

It was a messenger from the High Priest. Leoichan frowned. That man would have to go if things did not change, he reflected darkly. One of the boys, still panting, sank to his knees and bowed before him.

"Venerable One," the boy gasped and looked up with fear and wonder.

"Speak!"

"The Observatory!"

Leoichan's ears roared and his heart began to pound. No, it cannot be.

"What about it?" he whispered, hardly daring to believe.

"The dome opened and a shiny dish-like shape rose from within and started turning. Then it stopped and I was ordered to tell it to you."

Leoichan nodded and closed his eyes in quiet happiness. The gods were coming at last. He should have believed, he should have. Did not Kukll-nn promise he would come?

"Tell the High Priest and the King to assemble the people at the star nest," he ordered and smiled at the gaping faces. "The gods are coming."

He sat back and relaxed, content. He feared to die before setting eyes on Kukll and the goddess Oryana again, but he was an old fool.

He remembered how it was on that fateful and terrible day fifteen years ago. Seven of his priests and he were hidden in the mountains, far above Tiahunn-cc and the black lake. They could hardly see the massive walls of the fortress in the hazy

17

distance. The star nest on the plain far below clearly visible. They waited, wanting to see the anger of the gods, realizing that death may be their only reward for such presumption.

He watched as the last heavenly bird roared in anger, fire billowing from its base. He trembled in fear as it climbed into the sky. Fire and thunder followed it to the heavens and the ground shook beneath him. When the thunder stopped, only a column of writhing smoke remained. He remembered talking to one of his priests, arguing whether they should stay longer, when a flash of blinding radiance seared the hills around them. One of the priests screamed and tore at his eyes.

Leoichan turned to see a strangely shaped cloud hang over where Tiahunn-cc once stood. Then the wind roared and clutched at them, threatening to sweep them from the mountain. Terrified, they fled. That night, huddled together against the cold, he remembered Oryana's tears and he wept unashamedly for what was lost.

The memory of that cloud had stayed with him always.

Four of his priests died of a mysterious, wasting illness. Although he took sick, he recovered, the illness leaving him old before his time.

\* \* \*

Arms raised, the priests toned through the seventh chant of observance. The multitude buzzed with excitement. The King sat adorned in feathers and gold, hands folded as he stared at the emptiness of the star nest. Slowly, he turned his head, looked at Leoichan and nodded. Someone shouted and pointed and heads turned toward the heavens.

Brighter than a star and Leoichan squinted to look at it. It had been a long time, a long time since he witnessed the coming of a heavenly bird. He did not mind dying now. He watched the light sink swiftly and heard the first rumble of thunder.

# A Whisper from Shadow

Flame and smoke filled the small plain. The very air trembled as the pillar of fire hung briefly and touched the earth. In the sudden silence the echoes boomed in the distance and faded. The priests finished chanting and they waited. The smoke cleared quickly and a hole appeared in the side of the bird. Leoichan clenched his fists with gleeful excitement as an air chariot glided out, sank slowly and started toward them. He turned and nodded. The retainers moved his palanquin forward, away from the waiting priests and royalty.

The chariot drifted to a stop and sank toward the ground, but did not touch it. Its glittering bubble opened and Kukll-nn, all in red, stepped out and looked curiously about him. Oryana moved close beside him, her blue coverall shimmering in the heat. Leoichan stared at them with hunger, drinking in every detail. They were just as he remembered them, unchanged. They were gods, no?

Kukll turned and smiled as Leoichan stood and bowed low. "Lord, I have waited as you commanded."

"My faithful servant." Kukll placed his hand on Leoichan's shoulder. "I have come, as I promised."

Behind them, the chanting rose in waves.

Stefan Vučak

# Chapter One

Dark and heavy the sullen cloudbank reluctantly dragged itself eastward over a drenched landscape, trailing behind it ragged, torn streamers of fluff. In the north, slanting black sheets stabbed down in a downpour. Jagged lightning flickered, accompanied by a muted rumble. Overhead, the sky brilliant washed blue and the air had a clean, invigorating smell that always seemed to linger after rain. Tendrils of white mist drifted over the thick lush jungle, softening the sun's glare. Branches hung limp, laden with shimmering dew.

This early in the morning the archaeological site was deserted, not that the place was overrun even at the height of the tourist season. Comalcalco wasn't Palenque or Chichen Itza. An out-of-the-way dig, its origins were considered too humble to be part of the mainstream tourist path. Hands on hips, facing the ruins of Temple II towering beside her, Lauren pouted as she surveyed the dig, then gave a sigh of frustrated exasperation. It wasn't *supposed* to rain in January!

"Just look at it," she demanded in disgust. Her undergrad assistant winced beside her and nodded in sympathy.

It wasn't pretty.

The whole west side of the mound where they have been excavating was an oozing brown wound, scored deep by runoff channels. Both L-shaped test trenches dug between the mound and the eastern side of Temple II were completely filled with glistening yellow mud. At least the sorting tables were clean, scrubbed by the two-day downpour, which the makeshift canvas roof obviously wasn't able to protect. It would be impossible to do any further digging until the trenches were pumped out and dried. The rain also carved a deep channel down the west side of The Palace mound restoration site, the runoff spilling slush on either side of the completed Great Acropolis temples. Lauren didn't care, that was Imatlan's problem.

Her little roped-off kingdom had turned into a mire. This was the second time this month they'd been washed out, and the damage far worse now. The old Mayan gods were indeed cruel, she thought dejectedly. Her visa and permits will expire in three weeks and she harbored a nasty suspicion that Columbia U would not be renewing her grant for an extended stay. Especially as it would mean skipping some of the second semester classes. No, it wasn't the university. It was Boulcher!

The image of the archaeology dean's corpulent shape and sagging jowls, greasy hands fluttering in a grope and squeeze, made her squirm in disgust. He was her PhD thesis and research advisor and sat on her orals. She received her degree despite his negative endorsement after she failed to be suitably cooperative with his, ah, advice. Ever since then the repulsive man had hounded her career, pouncing on every opportunity to ridicule her work. Unfortunately for him, she was very good at what she did and her papers were generally well received by the Mesoamerican archaeological and anthropological communities. She had realized for some time that Boulcher was a clinging fossil, and the university should have buried him and his stuffy collection of dusty bones and rocks years ago. He had not published a paper in years and the closest he came to a dig these days was when he nursed his potted prize petunias.

Perhaps she should seriously consider the offer from Texas U. Their archaeology department was respectable and it wouldn't hurt to add full professor to her name. She was vain enough to want it, and the tenured security it would bring, realizing that while Boulcher sat as chair, it was unlikely Columbia would give her tenure. A woman needed to be twice as good as anyone else just to get to the starting line. In a purely unconscious gesture, she pushed back her sleeves and set her full mouth into a tight line.

"Two weeks of work down the drain." Lauren clicked her tongue and ruefully shook her head, setting the long ponytail swinging.

"Literally," Martin said with a marked lack of enthusiasm, realizing that *he* would be the one having to clean up the mess. Well, not completely alone. A murmur of restrained sympathy came from the other three Columbia U undergraduates who stood in a huddled group beside him dressed in shorts, T-shirts, and floppy green army hats. After two days stuck in their steamy Villahermosa hotel, they were not all that sure whether mud and wet grass was a better bargain. Either that or more of the doc's stern tutelage. The doc did not believe in idle hands or minds, and this was not a holiday. What they did here would earn them valuable course credits for the second semester, determined by the course coordinator; meaning the doc, of course.

Watching her, Martin knew the expression well. When the doc firmed her mouth, everybody the hell better be ready to get out of her damn way, for the lady played hardball and took no prisoners. Her single-minded drive could sometimes be frightening. He was in love with her of course, and everyone on the campus shared his amorous desire. When she walked into a lecture theater, the testosterone level of every male present spiked. The doc apparently oblivious to the devastating effect she had on her students, or presumably didn't even care. Which was too bad. The reality was, he thought morosely, she probably never dated anyone who wasn't at least a postdoc. Which was also too bad, for it placed her forever beyond his reach. Ah, unrequited love, a major drag.

Golden light bathed her oval face and clean complexion, highlighting the yellow streaks in her auburn hair. While on a dig, she unfailingly wore it in a ponytail, otherwise piled up high in a bun or left long to cascade down her back, with half of it covering her left breast. Her large brown eyes could suddenly turn from their glittering incisive hardness to soft, sensuous pools of churning emotion when focused on a particularly fine artifact. Slim, graceful and long-legged, at five-foot eight the doc was a walking fantasy. All her undergrads would murder for a chance to be her slaves on a dig and competition was stiff to see who would make it to Comalcalco. She worked everyone hard, but was fair and generous, caring more for genuine scholarship than a given tonnage of paper output. The doc only taught final year classes, serious students who had already decided on a career in archaeology. Looking around, despite the rain and primitive conditions, Martin enjoyed working on another professional dig. He fervently hoped she would consent to be his advisor when he took his master's.

First, he had to graduate this summer.

When he started the fall semester last year, graduating not altogether a certainty. He still squirmed at the memory of that awful first day. Busy copying summary notes displayed on the theater's eleven-foot by five-foot LED screen, he did not notice the doc walk in. He could almost hear the eyeballs click as the guys took her in. Unconcerned, she took one look at the screen and switched it off.

"Hey!" he yelled. "I was taking that down!"

"And you are?" she asked pleasantly.

"Teller."

"You have your Markson and Boon's, Mr. Teller?"

"Sure, doc. I thought—"

"You're not privileged to call me doc, and think you didn't." She stared at him like he was a discarded pot and frowned. "I've got bad news for you, Mr. Teller. For all of you. Come exam time the whole of Markson and Boon's will apply, not only my summary notes. Corner!" she snapped and pointed with a slim hand.

The theater became deathly quiet. Hands on shapely hips, she leaned forward and waited.

Coloring, his blood seething with embarrassment, he stood up and with clenched teeth walked to the back corner. Who the hell did the bitch think she was! Hushed murmurs rippled through the hall. He'd heard about the terrible professor from a master's graduate, but this swift demonstration of her wrath very unpleasant as it was unexpected.

What was she saying?

"People, I am Doctor Hopking, and I will be your lecturer for advanced Mesoamerican archaeology 304. Webster's defines a lecture as an informative talk to a class. That is exactly what I intend doing; give you information. How you take it will be up to each one of you. If anyone here expects this semester to be a tedious session of movies on past digs, quit now and avoid disappointment. I have no use for you. If you want to graduate, you'll need to pass 304, and you'll have to earn it. People, I don't take prisoners. Sucking up to me is a dead-end street. Mr. Teller, you can come down now."

He never forgot that day.

As others soon found, getting the corner was no big deal. Simply the doc's way of punctuating a dumb move and a very effective punishment for sloppy thinking. The doc did not mind misguided thinking. She just didn't have much time for idiots. From thirty-four hopefuls who were mostly there to drool over her sinuous figure, the second semester had only nineteen.

"Doctor Hopking!"

The piercing cry made everyone's head snap around. Lauren instinctively started walking toward the mound, then paused and turned.

"Martin, break out the gear and start cleaning this up," she ordered and swept a hand at the flooded trenches.

The pretty little black-haired Chatika appeared on top of the three-meter mound, practically dancing with excitement. Martin grinned at her and waved. He liked working with her and being near her. She was friendly, professional and very competent. He would not have minded exploring the relationship further. Unfortunately, she also had a big muscular boy-friend. Martin saw him once and had no wish to be the subject of his displeasure. He had two favorite women and both were out of reach. It just wasn't his summer.

Chatika was a graduate on loan from Mexico City's National Anthropology Museum, sweating out her master's dissertation. Her mentor, one Dr. Kareza Imatlan, a tall taciturn individual who exuded gloom and depression by his mere presence, thankfully still to arrive. After all, a learned figure of his stature could not be expected to be up and getting all sweaty and dirty before mid-morning. His team of local and international undergrads were doing that for him, restoring The Palace temples—the Great Acropolis—already having been rebuilt. The Mexican government forced Imatlan on Lauren as part of the price for allowing her to dig at Comalcalco. Martin knew that Imatlan resented the American undergraduates and had little patience with their questions, but he and Lauren got along surprisingly well.

It was a different story when they first met. What Imatlan could not have known, when the doc assumed her professional persona, there could never be any doubt as to who was in charge. The way Martin heard it, after a brief but fiery clash of wills, Imatlan unexpectedly capitulated with a gracious display of Latin gallantry. Martin wished he could have been there to see it. Thereafter, Imatlan mostly kept to himself and didn't bother Lauren much, for which Martin was sincerely grateful.

Lauren ducked under the perimeter rope, strode past the test trenches, winced at the mud clinging to her boots, and clambered to the top. She heard the roar of revving car engines and turned. Two jeeps emerged from the museum gate trailing blue exhaust smoke, Imatlan's group coming in for the day, still too early for the tourists. Chatika grabbed Lauren's arm and practically dragged her to the north face. When they stopped, Chatika beamed triumphantly and pointed down.

"O my gosh!" Lauren husked in awe. Imatlan forgotten,

she scrambled partway down the mound. Ignoring the mud, she knelt and ran her palm reverently along the smooth side of a yellow, stained sandstone block. Her heart hammered and she wanted to shout with joy. Absently, she pulled a broad brush from her back pocket and lovingly swept away loose dirt and dried mud smears. She did not see Chatika smile at the unconscious gesture. It was obvious what happened. The storm had washed away part of the artificial earthen mound of Temple II, exposing the stone. Instinctively, she knew this was old and clearly predated all the structures erected here. But how old? She would have to dig to the base and get soil samples for accurate dating. Goodness knows where the thing was quarried, probably Chiapas. Tabasco had no sandstone quarries she knew of, old or new.

She looked up and flashed Chatika a warm smile, revealing even white teeth.

"We just made the history books here, my dear, you know that."

"You were right all along, Doctor," Chatika said in soft accented English, her dark features split in a wide grin. "The mound had a purpose after all. It wasn't a simple foundation for a temple ruin."

"As to that…we need to peg this out, string and photograph it. Get the others, will you?"

Lauren longed to start digging around the block right away, but refrained. The stone wasn't going anywhere and she needed to handle this properly and with care. This single piece was proof positive, a clear vindication of her theory that the Mundo Maya, and even the much older established Olmec forerunner civilization that once inhabited most of Tabasco, were only a relatively recent phenomena in this part of Mexico. It was never clearly explained why the Mundo Maya first prepared earthen mounds at Comalcalco before erecting their unique brick pyramids on top of them. The fact they used brick, clearly indicated stone was not readily available, or not available in sufficient quantity, and not as some of her detractors suggested the eastern Mayans didn't know how to work stone.

She had little time for Boulcher or Kirmond's theories that the Mundo Maya were primitives, being the reason why they built their pyramids using only brick. Another accepted doctrine she scorned, claimed that since Comalcalco lay on a flood plain surrounded by jungle, the Mayans built mounds to ensure the temples would be seen from a distance. To her, a ludicrous proposition. With jungle all around them the local inhabitants would have no way of seeing the temples no matter how high they were.

Her theory was simple. When the Mayans moved into Comalcalco, they found the mounds already there. Although not conclusive, carbon dating of various soil strata samples provided some legitimacy for her position. Some of the samples dated to over five thousand years. Lauren considered it only logical the Mayans would then build on top of the mounds.

With this single stone, she now held an answer to some of the questions that plagued her ever since she first decided to carve her way through the male-dominated archaeology field. She could now start asking who were the people that laid this stone. Gazing at the block, the mound clearly not a tel, already established from earlier digs. Perhaps the mound hid something. She peered closely at the worked face. The side perfectly smooth and bore no trace of tool markings. Running her finger along the almost sharp edge, she marveled at the precision of the workmanship. This was not a product of a culture barely out of the Stone Age that supposedly only had copper tools. This stone took sophisticated technology to produce.

Martin appeared, towing behind him the other undergrads. They crowded around Lauren, chattering heatedly, maintaining a respectful distance. For them, this was the reason why they went into archaeology, even though everyone realized that most of their careers would in all likelihood be spent in museums and libraries, sifting through musty collections and chasing down

arcane references. In the main, all the interesting stuff was supposedly already dug up, or so they were told. Martin didn't believe it and the doc certainly did not, always prepared to challenge the envelope of accepted dogma. Besides, field trips were
always fun. Gazing at the stone, it was proof undeniable that
everything had not been dug up.

Conversation suddenly died and they stood in silence, con-
templating the shrine that was the stone. Martin looked down
and smiled into Lauren's eyes.

"Congratulations, Dr. Hopking."

Everyone broke into huge grins and clapped. The familiar
growl of Imatlan's four-wheel Toyota sounded from the other
side of the mound.

Lauren stood up and dusted off her jeans. "Thanks, Martin.
We'll hold off congratulating each other for now, but we'll
make up for it tonight with plenty of cold Margaritas." There
was an even more furious round of clapping, self-congratulation being thirsty work. "Until then, we have work to do.
Chatika, it looks like Dr. Imatlan has finally arrived, but this
cannot wait. Take one of my hopefuls and start stringing the
site—"

"What reference?"

"SSL1; sandstone level one. Use 500-millimeter grid
squares. Mark levels every ten centimeters. Martin, you take the
others and organize a one to twenty plan, context sheet, find
bag, and analysis sheets. Get this photographed and download
a brief to our website. You might as well send some pictures
down to Villahermosa in case someone wants to come and see
for themselves. We'll start on a group paper tonight. Oh, and
e-mail a photo or two to Boulcher and Kirmond," Lauren said
sweetly, her eyes glittering with ice.

She longed to see the condescending smirk vanish from
Boulcher's fat face when he saw the stone. She might at last get
some deserved respect from the man, but doubted that even
this would have any impact on that fossilized mind. More likely,

he would be maneuvering to make sure a percentage of any publicity limelight fell on him.

Archaeologists were a queer breed. They did not lust after riches or even fame. They lived or perished on recognition, and getting published first counted for everything. She would allow anyone to steal her thunder, especially Boulcher or Kirmond, which, of course, was a ridiculous attitude to have from the learned community who should know better. After all, they were just men, she thought comfortably.

Satisfied, she clapped her hands and grinned broadly, in her element, archaeology she loved.

"Right, let's break out the tools."

Martin stared at her in admiration. When the doc got activated, her enthusiasm infectious and irresistible. He cleared his throat.

"Ah, Dr. Hopking, haven't you forgotten something?"

"And what could the lovely doctor have forgotten, Martin?" a deep cultured voice inquired pleasantly, his accent barely noticeable. Lauren whirled and regarded the tall, swarthy Mexican. They were so absorbed, no one noticed Imatlan climb up.

"You, of course, you clod!" Lauren laughed and motioned to him. "Look at what we've found!"

Another numbered brick, he mused. Whatever it was, it couldn't be all that important, but he was prepared to humor her. Not wearing his field boots, Imatlan daintily stepped over a pool of mud.

"Driving up, I wondered where everyone disappeared to." At the sight of the exposed stone, he stared and color drained from his deeply tanned face. "Madre de Dios!" he muttered in a strangled whisper.

Lauren smiled with grim satisfaction. This would put the haughty Dr. Imatlan in his place. Apart from always trying to get into her pants, Kareza had been nothing but a monumental pain and an irritating distraction. She knew he resented her professional presence and held her theories in mild scorn. As far as he was concerned, Temple II and its mounds were a minor curiosity at best. Interesting, but hardly worth serious scholarship. After all, what was there worth digging that wasn't already thoroughly researched over the last century? Still, she admitted that when he dropped his amorous pursuits and was himself, Kareza could be charming, very knowledgeable about the Maya, and a good storyteller. He carried out a lot of valuable fieldwork, the latest at Belize, before getting more involved in archaeological politics. He and Boulcher would make an ideal pair, she reflected.

Imatlan cleared his throat, clearly dismayed by the find, and looked enviously at Lauren. She was smug and perfectly aware of what she had here. Her discovery made all his work at The Palace mounds seem like an amateurish waste of time, and he felt a chilling stab of childish resentment. This should have been *his* discovery. A galling and bitter pill to swallow from the *norteno* woman. Nevertheless, he put on a brave face and smiled thinly.

"I guess congratulations are in order, my dear Lauren," he said, his voice dripping with feigned sweetness. "It's a fantastic find and your theories have been vindicated. I planned on going back to Villahermosa later for supplies, but this is far more important. I'll go now! I'll organize a press release, with full credit to you, of course—"

"Don't bother, Kareza. Martin already has that in hand," Lauren said harshly, her eyes challenging him. Full credit, right. Out of her sight, strutting before the media, it would more likely be a professional stab in the back. She clawed with Boulcher and the Mexican authorities to be here, but Kareza, she could handle. In his view, if money was going to be spent at Comalcalco, it should be spent on restorations, not on aimless poking around Temple II and piles of dirt. Well, if any money was going to be spent now, it certainly wasn't going to be spent on The Palace. Eat that, Mister!

# A Whisper from Shadow

One of the undergrads coughed and rubbed his chin, embarrassed at this display of turf fighting. Imatlan straightened to his full height and his face clouded as he glared down at Lauren.

"As the site director—"

"And my liaison with the Mexican government, your contribution to my expedition has been invaluable, but don't go muscling in on my dig. You stick to your restorations. Do we understand each other?"

Imatlan pursed his mouth and shrugged. Formidable indeed. Although a personal setback, the development wasn't necessarily irretrievable. The extra publicity Lauren's find would undoubtedly generate can be turned to benefit his work on The Palace. It may also give him a way to peg back the arrogant lady doctor. Anyway, any ensuing publicity would flow his way as well. Another time, then.

"As you say, Dr. Hopking, this is your dig," he said backing down, the burn of jealousy a crawling pain deep in his belly. *There will be other moments.* He turned, walked a few paces, and snapped his fingers. "Chatika!"

With the look of a hurt child, her shoulders sagged as she shuffled toward him.

"Doctor?"

"I want to know everything that goes on here," he growled. When she didn't say anything, he turned and lifted her chin. "Am I clear?"

"Dr. Hopking—"

"This is our heritage and no outsider will rob us of our glory."

Chatika's eyes blazed. "*Your* glory, Dr. Imatlan."

He shook his head. *So naïve and innocent...*

"Your work here is a significant part of your dissertation, my dear. You wouldn't want anything to get in the way of that, like misguided loyalty?"

She hated him then. He was a piece of slime, but she

31

needed that degree. It wasn't like she would be cheating on Dr. Hopking. He smiled and patted her head.

"I am glad we understand each other," he said and walked down the mound.

Lauren watched Kareza disappear and bit her lip. Chatika looked desperately unhappy. Lauren walked to her, placed a protective arm around the smaller woman, and gave her a squeeze.

"The man's a pig, dearie," she murmured. "Beneath our contempt."

* * *

After a cautious start and careful excavation, measuring and pegging, the meticulously sifted detritus surrounding the stone was revealed to be ordinary soil mixed with crushed shells and limestone. So far, nothing out of the ordinary; the initial two test trenches on the other side of the mound now completely forgotten. Exacting work: meticulous recording, sample taking, level measuring, cross-referencing and labeling. Lauren did not spare herself either, often getting into the trench with a trowel and brush, talking to the students, always teaching. Every now and then, an archaeologist from The Palace site would wander over to chat with her, make appreciative noises, or simply stare at the dig.

They found nothing of interest; no discarded pottery, broken tools or indication of any sort the mound could be anything more than a pile of dirt. The undergrads showed disappointment, their eyes filled with visions of golden beads and semi-precious stone. Far from discouraged, Lauren kept nodding to herself as though the lack of artifacts confirmed something for her. She simply extended the excavation along the north face of the mound, which revealed more sandstone blocks laid out in a perfectly straight wall. They uncovered six meters and were yet to reach the end.

# A Whisper from Shadow

Occasional tourist groups clustered against the dig's perimeter rope, while the tour guide learnedly described the latest developments. Cameras clicked and camcorders waved unsteadily, the owners unaware of the horrible result that would ensue when they finally got to view their amateur efforts. Loners and couples wandered the grassed expanse between the temples, soaking in the palpable history of the place.

While the initial part of the dig next to the original stone continued to be scraped away with painstaking precision, ongoing work to completely expose the wall took on the scene of a construction site, and just as messy. To her surprise, Imatlan gave her four of his laborers. Although she suspected his motive was not altogether altruistic, she was grateful for the help and immediately put them to work clearing away the material; brute pick, shovel and wheelbarrow toil. Not exactly an orthodox approach to handling an archaeological dig, as Chatika diffidently pointed out. Secretly they all wanted to see more of the wall. Everyone in high spirits, the expedition already a success and the undergrads assured of obtaining postgraduate positions. During breaks, they mixed with The Palace archaeologists. Rough local red wine helped lubricate the sometimes heated speculations and wild theories about the wall.

In the stimulating environment, with the pleasant smells and sounds of the jungle around them, they revealed a row of blocks each 1.8 meters square, laid with the mathematical exactness of a machine. The joints were dry, but a needle would not penetrate the tight seams, and Lauren had tried. The blocks were remarkable and reminded her very much of Inca stonework. That also worried her. Although the Peru workmanship at Sacsayhuaman superb, no one could mistake those blocks as anything but simply well-dressed. What she had here rivaled the best that could be found at Giza. A coincidence? In archaeology, she reminded herself, there was no such thing as coincidence, only fact. Was there a link between the ancient Mesoamerican civilizations and Egypt, and as some of her earlier pottery finds suggested—definitely Mediterranean in origin—even old Rome? The markings found on the temple bricks by Steede and others were certainly suggestive, if controversial. She hoped to find out. She also hoped the information would finally stifle her opponents and bring her the recognition she deserved.

Nibbling at a fingernail, she watched the local laborers work. The top row of blocks, marked by the cornerstone that started it all, looked odd and out of place. These were narrower, only 900 millimeters high, and looked almost like…chamber capstones? She reigned in her excitement, chiding herself for jumping to conclusions. Still, a little speculation was stimulating and good for the soul.

A sharp clang below her made her head jerk around. One of the laborers looked up and smiled sheepishly. The other three chattered and grinned at the unfortunate man. They had reached the base of the mound and were starting to dig a trench along the wall. Lauren glared at him and scrambled down the side of the mound. She knelt beside the stone and ran a critical eye over the scuffmark left by his heavy spade.

"Chatika!" she bellowed and looked up where the Mexican girl was sketching the site layout.

Chatika lowered her drawing pad. "Yes, Dr. Hopking?"

Lauren scowled and pointed at the man beside her. "You tell this clod, if he marks another stone, I'll have him buried where he stands! Got that?"

Chatika looked startled, then broke into rapid Spanish. The guilty man lost his smile and bowed.

"Excuse, Senorita," he mumbled, obviously contrite.

Lauren's rage faded and she cursed under her breath. The local help useless, but she could not afford to bring anyone else from Columbia U, and she tried. Boulcher already called her twice, demanding an explanation for all the extra costs. The fossil even threatened to come down personally and take over the dig 'to make sure she didn't ruin anything'. What he really wanted was to bathe in some of the publicity that now surrounded the find. The man was pathetic. The image of Boulcher behind a spade almost made her smile.

"Just tell them to be careful, okay?"

"They understand, Doctor," Chatika said evenly and went into another round of Spanish. The four resumed their labors with renewed vigor, not daring to look at the terrible gringo lady. Hiding a grin, Lauren climbed back up the mound.

"Have you seen Dr. Imatlan?"

"Is there anything I can do for you, Lauren?" he said smoothly, suddenly beside her. She jumped and slapped his shoulder.

"I hate it when you do that!"

He smiled at her, his smoldering dark eyes burning, then turned away to look speculatively at the exposed wall.

"Absolutely remarkable. I wonder how far down it goes?"

"It will be even more remarkable once we see what's inside."

Imatlan peered at her. "What makes you think this is anything more than a supporting wall?"

"Don't be dense. Look at the first row of blocks." Lauren gestured impatiently. "The stone we uncovered is clearly part of a corner. The wall runs between the mound and Temple II."

"A chamber? But the weight of the mound—"

"Less than a meter of dirt at this point. Minimal load bearing stresses."

"Here, yes, on the outside of the mound, but farther in? If there is a chamber, unlikely as that is, keep in mind it must support the weight of the whole temple ruin."

"If it extends that far in, and it might not be a chamber at all. I can't tell yet, but the wall doesn't look to me like it's part of a solid structure. Still..."

He squinted at her mischievously and grinned. He couldn't help himself. As an archaeologist, he was also caught in the excitement of her dig.

"Like a good scientist, you want to scan the wall for a cavity?"

"Right! With all the oil companies in Villahermosa, someone must have a ground-penetrating radar unit we can borrow. I cannot believe that whoever built this thing would go to all the trouble of erecting these blocks with such exquisite precision simply to create a decorative pyramid wall, then have it buried. I've studied the analysis sheets, but we need to be sure."

"You're a romantic, Lauren. Always dangerous in an archaeologist."

"Can you lay your hands on the thing?" Lauren demanded, ignoring his affectionate outburst.

"Mmm. Pemex has a field office in Villahermosa and they might have a GPR unit. If they don't, they will know who does. Let me make some calls."

"Good. Be a lamb and get one for me, will you? And Kareza? I appreciate you taking time off your own work to do this."

The tall Mexican pursed his mouth. Lamb? When what he wanted was to be a lion, Imatlan mused. Looking into her captivating eyes, his hormones fizzed. *My lovely doctor, if you really wanted to show your appreciation…* He abruptly turned and walked off.

Wearing a heavy frown, Lauren watched him descend down the mound. He climbed into his brown four-wheel drive Toyota and headed toward the site entrance. She sensed trouble here, and not only of the romantic kind. Her find had disrupted restoration work on The Palace, if for a time, and despite his suave appearance, Kareza didn't like it. His archaeologists were wandering in and out all the time to watch the excavation of the wall, holding long debates about its nature, who put it there, and why. He'd been smooth and polite and resentful, and she didn't trust him. Kareza may not have sufficient pull to have her thrown off the site, but in the short term, he could certainly drown her in red tape and cut her off from local help. That would force her to do battle with the local bureaucrats who were not at all keen to cooperate with a gringo, and a woman too! She knew what his problem was, of course. He wanted total control over the whole site and the publicity limelight that went with it, and he would not rest until he got it.

Finding the wall generated only mild reaction from the Mexican media, which was disappointing, until Chatika pointed out that the papers were inundated by an almost constant stream of news tidbits from a host of active digs throughout the country. The reaction around the world anything but mild and triggered an acerbic debate among a handful of Mesoamerican experts, including Boulcher and Kirmond, which pleased Lauren no end. She relied on that very controversy to keep Kareza and the Mexican authorities from interfering with her. After all, this was good for business and drew in more visitors. If her hunch was right and the site indeed hid a chamber, Kareza would have to bulldoze her to get her out of here. Equally important, despite Boulcher's posturing, Columbia U promised to fund the dig beyond her initial grant, even though they were not willing to send her more people. She was pretty sure they would, and the assurance relieved her of a major administrative headache.

Damn! She reminded herself to ask Martin to get their immigration entry cards revalidated. They could be here all February. Exactly the kind of oversight Imatlan could use to get her thrown out of the country, especially if Boulcher kicked up a fuss with the university about her missing the start of the second semester. Would Kareza attempt to influence Mexico's immigration officials to keep her out? She wouldn't put it past him.

Deep in thought, she observed Chatika and Martin as they carefully scraped around the cornerstone. Chatika pried away the soil with a small trowel and swept away debris with a broad brush. Martin suddenly leaned toward her and peered closely at the exposed stone face. Chatika absently pushed back her short black hair that forever cascaded over her eyes, and muttered something to Martin, who looked at her in surprise, then shook his head. They made a good team, Lauren thought. Chatika, more experienced around a dig, methodical and exact, perfectly complemented Martin's youthful enthusiasm. The boy had matured immeasurably and should turn into a fine archaeologist. The experience of working on a serious dig reinforced better than anything else all the hours of staring at books.

"Found something?"

Chatika looked up. "Etchings, Dr. Hopking. It could be writing."

Lauren climbed down into the trench and Martin stepped back to make room for her. She knelt to study the exposed markings and absently pulled back a lock of wayward hair. The lines were expertly cut and looked almost stamped in their precision. What struck her was the haunting resemblance to Semitic text. Impossible, of course.

"These certainly don't look anything like Maya cursive," she murmured and smiled at Chatika. "Good work, you two. Get them photographed and uploaded to our website. Okay, tell me. Who is the most noted expert on Semitic text? A wrong answer gets the corner."

Martin suppressed a smile. With the doc the lessons never ended.

"Dr. Markinov at Ben-Gurion's Dept of Hebrew Language," he said and grinned at Chatika who promptly stuck the tip of her tongue at him.

"Right! Send him an e-mail and let him work on it. Tell him he can write the paper on anything he finds."

"Semitic text? Here?" Chatika asked incredulously and Lauren shrugged.

"Hard to believe, isn't it. The implications would be incredible."

Martin leaned back against the trench. "Incredible? Doc, this text is telling me there was communication between the old

Armenian and Euphrates civilizations and Mexico. There is no evidence in their writings to suggest either of them were seafarers."

"I know," Lauren said, apparently unconcerned. "We have Roman markings on temple bricks, also incredible."

"What do we have here then, doc?" Martin asked suddenly and swept his hand at the exposed wall.

One of the laborers below them paused, bent over his shovel and wiped his forehead. To the gringos the site had significance. To him, it was just hot, dusty work. Lauren bit her lip. She'd been asking herself the same question. She gazed at Martin and her brown eyes turned soft and dreamy.

"If you hope to graduate this summer, you tell me."

Martin often played these word games with the doc and enjoyed the sharp clash of ideas and the sparks they generated. The doc would sometimes throw a verbal grenade into an otherwise safe conversation and the resulting blast would leave rags of outrageous comments and theories hanging in tatters. Her inner group were dedicated students and their minds were not fettered by the stilted restraints of orthodox thinking. They were prepared to challenge established dogma using all the science and technology at their disposal to back up their ideas. A rebel herself the doc allowed and actively encouraged these jam sessions, to the disapproval and displeasure of some of the more stuffy faculty who did not seem to realize the dust in their offices was merely the fallout of irrelevancy that lay between their ears.

Theorizing was one thing, but the lettering etched into this stone threatened to turn Martin's orderly notion of archaeology into chaos.

Okay, he'll play the game.

"Not wishing to be swayed by wild claims from some of the more populist quarters—"

"Of course not," Lauren said with a straight face at the veiled reference to her own writings. Chatika's eyes sparkled.

Archaeology with Dr. Hopking was an exercise in self-discovery, not merely scholarship, and never dull. She worked with Americans on other digs and found them stuffy and opinionated, but the evening sessions with Lauren at their hotel, with Tabano's Bar as the watering hole that supplied the necessary stimulation, were anything but.

"—who shall remain nameless," Martin bored on unperturbed, "we have a bona fide puzzle here and the pieces themselves are a mystery. Item one. Take the unique manufacture of the stones. Item two. Being sandstone, how were they brought here and presumably already dressed, as we found no trace of discarded tools or stone chips, or anything else for that matter, to suggest the blocks were worked here. Item three. How did they lay such huge blocks? All this demonstrates a command of technology that is several quantum orders of magnitude greater than thought possible for the period."

"Have you considered that they may have had help?" Lauren asked, dropping one of her verbal grenades and Martin winced.

"Now you're asking me to commit myself, doc."

"Nothing of the sort. I only want you to consider all the possibilities."

"Since you're asking. It is clear if the local Olmec, and this is an assumption on my part, of course, didn't have the skill or the tools to do the job themselves—"

"And five thousand years ago, who had the necessary skill and technology?"

"The Egyptians. We have evidence that Egypt traded with the Americas. Coca leaves and tobacco were found in some of the Egyptian tombs, which predate the Roman period by several centuries, and those things are indigenous only to South America."

"Thin, but plausible. Okay, Martin. I won't scandalize you any further."

"Thanks, doc. Will this be on the menu for tonight?" he

asked looking glum.

"Count on it," Lauren said and he made a face. Chatika grinned broadly.

Built in modern colonial style, hotel Cencali overlooked the glassy 'Las Illusiones' Lagoon that pushed back the crowding buildings. Palms and fig trees lined the broad Avenue Juarez & Paseo. After a hard day's work on a dig the 'La Isla' restaurant provided a terrific outdoor wooded setting with gnarled branches hanging over the tables. Dropping leaves were thrown in for free. Not the flashiest hotel in Villahermosa, but it was comfortable and close to all the downtown attractions. Anticipating nights of fun and exploration when they first got there, the undergrads were quickly disappointed. Lauren saw no reason why the evening hours should not be used as tutorial sessions. At least the doc had a heart and did not torture them every night.

"What else have you got?" Lauren demanded.

"I thought you didn't want to scandalize me any further?"

"Just when things are getting interesting? What else?"

"The significance of the wall itself, of course."

"Good."

"It's obviously part of a larger structure—"

"Obviously?"

"Okay. What we have excavated so far *suggests* the wall *might* be part of a larger structure, but what is its purpose? The fact of its deliberate burial could imply the contents were not meant to be disturbed." Martin paused and gave Lauren his most charming and very engaging smile. "Doctor Hopking, if I told you what I think is in there, you'd have me certified."

"I might have you certified anyway. So, what's inside?"

Martin took a big breath. Here goes…

"An Egyptian boat."

Lauren smiled, but not with scorn. "No Roman chariot?"

"No Roman chariot."

"Comalcalco isn't anywhere near the sea," Chatika protested.

"It isn't now," Martin insisted, "but five thousand years ago the Gulf of Campeche was higher and boats could have come in quite far along the tidal estuaries. If the Olmec could transport fifteen-tonne granite blocks from Chiapas to make their head carvings, hauling a ten-meter wood boat would be child's play."

"Okay. Now for the big one," Lauren said. "The significance of the boat?"

Martin looked directly into her eyes. They really were such lovely eyes.

"I think it was a ceremonial boat used to transport someone important. I think Comalcalco could have been an administrative center."

Chatika stared. "You're saying Egypt ruled this part of Mexico?"

"Why not?"

"That's contrary to everything we know about the Olmec," she protested.

"So?"

"Martin, I agree with you that the unique manufacture of the wall suggests use of tools that should not have been available in the period, and I'm even willing to concede the possibility of Egyptian influence, but colonization? Where are your facts?"

"I don't have any facts to support a working hypothesis, not now. Ask me again once we're inside the chamber."

Lauren nodded approvingly. Martin applied sound reasoning and imaginative flare. Even if the idea turns out to be false, he was willing to test the limits.

"Okay you two, we'll be scientists for a little longer and wait for facts, but remember. Without ideas, even wild ones, you end up missing out on a lot of fun," she said and left them. Martin watched her climb up and shook his head.

"Believe me, doc, we're not missing out on any fun at all."

# Chapter Two

Terr leaned back against the warm sands, hands clasped behind his head, and stared into darkness. A drifting breeze gusted over the dune crests, its hot breath carried with it the burned smells of the Saffal deeps. Beneath the canopy of hard stars the dunes whispered to him. He allowed himself to drift through the silence, letting the night cradle him, keeping the flood of emotions at bay, if for a moment.

His breathing slow and even, controlled, like the icy calm of his thoughts. He knew it for the façade it was as rage threatened to burst through the flimsy barrier of his sanity. If that happened, he knew it would consume him and Death would walk unchecked, a destroyer unleashed. He felt it now, growing inside him, scheming and irresistible. He clenched his teeth and groaned as little blue lightnings slithered over his body. It would be so easy to let them loose. All he had to do was will it. Who would stand in his way if he did? Did he not walk in the shadow of the god of Death? A surge of power coursed through him and he shuddered at the keen thrill of its passing. A pulse of intense blue light rippled down his body and lit the faces of the dunes around him, and he felt their homage. Overhead, a low rumble made the sands tremble beneath his feet.

He was in a whirlwind of forces that raged restlessly within him. Surrounded with power, there was nothing he could not do, and he allowed himself to be swept up in the moment. Shrouded in light, he stood and held his arms high and touched the sky. Lightings played between his hands. His body tingled with pulsating energy and he grimaced at the almost painful waves of pleasure. Death settled on his shoulders and he felt the touch of its shadow. Immortal, one with the god, he chanted the words from the *Saftara*.

"I shall walk in the shadow of Death," he intoned and his voice boomed into the night. "And it shall be with me all the days of my life. With shadow shall I smite my enemies and with thunder shall I purge their land!" He cried out as the force of creation burned through him, searing away all restraint, and he welcomed the unholy joy of its touch. "And all who stand with me in the shadow of Death shall know my power and be comforted. With shadow and thunder shall I walk their land!"

The lust of destruction hot in his eyes, he savored its sweetness. With the dunes echoing his words, he loosed the lightnings. The sands moaned beneath his touch and thunder rolled across the desert. Reality flickered and he found himself staring at a crescent world, two stars suspended beneath his feet. His arms leveled, the lightnings ripped and tore at the blue planet, opening gaping chasms of fire. Billowing steam rose in silent agony from vaporized oceans and jagged chunks of the planet's crust were hurled into space. He laughed as the lightnings devoured the world, its cry only adding to his power lust. Streaming tendrils of yellow magma, the burned remnants of the planet's core bubbled, then vanished in a searing explosion of shooting debris.

He stood, suspended in space, two stars adorning his feet.

He slowly lowered his arms and the desert emerged to surround him, cradling him in its dark and warm embrace. The breeze tugged timidly at his cape. Death rode his shoulders and the image of his vision slowly faded. Looking up at the Stalker waiting to plunge the arrow into his enemy, he wondered if he would have the strength to stay his hand when the moment came. Was death and destruction the inevitable end of any lust? He clutched the surtaf and shivered, suddenly cold. The power drained from him and he felt the shadows part as Death left him.

Staring into the night's blackness, he could see the two paths of his future open before him. It would take a single step to fix his fate and the destinies of those close him. Both paths looked the same, but he knew that one of them ended with him suspended in space with two stars at his feet.

Did it have to be?

The warning from the gods clear. No matter what path he trod, he knew they would not interfere or guide his footsteps. The choice his to make. One path was shrouded in mist, and in it lay pain, betrayal, love and…he could not see, but his to shape. In the end, he didn't really have a choice. He would never knowingly stray down the path of total abandon and annihilation, no matter what the price or the pain. Where then free will? Was that too just a cruel delusion, a cosmic joke for the amusement of the gods?

It wasn't fair! He cursed silently at the fates that have trapped him. The lined face of his master frowned and the orange eyes burned at him in disapproval. His words were a soft rumble in the desert.

'Foolish creature, temptation is merely an exercise of will, whether you give into the act or refrain. The right or the wrong of it does not come into it, for you know it even as the need for gratification presents itself. The exercise of power should never be merely an indulgence.'

Terr nodded slowly and allowed himself a rueful smile. Apparently even feeling sorry for one's self was scowled at.

"I have indulged, master, for that, I crave your forgiveness," he murmured solemnly and the heaviness he felt seemed somewhat lighter. He fancied he could see the old Wanderer nod in approval. He sat down, stretched out his legs before him and idly stirred the coarse sand with his fingers.

It still wasn't fair.

The sands shifted behind him to familiar footfalls. They hesitated and stopped.

"Join me, Nightwings." Wrapped in his cloak, he relaxed and noticed the faint night sounds around him. His mischievous side snickered. It was all a sham, it said.

Dharaklin stood motionless and watched the dark shape of his brother, uncertain what to do. He hung back when the lightnings lit the sky and thunder shook the dunes a silent witness to the raw rage of Sankri's emotions. He sensed it would have been too dangerous to approach him then, while Death strode free to do Sankri's bidding. Not that his brother would consciously harm him, but his naked feelings could have lashed out indiscriminately as he rode the storm of his inner struggle. That was one aspect of his brother that had always disturbed him. The cloak of Death seemed to glow more brightly in him than it should have for someone who had undergone only the first trial. It was almost as if his power somehow became magnified.

Dhar checked the thought, profoundly troubled by its implication. On that fateful day when their spirits merged and he pulled Sankri back from insanity, Dhar left part of himself in his alien brother. Could he also have somehow left part of the god of Death's power in him? It could explain much. He would have to discuss this with Sidhara, but the realization was strangely disquieting. He was aware that for many nights the village Rahtir had deliberated over this alien child of Death, pondering the whim of the gods. They were still to reach a conclusion. What of his relationship with his brother?

The savage brutality with which Kai Tanard waged battle left him shaken and deeply disturbed. He knew that wearing the Scout Fleet uniform meant he would have to place himself in line of fire and test himself against Death. When the moment came and Death was unleashed, he found himself wanting. Not in physical courage, but in spiritual preparedness. The words of the *Saftara* were strangely unhelpful against the ravening slashes of an M-3 projector. His conscience protested and he now squirmed with guilt. He failed his brother, shielding his misgivings behind Sankri's orders, as he was now shielding himself behind the *Saftara*.

"Tah, the gods will tell," he murmured.

# A Whisper from Shadow

Seeing him sitting and apparently relaxed, Dhar was relieved to see the anguish that drove Sankri away from the village had now dissipated. He was not so naïve to believe that his brother's inner discord was resolved, but it appeared Sankri had reached a workable compromise. He took the two steps between them and slowly lowered himself to the warm sand. Sankri did not turn to look at him and Dhar allowed his eyes to travel across the dark dunes, content to share a quiet moment of completeness.

The night hot and the stars were restless. He felt good.

"It's always at night that I feel closest to the Saffal," he said softly.

"It's a lie, my brother, for the night merely hides the harshness of Saffal's day, as it hides the true face of its people," Terr said with a sour chuckle.

Dhar turned his head and stared at the dark form, probing for the meaning of Sankri's words.

"Are you saying the Saddish-aa are living a lie?"

"A delusion," Terr said after a while, not moving. He stirred the warm sand with the tip of his finger. "This evening you stood proud with your father at your side and your mother's arms around you and I basked in the glow of their love for you. I was also envious because my family is unable to show that pride in me. I chose a way of life they did not approve and in their eyes I have no shadow." He paused and the sands whispered to him.

"Watching you, I felt resentment. You know what I resented most about you, about all the Wanderers? It's the assured arrogance with which you carry your power. Even Sidhara, wise in the frailty of flesh and temptation, resorts to mouthing platitudes from the *Saftara* as though the writings were an end in themselves." He grinned sardonically at Dhar's startled expression. "Don't look so shocked. He cannot help it, none of you can. It's a real pain watching you all, bathed in the shine of self-righteousness, telling each other what great noble guys you are and how the Saffal cradles you all beneath the benevolent gaze of the god of Death. Cloaked in power and self-congratulation the *Saftara* fails to show the dark side of your nature, the bickering, the jealousies and the rivalries between the tribes. And the Resident is the worst example of the type, expecting me to bow before him in gratitude that he should condescend to see me worthy to join his grand scheme and fight for the Unified Independent Front's cause. I wanted to smear that smugness right off his face. If the Rahtir Council itself can hide behind such hypocrisy, maybe it would be better if they just sat before their mud huts and watched the sands move. You guys make me tired."

Dhar felt a stir of indignation at the flippancy of Sankri's accusation. He had been ready to console his brother, comfort him in his moment of trouble and doubt and be there for him. Certainly not prepared to have the Discipline thrown in his face, or the purpose that underpinned the Unified Independent Front movement shredded into mere political expediency. The tribes of Anar'on may have their disputes; that is the way of life, but they all supported the Rahtir Council. Prepared to lash back, he merely gaped at the amused upturn of his brother's mouth, mortified by the realization he was a breath away from spouting the *Saftara* himself. Were its words so ingrained in him that he could not form original thoughts?

Terr nodded and smiled at the irony of it. "So, Nightwings my brother, the shadow who walks at night. Tell me again that I should welcome being Death's harbinger."

"I…" Dhar completely confused, his cloak of moral superiority ripped off him, left behind…what? Was the Wanderer's rigid adherence to the Discipline and blind obedience to the *Saftara's* tenets the only things that sustained them? Were they a veneer that hid the base self, keeping them from exploding across the Serrll with Death blazing in their hand? Assuredly, but were the Saddish-aa so shallow and the Discipline so superficial? He rejected that, but he thought he saw something of what Sankri was getting at. The issue needed to be oversimplified or they could not grasp the essentials. Was that it?

He saw the wounded anguish of Sankri's spirit and followed him into the night to...to offer *his* platitudes? He accused his brother of lacking in courage to face up to the responsibility of his gift, and Sankri had now turned this into a trial of the Discipline, questioning the very faith in its teachings. Why did his alien brother war with himself so? Why couldn't he simply accept what he was now? Accept...

He felt his face drain and his breath hissed as the awful truth struck him. His brother did not question the Discipline, but himself and his place in it. It had always been an inner and singular struggle with a heritage forced on him. Dhar had seen it, masking it as an irrelevancy, not recognizing it for the struggle it really was. Terr had simply torn away the façade and forced them both to look at the underlying truth.

"Sankri..." A lump grew in his throat and he swallowed heavily. "I have wronged you, I see that now," he said gruffly, his voice a deep tremble in his chest. "When you lay there on the mat, your spirit wounded and I reached out to you, I did it for the noblest of reasons. I could not stand there to see you suffer and do nothing. You have to believe that. Our master wanted to stop me, but I was determined. As much for my pride and vanity as a desire to help you that I forced myself on you. Because of that one act of arrogance, you suffer now even more. For that, I am most sorry."

"Nightwings..." Terr reached with his hand, but Dhar drew back.

"No, hear me. Your words have provoked me as you intended, and this must be said. They have shown me the error of my actions and my hasty judgment of you. Instead of accusing you, it is I who lack courage, for the way of the Discipline is not a struggle for me as it obviously is for you. It is a joyful fulfillment. I could not understand why you resisted the God's gift. Now I know that for you, it was not something willingly sought and received. Walking in god's shadow, I expected you to behave like any other Wanderer, your alien nature merely a uniqueness of your individuality. I failed to see the pain of your struggle with a code of alien morality that must be so terrifyingly different from your own."

Dhar knelt and bowed deeply. "My brother, I would undo what I have imposed on you," he whispered into the sands.

Terr touched the scar on his left temple and shook his head. He did not intend to reduce this proud being to abject humility, cloaked as he was in anger and internal rebellion. Seeing Dhar kneeling before him only added weight to his brother's veiled accusation. He should embrace the superior framework of the Discipline, not resist it, but the power over Death requires its own responsibility. He wasn't sure he had the strength of character to meet that responsibility. Life would be so much simpler without having to be *correct* every time. It was one thing to have an aggressive argument with flying fists. That same argument with Death unleashed was unchecked indulgence. Who could stand before him to curb his excesses? The problem, he realized wryly, the Discipline allowed no room for fun. Given the harsh demands of just surviving in the Saffal, giving into fun could be fatal.

He touched Dhar's shoulder and the Wanderer looked up. Even kneeling, his towering form imposing.

"Then we wouldn't be brothers," Terr said gently and placed an open palm against Dhar's chest.

Hesitating, his emotions warring within him, Dhar reached out with his hand. He felt the touch and something flowed between them, something that more than friendship or love. They were one and in each other they were complete.

"All I wanted to say, Nightwings, I need some time to sort myself out," Terr said ruefully.

Dhar cleared his throat. "You have a damn peculiar way of going about it."

Terr smiled broadly, then chuckled. "The sorting out might

take some time. You'll have to be patient with me and forgive me my transgressions along the way."

"Restraint, my brother," Dhar admonished with mock emphasis.

"Yeah."

"And now?"

Terr brooded for a moment. Has he sorted himself out? He looked up where the constellations blazed bright in the sky and inclined his head at a pattern of stars.

"The Stalker carries a pretty big bow for the job," he said casually. "Must have taken some practice to bend it all the way back."

Dhar peered closely into Terr's face, but the shadows lay thick, shrouding them. Still, he did not have to see Terr's face to know what his brother had decided. In a chaotic environment one chooses a solution in irrationals. Sankri would explore the morality and limits of his power where the *Saftara* was helpless to guide him. Even though he walked in the shadow of Death, he was the man he was. The Wanderers would not march across the Serrll, but it seemed that a tentative step would be made nonetheless in the form of an alien adept. Fitting perhaps, but Dhar felt uneasy.

The gates of chaos have very wide doors.

* * *

Without hurrying, Marrakan slowly poured the thick yellow liquid into two tall glasses bound in oark-calf leather. The liquor glistened oily in the solid shafts of light that streamed through open windows. A dry desert breeze teased the room and made the office warm, but the two men didn't seem to mind. Ronowan waited until Marrakan placed the bound flask on the polished peelath table, then reached for the glass with both hands. Almost with reverence, he brought the tumbler to his nose and inhaled the delicate bouquet of the liquor. It smelled

51

of parched sands, burned rock, dry desert airs, and swaying fields of tarad grass. After a moment of contemplation, he took a small sip.

An infinity of tastes rolled over his tongue, the fragile flavors of peelath blossoms predominant; sweet but not cloying— pure. The prana water had a silkiness and smoothness that identified it as stock matured for at least eighteen years, stored deep in cool sands. He closed his eyes and allowed the liquor to diffuse through him, carrying with it images of far lands and memories of treks made long ago.

Prana water was one of Anar'on's prized exports, rare and astronomically expensive. In a year a village could hope to produce forty to sixty bottles, and there were not that many villages. The liquor was also a chemist's nightmare. Attempts were made all the time to synthesize the wine, some of it very good, but the imitation paled when one tasted the real thing. Prana water was much more than the combination of its parts, as with all things.

"She is all right?" Marrakan inquired solemnly over his glass and Ronowan smiled.

"She thought a flight in an M-4 the coolest thing. They even allowed her on the command deck, or whatever they call those things."

Marrakan allowed himself a small smile and nodded. The exuberance of the young would not be denied. Several of the delegates saw the plenary conference on Anar'on as a way to bring family members to Naklanor for a holiday. The Orgomy group's capital world had many attractions beyond Anar'on's means, the principal ones being its soft airs, warm seas and a temperate climate. Ronowan's youngest daughter took the opportunity to return to Anar'on for a break from the university and gotten more than she bargained for, as did the delegates. He still fielded complaints. Plucked from the comparative luxury of a civilian liner and dumped unceremoniously into the utilitarian comfort of an M-4, no matter what the reason, had not been an amusing experience. Their sensibilities were justifiably outraged, but Marrakan made no apologies for taking advantage of circumstances to defeat a plot that could have seriously undermined the Unified Independent Front and its cause. Their outrage only mildly tempered by the subsequent exposure of the Palean base on Italan and the existence of the AUP Provisional Committee. It was a calculated, but marginal risk. The delegates were never in any real danger and, as Prime Director for the Kaleen group, his call to make.

"And Kai Tanard?"

Ronowan's face hardened. He visited the raid commander at Tanarath General, shocked at the change in the Palean. Tanard looked old, his eyes cold and lifeless. The scars across his right cheek and chin were vivid purple malevolent lines. He lay on the bed unmoving, his arm held rigid in a restraining clamp. Looking at him lying there, without hope, without a future, Ronowan felt a twinge of pity. He fought down the emotion when he remembered who Tanard was and what he had done along the way. Death, broken minds and broken bodies were the legacy of a flawed policy. To the faceless men in the AUP Provisional Committee, engaging raiders as an instrument of their strategy may have been a logical move. To him, it showed a monstrous lack of regard for the value of life and ship's crews. The Serrll would be a grim place indeed if this Committee ever managed to claw to power. To ally himself with such, Tanard deserved his condemnation, not pity.

"He has a genetic abnormality, which means his arm will not regenerate. Genotherapy was tried, but failed. However, there are excellent cyberplasts available to treat such cases. His new arm will be almost indistinguishable from a real one. Otherwise, he is treated correctly."

Marrakan took a sip and regarded his aide with interest.

"I am sure he is, and I see that you haven't overlooked what he is. That is as it should be, but refrain from judging. Keep me advised of any relevant intelligence we get from him and his crew."

"Of course, master."

"Once we finish with him, hand him over to BueCult. Not before."

"Understood."

"I want you to start a penetration mission against this AUP Provisional Committee. We need to know who they are, their strengths, and weaknesses. If necessary, we shall take steps."

"The penetration has already begun, master."

"Good. We must not get caught like this again. Their next attempt may very well succeed. That, of course, we cannot permit."

"I don't see what we could have done to predict the existence of the Provisional Committee, master. A cabal operating outside the normal framework of the Palean and Sargon governments?"

"But were they operating outside the framework of their respective governments? To mount an operation like Lemos required considerable capital and staff. Suborning an entire Fleet outpost mandated complicity at the highest government levels. No, the signs were all there for us to read, my son. We just didn't see them. When the raids started on Pizgor's commerce, we should have been warned. All those deaths, a harsh penalty for our lack of attentiveness," Marrakan murmured and took another leisurely sip.

"Master, have you considered that the Alikan Union Party might not be the real objective of the Sargon/Palean merger, but is merely a front to absorb the Palean Union and usher in a Greater Sargon?"

"The thought had occurred to me," Marrakan said heavily. "And it probably occurred to the Paleans as well. They have always been very deliberate and calculating in what they do. They will be careful."

"The Provisional Committee may have failed with Pizgor and could now be eyeing other more vulnerable independent systems."

"Like Kaleen? Indeed, and the point has not been lost on me."

Ronowan nodded. "I presume, of course, the Karkans had not stood idly by while their coalition partner blatantly goes about usurping the Servatory Party's authority?"

"No, I don't imagine they have," Marrakan mused. "Although they wouldn't mind seeing the Unified Independent Front destroyed, they're not about to do it themselves."

"Preferring Sargon or the Paleans to do it for them?"

"Just so. I believe the Karkans anticipated the attempt on Pizgor would fail. A judgment call, relying on Sargon's impatience to force the merger and the situation allowed them to turn their attention on us. They are good at that kind of strategic maneuvering."

"Then the Servatory Party has conceded that the Unified Independent Front will become a recognized political block, and Illeran came to woo our support?" Ronowan ventured.

Marrakan did not bother to answer the obvious and stared thoughtfully at his glass. In life, only death was a guarantee. Still, there were seven years to go before the next general elections, plenty of time for the Karkans to derail the UIF.

"Make a note to highlight for my attention the next quarter's shipping volumes. I want to see if eliminating Italan will translate into a direct decrease in hull losses attributable to raider activity."

Ronowan stared at his mentor. "The more militant elements within the Alikan Union Party may be acting independently of the Provisional Committee?"

Marrakan raised an eyebrow in appreciation. "Wouldn't you? Is security in place for the conference?"

"Every offworlder intelligence operative is identified and tagged. When deemed necessary the individual was deported. The delegates will be safe."

Marrakan nodded. A single smuggled plasma charge in the

conference hall, that's all it would take. The success against Tanard would be nullified and the Provisional Committee would still have won.

"On the matter of First Scout Terrllss-rr. He appears to be a singularly unique individual."

Ronowan allowed himself a small smile. "I dare say. After seeing him, I understand why Master Sidhara speaks of him with puzzlement."

"An alien initiate. I had not thought it possible. Sidhara named him Sankri?"

"The ways of the gods are inscrutable."

"Apparently."

Sankri…Sarumajan, the destroyer of worlds. Sidhara told him of his dream where he saw the alien suspended in space with two stars adorning his feet, lightnings devouring a world. If true, Death would reign and untold billions would die before its thirst was slaked and the gods relented. It was no wonder Sidhara felt disturbed.

A warm breeze drifted through the open window, bringing with it the dry smells of the Saffal. Marrakan yearned to wander its desolate treks again and lose himself in the escarpments from where the gods so whimsically appeared to play with the Saddish-aa. Those days were behind him now and there were other obstacles to overcome, now seemingly from within the Unified Independent Front itself.

"The Resident," he mused, "it was a clumsy and misguided attempt to recruit him. I am not surprised that Sankri threw the offer back in his face. I understand why it was done, but the Resident allowed his zeal to override prudence and good judgment. We have erred somewhere, you and I, if the UIF is seen as another self-serving political machine. What did Sankri say? 'What I resent is your automatic assumption that I share your singular needs. I suggest Anar'on may be committing the same transgression.' Profound words from someone still so young. Profound."

"He could be right," Ronowan said quietly, impressed that his master was able not only to retain this level of detail, but also to recall it so exactly. "The objective may have become our cause and in its pursuit we have overlooked a lone cry of protest."

"Indeed. An alien perspective *can* sometimes be useful. The UIF must not become a holy war and room must be made for everyone or there will be no room for anyone. We shall achieve independence, that is inevitable, but we need to take care in selecting the path. I do not fear the obstacles that will be placed in our way. I fear those that will confront us once we reach the journey's end."

"How to exercise our Executive Council vote?"

"Very much so." Marrakan placed his glass on the table, pleased at his aide's perceptiveness, stood and moved to the window. His face hard and lined with deep wrinkles inscribed by years of political life. The eyes, with their vertical slits, used to be orange and the slits red. Now they were faded. Looking out over the city, he automatically lowered the thin membranes to protect the eyes against fine abrasive sand. His once ocher hair was developing streaks of brown and spilled around his shoulders in thick braids.

Dusk fell and the air became soft and intimate, no longer harsh and draining. The open sea a dark shadow, its shore lost in Tanarath's awakening glare. After the oppressive heat of the day the streets would fill, drawing people to its many attractions. The hanging gardens, always popular with offworlders—a sinful waste of water and greenery—would be crowded. A decadent reminder of bloated blue worlds, of easy life and soft citizens. Although shunned by the Wanderers, he rejected petitions from some of the more conservative elements to abolish the attractions. In themselves the hanging gardens were beautiful. It was the contrast between plenty and privation that most irked some. The sin was in the mind, not in the object, he reminded himself.

"Tell me, my son, what does the Unified Independent Front mean to you?" Marrakan asked softly, his eyes on the city, but he didn't see it. He was somewhere else, in his youth, when the power was new in his hands and the Saffal a wonderland and a plaything to be discovered and conquered. The worlds of the Serrll meant little to him then. They were just glinting points in a night sky. When did his perspective change? Sankri's words were loud in his mind and the question was suddenly very important.

Ronowan stared at the old Wanderer, seeing the subtle glow of power that hung about him like a cloak. He suppressed an urge to pay homage. Wryly, he recalled the awe and timidity with which he first approached the old Rahtir, to the point where he could not carry out his duties. One day Marrakan simply stood before him and extended his arm.

"You hand!" he demanded.

Puzzled, Ronowan slowly extended his arm, open palm up.

"What do you see?"

"I see two hands," Ronowan said uncertainly.

"And that is *all* you see. Two identical hands. So stop this foolishness and get on with your work!"

Ronowan remembered staring after the retreating figure and at his own hand, and he finally understood. Beneath all the trappings of power, Marrakan was still just a man—powerful, yes, and deserving of respect, not reverence. A valuable lesson, and one he should not forget now.

What *did* the UIF mean to him?

"As I told Sankri, master, the Unified Independent Front is more than mere political opportunism to exert influence on the Executive Council. In a self-serving environment one must develop defenses in order to stave off annihilation. The UIF is a defense mechanism for Kaleen, Orgomy and the surrounding independents against the predators who would absorb us. Admittedly, the threat is only a political one, but freedom is a precious commodity even though the cage might be gilded. With the Discipline, no one could stand before us. That course would lead us all to an even more terrible end and an ultimate betrayal of everything that we are. If the UIF is to achieve recognition, it must be through voluntary participation and a sharing of a common belief. Anything else will be duplicity. I believe in those words and I live for the day when our worlds shall be free."

"Freedom," Marrakan reflected and turned. "Such an elusive and subjective concept. You have spoken well, but in everything you've said, there is one glaring omission. You have not answered my question."

Ronowan opened his mouth in protest. Then the impact of Marrakan's words hit him. His master was right. He spoke of a glorious future for Kaleen, but what did all that really mean to him: greater personal power, political power, self-fulfillment? A legacy in history?

"To preserve our way of life…"

Marrakan smiled, but it was a grim smile. "Our way of life is to cling to the shifting mists of past glories. The purity of the Discipline has been contaminated by our contact with the Serrll. The ways of our ancestors may be irrelevant or even dangerous now. Why should we cling to that which is gone?"

Ronowan's brow creased in concentration. "We have the Discipline and the *Saftara* to guide us. These things are still true, master, whether the Serrll touches us or not," he said, floundering for meaning, aware of the inadequacy of his answer.

Marrakan nodded slowly. "I was thinking of the muneera…"

Ronowan saw the little desert predator: timid, yet ferocious, a master of desert survival where everything was an enemy, even the sands. It made conical traps in the sand to snare food. Things blunder into it and are unable to crawl out because the loose sand shifts beneath the hapless victim, carrying it to the waiting muneera at the bottom.

"Safe in its environment," he said cautiously, probing for

hidden meanings behind Marrakan's simple words, "but vulnerable to predators should it venture out of its lair. Still, venture out it must nonetheless."

"To grow and find a mate, it has to experience life and overcome its adversities, yes."

"And sometimes it too falls as prey."

"Death weeds out the unfit and the unfortunate with equal impartiality or regard for justice or cause, my son."

Ronowan leaned forward, clutching his glass. "When Kaleen ventured out of its isolationism to become more than a curiosity, we were helped by those who now seek to destroy us."

"Because then we were merely a cuddly muneera and not the predator that we really are," Marrakan said and watched Ronowan's reaction.

"Predator…"

"And Orgomy was our second kill."

"Second kill?"

"The first, of course—"

"The Kaleen systems, yes. When Anar'on took on the mantle of the Unified Independent Front, we were no longer timid frontier worlds reaching out into a hostile economic frontier. We became a political force, a predator." Ronowan sipped the prana water and his thoughts whirled in turmoil. "Master, are you saying to avoid becoming prey, the Unified Independent Front has unknowingly built a sand cone as a barrier and a warning?"

"Perhaps. What we may have overlooked is that a barrier is also an automatic invitation for those on the outside to tear it down. There need not be a reason or there may be many reasons. It's the way of things."

"In our zeal to secure political self-determination, you're saying we have become parochial and insular?"

"Not bad." Marrakan nodded approvingly. "Look at our relationship with the Serrll. Admittedly oversimplified, first, there is resentment that we've been placed within its political and economic sphere. That gives rise to inevitable rebellion and the scheming to overthrow the perceived yoke even when none exists. Finally, there is the cause to achieve freedom. After a time the cause swamps us all, sweeping away the resentment that gave it birth, carrying us to its inevitable conclusion where the struggle itself becomes the cause—without reason, heart or purpose. It promises nothing and demands everything. We serve only to perpetuate the struggle, the nobility of it now merely words of propaganda that allows no dissent. Sankri had it right more than he realized."

"Master, I still believe in the validity of the UIF."

"So do I. That doesn't mean we should not question or be critical of our tactics. The danger we always face when pursuing an objective we perceive is for the greater good of everyone, is that we may be imposing an individual interpretation that could in fact be a source of great evil, such as autocratic or dictatorial rule. For us the danger is even greater because we walk in the shadow of Death. The exercise of power, no matter how benevolent the intent, is always destructive. Should we ever stray down that path, the consequences would be terrible." Marrakan paused, momentarily lost in contemplation, then lifted his head.

"We need to place more operatives on Captal. See to it," he said evenly.

"It shall be done," Ronowan said. He drained his glass and stood up.

Marrakan watched his aide depart, then turned to the open window and gazed into the dark sky and the phosphorescent sheen of a black sea. It was far into the night when he stirred again.

# Chapter Three

It took four days of hard digging to expose the six blocks that made up the 10.8-meter length of wall. The far corner of the wall was cleared all the way to its base almost a meter below ground level. The dig made a sizeable trench and Lauren fervently hoped it wouldn't rain. The two blocks lay on top of each other supported by a stone platform that protruded .9 meters from the wall. Each floor stone 1.8m wide and .9m thick. They exposed enough of the corner to show that the wall blocks were also .9m thick. This combination of measurements not lost on them. However, the implication behind the 2:1 ratio eluded analysis. Was it allowance for the mechanical strength of the blocks? Lauren sent the data to civil engineers back at Columbia U and they told her it was not possible for the thin blocks to support the weight of the mound without internal pillars.

Next to the makeshift hut, having transferred their work tent from the other side of the mound, she adjusted the laptop connections and nodded to Ibanez standing in the trench. The Pemex engineer promptly started rolling the ground-penetrating radar unit along the floor blocks with maddening deliberation. Her team crowded about her, eagerly waiting for the image to be painted on the screen. Several archaeologists from The Palace site stood about, their work forgotten, observing the proceedings with consuming interest as Ibanez walked along the base of the wall.

Speculations regarding the possible contents of the chamber, if there was indeed one, were rife. Shifting in real time the image slowly built up. A reddish-orange linear pattern, a typical sandstone signature, stood out clearly above a uniform brown-gray and white of the twenty-meter-deep supporting soil strata.

Lauren did not expect anything there, but she needed to check. When Ibanez reached the end of the exposed wall, he looked up.

"Another run, doc?"

"Later. Right now, do a calibration sweep against the wall itself."

"What depth?"

"Twenty meters."

He waved at her and unclipped a small hand-held unit. Trailing an extension cord, he placed the emitter head against the wall.

"You getting an image?"

Lauren adjusted the tracker ball on the laptop's keyboard and the image cleared. Beyond the initial layer of reddish-brown lay a zone of black that indicated a cavity. Martin turned and grinned broadly.

"It *is* a chamber!"

The comment raised a torrent of theorizing from the expectant audience. Staring at the image, Lauren frowned. There didn't seem to be any pillars. So how did they support the roof? She absently pulled back the sleeves of her shirt.

As Ibanez walked back along the wall, the uniform line of black on the screen faded to show a grainy gray-white image of a large object. When Ibanez neared the corner of the wall the image turned a uniform black again.

"There is something inside," Imatlan breathed beside her. This prompted another round of excited comment.

"Scan the entire wall!" Lauren shouted. Ibanez nodded and moved the emitter back along the wall, then climbed up the excavated slope into the corner test trench.

It was almost impossible to visualize an image of the entire chamber from the jumble of confused colors in the moving scan, but something definitely lay inside, resting about a meter above the floor.

"A sarcophagus?" Imatlan ventured.

Lauren turned her head and scowled at him. Anyone else would have gotten the corner for such a dumb remark.

"Nine meters long?"

"Then what is it?"

"It doesn't look like stone, that's for sure. Take a break Ibanez," she told the engineer when he reached the top of the wall. "I want to run the imaging routine." She keyed in the drop-down menu and selected 'Image Processing', then 'Composite'. The laptop's hard drive silent as the computer crunched through the mass of captured data. After two minutes, color lines started to build from top of the screen. It took another three minutes before the composite image was complete.

Martin gawked. "Holy shit!" Lauren and Kareza shot him a withering glare.

The first pass image coarse and showed little detail, but it didn't have to. The gray pebble outline clear enough. Almost two-and-a-half meters thick at the center, it tapered off sharply toward the ends.

"What the hell is that thing?" Imatlan demanded, a mighty frown creasing his forehead. "Looks like an inverted boat hull."

Lauren shrugged. "Whatever it is, it's metallic. Look at the color profile. Wood would show as yellow."

Imatlan grunted like he'd been punched. "Metallic? That's not possible, Lauren. You must be mistaken."

"The Olmec or the Maya, or whoever built that thing, had copper and bronze, you know."

"Mmm. The wall blocks don't look to me like they could have been made by a copper chisel."

"So you're puzzled by that as well?"

"We have to get inside."

"Obviously. To get in, we'll need some special equipment and people."

"Already on hand, Lauren. Pemex will have them here in the morning."

Lauren touched his arm and flashed him a grin. He could

be nice when he wanted to.

"Good job."

"They're yours for a day and I wouldn't ask how much they cost."

"Don't worry, I won't," she said and laughed. "I want them here first thing. That will give us the rest of the day to clear away the entire wall base."

"Lauren, this is your dig and my government has given you full authority, but they never envisioned finding something like this. Even if the chamber is empty the wall itself is a priceless national treasure."

"Relax, will you. I won't be doing any blasting, if that's what's worrying you. I won't even scratch any of the stones."

"Ah, you'll cut along the joints, no?"

"Right, then push the whole block into the chamber."

"Push..." It made sense and he liked it. To pull the block out would require drilling into the face to attach eyebolts. The block would look unsightly even after the holes were patched. On the other hand, once pushed in, they could easily tip the thing on its side and drag it out later unmarked. The hole in the wall could then be re-plugged or left open as a permanent door-way. Either way, it was a minimum invasive approach.

"There is one other thing," Lauren said and looked at him intently. "I want the *policia* here tomorrow and the site closed to the public."

He raised a questioning eyebrow, then nodded. A sensible precaution against possible looters, and there was no telling what they might find in there.

* * *

Cool and deep, the sky clear, promising another fine day. An undisguised undercurrent of excitement and expectation rippled among the dig team. Everyone waited impatiently for the stone gang to make the breakthrough. A detachment of two police from Villahermosa were posted at the site entrance. They leaned idly against their cruiser and chatted. The large portable diesel generator thumped noisily beside the hut. It labored occasionally and belched dark smoke when too much pressure was applied to the enormous cutting wheel. Sandstone not a particularly hard rock, but the cutting wheel gave off an incredible screech as it chewed furiously along the joint. Even though water was pumped into the cut for lubrication, the process threw back a gushing plume of white dust and slush. Another pump was used to keep the trench from getting flooded. It was dirty and unpleasant work.

Lauren hovered over the gang like an expectant mother, driving the workmen to distraction. Finally, Ibanez exploded and dragged her bodily out of the trench, telling her in no uncertain terms he would down tools if she interfered again. Looking at her as she clenched and unclenched her fists, staring anxiously at the workmen, Martin had to smile. The doc not so unflappable after all. Beneath that hard façade lay a vulnerable persona like any other. Well, almost like any other. He sympathized with her.

For six years, she suffered rejection and vitriolic ridicule from her colleagues over her theory that the Yucatan civilizations were far older than anyone thought. The sandstone wall before him a most striking proof and vindication of her views. Already, fossils like Boulcher and Kirmond were backpedaling, pontificating learnedly how her find merely served to confirm their own suspicions, conveniently forgetting that as recently as last fall they denigrated her expedition to Comalcalco. Their peace overtures now were as hollow as they sounded and did nothing to deflect the spotlight from the doc. Why was she so nervous then? What did she think was in the mysterious chamber, and where did those markings fit in?

He saw the final GPR composite scan, they all did. With only one wall exposed and the whole of Temple II in the way, it was not possible to do an overhead scan and build a three dimensional image. They ran a scan over most of the mound's top as they could reach, but the image was broken by regular parallel interference stripes—frustrating. Still, what the ground radar profile did reveal was intriguing enough and he did not think it looked anything like a damn boat. Did the doc know more than she was telling? It wouldn't surprise him at all.

He turned his head and looked lingeringly at Chatika. Now there was someone who had it all together, someone who knew where she was going, like the doc. Chatika swept back her hair and caught him looking at her.

"This waiting…"

He nodded. "I know, but it won't be long now."

Chatika smiled. This was not the first time she caught Martin looking at her like that; a mixture of hunger, desire, and something else, almost like fear. Not that she would ever consider getting into a relationship with the American. She invested too much into her career to throw it all away in a moment of heated passion, but nice to be considered desirable. Besides, her boyfriend back in Mexico City, a civil engineer, would not be amused if she started to flirt.

The screech from the cutting saw suddenly stopped and vacant silence descended, broken by the thump of the generator and the gurgle of water from the pump. Ibanez removed his mask, gave a long sigh, and wiped his brow, then looked up at Lauren.

"We're still sixteen centimeters short, Doctor. The jacks should be able to push the block in."

"And if they can't?"

Ibanez shrugged. "Then we'll use the long drill as a saw. I would prefer not to do that if possible. It would be a very slow job."

"Drill a test hole first. I need to take an air sample from the inside. One man on the wall only and he is to wear a respirator."

Ibanez scowled and shrugged. The doctor explained to all of them the dangers of exposure to fungal spores, but he thought the gringo woman crazy. How can anything that's been sealed up for perhaps hundreds of years harm them now? Still, it was her money—an hourly rate plus bonus. He shook his head, but gave the instructions anyway.

Lauren ignored him. Ibanez may be a great mining engineer, but he knew nothing of the potential death that sometimes lurked inside sealed tombs. These days, archaeologists were prepared and it was rare for anyone to be caught out, but fungal infection nevertheless represented a real danger. Cryptococcus strains and aspergillus were only two of the nastier members of the family. Pulmonary infection was not unusual and sometimes spread to bone. In more extreme cases patients developed cerebral abscesses that lead to lingering madness and eventual death. A sealed, moist and presumably warm environment an ideal breeding ground for fungal pathogens. Even if the fungus itself was now dead due to lack of nutrients, its spores could lie dormant forever, waiting to become virulent once inhaled. The chamber could be sterile for all she knew, and she was not about to risk anyone's life on an assumption when modern precautionary measures were so simple.

The driller heaved himself up the makeshift wooden platform until his chest was level with the top joint along the 1.8m high block. He carefully positioned the one-meter-long, four-millimeter tungsten drill bit into the left corner of the joint and pushed it in. There was not much left of the protruding drill shaft when he stopped. The compressor suddenly chattered and a thin cloud of dust shot out. Martin made sure that everything was recorded on his video camera. A few moments later the driller lurched when the bit broke through and there was an audible hiss as a thin jet of escaping air pushed its way out. The driller immediately withdrew the bit, laid the drill on the platform as instructed, and climbed down. Another workman hosed down his coveralls with evident delight. Only then did he take off his respirator and grinned widely, his sunburned complexion slightly wild.

Lauren grabbed her bag and with a nod to Ibanez, quickly clambered into the trench and up the platform. She took out a cotton swab and wiped the corner of the wall around the hole, then popped the swab into a glass jar. She did the same thing to the tip of the drill bit. Once off the platform, she motioned to Ibanez.

"Wash down the drill properly before it's used again. Then wash down the wall."

"It will be done, Doctor."

She disappeared into the hut and quickly carried out the simple tests using a standard kit. The samples were clean, but she wasn't about to lower her guard. She strode toward the trench and waved to Ibanez. With mounting tension, everyone watched as Ibanez positioned two jacks with maddening slowness. He adjusted a set of protective wooden blocks against the trench wall and nodded to the two workmen. The pawls clanked over the ratchet as the workmen took up the slack. When the wooden pads were firmly seated against the stone face, Ibanez made a last check and the workmen started pumping the long jack handles. The pawls made two clanks and that was it. The block gave no indication it was about to move. With further pumping the supports groaned and shifted. Ibanez shouted and the retaining pins were hammered out. The pawls whirled around the ratchet with the relief in tension.

"It's no good, Doctor," Ibanez declared mournfully. "After all this time the stone blocks have probably cemented themselves into place. We'll have to cut."

There was a collective groan of disappointment from the audience, including the scientists from the restoration site. Lauren shrugged in resignation.

"Everyone is to wear a respirator," she cautioned him.

When one driller started protesting in a torrent of voluble Spanish, Ibanez stepped in and shut him up. The respirator made the already hot and unpleasant work even more uncomfortable, but he couldn't fault the doctor's caution. Drilling resumed. It took another two hours to push away the wooden platform, and the jacks fitted again.

A soft crack from the base of the block and the whole thing lurched inward. Someone gave a yell and there was a spontaneous outburst of furious clapping. Lauren and Kareza exchanged grins. Ibanez got the workmen to fit a hydraulic support beam under each end of the top block to prevent it from shifting under the weight of the mound material above it when the bottom block was pushed in.

With the block dislodged, it was easy to push. It slid in unevenly, scraping along the sides of the neighboring blocks. After 900 millimeters, it rested inside the chamber. Lauren yelled and the pumping on the jacks stopped. She grabbed a respirator and fumbled to put it on as she descended into the trench. The thing smelled ghastly and her skin crawled at its clammy touch. Peering into the dark crack between the wall and the block, she saw the floor as a continuation of the stone slab that formed the exterior platform. She feared the block might sink into soft earth inside and possibly topple over, crushing whatever priceless artifacts might be inside. She waved at Ibanez and the workmen started pumping the jack handles again.

With the gap wide enough, Lauren gave a signal. The workmen gratefully moved back and pulled off their respirators. She glanced up at Kareza and flashed him a tight little smile. He nodded to her. This was her moment and he knew what these rare snatches of history meant to a professional archaeologist. Basking in the glow of her find, his reputation already immeasurably enhanced. Gazing at her as she squeezed through the gap, he pursed his lips. *You can have it all, my dear Lauren—for now.*

Behind her respirator faceplate, her breathing sounded unnaturally loud. She wrinkled her nose in distaste, trying to ignore the rank smell of the mask. Gods only knew who had worn the hideous thing before and where it had been. Next time, she would bring her own. As her eyes slowly adjusted to the gloom, she cautiously looked about and absently ran her left hand along the interior wall. The surface polished smooth, without markings, drawings or anything. If this was some kind of burial chamber, it was a most unusual one not to be decorated, given all the trouble to build it with such astonishingly elaborate craftsmanship.

Apart from some drilling residue, the wall, happy to see, was clean, with no hint of dormant dust or fungal molds. She peered into the gloomy interior, her breath a fluttering rasp. Too dark to make anything out, but she sensed that the interior was large. She also had a strong impression of something looming before her. Unaccountably, she became suddenly breathless. She felt blood drain from her face and her mouth went dry and coppery. The oval shape from the GPR scan burned bright in her mind. Swallowing hard to clear the coppery taste, she slowly raised her flashlight and clicked it on.

"O my gosh!"

When she stopped trembling from waves of excitement that coursed through her, she played the light along the length of the object, captivated by its clean lines and elegant engineering. The gray polished surface looked smoky and sullen, refusing to glint even under direct light. Unable to contain herself, she tilted back her head and gave a whooping yell, almost deafening herself in the confines of the respirator mask. She quickly took swabs off the wall and floor and popped them into a specimen jar. Fumbling with the lid, she took another lingering look at the resting shape. This wasn't just a byline in some archaeology text, but a whole page in every history book in the world. This was unmatched professional success and a ticket to any university she cared to name.

*Eat your heart out Boulcher.*

She emerged, still wearing a broad grin, and ripped off the mask. The air tasted marvelous and she breathed deeply. The others crowded the edge of the trench and peered down eagerly. Prepared to be generous, she gave Kareza a flashing smile.

"We heard a yell," he said, his concern genuine. She laughed and threw the jar of samples to Martin.

"Run tests on these, will you?" she said and motioned to Kareza. "Come down! You won't believe what I saw."

Imatlan sensed her agitation and quickly descended into the trench. He saw Lauren fascinated, absorbed and angry, but never this excited. He took Ibanez's proffered respirator and strapped it on. Lauren glanced at him and disappeared inside. He looked at the gap in the wall and followed her in. He hesitated before the dark entrance, then cautiously eased himself through with a tight squeeze. What surprised him was the air. Despite the drilling, the shaft of soft light that spilled in relatively clear and free of the usual dust particles and floating matter. The chamber must have been hermetically sealed. Absorbed in thought, he twitched when Lauren grabbed his arm and spun him around. It took him a few seconds to comprehend what he was seeing.

"Jesu Christe!" he hissed, unable to grasp the ship was real.

The hull seemed to absorb all light as he swept his torch over it. It looked big, the confined space of the chamber accentuated its nine-meter diameter. Supported about a meter above the floor by what looked like helicopter skids, only sturdier. The belly relatively flat and the sides curved gently up. There was no prominent central bulge—a favorite of cinema films—only a gentle and pleasing slope that flowed down to a rounded edge. He could not see any access hatches or portholes. The gray metal looked perfectly smooth and unbroken.

With a lump in his throat, he stared at the ancient ship with almost religious reverence. Old folklore legends crowded his mind. Who could say now that Tepeu and Gucumatz were not their creators?

Human history as they knew it was now changed forever. He took a hesitant step closer to the ship and reached up with his hand. Gingerly, he brushed the unexpectedly raspy surface with his fingertips, then pressed his palm flat against the hull. It was surprisingly cold, given the chamber, although cool, certainly not cold. He wondered why the ship's skin should have such a temperature gradient. While he thought about it, he made the next logical connection and arrived at an equally quick and disagreeable conclusion. The ship was not something he or Lauren could possibly study. This would require a full scientific team and the whole site would probably be taken out of his hands. It also meant that work on The Palace would almost certainly be stopped, something he must not allow to happen if at all possible.

Lauren swung her torch over the bare walls and began to appreciate how large and empty the chamber really was. Apart from the ship, there was nothing else inside: no markings, writing, drawings or implements. The interior stark and utilitarian, apparently designed for one function only, simply to hold the ship. She looked up and pointed the torch at the glinting ribbons of metal that spanned the ceiling. Now she knew how a 900-millimeter block could support the tonnes of mound that covered it. She smiled when she noted the length of the blocks. There was no need to measure them. They were the same 1.8m as the wall blocks.

Her footsteps sounded hollow as she walked slowly around the ship. Not a disc, she realized, but an ellipsoid. She shook her head in amazed wonder, still unable to believe it was real. This single object would turn Mesoamerican archaeology on its head, not to mention the world's religions. Ancient writings would have to be dusted off and read from a different perspective, especially some of the Dead Sea Scrolls texts and the Indian Rig Veda.

Five thousand years, she marveled. Were the aliens of old still looking over a fledgling Earth civilization? She stopped in her tracks as an awful realization struck her. She was finished here. As soon as this became public the whole site would be crawling with scientists and probably the military as well, she thought in disgust. This ship is worth going to war over. Its technology could catapult Earth's sciences a hundred years into the future, or destroy it. A country that could deploy a fleet of such ships would rule the world. Was man ready to deal with what this ship represented? Did they have the social and moral maturity to look beyond political expediency to see how this find could benefit mankind as a whole? Whether they did or not the problem was out of her hands. The genie out of the bottle and there was no putting it back.

She rounded the curve of the ship and caught Kareza staring thoughtfully into nothing. He turned his head and their eyes met. It was obvious he'd been thinking along similar lines and reached the same unpleasant conclusion. Something else gleamed in his eyes she saw in Boulcher and others—envy, mixed with resentment. Some of the glory would rub off on him, but it was clear he wanted it all.

Imatlan shook his head and peered into Lauren's shining brown eyes.

"Perhaps it would have been better if you never found that first stone," he said soberly.

"But we did, and now we have to deal with it," she said sternly.

Just then, Martin squeezed through the gap and did a double take.

"Holy shit!"

"Your mask!" Lauren screamed at him.

Martin tore his gaze away from the ship and waved. "It's all right. There is no contamination. Wow! Will this cause some excitement."

Somewhat reluctantly, Lauren removed her respirator and took a tentative sniff. The air smelled dry and there was no hint of mustiness or damp. That was good. The chamber must have been sealed like a vault. She nodded to Kareza, who ripped his mask off with more energy.

"Disgusting thing! I feel like I've had my head in someone's boot."

Lauren laughed, glad to be breathing freely. Unencumbered by the mask, she had a much better view of the alien ship and the chamber. She still found it hard to accept the thing was real. Talking of reality…

"Kareza, we need to quarantine this place. With the exception of our team, I don't want anyone else in here. That includes your people. I don't think the *policia* should know what we have here, do you? We can hint that we've found valuable artifacts. Let Ibanez and the others think what they want. Once word gets out that we have an extraterrestrial craft in here, there'll be a riot."

"I agree. You'll be notifying your government, I suppose?"

"Were you thinking of stopping me?"

Imatlan glared at her. This was his chance to assert himself, take over, and he was not going to waste it. Let a mere *norteno* woman steal what was rightfully his? Never!

"My dear Lauren, you misunderstand your position here. This isn't just an archaeological treasure anymore. This is Mexico's future!"

"Idiot! This belongs to the world!"

"What has the world done for Mexico? This is ours by right! As the site director, I am officially taking over." Let her chew on that.

Lauren's eyes blazed. "Martin! Take pictures and send them to everyone in our e-mail address book. Now!"

Imatlan blanched and grabbed her arm. "You don't know what you're doing! You can't do this!"

She shook him off. "I know what I'm doing and I *can* do this!"

"You realize the implication? The UN will take over! America will take over!"

"The UN *should* take over! This isn't something you can keep secret. I'll make sure of that."

"The UN is America's puppet!"

"Don't be a moron. By getting the UN involved, it ensures Mexico's sovereignty and rights are respected. Instead of alienating everyone, you'll have the whole world on your side. It won't be easy for *anyone* to simply walk in and take this away from you, and you can dictate the terms how this will be exploited—if you're not greedy."

Imatlan sneered at her. "You, an American, should talk about greed? Mexico was always forced to take America's leavings and smile. We have to beg for help, then be grateful for the crumbs thrown our way while the IMF and the World Bank sucks our national blood by imposing impossible economic dictates not designed to help us, but rigged to keep us in perpetual servitude."

Lauren snorted. "The IMF didn't suck your national blood. It was a series of corrupt Mexican governments!"

"No, it was the IMF. Mexico repaid the IMF three times *more* than what we borrowed, and we're still just repaying the interest. For what? To bloat European and American banks while the multinationals set up factories that further bleed our resources and produce goods useless to us? We're forced to work at slave labor rates while those same multinationals repatriate profits that should rightfully be used to develop our agricultural and industrial infrastructure, but they cannot allow Mexico to become economically secure. Oh, no! That would undermine their profits. Is it any wonder then that we hate you?" He hooked a thumb at the ship. "This will give us independence!"

"It will give you war! This ship spells power. You try it alone, I tell you, and Mexico will be invaded. Who'll defend you then? A strongly worded protest to the UN?"

"I won't simply stand by and have this *stolen* from us. By you or anyone else!"

"No one will steal anything, least of all me. Not if you play it smart."

"Smart? You are naïve, Lauren."

"And you're a fool! Go ahead, then. Call the *policia*. Have us arrested, but you'll have to shoot us to stop us from talking."

He *could* have her arrested. Then, he would have to arrest all the Americans. No, he would really be a fool if he tried that. How long could he keep them silent, even if the authorities co-operated? Eventually, Lauren would talk and he would be exposed, ridiculed, ruined.

The fire in his eyes slowly died and his shoulders sagged. He had no way to win. He turned suddenly and slammed his fist against the hull in anguished frustration.

"I wish I had never seen the damned thing. Take it! I won't stand in your way. This isn't our salvation, it's a curse." He made to push past her, but she stood firmly in his way.

"You don't get it, do you?" she said harshly. "I can't right the past or change the IMF, but we can do something about the future—everyone's future."

Martin coughed. "Ah, Dr. Imatlan, cutting in the others doesn't necessarily mean that Mexico has to give up its rights or intellectual property."

Imatlan whirled on him. "Stay out of this, boy!"

"You need to listen to this, sir," Martin went on stubbornly. "This ship is yours and no one can dispute it, but you've got to play it smart like the doc said. I cannot even begin to imagine the patents you'll be able to take out from this: new metal industries, material composites, novel power and propulsion systems. Who knows what else? These industries will be yours to license."

Imatlan looked at Martin with a spark of hope, then shook his head.

"You don't know how these things work. The UN will find a way to rob us."

"You mean America," Lauren said bitterly.

"Everyone! The Security Council will pass a resolution and they will have ships blockading us and bombers flying overhead to make sure we do nothing."

"Perhaps, *if* you go it alone. Listen to me, Kareza. You may not have much love for corporate America, I don't either, but the ordinary man on the street is something else. Instead of fighting us, get us on your side and defuse the situation."

Imatlan was silent as he chewed that over. "I don't have much choice, do I? I never did." He strode to the entrance and stopped. "I'll talk to my government and you talk to yours."

"Kareza—"

"You've won this round, Lauren. Enjoy your moment of glory."

"Wait! This isn't about me, you idiot. This is about all of us!"

"All of us? The UN will send a team and our usefulness here will be at an end. You and I'll be forgotten."

"You give up too easily," she said sweetly, but her eyes flashed. "We'll just have to see to it that it doesn't happen, won't we? Before we talk to anyone, we have to plan what we're going to say. In the meantime, we have work to do. Martin, get everything recorded. I want it all on film: walls, ship, everything. Then get it uploaded to our website. Kareza, I think it would be a good idea if Ibanez were to run some scans on the other mounds, eh? No need for all that lovely equipment to go to waste, is there?"

Imatlan stared at her, then shook his head. Formidable indeed.

# Chapter Four

"Illeran, a pleasure as always," Ed-Kani Takao remarked pleasantly and snapped his delicate jaws several times.

The Karkan hissed, his fishy black eyes probing from horizontal slits, hidden by a thin ridge of dark green scales. He inclined his slightly flattened head with a precise twist of a long slender neck, a purely reptilian gesture.

"I dare say it's more pleasurable for me than it is for you," Illeran ventured with a subtle flick of his pointed tongue. The Pizgor fallout had started eight days ago, but he refrained from talking to his coalition colleague. Sargon had plenty on its mind right now without being patronized by the Karkan Federation. That did not prevent Illeran from enjoying a rare moment of satisfaction watching Sargon try to extricate itself from a slippery slide of its own making. He was allowed a *little* fun in his job.

Ed-Kani squirmed, his smile somewhat forced. Completely hairless that offset the deep character lines around the eyes and mouth. Icy blue-white eyes were blank windows set wide on a narrow bony face. His office reflected the subdued opulence accorded an Executive Council Director. Illeran preferred lush greenery, hanging moss, and potted plants, a reminder of Karkan's humid and swampy climate. The Wall made the image so real that Ed-Kani could almost feel the heat.

"I don't doubt it. Lemos has been somewhat of a setback," he admitted candidly, an understatement if there ever was one. A disastrous one for the AUP Provisional Committee, he hissed under his breath, one compounded by the Italan folly. Kai Tanard also lost, and with him incalculable value in intelligence, now in the hands of the Unified Independent Front. The damage in that alone may have set back the merger for decades. He didn't have decades. He only had seven years before his last ten-year Assembly term ended and his career as a major political force in the Serrll was over. He needed to leave behind something more than merely thirty years of unremitting service. He wanted history to remember him as another pivotal figure that had shaped Serrll's fabric. Another debacle like Italan would definitely leave a mark in history, but not necessarily the one he wanted. May Ti Inai roast in whatever pit the Paleans favored.

"A bold plan nevertheless, my friend," Illeran said softly, offering a grudging sign of sympathy.

"But…"

"Are you asking me as Sargon's representative or a Servatory Party coalition partner?"

Ed-Kani grinned at Illeran's pointed humor. Was he joking? Hard to tell sometimes. The Karkans loved to play their little mind games and they played them at many levels. He had little patience with subtlety. To the pits with all of them.

"Lay it on the line, Illeran, man to man."

Illeran smiled briefly and inclined his head. He knew Ed-Kani and his kind very well: mercenary, ruthless, mere barbarians, but still worthy of cultivation. Pizgor may have been a disaster for Sargon, but at least they were starting to approach the problem from other than purely military terms, even if the thing was crudely executed. They would learn, but will they be able to afford the price the lessons exacted? Would the Servatory Party coalition survive the experience? Sargon was not a natural ally and they both knew it, the coalition nothing more than a union of convenience borne of a mutual desire to topple the Revisionists.

"In my view? Your premise was fatally flawed from the onset. Paleans have always been risk-averse, my friend. Just look at their history. Their moves are slow, calculating and deliberate. Often interpreted as a sign of indecision, a fatal mistake to make against a dangerous adversary. They may look nervous and twitchy, but make no mistake; they are polished predators. You don't occupy twenty-eight systems by bowing and scraping. Had you secured key Palean Congress policymakers before making your move, it's conceivable that you could have pulled it off. As it is, the merger relied on too many variables having to come together just right. Regardless of its long history the common Palean still does not trust the Alikan Union Party movement or its policies, considering them militant and extreme. With Lemos you pushed the envelope too far and forced Captal to act."

Ed-Kani peered closely at Illeran. Age had faded the scales on his face and he no longer carried himself with youthful grace. As Karkan's senior Assembly representative and a maluran in the home planet's government, Illeran could afford to move with reserve and dignity. His power was established and he exerted enormous influence within the Executive Council by sheer force of his personality. Dignified or not, Illeran was also a tortured being, seeing his and Karkan's efforts frustrated in toppling the Sofam-dominated Executive, and with it, Captal's government. Ed-Kani grimaced. Perhaps Illeran's quest for a mark in history wasn't so different from his own. They differed only in the method used in pursuing their respective goals. The realization both irritated and amused him.

Nevertheless, he relished these moments of candor with his sometimes ally. Too often their discourse was shielded in diplomatic overspeak. Moments of plain talk were rare and to be seized upon. Everyone should indulge in it from time to time, he thought morosely and shifted in his seat. It could avoid so many messes. That, he reflected sardonically, would detract from playing the game. Still, how many opportunities were lost in that vain pursuit?

"I know you don't agree with what appears to you is Karkan's preoccupation with gaining the Executive Council majority," Illeran went on and his tongue flickered. "It's an understandable point of view from an aggressive and martial culture such as yours. No intent there to disparage Sargon. I am merely stating an evident fact. Your military conquests have won you thirty-two systems. However, this predilection toward the use of force also makes you impatient and quick to act, and that my friend, is a fatal shortcoming in any game of political counterthrust, especially for someone who aspires to rule the Serrll."

"A silent, quick slip of a verbal blade, is that it?"

Illeran smiled broadly and his eyes glittered. "Or a prolonged campaign that by degrees leads one's enemy toward inevitable self-destruction."

"And Sargon is too impatient, right? Not at all like you. After all, you've only been after Sofam for, what is it? Sixteen hundred years?"

Illeran gave a graceful nod, ignoring the veiled barb, which in his mind typified Sargon and all its collective barbarians.

"We prefer to take the long-term view."

"Hah! I cannot afford the long-term view. Since you seem to understand it all so well, Illeran, why hasn't the Karkan Federation attempted to take over the Palean Union itself?"

"To what end? The power balance between the Servatory Party and the Revisionists would not have changed. We would still hold only three Executive seats. We need a fourth seat to threaten Sofam and its Revisionist coalition."

"It would have denied the Palean seat to the Revisionists!"

Illeran shook his head. "As in your attempt, too many variables would have had to come together just right, and there was a real risk of military confrontation with Sofam; bad for business, not to mention ongoing open rebellion from the Alikan Union Party and the general populace. The Palean Union would have been a conquest of occupation and an impossible drain on Karkan's resources to maintain an unattainable peace. It would have left us bereft and unable to pursue our real objective, which is to overthrow the Revisionists. In your case the stakes were not as high. You only needed five systems and the Paleans were willing. Most of them, anyway."

This was the second time Illeran had mentioned the Alikan Union Party, warning his friend that the Provisional Committee may be working with the AUP. It did not necessarily mean the AUP was subservient to the Committee's demands or its agenda. Was he being too subtle and Ed-Kani had missed the point?

"Pizgor's lousy five systems." Ed-Kani snorted, his thoughts on the aftermath. "As you said, we pushed the envelope and Sargon is suffering the repercussions of its folly and lack of finesse—"

"As are the Paleans," Illeran reminded him.

"It isn't a happy time for either of us, I admit. We both lost a lot of credibility within the Serrll and the opportunists are snapping at our heels, baying for blood. Our enemies have revealed themselves and Sargon has a long memory," he said with relish, his teeth bared at the prospect of grappling with the enemy.

"Karkan isn't gloating."

"No, I have nothing to reproach you for, and getting you involved, even if you were willing, would have gained you nothing. We have chosen our path and now have to reap the consequence of our actions."

Despite the presence of M-9s and M-6s over Palea and Hakran—such impudence—there was little risk of real military punitive reprisals. Captal was merely sending a message. Friendly takeovers were okay, but using standover tactics had crossed the line. Embarrassing as it was to have warships over your planet, the resulting economic backlash had been far more devastating and the message more pointed. The scavengers were carving out what they could while they could. Sargon would remember…

"Sofam isn't gloating either," Illeran added softly and Ed-Kani's cold eyes flared.

"But the cowards lost no time in bringing their economic might to bear on our commerce and almost crippled our financial systems in the process. Instead of fighting us openly with the Code, they hide behind traders and merchants!"

Illeran gave a hissing chuckle. "That's merely business, my friend. What did you expect? You will note, though, they stayed their hand and have not pressed the advantage."

"How noble of them! Crippling Sargon would have damaged their own interstellar interests and they know it, including those of their precious Paravan Trading Association. Bah!"

"It may have been a hollow victory, I admit, but they could have savaged you and weathered a gyrating market. They chose not to because they didn't want to precipitate long-term disruption to Serrll Combine's stability, as your attack on Pizgor threatened to do. Nevertheless, as the senior Revisionist Party coalition partner, Sofam was forced to show its displeasure. Believe me, my friend, you don't want them as an enemy."

"We had them as an enemy at the battle of Anantor and left the remnants of their broken fleet scattered in space."

"That was eleven hundred years ago," Illeran said gently. "And did you win that war?"

Ed-Kani squirmed. No, they had not won that war…

"When the Executive voted to endorse Sofam's retaliatory action, you did nothing!" he snapped and immediately looked contrite. "My apologies, Illeran. You abstained, which under the circumstances was the correct thing to do. Your way of telling us that Sargon's behavior had damaged the Servatory Party cause."

"Correct. Whatever our internal differences might be, my impatient friend, and I am wholly aware of them, our public image must always be a united one."

"Hypocrisy!"

"Perhaps, but our posture has its value. For those who would see the Revisionists removed, we must be held up as a viable alternative government. Destroy that and we face political oblivion. Public trust is notoriously difficult to gain and easily lost."

"You don't have to worry about public perception when standing behind an M-6 projector," Ed-Kani growled and Illeran laughed.

"Tell me. Had you succeeded in every respect, would that have delivered to the unified Alikan Union Party a government majority on Captal? Would the Serrll worlds have trusted you to maintain peace and stability if it did?"

"There would have been order! This silent scheming and plotting violates everything the Code teaches. Sargon has little taste and patience for it."

"And that's why you failed with the Paleans," Illeran reminded him and his tongue flickered.

Ed-Kani winced, silently acknowledging the wisdom of Illeran's words. Right now, his anger was not directed at the Karkans.

"One day, I shall see Sofam humbled. Crawling canal worms. Still, it was a fun game we played."

"Throwing bricks at each other, my friend, is always dangerous. One never knows where one will hit."

"Ah, another example of Karkan subtlety? You, of course, would never resort to such crass tactics."

Illeran hissed, his eyes bright. "It is beneath us, really," he said and they had a good chuckle. "As much as I appreciate this interlude…"

"You're right to remind me. I wanted to talk to you about the CAPFLTCOM tender for the new Fleet base."

"Given my position on the approval committee, you know I cannot discuss it."

Ed-Kani spread his hands in mock outrage. "I'm not asking you to compromise yourself. I only want to know where we stand and to remind you of Sargon's—"

"Spare me the propaganda! I've had enough presentations

already. Let me say the Committee is handling a delicate problem. As Sargon's representative, I would advise you to keep a low profile here."

Tempted to tell Ed-Kani the Paleans have put in a bid of their own, he refrained. Ed-Kani would find out soon enough and revealing the information could backfire on Illeran, compromising his position on the selection committee. There was another consideration he must keep in mind. Sargon had created a problem for itself in its haste to secure the merger, and he saw no reason why he should help them solve it. Let them stew for a while. A salutary lesson in the value of subtlety.

"My head might be chopped off, is that it?" Ed-Kani said. "Tell me this, then. How favorably is the committee looking at the Rolan bid?"

"I cannot talk about that either," Illeran said and his tongue flicked out.

"Coward!"

Illeran grinned. "Just being discreet, my friend. I can tell you this. Rolan would make a good choice. It's in an ideal location, but it's also a poisoned chalice. The Rolan group is a bunch of meddling self-serving independents, and the sooner Sofam tires of kowtowing to their demands and annexes them, the better."

"Sofam wouldn't do anything of the sort, and you know it. Worm slime!" Ed-Kani snapped, then smiled slyly. "Besides, giving Sargon the base would show that Captal has no hard feelings over Pizgor."

Illeran shook his head in rueful amusement. With Sargon, it was always push, push until something broke.

"I'll get back to you—"

"Make it soon!"

"—once I have studied CAPFLTCOM's recommendation."

"Good enough. And Illeran? With Pizgor, there was never anything personal in what I or the AUP Provisional Committee did."

"I know."

*And that's what makes you so dangerous, my misguided friend*, Illeran thought as he cut contact.

Ed-Kani watched the Wall pool through a tortuous pattern of color and realized that he meant what he said. Of course, that would never stop him from trying to usurp Karkan's dominance of the Servatory Party, and subtlety be damned. He suspected Illeran knew that also, and gave a low sigh. Why did everything have to be so complicated?

Absently, he turned and gazed out the window screen at a fine afternoon. Fleecy white streamers smeared a reddening western sky. A Hakran lobbyist group was taking him out to dinner later and he looked forward to catching up on the latest juicy gossip and dirt digging from home. The refined art of politics had much more to do with whose levers you could pull than promoting policy or sponsoring major public works. That was the kind of subtlety he approved.

Enough of brooding. He leaned forward and touched a pad on the inlaid comms panel.

"Next!" he barked at the Wall.

"Ratalian is here to give you that brief you wanted, sir," Keana announced primly and he frowned.

Keana was plain, dour, frigid and a priceless organizer. He would have found it impossible to run his office without her. She stood steadfastly with him and helped run a cutthroat campaign to secure him a third nomination to the General Assembly. Over the years, he ticked off a number of influential power brokers throughout Sargon and they saw the elections as a means to derail his career. There was talk of giving him lifelong tenure as a Pro-Consul in the Dumas Conclave, a reward for two decades of faithful service; in reality a stab in the back. He weathered the campaign and brought Keana to Captal as his personal aide. He hated to admit it even to himself how much he grew to rely on her and her judgment. He hated even more the realization that she saw through him and was the one person whom he could not dominate. Later perhaps, that would have to change, he told himself firmly. Everyone had a handle, even the prim indispensable Keana. If he did manage to subdue her, would she lose that spark of vitality and intuitiveness that made her so effective? An interesting quandary.

"Show him in," he said smoothly and looked out the window again. His admin assistant better have something new for him or the kid would find himself assisting on Cantor.

Ed-Kani enjoyed the trappings of power.

As a member of the ruling Executive Council and Director for the Bureau of Economic Affairs, he climbed the pinnacle of Captal's hierarchy. Admittedly, the responsibilities far outweighed the privileges, but the position wielded undeniable authority and he wielded it with relish.

When he became a newly minted member of the General Assembly, he was thankfully spared the humiliation of having to be broken in by serving years as some Commissioner's flunkey in order to learn how business was done in Captal. He knew full well how to do business in Captal. He crafted his political career with all the care and attention of a military takeover. His every move calculated to the last variable with a single objective in mind: reaching Captal. Getting into the seat of Serrll power merely the first step. Staying there demanded different skills and tactics. For what he contemplated, he could not afford on-the-job training.

Patience came hard to him, which only served to prove Illeran's veiled accusation. Over time, he learned to curb his disdain of fools. Eleven long years serving in Hakran's Dumas had seen to that. He rose steadily through the Party, using the silent and ruthless tools of character assassination to sweep away those who would oppose him, until after several ambassadorships and emergency chairmanships the coveted post of Hakran's Controller was his. It had been a sweet moment. That single step opened a vital doorway to understanding Serrll's political machinery, overshadowing as it did the working of the Sargon Directorate. After a single five-year term, he shocked everyone by resigning to take a lobbyist post on Captal itself. Many called him a fool for seemingly throwing away a promising career, the post of Prime Director of Sargon being the next logical step, but he knew what he was doing. Wiser and more experienced heads on Hakran quietly approved his move. The promising career he sought was not in Sargon, home or not. He sought to influence events from a much broader platform. To realize that ambition, he needed to do it where that influence would count the most. Power was there to be wielded by those willing to grasp the burning blade.

He considered himself sophisticated, and to an extent he was, but stepping onto the Serrll's capital world for the first time had shaken him. Intellectually, he knew Captal to be a seething conglomerate of all the races that made up the Combine, but to be actually immersed in the impersonal vastness of the city almost smothered his resolve. It took him three long years of navigation through the tortuous labyrinth of Captal's Bureaus as a lobbyist before he felt confident enough in his abilities to use the system to serve his ends and avoid the inevitable pitfalls that waited to chew up the unwary or the presumptuous. During that time, he had not forgotten Hakran, and the home government was suitably grateful, endorsing his nomination as Hakran's Assembly representative. That also made him the official senior rep for Sargon. The position carried with it considerable prestige and in the Assembly's caste hierarchy, it all counted, and he wasn't shy at exploiting it. After only a year as a backbencher, he was posted as a member of the Bureau of Defense's influential Strategic Initiatives Committee. The appointment made him a comer, and there was even talk of a Commissioner post; an unprecedented and ludicrous move for someone who many naively considered too inexperienced. Well, he left their ruined reputations in his tracks.

Looking at Celean Park and the sprawl of Captal beyond, he felt himself destined for greatness, and today was a good day to make another step toward achieving it. Nodding solemnly, he pulled at his long chin.

The white translucent doors split and hissed into the wall as Ratalian strode through. Young for a Deklan, only one of the twin bands of gray showed in his otherwise white hair. Tall and wiry, thin eyebrows outlined large, liquid wide-set blue eyes. His face full beneath an olive complexion. As a professional staffer, he served all those who walked the halls of power, and in his time, he'd seen his share of them. Only a few managed to impress him, while the opportunists either faded or toughened to become the shakers and the movers. He'd made up his mind early that he didn't like his boss, undecided in which category Ed-Kani belonged. The man bore the mark of a schemer and manipulator, and Ratalian didn't trust the type, but he never allowed that to interfere with his professional duties. Of course, everyone who strode through the corridors of Captal had to be to a degree a schemer—a characteristic of the individual who sought political power—but Ed-Kani was being far too clever at it. He gave a mental shrug and recited a litany of acceptance for the righteousness of the Path and walked quickly to the wide desk.

Ed-Kani looked keenly at his assistant, appraising the youngster with ice-cold eyes. There was an air of detachment about the Deklan that made him uneasy. Nothing he could put his finger on, and the boy always unfailingly respectful. Lack of servile commitment? He pushed the thought aside. He would wait before replacing him. After all, even for an Executive Director, staff not easy to come by.

"I have the preliminary analysis you asked for, sir," Ratalian piped coolly, his voice surprisingly thin despite a broad and full chest. "The complete report is in your Comsec."

"Take a seat and give me a summary," Ed-Kani commanded and nodded at a vacant formchair.

Ratalian made himself comfortable and placed the tips of his fingers into a pyramid.

"Predictably, CAPFLTCOM has narrowed its choice for a site to the two obvious options; the Sargon Directorate and the Sofam Confederacy, of course. Ach! Both sites are near the Rolan border. Placing the new base in any of these locations will close the Scout Fleet's strategic exposure in that part of the Serrll Combine. The resulting logistical facilities will also support the Bureau of Colonial and Protectorate Affairs' initiative to launch an exploration and expansion program beyond the Rolan group. Your proposal, Director, to site the base in Sargon's Fourth Directorate meets the tender criteria with a better than a ninety-four percent fit. Ach!"

"Tell me something I *don't* know!" Ed-Kani snapped. "What's the political dimension, man? I'm paying you to think, not to report!"

Ratalian shifted and the chair remolded itself around him.

"Ach, that analysis does not lend itself to straight-line determination, sir."

"Answer the question!"

"Very well." Stung, Ratalian composed himself. He hated these sessions. They gave you a strict brief, then expected you to be omniscient, with a dressing down if things turned to slag. "If I may speak bluntly, sir; you must know, although CAPFLTCOM is not a political organ and we can rely on the Fleet to make an objective assessment, the Bureau of Defense most certainly is a political organ and they'll be the ones giving the final site approval. You know why everyone is scrambling to secure the tender. The chosen system would instantly become a very influential economic hub. Although BueDef is run by Director Illeran who is a senior Servatory Party member, and under different circumstances, Sargon could expect preferential treatment, Sofam controls the government, and it will do its utmost to see to it that the base ends up in one of their systems. Ach! They'll not want to strengthen your position by handing it to you. It could be interpreted as tacit approval of Sargon's attack on Pizgor."

"That's where you're wrong," Ed-Kani boomed and banged the desk with his hand. "They may not have much of a choice. This is a hot button, son, and in these delicate times the General Assembly is closely watching all the players. Sargon may be in the cellar over the Pizgor debacle right now and no one is feeling particularly sorry for us. Serves them right, they'll say…little tin dictators. Many on the Assembly floor also feel that Sofam has unfairly exploited the situation to expand its trade tentacles. Very naughty. Whatever the rights and the wrongs of the interpretation, and I don't care, the Bureau of Defense will not stand for any interference from Sofam. There would be an outcry. They'll be objective."

Despite himself, Ratalian was impressed by Ed-Kani's ready grasp of the political realities. He expected nothing less.

"Perhaps, sir. Outcries die away and the public has a noto-riously short memory. There is always a new issue tomorrow."

"You weren't thinking of the Alikan Union Party by any chance, were you?" Ed-Kani asked darkly and noted the pained expression on Ratalian's face. He wondered what Ratalian would think if he knew Ed-Kani to be a senior member of the AUP Provisional Committee? Probably turn pale and flee. The thought amused him.

"As a matter of fact, I was, sir. Ach! The AUP may not be exactly a new issue, but given the current turmoil in the Palean Congress, CAPFLTCOM may want to bolster its presence in the Palean Union in case the Alikan Union Party becomes openly militant. The Executive Directors may need an occa-sional prod to get them to move, but they're not fools, begging your pardon, sir. A militant AUP would be a very destabilizing influence, and CAPFLTCOM has already asked for a change to the tender terms of reference for an option to site the base in the Palean Union."

"Nonsense!" Ed-Kani waved his hand in dismissal,

alarmed at the thought. "After Lemos and Italan the Paleans are lucky not to be invaded. No one is about to hand them a prize like this base. Not now." Could it be possible? Would the Paleans put in a bid? He would have to ask Keana to follow it up.

"True in the short term only, sir, ach! Like it or not, an aggressive Alikan Union Party has introduced a new strategic element into the Serrll defense posture that must be honored. Whether it wants to or not, BueDef would be compelled to consider the Palean option. However, my analysis still favors Sargon. The proposed location would accommodate any strategic and long range exploration scenarios that Captal may want to pursue, and there are sufficient bases in the Palean Union itself able to handle any future Alikan Union Party overtures."

"Mmm." Ed-Kani looked pointedly at his staffer. "I would agree with your wild fantasy *if* the Alikan Union Party were a recognized power block, but it isn't. At least not yet. Take it from me, son, the AUP is an idea, a concept that one day will become a reality once Sargon affects the merger with the Paleans."

"Ach! That's a somewhat extreme interpretation, sir, and perhaps one that might take a long time before it becomes a reality," Ratalian said diffidently and Ed-Kani chuckled.

"You don't believe me? Never mind. Forget the Paleans. What's my lever to site the base in Sargon?"

Ratalian didn't avert his gaze. "Ach! Given recent events, I don't see that you have one, sir."

"You're no good to me. Get out of my sight."

Ed-Kani waited for the doors to close, then slammed his fist against the desk. Bureaucrats! Bah! Ratalian was a fool. He met the type on Hakran where he first learned how to handle them. Captal's parasites were no different, only more polished and harbored grander delusions of personal power. Eager to please and obfuscate, but in reality delivered nothing. Why couldn't they get outside the box and explore *all* the possibilities! He knew why, of course. Bureaucrats everywhere hated change, and change represented uncertainty—an anathema for a bureaucrat. By the time field information was filtered, analyzed, summarized and predigested before it reached him, its value hardly better than blinkered opinion. He got better intelligence from a newscast.

So, he had no lever, eh?

He cleared the Wall and punched a pad.

"Keana! In here!"

His fingers tapped impatiently against the armrest of his formchair, his mind a whirl of ideas, trapped with seemingly no way out. The doors finally slid apart and Keana walked in. Without waiting for an invitation, she sat down, folded her hands in her lap, and waited without expression. He scowled at her.

"That pup Ratalian just sent a blast through my proposal to site the new Fleet base in Sargon."

"I regret that," Keana said unmoved.

"You regret that," Ed-Kani sneered. "You know how much work I've put into this bid?" Actually, Keana and her staff did most of the work, but that was a detail. He outlined the strategy, set the tactics and guided the bid hearings through the Fleet bureaucracy. "Well, I'm not giving up. There has to be a way to swing the deal my way."

"There is always a way if you're willing to pay the price."

"I'll sleep with the devil if that's what it'll take."

"You may have to yet," she mused and chewed her lower lip.

"Oh? What do you have in mind?"

"Whether you like the idea or not, the approval committee will be looking hard at Rolan. Given Sargon's current predicament—"

"You've been reading Ratalian's brief?"

"Of course."

"Hah! Go on."

"Approach the problem from a different perspective."

"Oh?"

"Don't look at getting the Fleet base as an end in itself. See it as an opportunity to achieve a broader objective. Sargon and the Paleans want to merge, right? They want to merge because as a single entity, they'd be entitled to an additional seat in the Executive Council. The AUP Provisional Committee has one problem. Consider what Pizgor was all about."

"Numbers," Ed-Kani breathed, starting to get a glimmer of what Keana was driving at.

"That's right, numbers. Instead of lobbying for the base, convince the Dumas to throw its weight behind the Rolan bid. The move would short-circuit Sofam's opposition to Sargon's bid and show the rest of the Serrll that Sargon can rise above parochial interests and stand behind an idea that's for the greater good of all. The public may be dazzled long enough by the maneuver to forget its pique over Pizgor. While they're dazzled, you ask Rolan to cede to Sargon in return for getting the base, and the Provisional Committee gets its five systems without raising a sweat." She lifted her eyebrows and smiled brightly, pleased by her bombshell.

Ed-Kani looked hard at Keana, impressed by her reasoning. The notion was incredible, and what was more, it could just work. More importantly, the Provisional Committee would have seized the initiative again. *He* would have seized the initiative and regained some of the face he lost over Lemos. He did not doubt Rolan would be titillated by the idea. They would finally be able to throw off the stifling interference into their economic and trade policies by the Paravan Trading Association and secure legitimate autonomy. Strategically, Sargon would still be in effective control of the Fleet base and that's what counted. Sargon had no interest ruling Rolan directly. Equally importantly, the secession would cause immeasurable damage to the independents and could set off a rash of secessions and annexations. If the thing cascaded, it could even destroy the single Executive Council vote now wielded by the meddlesome independents and remove a singular thorn from the Provisional Committee's side; a perfect outcome for everybody. Not only that, once Sargon had Rolan, the Committee would have a powerful lever to dictate new merger terms to the Paleans.

He realized this lever would have to be pulled with delicacy, as four of the nine Committee members were Palean. Each and every one of them committed to the Alikan Union Party, the recent demise of two of their own showed how committed they really were. However, if not handled properly the Provisional Committee could splinter and decades of patient planning by the Dumas Conclave would be wasted should the Rolan secession be perceived as nothing more than a puppet instrument to achieve a Grater Sargon.

If Sargon did manage to secure Rolan, the Dumas could use the Sargon arm of the Alikan Union Party to peel off Palean splinter groups and sow internal discord within the Palean Congress until the government eventually collapsed and the Palean Union would effectively cease to exist as a viable entity. There would only be a Greater Sargon. An audacious idea, but if it could be pulled off, it would be a masterful stroke of tactical organization worthy of Karkan subtlety. Illeran would be pleased.

To win in Captal's high-stakes game, you sometimes have to be prepared to throw in some serious chips. A lazy grin slowly spread across his face.

"I love it! You're beautiful and your talents are wasted here, my girl."

"I know," she said dryly, but the irony was lost on him. "For the plan to work, though, you'll need support from two key men: Mariawa, Hakran's First Pro-Consul, and Karshwin, the new Prime Director. Mariawa could be a problem. He is cautious and averse to taking risks. He has grown complacent surrounded by the trappings of power."

"I've got a few levers I can pull to bring old Mariawa around," Ed-Kani said comfortably. "I haven't spent my time as Controller without unearthing a few skeletons. Leave Mariawa to me. As for Karshwin, I know of him. All he craves is an important title and a Field-sized office. What we need to do is bring on board the faceless powerbrokers who stand behind them."

"I'll work on it," Keana said, then paused. "Of course, you know the downside to this?"

Ed-Kani gave her a sly smile. "Sofam may offer Rolan the same deal if the alternative secures Sargon a second Executive Council seat."

Keana raised an eyebrow in appreciation. She looked at her boss with a tad more respect, managing to stifle any gush of emotion. Ed-Kani was getting tired of her; she could read the signs. The prospect didn't worry her and she was ready to return home anyway. Her work with Ed-Kani would be good for her own Pro-Consul election bid. Besides, after two years, Captal's silent byplays were getting wearisome, and she missed Hakran.

"Get me Karshwin," he ordered. "I will want to talk to Trianon then, Rolan's senior Assembly rep. I also want you to organize a Wall hookup with all the Provisional Committee members. We need to move on this before Illeran's approval committee sits again in forty days' time."

* * *

"Vlad, what do we know about this Dr. Hopking?" President Rodney Harford asked mildly, sitting in a striped beige chair that at the moment was positioned over the great seal. His National Science Advisor took most of the three-piece couch on his left. Lincoln's portrait hung on the wall behind him. Although Harford looked calm, his voice could not completely hide his irritation. The woman had the temerity to dictate terms! It was blackmail!

Vlad put on his characteristic frown and his thick black eyebrows came together. Of Rumanian ancestry, he was a lumbering presence that belied an incisive and formidable intellect. With PhDs in nuclear and aeronautical engineering—he picked that one up while still a fighter jock in the Air Force and much thinner—Vladimir Gorkanin was infamous for his demolition sessions of ill-prepared staffers and lobbyists. He hated to have his time wasted. What he did to military appropriations and new weapons projects made Pentagon three star generals go pale and think of retirement. Armed with a deceptively smooth and beguiling voice, Vlad led his trusting victims down a path of utter destruction that afterward left them wondering what had happened. Often caustic, his sarcasm rubbed people the wrong way, and that was exactly the way he liked it. In two years, general elections would sweep in a new president—probably Kurtland Hennery, a Republican Texas Governor—and he'll be out of a job. Not quite true. There were plenty of universities, think tanks, and global corps willing to take him on at any salary he cared to name, but that was in two years' time. Right now, he still owed his loyalty to this administration. He removed his rimless glasses and scowled.

"By all accounts, Mr. President, she's a very capable archaeologist. Associate Professor at Columbia U's Department of History and Archaeology—"

"Boulcher and his crowd?" Morris Paddington II cut in.

Vlad regarded the White House chief of staff as though examining an insect specimen. There was no love lost between them and he didn't hide his disdain of Paddington the Second's Harvard veneer. Morris was Harford's second chief of staff and it looked like he was going to survive the term of the Administration. A former DuPont executive and self-made millionaire, Morris was yanked out of his ambassadorial posting in London and into his present job barely eleven months into

Harford's first term after the former chief of staff failed to cut it. Never wealthy himself, Vlad resented the man's arrogance that money invariably generated, and his presumption that everyone should defer to him. As the last barrier between the president and the rest of the world, he conceded that Morris had some basis for his conceit. The problem was, Vlad hated to admit it, the man was insufferably effective and managed the White House and the various Congress factions with equal skill. He had to give the devil his due.

"The same."

"I feel sorry for her already," Morris said, which raised chuckles around the table.

"I would reserve my sympathies for Boulcher."

"Gentlemen! You were saying, Vlad?" Harford prompted, the authority in his voice unmistakable.

"My apologies, Mr. President."

Vlad liked Harford. A former Senate majority leader from New York, the president had an enormous capacity for detail and a discriminating sense of fitness in handling local and international crises gridlocks. He would need that fitness now, Vlad mused. Relatively young, only fifty-eight, Harford's hair already peppery, he wore deep lines around his smoky gray eyes and thin mouth. Why anyone would want a job that guaranteed to take fifteen years off your life, Vlad could not imagine. No, that wasn't really true.

He knew exactly what drove men like Harford and Morris—power. Power to shape the world in their image. Heady stuff, and he did not mind a whiff of it himself now and then. The only criticism he could level at Harford, the president often sought neatly polished solutions to intractable problems that in the end delivered nothing and left the Administration looking weak and indecisive.

"As I was saying, Professor Hopking has done some fine fieldwork on the Inca and Mayan civilizations. Several of her theories on African and Egyptian influences run contrary to accepted dogma, which earned her a measure of ridicule from the establishment."

"Professional jealousy," Harford remarked dryly. "I dare say this find of hers will change all that."

"With mixed results for some, sir. She seems to have weathered the deprecation of her colleagues without lasting scars, while managing to gain a measure of popular appeal along the way. Her book, *The Inca Sphinx*, had raised quite a furor in the archaeological community, and not a little embarrassment for Columbia U. The work published without their endorsement."

"You mean, embarrassment for Boulcher," Morris said comfortably.

"Right. Until recently, she was his protégé. Her theories in that book are not exactly orthodox and contradict everything he stands for. Nevertheless, she has a reputation as a solid researcher, organizer and planner, but is sometimes impatient with the administrative due process required to secure grants. She has little tolerance for dogma of any kind and seems to enjoy the admiration and respect from her undergraduate and graduate students."

"You've spoken to her?" Harford demanded.

"Yes, sir. She bulldozed through our Mexican ambassador, insisting that she speak to me."

"Shows nerve, and Barney never could say no to a pretty face," Carl Mansky ventured with a smirk that brought fresh smiles. As the National Security Advisor, he also sat in for the Secretary of State Karlovich hurriedly recalled from Tokyo when the news broke, and because this was his business.

Vlad shot Carl a penetrating frown. Sitting in a chair before the cold fireplace, the room air-conditioned, Carl looked relaxed, and his gangly body somehow managed to make his rumpled suit look elegant. Carl was competent enough and seemed to have an encyclopedic knowledge of just about everything, and he was very, very smart. His easy and engaging manner could suddenly turn into an icy interrogation, an extremely unpleasant experience for anyone unlucky enough to be on the receiving end of such a session. Divorced, his two girls living on their own, Carl now threw all of his considerable energies into his job. They got along.

"Morris?"

The chief of staff pushed himself back into the couch and let out a soft hiss.

"I am more worried about what the Mexican government will do, Mr. President. They haven't been in touch, but I would say it's only a matter of time. After all, the ship *is* theirs. If they want to sit on it, there's not a damned thing we can do about it—officially. After all, we cannot simply invade the place and take the thing. Unofficially, we can dangle some nice carrots for equal access rights."

"Such as?"

"Ease off on cross-border incursions. Loosen our immigration policy. There are things we can do with NAFTA and the IMF loans to make their life easier. It's ridiculous for a country to have to keep paying even after the loan itself has been repaid several times over. Mexico isn't alone in its resentment of the IMF. Talk to any South American or African country."

"I am not unaware of the problem, but this isn't the time—"

"Pardon me, Mr. President, this is *exactly* the time to address a festering injustice," Morris said firmly. Harford locked eyes with him, then nodded.

"We'll talk about it later. What else?"

"Mexico will want to make a deal. They'll have to, if for no other reason than to protect their ass from any international backlash if they try to shut everyone out. The first thing to do, sir, is talk to President Hernandez Maguela and ask him to speak to the new UN Secretary General, Nikita Bandrik. We may not like it, but in my view, this has to be a cooperative UN effort, and we'll be just one of the players—with a big say, of course. Once this hits the media, and it will, all bets will be off. This find will touch the whole fabric of our civilization. There is bound to be an economic impact, probably religious and social hysteria, marches and protests, and God alone knows what else. If this isn't handled just right, Mr. President, the whole world could go into a meltdown."

"Vlad?"

"I agree with Morris. There is one other thing we need to consider, though, perhaps even more important. Something that might threaten our national security."

Carl glanced sharply at Vlad.

"Technology transfer?"

Harford looked hard at the two men. "Explain."

"What we have here is a technological Rosetta Stone," Vlad said.

"Rosetta Stone?"

"Yes, sir. Think of it in terms of building a radio. Instead of using chips and printed circuits, meaningless to someone sixty years ago, we have a box of old-fashioned valves and coils. Hopking's ship is our box of valves."

"Sufficiently advanced to take us to the next level without being totally incomprehensible, is that it?"

"Precisely!"

"And that also makes the ship a very tempting target. Very good," Harford murmured and inclined his head at the 10" by 8" glossies. "Are these the photos?"

"Downloaded from Dr. Hopking's website," Vlad said and handed them over. Harford glanced up, one eyebrow raised in query and Vlad smiled. "It's in the secure part of her site, sir."

"I'm glad to hear that! What am I looking at?"

"The ship is approximately twenty-eight feet in diameter and nine feet high. If I'm right, Mr. President, it's a reactionless drive vehicle."

"You mean it's not spewing out propellant to push it?"

"Yes, sir. It's likely to be a variation of the diametric or pitch drives. The NASA Glenn Research Center and the Marshall Space Flight Center have been tinkering with the concept for decades. If this vehicle is indeed based on modifying the local gravitational field associated with zero-point fluctuations of the quantum vacuum, we would have something that could reach Jupiter in a week, if not sooner."

Harford cleared his throat. Vlad sometimes got carried away, forgetting that not everyone was as brilliant.

"Thomas Townsend Brown's experiments with spinning superconducting electrogravitic disks, right?"

Vlad was impressed. "Yes, sir, but we've made some progress since then."

"I should damn well hope so, given the money that's been poured down that black hole. We should have gotten more out of that effort than just a B-2 Spirit." Harford scowled as he stared at the photos. He pursed his lips and shook his head. "Getting back to reality, what's your assessment, Carl?"

The National Security Advisor was used to these round table sessions. It forced people to commit themselves, and not everyone enjoyed the process. The fence-sitters, and there were always a few around, especially detested the limelight. Morris eased such people out as quickly as he found them. The White House staffers learned early to cut it the way they saw it or got the chop themselves. They didn't have to be *right*, but they did have to commit.

"Vlad and Morris have touched on most of it, sir. Once this thing becomes public the key question, as I see it, what happens then? How do we handle the Europeans, the Russians, and the Chinese, to name a few? They'll all want a piece of the ship and afraid that someone else will gain an advantage."

Harford snorted and made a face. "UFOs aren't news. Everyone's been tinkering with alien technology since the '50s, except that no one has come out into the open and said so. What do you think the MAJI twelve program is all about? Our SIGMA and PLATO channels have more comms traffic than the stock exchange."

"That's deniable, Mr. President. This isn't. If Vlad is right, this is vastly more significant than anything we have at Wright Field now."

"Truman should never have created MJ-12," Harford growled. "It was stupid, and one day it's going to bite us on the ass. Okay everyone; let's deal with this. Unless you want to contact the Serrll Moon Base—"

"We certainly don't want to do *that*!" Morris said firmly and the others nodded.

"—what's your recommendation?"

"The Serrll will find out soon enough," Carl said. "In the meantime, I suggest we get the UN to establish an international research team to study the thing and take it apart. That way, no one gets left out and everyone gets a slice of the pie. With a lion's share to Mexico, of course."

Morris nodded. "Sounds good to me."

"You'll want Professor Hopking," Vlad said firmly.

"She's not a scientist!" Carl snapped.

"Oh? Her degrees are for basket weaving, eh? This holds as much significance for Mesoamerican archaeology as it does for NASA."

"The security—"

"Hell, Carl! We have an opportunity here to take a genuine leap that could benefit everyone on this stinking planet and you're worried about security and military potential."

"Now wait a minute—"

"Keep the thing for ourselves and enhance our competitive advantage, right? You try a stunt like that and someone is liable to lob a tactical nuke at the site, or at us. Don't you see? Who cares if everyone shares the information. With our technological base, we'll be in the best position to exploit this find anyway. Nothing else matters. The Midwest is turning into a desert, and what used to be the world's breadbasket is now a begging bowl. The Japs are eyeing the oil-rich Spratly islands and are ready to shoot it out with the Chinese over them, with the Philippines in the middle. What do you think Secretary of State Karlovich was doing in Tokyo? With all that going on, do you really want to risk an international backlash by being clever? And it's so unnecessary!"

Thick silence hung over the Oval Office, broken by soft ticking from the golden Faberge egg clock on Harford's *Resolute* desk, a gift from the late Russian president.

Harford pulled at his long chin and glanced out the window. Snow sparkled on the lawn outside, piled in drifts along Pennsylvania Avenue. Plows kept the slush from clogging the roadway, but traffic was light. Lafayette Square deserted, the tourists preferring the warmth of Florida. He couldn't blame them, preferring Florida himself. Frowning heavily, he turned away and looked at the hard men before him.

"You make a persuasive case, Vlad, as always," he said. "And you're right, of course. I agree with you that if this isn't handled right, it could have serious international repercussions. I don't like the idea of Professor Hopking holding a gun to our heads by threatening to go public, but we've got to keep an eye on broader problems. That ship may have technology we can apply to our current difficulties. You never know. Like climate change, for instance, and I'm not convinced that man is the cause, although our pollution isn't helping things. Damn it, *something* is drying up our bread bowl states. It that wasn't grim enough, the Saudis and OPEC are raking it in. It's intolerable, I tell you. What we need is to secure a stable supply of alternative energy unfettered by Arab influences."

"Go into a partnership with the Japs over the Spratlys?" Morris suggested slowly and Harford shook his head.

"No, that wouldn't work. The Chinese and the Philippines wouldn't stand still for it. They want the stuff for themselves. Not that I blame them. It could drive us into conflict with the

Japanese, of course. The economic and resource scenario they face now is the same one that pushed them into the Second World War when we blockaded them. We cannot allow the situation to degenerate that far, but we have to be prepared. How is the refurbishment of Eielson AFB going?"

"Six, nine months tops," Morris said. "Alaskan weather—"

"We may need that base. Set up a debrief with Secretary Karlovich as soon as he gets in from Andrews. I want to know what Tokyo had to say. Getting back to the issue at hand, there is no question that we steal the ship and hope to get away with it, and I don't even want to try. As for Mexico, they must know they have to share. About Hopking, she's on whatever team the UN sets up, and I fancy the Mexican government will be equally insistent about Doctor—"

"Imatlan," Vlad prompted.

"Mr. President, we're assuming the Mexican government *will* share," Morris said.

"I'll talk to Maguela."

"And if he refuses to play?"

"I don't see that he has much choice. I don't doubt he'd prefer to keep the thing for himself. Hopking's threat applies to him as well. Mexico is in as much of a bind over this as we are." Harford smiled, but there was a glint of steely determination in his gray eyes. "Another thing. We may have to start getting very polite with Maguela, especially if he elects to exercise proprietary rights over any discoveries that will be gleaned from the ship. I know, I would. Vlad, get in touch with Hopking and tell her to sit tight. We will do it just the way she wants, with repercussions later. Morris, after I've finished with Maguela, get me Nikita Bandrik. He'll want to call a special session of the UN Security Council. Thank you, everyone," he said and the meeting was over.

* * *

# A Whisper from Shadow

FLYING SAUCER FOUND IN MEXICO!
BURIED SAUCER UNEARTHED IN MAYAN PYRAMID!
HYSTERIA SWEEPS THE WORLD!
MEXICO READY TO HAND OVER SAUCER TO THE UN!
SECURITY CORDON HOLDS BACK SIGHTSEERS!
RUSSIANS SENDING NAVAL FORCE AS 'PROTECTION'

"Jack Willison reporting from the CNN center in New York. Finding a five-thousand-year-old interplanetary craft in a small Mayan tomb in Tabasco that borders the Gulf of Mexico has generated waves of crisis around the world. A special session of the UN Security Council will decide tomorrow how best to exploit this find for the benefit of mankind. The Mexican government has extended an open invitation to the world's leading scientists to study the craft. The find, President Maguela said, represents hope for all humanity. That may be, but Mexico has declared a ten-mile exclusion zone around Comalcalco. Aircraft within the zone will be forced down. Those that get within five miles of the site will be shot down without warning. That, I'm told, includes media helicopters. The site itself is under heavy military isolation, presumably designed to prevent thousands of sightseers from flooding the place, and F-16s from Chiapas are maintaining patrol over the area.

"International tension is mounting, following a declaration by the Russian Federation it will station a naval force off Mexico to forestall any interference with the UN mission by potentially hostile and unnamed powers who could disrupt the peaceful study of the craft. The White House declined to comment, beyond saying that international waters are open to everyone. However, it's known that the Second Marine Expeditionary Brigade at Camp Lejeune in North Carolina has been placed on a readiness alert. A carrier group near Hawaii is in position to intercept any force if necessary. Other elements of the Pacific Fleet closer to Mexico's western coastline will provide additional support. It's not clear why the Russians are taking this posture, as they will undoubtedly have members on the UN-sponsored research team. Undeterred by these developments the UN will have its hands full deciding who will get picked and who will miss out on the Comalcalco preliminary investigation group. Information from the site will be passed to other teams based at Geneva via the Internet, a political compromise tolerated by everyone. Stay tuned."

\* \* \*

"This is Mark Rown for NBC news. Archbishop Waller, the newly appointed Cardinal for the New York Diocese, dismissed any connection between the found saucer and Earth's major religions. Even if Earth was visited by extraterrestrials in the past, the Archbishop contends that these events could not possibly have any impact on Christianity as the life of Jesus and his miracles are divine in origin. He dismisses the more extreme of the populist views that claim Jesus was an alien as products of misguided minds, and that these persons should seek guidance to absolve them from such heresy.

"The recently formed Friends of Aliens is sending a delegation to Mexico to make sure the major powers don't attempt to cover up the find. 'We will be there to protect the interests of the people against the greed of the multinationals', said the spokesman. In the meantime the discredited works of the '70s author Erich Von Daniken are enjoying a sudden revival and UFO societies everywhere are smugly saying 'I told you so'."

\* \* \*

Enllss-rr skimmed over the Comsec message displayed in the full-dimensional holographic Wall communication extension and gave a low growl of irritation. Scowling, he tapped the comms pad in the inlaid console of his desk.

"Ree-Lee? You tell Gershowan I want his butt in here

now!" he bellowed and cut contact. His new First Assistant capable enough, but if the individual insisted on acting like a still-moist Assemblyman, Enllss would accommodate him, by damn! Another mess and it wasn't even lunchtime. What's come over everyone these days? Did they think that once they made it to the Assembly it would be all perks and a free ride? When *he* started, he served a three-year internship before even *thinking* about getting an appointment to a committee. Now, these young bloods expected executive appointments as a matter of course, looking at Assistant positions with scorn. It was ridiculous.

Absently, he reached for his cup of special herbal tea and took a sip. Gagging, he grimaced, swallowed the cold mixture, and slammed the cup against the desk.

"Pits and damnation!" Nothing was going right today. He stabbed the comms pad again. "Ree-Lee? Fresh tea!"

Suddenly restless, he got up and stepped to the floor-to-ceiling window screen. Far below, Celean Park awash with autumn color. Greens and purple blues competed with the profusion of gold, red, and brown. The air still had that wintry chill to it and the rains were getting more frequent. Today the sky clear and blue-green, perfect for being outdoors and digging up a garden. Perfect or not, it was unlikely he would get a chance to do any digging. The day was shaping into another long administrative drag, longer if he needed to field Gershowan's tasks, and it would be well into the night before he went home.

He wasn't complaining. He reached for power quite prepared to pay the price. Well, almost, even if the mortgage was a lifetime commitment. He thanked whoever managed the stars that he had an understanding and sympathetic partner. Without Rhea's silent and stoic support, he was sure the pressure to succeed in Captal's boiler environment would have driven him to insanity. The problem was keeping impersonal detachment. Once he allowed himself to actually care, he would be doomed. Sacrifice the individual for the greater good, was that it? He didn't believe it. In his book, it was the individual who made up the seething masses, and the individual always mattered. As a policymaker, he *should* remain detached. Difficult not to care, and caring was his job, wasn't it?

Lines of communals, commercial carriers, and sled-pads made a hash over Captal's sky, but overhead it was clear. Center overflights were forbidden, even if the traffic control system had allowed it. Slim towers of color-reactive ceramic and crystal soared up about him. The linking tubeways were transparent ribbons of light. Running the Serrll government took up a lot of space. The redolent smell of hot tea stole through the office and he strode back to the desk. The panel in the desk closed where a fine porcelain pot was deposited. He poured himself a cup and sipped appreciatively. On his right, in a little L-shaped alcove stood an oval table. Its patterned wooden surface lovingly hand-polished into hues of deep reds. Elaborately carved matching padded chairs were arranged around the table with mathematical precision. A thin-necked rock vase occupied the center of the table. Dry flowers arched from its long neck. They gave off a subtle mixture of fragrant scents, reminding him of deep forests and rolling fields of his native Kaplan.

Deep in thought, he was distracted when the translucent halves of his door slid into the wall.

"You wanted to see me, Mr. Commissioner?" Gershowan said diffidently as he walked in.

"I wanted to see you, yes." Enllss lowered the cup with a harsh click and turned to the Wall. "What is this drivel, eh?"

Short, with powerful arms and legs, products of his native high gravity environment, Gershowan stared blankly at the Comsec message. He wore his blonde hair clipped short and combed straight back. His pale features were hard and angular and looked unfinished, hurried. He turned to Enllss, his startlingly blue eyes squeezed into buttons.

"A routine message for your information."

"If it's so routine, why haven't you dealt with it? Why did I have to see it and what did you expect me to do with it?"

Gershowan looked confused. "I thought I summarized the situation well. You have my recommendations."

"Then you bungled it by dumping the thing in my lap."

"Sir?"

"You can delegate authority, but you cannot delegate responsibility. As my First Assistant, it was your job to deal with the problem, not hand it back to me. You're no good to me if I have to do your job. I don't have enough hours in the day to do *my* job! Why didn't you action it? You had the solution. It's right there in one of your recommendations."

"Given the delicate nature—"

"Drivel! You're supposed to *handle* delicate situations, by damn! Now, what are you going to do about it?"

Gershowan blanched at this blast from his boss. Proud to represent his system in Captal, he thought himself capable and efficient. Faced with the Commissioner's rage and the realization he somehow failed was crushing. He'd worked diligently on this particular problem, given the sensitive and prickly nature of its history. If old Enllss wanted him to handle it, he would handle it.

"I shall order the ship destroyed. The adverse impact of the find—"

"Good! Do it. Get out."

Enllss smiled when the panels clicked shut. With a bit more polishing, Gershowan would do all right. After all, he had to have *some* potential to have made it into the General Assembly. He did not care to press that line of thought too far or he would start to worry about the future of the Serrll Combine. By damn! He sat back into his formchair, leaned against the armrest and sipped his tea. Ree-Lee made it just right, perhaps a touch on the strong side this time. Allowance for his temper? He smiled again.

Awkward business, Earth finding that old C-32. After reading Gershowan's report, he dug deep into the archives to find out what exactly the infernal thing was. As a museum piece, the ship was priceless and in its day represented cutting-edge technology in reactionless drives. In Earth's hands, though, a fusion charge that could rip apart their whole culture. The place was unstable as it is without adding the C-32 into the equation. How in the pits the damned thing got left behind was beyond comprehension. It wasn't something one could forget to slip into a pocket. Unfortunately, after five thousand years there wasn't anyone left he could blame.

He tapped the comms pad. "Ree-Lee? Get me Commissioner Sill-Anais at the Bureau of Cultural Affairs."

You can delegate authority, but not the responsibility.

He spent the next few minutes sorting through his Comsec messages. Even though his battery of assistants spared him the drudgery of minutiae, Comsec was starting to get cluttered again. Originally set up as a secure message conduit between the Commissioners and the Executive Directors for issues that required his personal attention. Instead, it had degenerated to a private chitchat bank. He must remember to ask Ree-Lee to send another memo to the Executive Council Moderator's office. If something was not done, and soon, he'll end up spending his whole time sifting through Comsec drivel. That was why he had a staff. He was a policymaker, not a sucking bureaucrat. It simply wouldn't do.

The comms alert beeped and he turned to the Wall.

"Sill, you old sand slug!" he boomed as the Deklan's gaunt features cleared. "How's the mole catching business?"

"Ach! Better since you've left the Bureau," Sill remarked dryly. "I'm kind of busy right now…"

"No small talk?"

"What do you want?"

"You're heartless."

"Ach! I'll live with it," Sill grunted and combed his fingers through his long white hair, streaked with twin bands of dark gray that denoted a mature male. His clear wide-set green eyes squinted beneath thin white eyebrows.

Enllss laughed.

The two men could not present a more striking contrast of presence and personalities. Enllss muscular and powerful, his bearing commanding instant attention. His aquiline nose stood out sharp above a firm full mouth. Dark gray eyes glittered with intelligence and his square jaw thrust out with determination. Sill was thin and wiry, and the olive complexion only accentuated his pinched, dry face. Although both were Revisionist Party Assembly representatives, they started their careers—only twelve years ago—as adversaries. Time and experience had turned antagonism into grudging respect, then firm friendship.

"A memo crossed my Comsec this morning, a Serrll Moon Base intercept. An archaeological team on Earth has apparently dug up an old C-32."

"A what?"

"A first-generation direct drive scoutship, you ignorant barbarian."

Sill frowned, then his eyebrows climbed. "Ach! That would place it at the end of the genetic experiments period. You've got a problem then."

"I don't have a problem. Earth has a problem."

"A matter of perspective, ach! I suppose you want my help in sanitizing it?"

"A directive is being relayed to the Diplomatic Branch, but I wanted to make sure you were in the loop. Whatever Anabb does, Earth mustn't know that we were involved."

"If they ask?"

"They won't. The Americans will not risk public exposure of MJ-12. This is not to say they'll give up the craft willingly either. We need to defuse this before there is escalation in international tension and the thing blows up in their faces. Prickly lot, they are."

"Not like us at all, of course," Sill said with a straight face.

"This is serious, Sill."

"Ach! Anabb will handle it."

"Let me know when it's done." Enllss picked up his cup and took a sip. The tea cold again. By damn! "How are you getting on with the Lemos raiders?"

"The net is unraveling and I'm especially keen to get a brief from Anar'on on any intelligence they've gained from Kai Tanard."

"They're still sitting on him?"

"Sucking him dry, more likely. Can't blame them for that, given what he tried to do to the delegates. Ach!"

"Sill, this AUP Provisional Committee. What do we know about it?"

"It's compartmented and you don't have the need to know."

"I do have a need to know, by damn!"

"Ach! Get clearance from Illeran and I'll talk to you."

"You're a stuffed asshole."

"You ran BueCult yourself, Enllss, and you should know how these things work."

"Remind me when you come crawling for help, you Deklan hypocrite."

"I will. If there is nothing else, I've got real work to do."

"Don't forget the moles, Sill! There are always moles!"

"Ach! There would be fewer if you pulled yours out," Sill remarked darkly and cut contact.

Enllss chuckled. Sill was his friend, but he served a different master. Running the Bureau of Colonial and Protectorate Affairs required a lot of information from every government department. Not all were willing to part with it, but there were ways of getting what he wanted without necessarily having to go cap in hand through the front door. Conducting the business of the Serrll government sometimes demanded a circuitous approach.

Should he go through Illeran for that raider data? His boss would probably okay the information request, but he did not want to alert the Executive Director that he trawled for information. The problem he had, Illeran was a senior Servatory wheel and a political opponent. Enllss felt uncomfortable about broadcasting his intentions, however innocuous they may appear. No telling who might get to hear about it. Then he smiled, realizing he was being a paranoid old fool.

Still, just because he was paranoid didn't mean that they weren't after him.

* * *

"Ariane! Where is Terr? And where is his report? I want them both right now!" Anabb demanded unreasonably. As director of the Diplomatic Branch, he didn't have to be reasonable. Not today at any rate.

Outside his office, Ariane gracefully bent her long neck and ran her fingers along prominent cheekbones. Lips pursed in a delicate frown, she tilted her narrow head. The boss knew very well where Agent Terrllss-rr was. Anabb knew where his agents were. He was simply being difficult and in one of his raspy moods again.

"He is three days out from Taltair after authorized leave on Anar'on, sir," she said immediately. She also knew the location of every one of Anabb's agents.

"I don't pay my agents to be on leave. If they want to be on leave, retire they can."

"Yes, sir."

"Signal him," Anabb ordered. Thunderation! A month on the job and already taking leave. Absurd! The boy may have had a rough day with Kai Tanard, but leave? No wonder the building looked deserted. Everyone goofing off. About time the Diplomatic Branch did some real work. "Another thing. Cancel all leaves. Running a resort I am not."

"Sir?"

"And a department heads meeting I want in two hours.

That means everybody!"

Feeling better, he stood up, clasped his hands behind his back and began pacing. After tackling Tanard, Terr might be understandably filed down, but what he had in mind for him was a simple mission. Time the boy got a taste of the routine.

It poured outside, the rain blurring and softening everything it touched. Dark heavy clouds smothered the taller buildings and obscured the skyline. The slim towers glowed with inner pearly light. The bright tubeways that wound between them were filmy ribbons of white. Staring out the window screen, his eyebrows knitted. It took him a few seconds to realize what was missing…no traffic. The network either buried in low clouds or more likely was above it. White lightning slashed down. A moment later came a sharp crash and thunder rolled, grumbling to itself. He rubbed his hands with satisfaction. A perfect day for indoor work.

The comms alert beeped and he frowned. Well, maybe not that perfect.

"What is it, Ariane?"

"Sir, Commissioner Sill-Anais."

"Hah! Put him through," he growled and turned to the Wall.

Sill looked tired and distracted. Well, Anabb felt somewhat tired and distracted himself. He suppressed a gush of sympathy for his boss and squared his shoulders.

"If you're looking for that Lemos brief, Sill, it's not ready yet."

"Ach! I'm not about to rain on your shoes, Anabb," Sill piped and brushed back his hair. "Just wanted to give you a heads-up."

"Oh?"

"BCPA is sending you a full brief, but the short of is that we need to remove an old C-32 scoutship Earth managed to dig up at one of their archaeological sites," Sill said and paused. "Be careful on this one, Anabb. Here is one of those nasty things where a slipup could have very unpleasant ramifications—for everybody."

"Thunderation! If everything goes well, I won't even get a thanks. Otherwise my ass will be in a sling."

"Ach! Crude, but accurate."

"Thunderation!"

"Talk to me once you get that brief. On that other matter, I don't want to put you on the spot regarding Lemos, but do you have *anything* that I can use?"

"Like hell you're not putting me on a spot," Anabb grumbled, not really resenting Sill's question. "The returns are still coming in. I suspect the raider networks will turn out to be far more extensive than anyone imagined. Although mainly a Palean pastime, there are strong indicators that Sargon and Karkan hypercorps are attempting to level out the competition by renting out raiders."

"That's no surprise, ach!" Sill pointed out evenly. "Any indication the Paravan Trading Association was involved?"

"None as yet. Paravan plays tough, but there is no evidence to suggest they're involved with raiders. It's a mug's game and Paravan are too smart to go down that path."

Sill frowned and nodded to himself. "Remember what you said before? That raiders are a social mollification index, a barometer of Serrll's general wellbeing?"

"A drastic example of the type if someone has to die to contribute a dot in some department's graph," Anabb added dryly.

Sill raised an admonishing finger. "Ach! You must remember that Captal's purpose is not to reform the society. It's there simply to maintain sufficient stability for natural social forces to evolve. As it is, we face a lot of flack because of what many systems see as inaction by an entrenched and bloated central bureaucracy. If Captal did act, in whose image should it shape the social fabric?"

"Acting for the elusive public good is a slippery concept,

which I know. I'm not surprised Captal more often than not does nothing."

"Most problems solve themselves by outliving them. Ach!"

"How does all this reflect on my program to clean out the raiders? Is Captal merely basking in the transitory limelight of public approval by my clampdown, knowing full well that in the long run, any action will be futile and a counterproductive gesture, forcing the survivors to become even more sophisticated?"

Sill laughed, his amusement tinged with genuine admiration. His Branch director had obviously thought this through and realized some of the implications.

"Cynical you are, Anabb, ach!"

"Thunderation! I have to be cynical or none of this makes sense."

"I don't pretend to know the government's policy on everything," Sill said wryly, "but I do know this. BueCult serves to protect the Serrll Combine from internal and external threats. Its ultimate purpose is to keep a finger on the pulse of social development and change, and to stop governments from meddling. The Executive Council deliberated long whether limited wars should be allowed to run their natural course, destruction and suffering notwithstanding. Violence, after all, is a reaction against a situation that has become intolerable, and there is a lot of suppressed violence out there. As a former military commander, Anabb, you must be aware of the risks associated with maintaining apparent stability that merely serves to raise the social temperature between the protagonists. When the lid eventually does blow off, the resulting mess can be even more catastrophic."

"Safety valves should never be screwed down," Anabb agreed. "Does the government view raiders as one of Serrll's safety valves?"

"Ach! You know the answer to that one," Sill said.

And Anabb did. Because raiders were a social symptom

and part of the nature of the races that made up the Serrll, they would always be there in some guise. His current action would merely serve to lower the pressure for a time. From a more immediate and cynical point of view, Captal probably wanted to make sure that relocating the Diplomatic Branch to Taltair had not been a mistake. While pursuing that line of thought, it was also likely that Sill wanted to satisfy himself that his brand-new Branch director could do the job.

His mouth twitched in a grin.

Well, if the Executive Council was happy for him to chase shadows, he was equally happy to accommodate them. He had a job to do, and social impact be damned. The Council can worry about Serrll's social health. That's why they held those lofty positions. If he thought too much about things, he would start questioning himself, and that was a path to insanity. Was that why his predecessor left so suddenly?

Thunderation! He was doing it!

"Keep me posted on that C-32," Sill said and cut contact.

Wearing a wry smile, Anabb strode to his desk and slid into the formchair. The tooled leather creaked beneath his weight as the thing molded itself around him. He hooked his fingers behind his head and leaned back. The comms alert beeped and he reached for the pad.

"What is it, Ariane?"

"Agent Terrllss-rr, sir."

"About time. Put him through," he said and turned to the Wall.

Terr looked relaxed, his gray eyes clear and penetrating. A healthy tan had turned his skin to a golden hue. He wore a native short-sleeved shirt, open to the waist. Strictly against regulations and Anabb was about to give him a dressing down, but managed to check himself. The boy wasn't officially in the Fleet anymore. Still, there were limits. Terr's shock of brown-black hair unruly and needed cutting, but the boy obviously didn't

give a damn. The face finely molded without appearing chiseled. A ragged scar above his left eyebrow that ran to his temple
barely discernable. The slight cleft in the chin suited him and
added character to his maturing features.

Given Sill's new orders, he wondered if Terr would be up
to doing the job.

"Took you long enough. You think I spend my time waiting for your call?"

Against the background of *Sheeva's* command deck, Terr
regarded his boss and blinked. The old fart was never satisfied.

"I regret if I caused you any inconvenience, sir," he said
easily, his voice even with a pleasant timbre.

"You're breaking my heart." Anabb paused, making up his
mind. This could be tough on the boy, but there was no easy
way to do it and Anabb needed to know if he'd made the right
choice by picking him to join the Branch. "I've got orders for
you. You'll get a full brief shortly, but I want you to make for
the Serrll Moon Base at max boost. You'll penetrate an archaeological site on Earth and destroy an old C-32 the locals have
managed to dig up. Your after-action report with Kai Tanard
and his merchant auxiliary will have to be done through a Wall
linkup. You'll have a full debrief when you're finished with the
C-32."

Terr's face was a mask and he must have had a raft of questions, but he didn't ask them. Anabb liked that. The boy realized that everything would be explained in his brief. In the
meantime, he was prepared to contain his curiosity. That
showed discipline.

"Two questions only, sir."

Well, partial discipline…

"Shoot."

"What's my level of authority?"

Although this would be covered in his orders, Anabb appreciated why Terr wanted to have verbal confirmation.

"You'll have full authority to ask the SMB commander for

anything you want."

"He might not like that."

"He'll like it even less if he fails to comply!"

"As a First Scout—"

"A First Scout you're not! You're one of my operatives. As such, you carry the authority of the Diplomatic Branch. Don't worry. You'll have appropriate clearance and authentication codes, and SMB will be alerted that you're coming. However—"

"I'll try not to let the power go to my head."

"Hah! I'm glad you understand. Remember, every organ of the Serrll government is at your disposal to help you. Just don't bend them."

"Aye, sir."

"Another thing. I want you to stop over at Salina, pick up a Captal science team and ferry them to the SMB. I have special reasons to keep this out of normal Fleet channels and your presence is fortuitous."

"How many of them are there?"

"Four, including Scholar Laraiana who is heading the team."

"An M-1 is not exactly a luxury—"

"They'll live."

"May I ask—"

"You don't have a need to know. Don't worry, this is a milk run."

Terr recalled what happened last time on one of Anabb's milk runs and his skin crawled.

"Your second question?"

"Is it too late to resign?"

Impertinent scamp. Anabb suppressed a grin and glared instead.

"If you're discovered, don't bother coming back!" he snapped and cut contact. He stared at the pooling colors in the Wall for a moment, then chuckled.

# Chapter Five

Squads of armed UN soldiers guarded the last kilometer of the approach to the archaeological site. People were parked and camped at every available clear patch of ground in a profusion of colored tents and trailers. Some walked about wearing Darth Vader headgear or green plastic alien heads with enormous slanting black eyes. An almost carnival atmosphere surrounded the road as Lauren's olive Land Rover threaded its way past gawking teenagers who seemed oblivious to the fact they were reveling on a public thoroughfare. Some of the fun died when a stringy-haired girl, her face contorted as she shrilled abuse, lobbed a bag of tomatoes at Lauren's windscreen. Placard-waving teenagers crowded around the car, protesting against everything from save the whales to anti-globalization and corporate greed.

"Repent, harlot of Babel! You have sinned against God!" a bearded face yelled from the side window. It startled her enough to grip the steering wheel hard.

"We want to see the aliens!"

"You cannot keep us out forever!"

"We have a right!"

Similar invective followed her the rest of the way until they reached the heavily patrolled exclusion zone half a kilometer from the site. Lauren found it hard to understand the mentality of the people mobbing the approaches. The UN engineers had erected three giant LCD screens outside the exclusion fence that provided constant coverage of the uncovered chamber, with regular segments that showed the saucer itself. It still wasn't enough for the chanting mobs, apparently determined to saw off a souvenir before they were satisfied. Smashing one of the screens was a start.

In Comalcalco the town seethed with masses of humanity impossible to move through, and tensions were running high against the heavy presence of the *policia*. She found it unbelievable that ordinary well-mannered individuals seemed to take on a different personality when inserted into a mob. Then again, it took a certain type to be here at all. What did they expect? Elvis to come out? She had not done any of the shopping she needed and didn't want to drive all the way to Villahermosa. The whole experience left her in a particularly foul mood.

She drove to the main gate and flashed her plastic badge at the unsmiling soldier. Wearing the familiar blue UN beret, the soldier carefully checked the badge, compared it with the printed list, then waved to his companion in the guard box. His eyes barely flickered at her passenger. Motors whined and the barrier boom lifted. She took back her card and the car surged through, throwing back a shower of gravel. Simmering, she drove along the now worn track toward a cluster of prefabricated huts that cluttered the clearing between Temple I and the Great Acropolis. A white-painted helicopter that looked to her like a Vietnam Huey, clattered overhead, the black UN insignia prominent on its side. A squad of soldiers decked out in striped jungle fatigues, were going through a series of close-order drills urged on by a bellowing sergeant. A row of drab khaki-colored tents housed the military detachment. Stacked piles of supply crates clustered near the barbed wire fence at the jungle's edge. The place was a mess.

Five days, that is all it took to transform her little secluded kingdom into an armed camp. When the UN detachment arrived with their trucks and jeeps and soldiers, she protested. Now she appreciated the scale of the operation needed to set up an impenetrable cordon around the archaeological site. If allowed in the crowds would have torn up everything, doing incalculable damage. She shouldn't complain. The Mexican government had permitted her and Martin to stay. All other work at the site suspended, to Kareza's intense annoyance. In reality, apart from trying to decipher the etchings found on the original stone, there remained very little for her to do. With the military trampling about, it was impossible to do any serious archaeological work, her heart no longer really in it—she had reached the end of her rainbow. Her GPR scans of the other mounds revealed nothing. With typical bureaucratic single-mindedness, the UN team covered every inch of the site again.

Perhaps it was time to get back to Columbia U and get the second semester lectures organized. She also had a paper to write. At least Martin seemed to be enjoying himself. Already responsible for photographing the initial expedition, he became the semi-official historian and record keeper for the UN investigation team. In the rush to get the team to the site, the official photographer was left behind. He arrived a day later, armed with camcorders, cine cameras and a virtual photolab. By that time, Martin was accepted as one of the team.

Soldiers in green issue T-shirts were stringing the last of the electrical wiring along makeshift poles from the site's main entrance distribution board. Power allowed some welcome luxuries to be installed in the huts, like lighting. She learned to hate the hissing little gas lanterns in her makeshift hut. Everyone shared a common mess and bathroom facilities. As the only female on the site didn't faze the engineers at all. They simply walled off part of the shower area for her. There was no question she would commute every day from her hotel in Villahermosa. There wasn't any need. Apart from Martin, all her other students had already left, including Chatika. She missed the company of another female.

She drove past Temple II and pulled up beside the second of four prefab huts that served as her new base camp and quarters. Taking a deep breath, she switched off the engine and glanced at the young captain sitting beside her. Her escort returned her gaze without expression.

"I'm sorry," she said simply.

"I guess you had to see for yourself, Doctor," he said in what she figured was a Boston accent. He was big and powerful and intimidating. Perhaps that's why they assigned him to her.

"Yeah." She jerked the door open and climbed down. It gave her a measure of satisfaction to slam the thing shut. She didn't see the captain's slow grin as she stalked to the hut and pulled open the door.

Inside, Martin looked up, saw the doc's dark scowl and brightened. The doc was mad, and that meant trouble for someone. He fervently hoped it wouldn't be him. Silently, he got up and poured a cup of coffee from a simmering percolator jug and held it out. Lauren's eyes crinkled and she smiled, accepting the peace offering.

"Thanks." She sipped and sat down beside him. She pushed back her sleeves and glanced at the laptop screen. "Still nothing?"

"Your hunch was right, doc," Martin said. "The script definitely contains Semitic root characters. I had to look up some really old texts from Euphrates and Armenia to see it. Kirmond is beside himself. He's chewing glass shards rather than admit there is a connection."

Kirmond had been her master's advisor. At first, she was flattered that such a prominent personage would be interested in her work and dismissed warnings from her colleagues as jealousy. Fortunately for her, Kirmond soon revealed himself for the predator he was. Although not a groper like Boulcher, his interest turned out to be far more insidious. Excited at discussing her work with him, that excitement quickly turned into disillusionment when she found he plagiarized her work, publishing it in his own name. What infuriated her more, the university did nothing about it. She finished her master's without him.

"Is there a connection?" she prompted.

"Doctor Markinov at Ben-Gurion thinks there is. He sounded very animated. He could assign the most general interpretation to only eleven symbols and he's guessing at the rest. He thinks the lettering is an inscription, a memorial to the gods who would return as promised."

Lauren nodded. That in itself was tantalizing, and not altogether surprising. She accepted the likelihood the aliens had fostered many of the Earth's fledgling civilizations over a long period of time. Speculation that needed backing by solid research. What intrigued her more, who built the chamber and how it was done?

"And the scrapings. Anything from Columbia?" Referring to scrapings made from inside the grooves in the lettering. Tools used to chisel out the text would have left microscopic particles of metal embedded in the stone. She hoped the electron microscope scans would give her a clue as to the type of metal, provided that after five thousand years something remained to be scanned.

"They didn't find any metals, but they did find pigments."

She tapped her teeth with a tip of her finger. "Paint!"

"They found one other thing, doc. Glass vitrification."

She stared at him, her mouth a round O. "Laser! O my gosh! The lettering was cut by a laser!" The process would have melted the grooves and turned the stone into glass, which over centuries would have slowly decomposed. "Have you told Dr. Markinov?"

"He knows. It forced him to rethink his initial translation."

"I bet. The inscription could say 'Do not store below five degrees Centigrade'."

Martin sat back and regarded the doc with affection. "What I'd like to know is whether the aliens wrote that inscription, or if they just happened to leave a laser behind?"

"The latter, I'd guess."

"Very untidy of them, doc. They must have left in a hurry."

"Mmm."

"You know, they're starting to call it the Ezekiel saucer."

Lauren snorted. "Just as long as *you* don't call it that. Where is Dr. Imatlan?"

"Left an hour ago; a call from the National Anthropology Museum and some government bigwig. He said he'd be back tomorrow."

She chewed her fingernail. She worried every time Kareza was out of her sight. It took a stormy General Assembly session, followed by a rowdy meeting of the Security Council, to affirm Mexico's ownership of the saucer and work out a deal acceptable to the major powers, but Kareza was still plotting and scheming. Things were difficult enough with the site overrun by the military without having to play his childish games. She inclined her head at the door.

"Anything new?"

"They're trying to find a hatch."

"Hah!"

"Doc? Will they really try and move the saucer?"

"Probably. Romantic as it might be to leave the thing here, this is no place to conduct serious research." She placed her cup on the sink tray and walked out, leaving Martin looking thoughtfully after her. Once the saucer was gone, what would the doc do? What was *he* going to do? Write his graduate dissertation probably. The thought didn't cheer him up.

Outside, she walked briskly over steel grating placed on bare ground after all the soil was cleared away by a backhoe between Temple II and the mound, exposing the entire length of the side wall to its base. The 4.5 meter-high structure looked imposing as she hurried, absently trailing her fingers along the stone. When the UN engineers wanted to dig out the front of the mound as well, she stood firm and entered into a shouting match with an English major. This was her dig and no one was going to disturb the site more than absolutely necessary. Even now, much of the roof had been cleared with needless enthusiasm, necessary if they were planning to move the ship. Was that part of the reason why Kareza had flown back to Mexico City?

To move the ship, they would need to demolish one entire wall and remove all the capstones that made up the chamber ceiling. The Mexican government may not like desecrating the mound or the chamber, but to the politicians it probably wasn't even a consideration compared to the knowledge that would be gained by studying the ship in a properly controlled environment. It pained her to admit it, but they were right. After all, the chamber could be rebuilt and the mound restored. The UN would pay for it and everyone would be happy. Cynical perhaps, but she felt she had the essentials right.

That didn't mean she liked any of it.

Where would they move it, and how? Once outside the site entrance a convoy would be mobbed. The idea made her shudder. Maybe they didn't intend moving it all, but simply bring in more equipment. She didn't believe it.

She rounded the corner and stopped. A burly individual was untangling a thick white cable from a drum. Another stood on a ladder next to the entrance, brandishing a drill. He was about to ram the bit against the wall and she screamed.

"Stop! You mark that stone and I'll have you shot!"

The soldier looked at her in astonishment. "I was just—"

"You were about to damage a priceless Mexican treasure."

"But—"

"Get down from there!"

"What seems to be the trouble, Dr. Hopking?"

She turned to the tall figure beside her. It was her hulky escort. She didn't need to have her hand held here, thank you.

"This clod was about to put holes in my wall."

"The scientists inside need more power and lighting, Doctor," the young captain said reasonably.

"Fine, then give it to them, but not by drilling holes in my wall! Got that?"

The captain nodded and jerked his head at the soldier, who shrugged and climbed down the ladder. Lauren snorted and marched into the chamber. With floodlights tucked into the corners, the ship had lost its dark brooding demeanor. Now light gray and seemed to have shrunk in the roomier looking chamber. Banks of blinking instruments, glowing PC screens, tools and assorted electronic gear stood piled on trolleys and makeshift benches shoved against the left wall.

Professor Babich, a British nuclear specialist from CERN and Europe's contribution to the team, stood beside the hot water urn, gesticulating with the stem of his pipe at Dr. Sheppard, a plasma physicist from the NASA Glenn Research Center. Babich always prodded somebody with that pipe as Lauren came to learn. She suspected that one day, someone would take the pipe and ram it down Babich's throat.

Zaminski and Fillipe Kopan sat huddled near an oscilloscope; both wearing worried expressions as they stared at the wiggling lines. The Russian, an advanced propulsion expert and Fillipe, Mexico's leading aerodynamics physicist, made an unlikely pair. Zaminski rolled back his chair toward the ship and adjusted a coupling taped to the hull. Wiggly lines danced and peaked in the oscilloscope.

Hirohito Oshigawa leaned back from the microscope and nodded to Dr. Zuang Kui Chee. The Chinese metallurgist craned forward and peered into the eyepieces. Dressed in worn jeans and loose sweaters, both looked like teenagers.

Staring at them, Lauren wondered how much politics went into selecting the UN team. They were certainly a colorful lot, but had slotted into a cohesive team surprisingly quickly. Reflecting on digs where she'd been a part of an international team, she wasn't really surprised. Driven by a common purpose, they were first of all scientists. Physical and cultural differences hardly seemed to be noticed. The same with this group, and she enjoyed the clash of sharp minds.

She strode toward the urn, picked out a cup that looked clean and proceeded to make herself coffee. Babich and Sheppard made room for her without a break in conversation and walked to one of the PCs. Bill Faroway came into view around the curve of the ship, spotted her and waved. He was a theoretician at the secretive Lawrence Livermore National Lab and walked about with a bemused expression, almost as if he was sharing some cosmic joke. She found him easy to talk to and he was very patient with her silly questions, something she appreciated.

"Absolutely amazing," he gushed at her, beaming from ear to ear.

He said that about twenty times already and she tended to ignore it now. In his mid-thirties, completely unpretentious, unmarried, Faroway had an innocent charm she found appealing. He wouldn't talk much about himself, but she sensed a wariness and a vulnerability she wanted to find more about. He held three PhDs, and that didn't surprise her. When he started talking, everyone listened. It was clear his disarming smile hid a considerable intellect. He was also cute to look at. Not tall, but well muscled and assured in his movements. She found his blue-green eyes particularly captivating, and his voice sent shivers down her spine. Was she getting infatuated?

"Found anything new, Bill?"

"Feel the skin," he said and placed his palm against the hull. She brushed her hand along the rough metal.

"I know, it's cold."

"Exactly! What I cannot work out is why it's cold. See those two?" He pointed at Babich and Sheppard. "They've been arguing about it for two days now. You see, this thing should behave like a black body, only it doesn't. With all these lights shining on the hull, the surface should have warmed, but it's reacting more like a glass, reflecting everything. It's got me. Babich is half convinced the ship is violating the first law of thermodynamics."

Lauren didn't know anything about the first law of thermodynamics, and wasn't about to ask.

"What if the skin isn't reflecting at all, but is absorbing, like a one-way mirror?" she said.

Faroway chuckled and she felt foolish. She was discussing black body radiation with one of the eminent scientists in the world as though she knew what she was on about.

"Funny you should say that, and it's a very good point. That's precisely what has me so intrigued. From the scrapings Oshigawa and Chee made, we know that the hull, although metallic, is more like a fiberglass composite. If the material isn't radiating, where is all that energy going?"

"Charging its batteries?"

He shrugged. "Perhaps. Until we get inside, that's as good an explanation as any."

Oshigawa saw them and walked over. He nodded to Lauren.

"Dr. Faroway, about the laser scans. Dr. Chee thinks the hull was grown into those shapes. No manufacturing process could have made those rods and cones."

"Rods and cones?" Lauren stared at the metallurgist and sipped her coffee.

"It would explain why the skin is so rough," Bill mused.

"It's a spaceship. Why make the skin rough?" she asked.

"It might be a spaceship, Dr. Hopking," Hiro said in softly accented English, "but it's also an atmosphere craft. Those little rods and cones create miniature vortices as the ship travels through the air and smoothes the flight, much as a shark's rough skin enables it to travel through water with minimal resistance."

"Sounds counterintuitive," Lauren commented.

"Yes it does, doesn't it," Bill said. "However, that roughness wouldn't do the ship much good at high Mach numbers."

Hirohito nodded. "True enough, and I think they are something else. I think they may be sensor nodes, part of a countermeasures mechanism. Radiation striking them would bounce around from one point to another in random reflection, or—"

"Be absorbed, like light hitting the retina," Bill said. "The thing would be radar invisible."

"Exactly!" Hiro mused, then pulled at his chin. "You mentioned a retina, Doctor. I wonder. Do you suppose they could also be a vision array?"

Bill looked startled, then chuckled. "Why not? Anything is possible."

Hero glanced speculatively at Lauren. "It occurs to me that Dr. Hopking should try the sensor."

"The sensor?" she demanded, automatically suspicious.

"Good idea," Bill said and pulled at her arm. "This way."

She put her cup on the table. Wearing a secret smile, he led her around the ship and stopped beside a strip of blue duct tape stuck to the hull.

"Press your palm against the pad," he invited.

She peered closely at the hull. A polished area some fifteen centimeters square glinted at her. She glanced at Bill with her unspoken question.

"We think it's an access sensor of some kind. Logical if you think about it, and much more practical than having to worry about losing your keys."

"The chances of my palm—"

"We don't believe it's a palm recognition device at all, Lauren," Hiro said with a boyish shrug. "We think it's just one end of a circuit, the other being the individual electrical patterns of the ship's crew keyed for access."

Bill noted her reluctance and grinned. "We've already tried everyone else."

Lauren blinked. "Everybody?" That was over two hundred people! "If this is a door, what makes you think it'll still function after five thousand years?"

"Not a thing, but I would rather not have to cut our way in if it can be avoided, for obvious reasons."

She shrugged and pressed her hand against the plate. A tingling shock raced up her wrist and she snatched back her hand. "Hey!"

"You felt something?" Bill looked at her with concern.

"A funny tingle. It startled me. I'll try again." Frowning, she extended her arm.

"What are you doing?" Sheppard demanded as he strode toward them with Babich in tow.

"Lauren's got a reaction from the pad," Bill said brightly. "Why?"

"The IR reading spiked."

"Interesting," Bill murmured and touched the hull. "I'll be damned. It's warm."

"Active after five thousand years?" Babich mused and Sheppard glared at him.

"Why not? It was obviously built to last, not like our obsolescent consumer rubbish."

"What have you done?" Zaminski roared as he rounded the curve of the ship. The burly Russian skidded to a stop, placed his huge paws on his hips and glared at them. "All my instruments have suddenly jumped off the dial."

Dr. Chee appeared behind him and waited expectantly.

Bill inclined his head at the taped pad. "We have a reaction."

"Do I need to be here?" Lauren asked tartly and Bill chuckled.

"Quite right, one thing at a time. Go ahead," he said and gave her a reassuring nod.

She lifted her arm and gingerly touched the pad. The tingle hardly noticeable this time. When nothing happened, she pulled her hand away. There was a sharp hiss of escaping air and beside her a section of hull silently swung down. She gasped and jumped back. There was a soft click as the section locked into place, revealing six steps.

"My god, will you look at that," Sheppard whispered.

The lit interior chest-high above the stone floor. They could see the back of what looked like padded seats that faced a curved instrument console and sloping flat screens. The walls glowed pale beige.

"Would you believe it?" Babich breathed in awe.

"Amazing," Zaminski said and shook his head.

Dr. Chee kept his face impassive as he stared in wonder into the ship. He would have to inform Beijing, although the purpose behind his daily transmissions tended to discommode him. He didn't like playing the spy. He was a scientist and did not share his government's hatred and fear of the imperialists, having earned his doctorate in advanced metallurgy at MIT. As it was, in the eyes of his superiors, his contact with the West had contaminated him. He was damaged goods, but he was also the best they had. And he had a family to protect. America was incredibly advanced and its people undisciplined and racist. Contrary to propaganda, they weren't warlike and didn't seek conquest. He knew them to be generous in peace and made implacable and awesome enemies. Perhaps he could still avert a confrontation, one that could send his homeland down a path of total destruction. For what? Hollow pride and personal political power? What good would those things be in a radioactive cloud?

"Who wants to go in first?" Bill invited with a quizzical smile.

"As the senior UN representative—" Babich began, but Sheppard cut him off.

"Let's not start on a whole lot of damn protocol."

"Not protocol!" Zaminski boomed. "Procedure!"

"Nobel laureate or not," Kopan started and prodded Zaminski in the chest, "this is Mexican territory and—"

Lauren snorted and lifted her arms. "Enough already! We should test the air before anyone goes in there. We may already be contaminated as it is."

"Is this really necessary, Dr. Hopking?" Zaminski demanded. "Any alien microorganisms—"

"I was thinking more of homegrown fungal spores, Doctor."

"Can you run the tests, Lauren?" Bill asked.

"It'll take a minute, and nobody moves!" she snapped and hurried to get the test kit from her hut. She banged the door open and laughed at Martin's startled expression.

"We have it open!"

"Holy shit!"

"Come on!"

She frowned when she saw everyone still clustered in front of the open hatch. Men! She placed the kit on the second step and took out swabs and two reagent bottles. Carefully, she wiped the sixth step and the deck, and popped the swab into the bottle.

"Check this," she told Martin and scrambled up the steps. She should really be wearing a mask, damn! The deck felt hard, but had some give to it, like cork, the thought flashed through her mind. The central dome was some two meters above the deck and emitted a dull milky glow. Three couches faced a down-sloping console that filled a quarter of the rounded interior. Large square display screens stared at her, gray and non-reflective. The consoles were filled with patterns of square and rectangular pads whose function was completely meaningless to her. She couldn't see any other controls. How did they steer the thing?

She tore her eyes away from the console and swabbed the left couch and the deck. With a last look around, she climbed out. Martin was holding a test flask against the light.

"Looks clean, doc."

"Good. Try this one."

To her relief the sample also came back clean. She turned to Babich and grinned impishly.

"You were arguing who should go in first?"

"*Touché*, dear lady. Dr. Kopan?" Babich said with a small bow and extended his arm.

Looking flustered, Kopan cleared his throat, realizing how silly the whole thing was.

"No, no. We're all on the same team, Doctor. You should—"

"Boys..." Lauren muttered and climbed in.

Standing in the middle of the deck, she sniffed. The air dry and smelled musty. She brushed her fingers against the center couch and her hand came away dusty. She wiped it absently against her jeans.

"Impressive, isn't it?" Dr. Chee said beside her. She looked into his deep black eyes and nodded. The others crowded behind him, protocol forgotten as they peered curiously like children at a carnival.

"Where is the power coming from?" Sheppard demanded and swept his arm at the glowing walls.

"We could be looking at a purely passive emergency system, my dear Sheppard," Bill suggested and Zaminski shook his head.

"Like batteries? A fanciful idea, Doctor, but unlikely."

"Considering the ceramic composition of the hull, it would take a lot of energy to warm it," Hiro said.

"Exactly!" Zaminski exclaimed.

"Not if the hull material was a superconductor," Bill murmured. "It might be converting gravitational energy directly into electromagnetic energy. I've done the experiments myself and the application would explain a lot, especially if the ship utilizes a variant of a diametric or pitch drive."

Zaminski stared at him. Babich stuck the mangled stem of his pipe into his mouth and chewed thoughtfully. Sheppard winced and shook his head.

"I have never been comfortable with the diametric drive theory. Creating a negative mass sink into which the ship would 'fall' to create propulsion sounds too much like hard work to me. Where would they get the power?"

"Fusion," Zaminski said promptly. "A field reversed configuration using rotating magnetic fields would be easiest."

"Have you noticed the shape of this thing?" Bill said quietly. "This craft could just as easily be an electrogravitic vehicle that uses an asymmetrical E-Field gradient to generate unidirectional thrust. Much more economical than bending the fabric of space."

"NASA's lift vehicles!" Babich exclaimed and everyone started talking at once.

Not really understanding the highly technical discussion, Lauren swung one of the couches toward her and sat down. The material squirmed and molded itself around her. It was a most comfortable feeling. On the console before her, several rectangular pads began to blink brown and green. She jumped and the pads faded.

"Interesting," Chee pronounced beside her. "Do that again."

Lauren sat down and the pads lit up. On impulse, she touched the left one. It stopped pulsing and glowed a steady amber, while an array of other pads lit up on the two side consoles. The central screen cleared into flowing color patterns.

"Tirumal akaina halium shanas," an even masculine voice said pleasantly out of thin air. Babich jumped and dropped his pipe.

"Shit!"

Lauren grinned at him in delight.

"Look!" Martin pointed and everyone crowded next to the couches. Three-dimensional schematics flickered in the central screen while the console pads lit up in cascades of shifting lights.

"What's it doing?" Sheppard said.

"Probably carrying out a status check," Bill said in a hushed voice, mesmerized by what was happening. The frantic activity suddenly stopped, leaving glowing brown, green, and white pads on the consoles. The central screen resumed its color pooling.

"Safasti datarak celevis karaman," the voice said with some finality.

"Now what do we do?" Kopan asked.

"That's probably what *it* said," Sheppard observed with a

smile.

"A computer able to function after five thousand years?" Kopan looked dubious.

"With solid-state chips and no moving parts, as long as it has power, why not?" Sheppard said with a wave of his hand.

"Safasti datarak celevis karaman," Lauren repeated slowly.

After a moment of tense silence, Sheppard cleared his throat. "Ah, I'm not sure you should have done that."

"Relayuan karaman," the computer said.

Bill touched Lauren's shoulder. "Before we get carried away, let's consider where this is leading us."

Lauren looked deep into his eyes, suddenly aware how clear and penetrating they were. The curve of his chin strong without being angular and she had an urge to stroke it. *Pull yourself together!*

"Bill, the computer is trying to communicate with us."

"Dr. Kopan may be right, and this could be random garble from decayed circuits."

"If we can get the computer to talk to us—"

"Talk to us," the computer said suddenly and everyone jerked like they'd been shot.

* * *

Captain Rashin Amanyev stared pensively through the armored glass of his bridge at the quartering seas that pushed foaming whitecaps against the ship's port side. The sharp prow bit into green seas and sent sheets of white spray high above the bow. *Pyotr Velikiy* shuddered and easily pushed its 26,000-tonne hull through the swell, its forward weather decks swept with churning froth. The helmsman leaned easily against the roll of the ship, his hands lightly holding the small wooden wheel, his eyes flickering constantly at the digital compass. The wheel a mariner's embarrassment. Connected to steering servo-motors the twenty-centimeter wheel a far cry from the oaken creations of old. In those days a man could feel the ship and the sea through the spokes and the tug of tiller ropes. Watching the helmsman, Amanyev shook his head. Technology, he mused, had taken the soul out of sailing. He looked up. The sky torn with white remnants of a storm that had dogged the *Kirov*-class heavy battlecruiser for two days. For five days, he'd steamed directly due east from Taiwan along the twenty-degree latitude line after being diverted from his Philippines run. Almost eight more days and 8,000 kilometers remained of pushing the hull at thirty-one knots before they reached their station off Mexico's western coastline. This overstressed the reactors and the main drive train way beyond prudence, but Amanyev had his orders.

It would be a long haul for *Pyotr*, but he was proud of his aging nineteen-year-old ship. Beset with economic problems the Russian surface ships were languishing in port or sold off to the likes of China and India, or anyone else with hard American dollars in their pocket. The in-service ships hardly ventured out anymore. From once having a premier blue water navy, Russia reduced to scrapping its assets, turning the steel into consumer cans. He saw the rotting hulls of the proud Pacific Fleet submarine force at Petropavlovsk, their uncared-for reactors a major environmental disaster waiting to be unleashed on the Kamchatka peninsula, Vladivostok and Japan.

Right now, he could not afford to think about these things. He had a mission and a ship to make ready. Stressed or not, *Pyotr's* twin reactors were performing at peak efficiency, he ordered the two backup oil steam boilers tested, base maintenance being the way it was. At least his ship was well armed to confront any enemy: three Ka-34 Helix helicopters for ASW work and an array of missile launchers and gun turrets. In the old days, the Soviet navy would have sent a *Kiev*-class aircraft carrier and escorting *Akula* submarines to project its power. The best it could manage now was a single scarred cruiser. It would have to do. After all, this was a peaceful mission. Wasn't it? There was one change he did not mind in this new Russian navy. He didn't have to share power or have his every order questioned by a *zampolit* political officer. Things can't be all that bad then. Staring at the green seas, he wondered about his secret orders to be opened once he reached his station.

Commander Grishnakov strode up to him and Amanyev nodded to his exec. Lanky, his uniform looking like it was draped over a coat hanger. Another doomed soul in the Russian navy. A commanding officer in his own right, he took a reduction in rank in order to serve with Amanyev. Whatever he may have thought privately, Grishnakov was phlegmatic about it. They were both seamen first and did what had to be done to be at sea, however tortuous the relationship.

"Captain, Vladivostok confirms initial intelligence the Chinese have sortied one of their advanced Type 52C *Luhai*-class multi-role large destroyers, the *Kiensan*, into the Pacific. Satellite intelligence shows the ship heading east at twenty-eight knots. This makes them two hundred and forty kilometers north-north-east of us."

That was close, Amanyev conceded. Why was the Chinese ship steaming toward Mexico? He was wary of the Chinese and suspicious of a coincidence that placed both ships in the same patch of sea at the same time. If it was coincidence. Whatever the reason, this was developing into a dangerous concentration of forces he didn't like.

"How far are we from Hawaii?" he demanded as he walked to the plot table.

"Around 2,900 kilometers, Captain," Grishnakov said. He leaned over the lit 1,000mm by 800mm glass chart table and pointed at the island group. "The *Kiensan* will reach Hawaii in three days. If we maintain our course and speed, we'll head-reach them by over eight hours."

"Mmm." At fourteen knots the *Luhai* had a range of almost 16,000 kilometers and well able to reach the Mexican coast.

Powering at twenty-eight knots, its range would be severely curtailed, unless the warship was able to refuel before returning to its home waters. "From Hawaii, how long before we reach our station?" Amanyev asked.

"Five days. It'll take the *Kiensan* at least half a day longer," Grishnakov answered his captain's unspoken question, then added, "and if their power plant hold together."

"Unfortunately, their Ukraine-designed gas turbines are reliable," Amanyev said with a grimace. "We used to build them well, Commander. Skirting Hawaii will slow us down, though."

"Unavoidable."

The exec didn't have to elaborate. Only a fool would attempt to drive a capital warship through American territory without having previously obtained clearance. For this mission, Russia hadn't even bothered.

"And where are the Americans?"

"Intelligence reports a cruiser-destroyer group approximately four hundred and sixty kilometers to our southeast. They believe it's Group One, USS *Constellation*."

The carrier old and not nuclear-powered, recalled to active duty after the Americans blockaded Panama in 2008 to counter Al Queda attacks. However, with its seventy-five strike aircraft, it didn't have to be nuclear.

"A chance patrol, Captain?"

"Chance or not, one of their cursed augmented Aegis cruisers is all it would take to give us a bad time."

"*Pyotr* will give a good account of itself, my Captain."

Both knew the capability of the American warship and its powerful anti-air and anti-surface warfare weapons systems. Although *Pyotr* was some seventy-seven meters longer and almost three times heavier than the Aegis ship, the American more than a match in any standoff confrontation. The *Kiensan* on the other hand, although slightly smaller in size and weight than the Aegis, was well matched. It mounted two P-800 Yakhont, NATO designated land-attack capable SS-NX-

26/Sunburn derivative anti-ship system cells. At Mach 3.6 the supersonic Yakhont was a formidable front-line weapon. The ship also mounted HQ-7/Croatale short-range SAM launchers and two HHQ-9 medium/long-range launchers. The *Kiensan* also bristled with anti-air defense guns.

Amanyev rebuked himself. He should be thinking more like a strategist than a tactician. Faced with the might of the US Pacific Fleet, he would be crazy to seek an engagement. What exactly was he doing here? He hoped his secret orders would tell him. Peaceful mission or not, he did not relish loitering in America's backyard.

"I'm not worried about the Americans so much, my friend. They'll be nosy, but they will leave us alone. It's the heathen Chinese that give me gray hairs. Rash and unpredictable, there's no telling what they'll do."

"Excuse me, Captain," the officer of the watch said respectfully as he approached the two men. They didn't have to say 'comrade' anymore either, also good. "Air defense has identified two F/A-18E Super Hornets inbound. Range, ninety-four kilometers. They should be here in three-and-a-half minutes."

"So, it has started."

"Shall I energize the Osa-MA?" Grishnakov asked, referring to the missile/gun system spread in two twin-launcher modules around the ship, capable of engaging multiple threats within twelve kilometers.

"No. This will be a reconnaissance flight only," Amanyev said casually. "We're in international waters and have as much right to be here as they do." Theoretically, that was true.

At 1,545 kilometers an hour it didn't take the Hornets long to reach the battlecruiser. Six kilometers out the Hornets dropped to 1,000 meters and lit off their APG-73 radars. The deck watchstanders tried hard not to react to the automatic warnings from the defense system.

Amanyev walked to the weather deck and looked up. He

saw a blur of two black shapes flash overhead and they were gone. The sonic boom hit him then, trailing after the aircraft. Staring into the empty sky, he breathed deeply of the warm air as spray stung his face. The ship shouldered through a wave, leaving creamy white water trailing alongside.

He loved the sea, but it would be torn from him when his tour of command ended in eight months. There were too many officers and not enough ships. Crew rotation now standard practice in the new Russian Federation. He lived for the *rodina*, but it had turned its back on him after twenty-two years of faithful service. What use were ships and submarines and aircraft when a man could not put bread on the table for his family while profiteers and racketeers drove flashy Western cars, protected by the very laws meant to exterminate them. Cash strapped, Moscow plowed wearily from one crisis to another, like this old ship, he mused. Things were getting better, but not quickly enough to save him and others like him. He shouldn't complain. He had an apartment in Vladivostok where his Viljana waited patiently for him. A battered old Honda got him around, and there was a pension; enough to buy bread twice a month. A lot waited for him on shore, all right.

The ship leaned into a wave, seemingly nodding in sympathy.

\* \* \*

Lieutenant Mike 'Chips' Grazier glanced at the ATFLIR display. The color infrared image clear as a television picture. At the moment it only showed gray clouds and choppy metallic seas. It would be a few minutes yet before they sighted the Russian cruiser.

"Strike Two, ready to drop to 3,200 feet," he ordered and looked at his wingman sitting fifteen feet off his port wingtip. A skull, holding a knife in its mouth, surrounded by the sign of the atom, prominent on the aircraft's starboard stabilizer.

143

"Roger One, ready to light him up," came back a lazy Texas drawl.

Grazier shook his head. 'Spike' Turner was a superb instinctive Hornet driver, but if he hoped to get his next half stripe to full lieutenant, he better start getting his shit together. The Navy had too many good sticks to tolerate individuals who constantly challenged the envelope. One reason why Spike hadn't gotten a conduct unbecoming, he was simply one of the best electronic dogfighters that VFA-151, the 'Vigilantes', had. As a still-moist jay-gee, he walked away with top marks from the Naval Strike and Air Warfare Center at Fallon, Nevada, that replaced the famed Top Gun Miramar facility, leaving seasoned aviators bemused and outraged. Trophy or not, today's right-sized Navy had only so much slack and Spike had just about used all of his up.

"Check master arm off," he ordered.

"Master arm off, One."

Bearing in at Mach 1.2—1,100 knots indicated airspeed—the two Super Hornets cut through the clearing sky with barely a shudder. The multi-mission strike fighter ideally suited to its job, being night and all-weather capable. Using its upgraded mid-wave infrared (MWIR) staring focal point plane technology the aircraft could deliver an awesome range of missiles and smart ordnance. Today, both carried a basic payload of heat-seeking AIM-9P Sidewinder and AIM-9H Sparrow radar missiles in addition to its M61 Vulcan rotary nose gun. Its multi-sensor integration meant the Hornet was always in touch with *Constellation*, the Group One flagship.

At eleven miles the Russian heavy cruiser stood out clearly against the choppy seas. Looking at the long sleek ship, Grazier admitted the Russians built them pretty—and deadly. The warship bristled with AA emplacements and missile launchers. The augmented Granit and the Osa-MA were particularly grim news. Although the Granit was primarily a land-attack/anti-ship weapon and would not bother his Hornet, its Mach 2.5

plus speed would give *Constellation* and any other surface ship a very bad time. If this was a for-real strike, he would now be flying through a cloud of radar-controlled AK-130, AK-630 and Koshstan air-defense rounds, not counting assorted missiles. The Russians didn't believe in stinting on air defense. He doubted his chances of getting through.

This was just a friendly overflight, right?

Breaking through three miles, Grazier gave the order to drop to 3,200 feet. The Hornets dived and lit off their APG-73 radars. This was to let the Russian know that Uncle Sam was in the neighborhood and wasn't about to take any shit off no Russian. He needn't have worried. Apart from getting painted with normal nav and weather radars, the cruiser ignored their presence. What the *Pyotr* was doing in these waters, he didn't know and didn't care. That was someone else's problem. For a second the ship loomed large before him and filled the canopy, then it was gone. In perfect synchronization the F/A-18Es went into afterburner and tilted up, pushing the GE F414 turbo-fan engines into a sixty-degree climb before leveling off at 20,000 feet.

"Home Plate, this is Strike One. Flyby completed. Returning to roost."

"Roger Strike One. Well done." CAG's fruity chuckle a comforting sound to Grazier as he settled the two-flight element for home. If he trapped without problems, he might be in time to catch an afternoon snack of leftover sliders and bug juice. Before he could make himself comfortable the radio crackled again.

"Strike One, proceed to the alternate package and provide a visual."

Damn! That would add more than three hundred and twenty miles to the flight. Didn't the navy have any feelings? Well, as the old saw said: if you can't take a joke, you shouldn't have joined.

"Home Plate, this is Strike One, roger. Turning now." He

clicked another button. "You with me, Two?" There was a double click of acknowledgment in his headset.

The fighters reefed into a tight turn pulling four g's and accelerated on a new course to intercept the PLA-N force. At Mach 1.2 it took less than ten minutes to sight the big Chinese destroyer. The *Luhai* not bashful lighting off its Rice Shield 3-D air search radar. When the Hornets crossed fifteen miles, the insistent *deedle…deedle* threat receiver warned Grazier he had Croatale and HHQ-9 SAMs locked on him using powerful Thomson and Castor fire control radars. He was pretty sure the *Kiensan* wouldn't really fire on him, but no aviator enjoyed hearing the threat warning in his headset. The consequences were too terminal. At ten miles a singsong voice broke through the Guard frequency.

"American aircraft, you are approaching a People's Liberation Army warship. Break off immediately or you will be fired upon."

Grazier grinned, but it was without humor. *Eat shit!*

"Strike Two, at five miles drop to 1,000 and peel to port. I'll take starboard. Form up on me when we blow through."

"Hey, Chips! At the rate that there Chinese tub is burning gas, she's gonna be sucking vapors by the time she gets close to home again."

"Maybe we can convince her to turn back now and avoid all that pain, eh?"

Two clicks.

The Hornets dropped as one through breaking clouds and raced toward the destroyer growing large before them. White wash curled off its sharp clipper bow. Although much smaller than the *Kirov* battlecruiser, at three miles the Chinese warship appeared far more menacing. Grazier saw tracking missile launchers and a single mount 100mm main gun on the stylish ship as he flashed across her bow. The threat receiver kept chirping in his ears until both aircraft crossed fifteen miles and were climbing toward 20,000 feet again.

"Home Plate, this is Strike One. Alternate package sighted. Received cold reception, over."

"Acknowledged, One. Your downlink is in the can. Return to Plate."

Grazier set his vector for the *Constellation*. Well, if he couldn't have an afternoon snack, maybe he'll have an early dinner. As his stomach stopped churning, he decided he would give the sliders a miss.

* * *

EZEKIEL VISITED BY ALIENS, ISRAELI SCHOLAR CLAIMS!
MEXICO PREPARES TO MOVE SPACESHIP!
RUSSIAN AND CHINESE NAVIES SET TO CLASH WITH US PACIFIC
FLEET!
THE SPACESHIP CAN FLY, THE GENEVA TEAM CLAIMS!

"Jack Willison reporting from the CNN center in New York. Grilled at the White House today the Russian ambassador was at pains to point out the heavy cruiser steaming toward Mexico's west coast was there to support UN's efforts to secure what has popularly become known as the Ezekiel saucer. The UN Security Council denies requesting such support, given the presence of US carrier groups in the area. The ambassador refuted rumors that Russia planned to seize the craft for itself, claiming it an absurd idea.

"Meanwhile, Beijing reputedly sent angry letters to Washington protesting what it sees as harassment of its ship by American fighters in international waters. Such unprovoked action by the US could lead to a regrettable accident. The statement is widely interpreted as meaning the Chinese guided-missile destroyer was prepared to shoot down patrolling US fighters. Uncharacteristically blunt, Cliff Bligh, the White House

Press Secretary, announced that President Harford has authorized elements of the Pacific Fleet to sink the Chinese destroyer if it fires on any American ship or aircraft. It is still unclear why China sent the destroyer to Mexico, or what its objective might be. This unwarranted escalation in tension between the major powers is a dangerous development and overshadows what should have been a celebration of an extraordinary discovery."

\* \* \*

"The UN contingent protecting Comalcalco were forced yesterday to use teargas to break up unruly Leave Earth Alone Society protesters when they tried to force their way onto the archaeological site. Clashes broke out with elements of Friends of Aliens who welcomed the revelation that Earth has been visited by extraterrestrials in its formative past. Comments by Dr. Markinov from Israel's Ben-Gurion University, linking Semitic text with cursive found in Mexico, only served to fuel the controversy surrounding possible historical alien visits and their role in shaping our civilizations. The world's three major religions, Islam, Christianity, and Judaism, are still grappling with the impact of these latest revelations. Iran's Guardian Council called for a holy jihad to destroy this blasphemy found in Mexico, claiming the saucer is a fake planted by the imperialists designed to undermine Islamic teachings. So far, there has been no word from Rome. This is Mark Rown for NBC news."

# Chapter Six

The Karkan positively hissed with displeasure and his thin tongue flickered from his mouth. Looking ready to tear strips off somebody, his large black eyes were now small points as he regarded Terr like he was some smelly specimen. The green scales shimmered when he tilted his head.

"Your clearance codes have been authenticated, Mister. It appears I'm required to extend you my full cooperation."

Terr nodded gravely, careful not to show satisfaction at winning this clash of wills. His earlier conversation with the prickly SMB commander was less conciliatory. Not satisfied with Terr's orders, Sariman must have queried Anabb himself. Terr could well picture how that conversation went. He learned the hard way that Anabb liked it cut thin and served plain, and had little tolerance for attempted worm crap. As much as he disliked the fish face, Terr knew that to carry out his mission, he had to get him onside.

"Believe me, I regret this inconvenience, Master Scout, and I'll try not to get in your way."

"What exactly do you want?" Another hiss.

"I lack on-site information. If you could send down a probe and get me some real-time data, it would help me a lot. I'm still eighteen hours out from Sol and I've done all the planning I can with what I have. A peek at what they're doing down there would parameterize my options. By the time I land, I should be ready to move."

"Anything else?"

"Plasma demolition packages. If you can upload me the specs of what you have—"

"Anything else?"

"I want to borrow your GS-4 shuttle."

"You want to go down there?"

"Remotes are fine, but I need to make an on-site assessment for myself."

"I wouldn't advise it. If you're detected—"

"That's why I need a GS-4," Terr said and the Karkan glared. Terr had served a tour of duty at the SMB and they both knew what went on to relieve boredom. Earth was a big and very attractive world, and the Moon wasn't exactly replete with tourist spots. The shuttle was fully stealthy and totally invisible in the infrared, radar, ladar and visible spectrums that Earth's current technology could mount. A perfect vehicle for snooping around where one wasn't wanted, or taking a nap on a deserted beach.

"I still don't advise it."

"Has Earth compromised the GS-4's stealth capability?"

Sariman glared through the main display plate. "The shuttle is already assigned to Scholar Laraiana and her program. You'll need to ask her to release it to you."

Terr looked hard at the Karkan. "Master Scout, until further notice there are to be no unauthorized flights, excursions or landings on Earth. This will include flights by Scholar Laraiana and her team. The situation on Earth is volatile enough without us adding to the equation."

"But her program—"

"Will have to wait."

"Since she is aboard your ship, you can explain that to her."

"I will."

The internal struggle on Sariman's face obvious. He clearly wanted to add something more. In the end, he gave a jerky nod.

"Very well. The shuttle will be prepped and waiting for you, but I'll note in my log that your action is against my express recommendation and you're needlessly interfering with an important Captal scientific mission."

"Your privilege."

"In eighteen hours, then," Sariman said curtly and cut contact.

Terr glared at the main plate and bit his lip. "Asshole!"

Dhar shook an admonishing finger. "You're being disrespectful to a superior officer."

"The fool is more worried about sucking up to Laraiana than exercising command. Can't he see what a disaster the C-32 is for Earth?"

"Sankri, if our mission is so urgent, why didn't Anabb simply order Sariman to destroy the C-32 instead of dragging us all the way to Sol?"

"Obviously the mission isn't *that* urgent." Terr climbed out of the couch and stretched his arms. "And you've forgotten another and more plausible explanation."

"Anabb wants to see us in action?"

"You've got it. Wouldn't you want to see how your two brand-new agents handle themselves? If we screw up, the situation is still retrievable."

"The last SMB report indicated surface combatants moving toward Mexico and the Americans have positioned elements of their Pacific Fleet to intercept them. If someone starts shooting, the mission will take on a different and more unpleasant dimension."

"I dare say. Earth is a protectorate, Nightwings, not a basket case. We cannot hold their hand every time there's a crisis."

"Perhaps, but the C-32 makes it a problem of our making, and that's why the Bureau of Colonial and Protectorate Affairs should have removed it as quickly as possible."

"What does the *Saftara* say? In adversity the spirit grows?"

"One slight difficulty with that, my brother. Earth has never read the *Saftara*."

Terr chuckled and looked up. This far out in the spiral arm, the stars didn't crowd each other. Here the warmth of the core just a pearly glow. So many islands of light out there. Were galaxies merely stars in some super galaxy? A charming and romantic notion. Brown and yellow gravity waves snaked and coiled past the ship.

Laraiana…Her presence had definitely added another dimension to his mission, and an irritating one at that. Anabb must have known about her when he ordered her picked up from Salina and the disruption to her program Terr's presence would create. Was this another test to see how Terr handled Captal officials? Crafty old bastard.

He looked forward to getting rid of his tiresome passengers. What he'd seen of Captal's mission scientists had not impressed him. His attempts at striking a friendly conversation when one of them came up to the command deck were met with cold rebuffs. As for Scholar Laraiana, he was tempted to dump her out the lock—especially after coming close to being left behind on Salina.

Approaching the cool watery planet, with the bloated red primary casting a copper sheen over *Sheeva's* gray hull, he had no idea what waited for him below when Salina's SC&C, Surface Command and Control, took over nav and the M-1 slanted down through the green-tinged atmosphere. The ship plunged out of low cloud sand Cel Field lay spread like a toy erector set. Ships clustered about the terminal complexes, their pale nav bubbles glinting. Brown smog smeared the city, its tall slim towers glistening in pale afternoon light. *Sheeva* hovered above the landing ring, then settled on the ramp. An access tube slid from the terminal and connected with a dull clang.

As a courtesy, he went into the austere military terminal fully expecting to find Laraiana and her team waiting to board. After fuming for fifteen minutes with no one in sight, he managed to make a Wall connection with one of her flunkeys. Terr politely inquired when the Scholar would deign to make an appearance, only to be told he was to stand by. That did it. Who the hell did she think he was, a hired communal driver? With icy formality, Terr told the individual if they were not on board in forty minutes, they would be left behind, and cut contact.

At forty minutes exactly, about to detach the access tube, the lady and her entourage appeared. Surrounded by what to him looked like a mikan of baggage, Laraiana and her team boarded with sullen grace. Of medium height, her one-piece dark blue uniform outlined a nice figure. A native of Hakran, Sargon's capital world, she was hairless, but her pale blue eyes more than made up for that deficiency. They could have been chips of ice for all the warmth they held. She didn't have what Terr would consider an engaging personality. As far as he was concerned, she was a typical officially stuffed shirt: pompous, overbearing, and condescending. An hour out from Salina, she complained bitterly about her cramped quarters. Terr suggested sweetly if the Scholar were to discard some of her excess luggage, she would have more room. That infuriated her even more and caused her to stomp off the deck, which made him feel a whole lot better.

Eighteen hours, he told himself—if she didn't drive him to murder first.

He allowed himself a quick scan of the consoles, automatically taking in the status of the ship. Although the computer would warn them of any problem, it was an instinctive thing borne of years of intensive training and watchkeeping. In a spaceship every problem was serious. The cold emptiness beyond the hull always hungry. He pushed *Sheeva* hard for four days at close to maximum boost to cover one hundred and fifty light-years, risking overstressing the main drive. Anabb would not be amused if he did that. The last fourteen lights to Sol were done at an easy three-quarter boost.

Noting the occasional flicker from the touch-sensitive pads, he felt a wave of nostalgia for his old M-3 and wondered about Mati and the others. A new commander, a new mission, possibly a different ship, life went on. Then he remembered that Mati was dead. He also remembered the spilled blood on Tanard's auxiliary, the stink of burned flesh and Razzo almost dead. The images were vivid and would not leave him. Tanard wasn't worth any of them. Next time, Terr would not be so chivalrous.

"I'll relieve you in a couple of hours," he said moodily and walked to the cable-tube.

Dhar watched him go, powerless to say anything. Only time would heal the scars in Sankri's soul.

* * *

"Stop speak," the computer said and Lauren paused. "Turn pages."

Obligingly, she began to turn the pages from the secondary school English primer designed to give the computer a grounding in grammar and its idiosyncrasies. It obviously had a sensor that enabled it to read text, but she couldn't see anything that looked like a camera. That didn't bother her much; she was just grateful for the interlude. It took her over four mind-numbing hours to read aloud a basic pocket Webster's, the computer refusing to listen to anyone else. Bill reasoned it probably had something to do with her opening the hatch and the computer became sensitized to her. She found it a pain, but resisted doing the sensible thing—authorizing the computer to accept someone else's voice. For now, she preferred to retain the illusion of control.

Six minutes later, she slammed the book shut and leaned back into the yielding couch. The thing squirmed to accommodate her. *I really must get myself one of these*, she mused with a contented sigh and rubbed her tired eyes.

"I'm glad that part's over!" she breathed with a sigh.

"I guess we just have to wait now," Bill said beside her and she flashed him a warm smile.

"Thanks for being with me. I appreciate it."

"No problem. I read a bedtime story to my computer every night," he said with a straight face and she laughed.

"Evil man! Do you know what I miss sometimes?" she said dreamily, her eyes closed. "Just working on a dig, lost in the moment, letting my imagination carry me into the past."

"I know what you mean. I think I had the most fun when I was doing my master's at SLAC—Stanford's Linear Accelerator Center. It's an outdated device by today's standards, but I couldn't have been happier. It was pure research, genuine atom smashing. I didn't have to think about grants, faculty politics, or worry I wouldn't get published."

"Or having to run classes!" she gushed. "I did part of my PhD research at Belize. Boulcher still a human type then, but his interest in me already becoming more than just professional. The time I spent at Altun Ha was pure magic. The site is huge and it's mostly jungle with ruins poking up everywhere. I had my dig in a little corner of it. You would get an occasional tourist group wandering through. Most of the time, I was alone in my Mayan kingdom. A shy, gangly undergrad did most of the digging, but he didn't seem to mind. The place was terrible; hot and steamy and sweaty, but that didn't seem to matter to me and I was happy. History spoke very loudly there. Surrounded by temples, I could easily imagine myself living in those times."

Bill nodded thoughtfully, enjoying listening to her speak. He loved the sound of her voice: soft and silky, strong and captivating. She was probably a very good lecturer. Lingering over her every feature, he traced the outline of her face with his eyes. Her skin looked so smooth and perfect. The way her nose curved up, the gentle rise of her cheekbones, the curve of her ear…He blinked and cleared his throat.

"You didn't finish your graduate work at Belize?"

"That was merely follow-up work I started at Caral."

"Caral?"

Her eyes grew large. "You haven't heard of Caral? O my gosh! That's terrible!"

"I've led a sheltered life, I'm afraid," he murmured and a smile tugged at the corner of his mouth.

"Evil man! Anyway, Caral is a site in Peru and is about the oldest city there is, inhabited since at least 3,900 BC. They lived without war for a thousand years, as far as we can tell. Can you believe it? It must have been enchanting." Suddenly self-conscious, Lauren pulled back a lock of hair.

"We all yearn for a moment in some past time we thought idyllic," he said gently, unable to tear his eyes off her face. *God, what a breathtaking woman!* "Why is it that after we struggle and claw to get where we are, all we want to do is go back to the simple and the uncomplicated?"

"Escape!" she said promptly with a lift of her chin.

"Of course, but—"

"I think it's the responsibility and the desire to let it all go, not having to care. I sometimes bury myself in work just to get away from reality. Believe me, reality can be dreary. There are bills to pay, a mortgage, not to mention a never-ending war with the university bureaucracy. Goodness! I make it sound so horrible." She gave a nervous laugh, aware of a flush rising to her cheeks. This was ridiculous, blushing like a freshman. Bill smiled at her, his green eyes gentle and mysterious.

"I also think people like us are cursed," he ventured, afraid to open himself, afraid of getting hurt again. "We've seen what lies beyond the next hill and the knowledge will not give us peace."

She looked thoughtful. "I saw an old war movie once. A German submarine captain said we shouldn't think, that we pay a penalty for thinking. We cannot find rest."

"He might be right."

"Why do we have to do this to each other, Bill? Warfare, I mean," she asked soberly.

"The Russian and Chinese ships? I heard," he said and chewed his lower lip. "Idiots! What do they hope to gain?"

"Prestige, Dr. Faroway. Prestige!" Zaminski boomed behind them, shattering the intimacy of the moment. Lauren swiveled her seat to see the burly Russian climb up the steps.

Reaching the deck, he patted his generous stomach and perched himself on the edge of the console.

"Prestige?" she asked.

"There is something you must know if you're to understand us, my dear Lauren. Under communism, we may have been misguided, but we had pride of sorts. We were respected and even feared. Now, we're just poor; another third-world country. Sending a ship here tells the world that Russia still wields power. You Americans don't know humiliation, being a world power ever since you defeated the British to gain your independence."

"We had Vietnam," Bill said mildly.

"Bah! That is nothing. A political setback. I am talking about national shame and frustration. We have so much and have squandered most of it."

"A lone cruiser, my friend. Not much of a display."

"It doesn't take much, Dr. Faroway," Zaminski said darkly.

"Take much to do what?" Bill insisted. "Its presence here is other than peaceful?"

"Please! I don't want to talk about it," Zaminski growled, then glanced at the flickering screens and brightened. "So, Lauren. What can your problem child tell us about this astonishing ship?"

"No speeke English," she said and Zaminski laughed heartily. He was easy to like, jovial and always in good humor. Still, the lines around his eyes and mouth did not come from laughter. And he seemed burdened by some dark secret.

"Very good. American humor, it always, how do you say it, cracks me up. I must study your quaint idioms. Who knows? They just might give me another Nobel Prize for it!" he boomed and gave a fruity chuckle. "Seriously, even if we do get it to talk, how much can it tell us?"

"What do you mean?" Bill asked. He wanted to talk about the Russian cruiser and suspected that Zaminski knew more than he was telling. Clearly, the Russian would not or could not discuss it.

"Consider. The computer will lack a meaningful technical vocabulary it needs to give us useful engineering information. Even if it had the words, does it know anything? After all, it only needs to pilot this ship. It isn't a library."

"I partially agree with you, but we'll find out a hell of a lot more with a talking computer than by simply poking at things."

"Let's argue it over coffee," Lauren said brightly and jumped up. The two men stared after her as she hurried out.

"A very sensible idea," Bill said and extended his arm at the doorway. "Doctor…"

Zaminski gave a small bow and walked toward the steps.

Holding a steaming mug between her hands, Lauren watched Bill emerge around the curve of the ship. He turned to Zaminski and she captured a frozen moment of his profile. She realized he had a strong nose, not large, but…manly, the word popped into her head. His features were firm without being angular, mature.

Imatlan peered at her, then looked at Faroway and his mouth tightened. She rejected him for *that*? He could not understand what she could possibly see in that dried-up short runt when she had him! What could Faroway know about love and things that set a woman's mind and body on fire? Americans didn't make love. They merely copulated.

Babich nodded to Zaminski and resumed his chattering with Chee and Kopan. Zaminski poured himself a cup, added sugar, and glanced at the chamber entrance.

"It's getting dark outside. No wonder I feel hungry. At least the UN feeds us well," he said and chuckled hugely at some private joke.

"Anything from the computer?" Hiro asked Lauren and she shook her head.

"Her pet is sulking," Zaminski declared amiably.

"I'll tell it you said that!" She laughed. "And what have you guys found?"

"Not much," Hiro admitted. "We lack the facilities to do proper analysis, but we have confirmed Dr. Faroway's assertion that the hull is a room-temperature superconductor."

"So?"

Hiro smiled and looked twenty years old. "Dr. Hopking, if we could harness that knowledge and reproduce the process—"

"Earth would have a channel to an inexhaustible power supply," Babich said, prodding Hiro with the stem of his pipe.

"If they don't classify it first," Lauren said darkly.

"Ah, the military. Always there to spoil things for us scientists," Babich said with an indulgent smile.

Lauren shot him a sharp look, not sure whether the European scientist was serious or having a personal little joke.

"Why would you want to classify something that has the potential to finally bring prosperity to the world?"

"Because, my dear naïve Doctor," Zaminski said indulgently, "prosperity would interfere with those who hunger for power, not peace."

"You have a morbid attitude, did you know that?" Lauren told him darkly and walked back to the ship.

Zaminski smiled after her and shook his head.

Inside, she paused and looked about. After six days the ship had grown familiar. She still found it hard to believe it was all real. She sat down and sipped her coffee, reflecting on what Zaminski had said. Could he be right and she was being naïve? She kept up with world events, but it came as an afterthought, a distraction while eating breakfast. Buried in her work, her perspective may have narrowed. She preferred to think of it as focused.

Much as she enjoyed the lively discussions with the others, a reality of a different kind started to crowd her. Once they moved the ship, what then? Resume poking around the mounds? She found what she wanted. Perhaps not in the way she imagined, but more than good enough. Nothing remained at Comalcalco left for her now. It was time to face up to her responsibilities back at Columbia U. The first thing she would need to do is renegotiate her position there. If they wanted her to stay, they would have to give her permanent tenure and a full professorship. Working under Boulcher no longer a possibility. If they refused? Well, there were other places that would be more than eager to take her on, and she suspected that Columbia would know it. She took another look around, wishing she were a physicist. Now, why did she think that?

"Dr. Hopking?" the computer inquired politely, the qualitative difference in its voice instantly recognizable. She sat up and placed the mug on the console.

"Yes?"

"Language assimilation completed. State your command."

"Wait!" She leaped off the couch and scrambled down the steps. "Bill! It's talking!" she shouted and ran to the others.

Babich looked up from his PC and raised an eyebrow. Zaminski broke off his conversation with Kopan and hurried toward her. She grabbed Bill's arm and tugged.

"It's talking in English!"

"Then let's hear what it has to say," he remarked calmly. For some reason, that infuriated her and she stomped away, her mouth a tight line. Bill looked helplessly after her, then turned to Babich. "What did I say?"

Zaminski smiled indulgently. "You Americans. She wanted you to share in her excitement and you reacted like you received a telephone bill."

"Oh, but I *am* excited!"

"Then you should have told her so."

Bill stared at Zaminski's amused expression and exhaled loudly. "I don't get it."

Babich pulled the pipe out of his mouth and patted him on the back.

"Three doctorates and still dumb," he remarked sadly and shook his head.

"The woman loves you!" Zaminski boomed and the others chuckled. Imatlan paused, the cup halfway to his mouth. "She just doesn't know it yet."

Bill gaped. Sure, he felt comfortable near Lauren, and she had a keen and incisive mind. Simply professional respect. Wasn't it? The fact her presence made his skin tingle and her perfume melted his insides, were normal physiological responses. After all, she was a very beautiful woman, but romantic attraction? No, it wasn't possible.

"You're nuts," he declared and walked toward the hatch.

"I lay you odds," Zaminski offered and Babich laughed.

"Do I look like a sucker? Get inside, will you."

They crowded into the ship and Lauren was all smiles again. She was in control here, if only for a while longer.

"Ask it if the ship is flight operational," Kopan demanded.

"Computer, is the ship flight capable?" she said.

"Cannot achieve flight mode. Secondary fuel cells drained and there is corrosion in the fuel inlets to the fusion chamber. If repaired and reaction mass provided, fusion ignition could be achieved. Primary drive activation is possible, but cannot be controlled due to degradation of number four, eleven, and seventeen asymmetric field modulation nodes. Self-diagnostic checks indicate several deteriorated power junctions and circuit board faults. Repair not possible with available spares."

"Ask it if it's weapons capable," Dr. Chee said and Lauren shot him a hard look.

"Computer?"

"Negative. Navigation deflector grid only."

"Ask it where it's from."

"Question has no valid term of reference."

"Display star system of last port using present location as reference," Bill said.

"Dr. Hopking, do you authorize command?"

"Yes."

The large central display screen cleared to reveal a dense

cluster of stars in a three-dimensional image. A black emptiness obscured the bottom left part of the display. In the upper right corner a ragged red and orange nebula lit the backdrop between the stars.

"Wow," Kopan whispered in awe.

"This could be anywhere," Babich muttered.

"No! Look! That looks like the Southern Cross!" Sheppard exclaimed with repressed excitement.

"That patch must be the Coal Sack," Zaminski breathed.

"We're a long way off, then," Kopan murmured. "You're looking at ninety light-years at least."

Hiro shook his head and winced. "Physicists! This isn't getting us anywhere. What we need is a directory of information the computer carries."

Babich stared at him, then pointed his pipe at Bill. "He's right, you know."

Bill looked at Lauren.

"Computer, state categories—"

"Astro navigational data—"

"It understands what we were talking about," Babich hissed to Bill.

"Of course, you fool. Shut up."

"—power management, automatic flight control, diagnostic and autonomous repair systems, communication protocols, life support and emergency procedures."

Babich raised an eyebrow at Bill.

"What did you expect?" Bill said. "A Library of Congress?"

"But—"

"It's a flight control system," Hiro said. "Sophisticated, but still just a computerized pilot."

Bill sat beside Lauren and looked into her eyes. "Lauren, I need you to do something and I think you know what that is."

"You want access to the computer."

"It doesn't mean you'll be sidelined—"

"There is no need to explain. I understand," she said wood-enly and stared at the central display screen. Inevitable really, and she'd enjoyed her fleeting moment of power. "Computer, you are authorized to grant unrestricted access and carry out any instruction issued to you by the individuals in the ship, understood?"

"Command acknowledged."

Bill touched her shoulder and nodded once. "Thank you."

A larger square pad glowed amber on the right console. "Individuals are requested to place their palms on the sensitized area."

After a few moments of shuffling around, everyone settled back. Lauren looked at Kopan and Kareza.

"Is the Mexican government planning to move the ship?"

Imatlan glanced at Kopan, deferring to him.

"You must understand the need for that, Dr. Hopking," Kopan said gently.

She did. "All the way to Mexico City?"

"No. Villahermosa. The government doesn't believe the ship would survive the, ah, obstacles a trip to Mexico City would undoubtedly present. The move will be difficult enough as it is."

Lauren nodded, then stood up and walked out. Bill hurried after her. Imatlan made to follow, but Kopan held him back with a shake of his head.

"Lauren! Wait!" Bill caught up with her at the chamber entrance. She went rigid when he touched her. "Where are you going?"

"Back to Columbia U," she replied coldly without looking at him. "Let go of me. I'm a useless artifact here, just like that pile of stones out there."

"What are you talking about? The project needs you!"

She faced him. "Needs me? For what? To make your coffee? Let's be realistic. I've had my fun and we can stop pretending." She gave a bitter chuckle full of pain and loss and Bill went pale.

"Lauren, if it's the computer—"

"Oh, for heaven's sake! Don't talk like a fool. It had to happen and has nothing to do with the computer."

He waited until she crossed the threshold. "You're going to leave it all to Imatlan then?"

That stopped her. She spun around and glared at him. "Leave what?"

"You're the archaeologist. You tell me."

She pushed back a lock of hair. It caught the overhead light and turned it into filmy gauze of gold.

"There is nothing left for me here—"

"Nothing?"

Her eyes flashed fire. "Maybe I should start studying astrophysics, is that it?"

Bill smiled at her frustration. She really was very striking when angry.

"You're getting close."

"I hate you," she snapped and whirled. She only took one step before it hit her and she froze in her tracks. "O my gosh! The aliens."

"A whole new field of anthropology," he said softly and felt a warm glow of satisfaction at seeing her spirits lift. When she turned, her brown eyes were big and round and there was a new sparkle in them. A breeze stirred her auburn hair and he had an urge to run his fingers through it. "The computer will need careful questioning, and you'll know what questions to ask it. I'm surprised the UN hadn't thought of it itself. Who knows what we might learn about our ancient visitors and what they were doing here."

"Speculation."

"So?"

"Didn't you hear what Zaminski said? It's simply a flight control system."

"You're still angry and you refuse to see the obvious."

"See what?"

Bill smiled and looked at the fingernails of his right hand. "Well…"

Lauren pursed her mouth and glared at him. "If you don't—"

"The star chart," he said slowly and let her think about it.

"What about the star chart…" She trailed off when the meaning of Bill's question became clear. The ship's computer must have complete knowledge of every planet, moon, asteroid or space station the aliens had in order to navigate, or was it astrogate? It'll have names and possibly even knowledge of political groupings, however rudimentary, a staggering wealth of information.

"I should have seen it," she whispered and her expression softened. "Thank you." She walked up to him and her lips brushed his cheek. "You really are a very clever man."

Her touch electrified him and he could feel his face grow hot. She wore a light perfume that was lavender and citrus and sent his head spinning. Her closeness terrified him, yet he longed to reach out and hold her. Was he falling for her? He needed to clear his throat before the words would come out.

"I didn't want you running out on me," he said lamely, aware of how stupid that sounded.

Her mouth lifted in an impish smile and her eyes grew misty. "You didn't?"

"No."

"Why not?" she husked, then leaned against him and traced one finger along the stubble of his chin.

"You're teasing me."

"No, it's just a simple question," she purred, her breath hot on his face, smelling sweet and intoxicating.

He lifted her chin and brought his lips down on hers, marveling at how soft and yielding they were.

"Because you're starting to mean something to me," he murmured breathlessly, realizing it was true.

She closed her eyes and smiled contentedly. Slowly, she rested her head on his shoulder and felt him tremble. His fingers sank into her hair and brushed the strands down her back. She moved closer against him and breathed deeply of his scent. His arms suddenly held her tight.

"You're a pretty special person yourself, you know," she mumbled into his chest, taking in his man smell, feeling the faint rumble of his heart. It felt right doing this, being in his arms. It was also madness, but reason didn't matter. It was enough just to live the moment, to abandon herself to the raging and delicious feelings that ran through her.

The moment passed and she pulled away.

"Bill, where is this going?"

"I don't know, but I look forward to exploring the possibilities." Suddenly aware of the ambiguity of his words, he blushed. "I didn't mean—"

She smiled and touched his mouth with her fingers. "I know, but this could be complicated." She pulled back. "Good night, Bill, and thank you again." She turned abruptly and walked into the night.

Still not sure what just happened, he wiped his brow and exhaled loudly.

"Whew!"

Walking back toward the ship's hatch, he pondered Lauren's question. Getting involved with her would create a major disruption to his lifestyle just when things were settling down and his life was again becoming secure and predictable. After six years, Dheera's ghost still haunted him. He loved her without reservation, opening himself completely to her. He was ready to die for her! He'd been young and naïve and inexperienced, and believed she also returned his love with the same unreserved passion. His colleagues tried to warn him, but he took it as jealousy because she was so beautiful. His world crumbled when he saw her on the campus grounds one day in someone else's embrace. It made him feel like a fool to realize

Dheera saw him simply as just another conquest. The row that night left him deeply scarred. He wasn't sure he wanted to risk having the old wounds opened again. Instinctively, he knew Lauren wouldn't do that to him. To take that next step, he would have to trust again and he knew Lauren was a woman who would not be satisfied with half-measures. Would he?

He almost bumped into Imatlan coming down the ship's steps.

"Have you seen Lauren?"

"I think she went to her hut," Bill said absently, not seeing him.

"Thank you," Imatlan said stiffly and hurried past him, trying hard to control a stab of raw jealousy against the American. He could not help what he felt for Lauren. Well, what he had to say would peg her down a bit. He may not have her, but this would be enough, and perhaps even sweeter. He walked quickly to her hut and knocked.

"Come in!" her muffled voice came from inside and he opened the door. She looked up from her laptop in surprise.

"Kareza, what brings you here?"

"I sensed your discomfort when you heard the ship is being moved," he said quickly, glancing around the sparse quarters.

"Oh, that. It had to happen."

He frowned, expecting to find her dejected. It would have made his triumph all the more satisfying, but her cheerfulness disturbed him. What was going on?

"I didn't want to tell you this in front of the others. My government appointed me research director of the Villahermosa facility that's been prepared to hold the ship. It will be part of the La Venta Park Museum and affiliated with the Juarez University and all the other major learning and industrial centers throughout Mexico. You can come and work for me if you want," he added offhandedly, clearly pleased with his new position.

Lauren sensed Kareza's jealousy of Bill, and also what he

saw as a final triumph over her for resisting him. Latin pride. Kareza could never understand that a woman needed more than a passing infatuation. Here she was, about to offer him a collaborative partnership in a joint paper on the alien civilization. Well, if this triumph meant so much to him, she was quite happy to publish it alone.

She smiled sweetly and offered her small hand. "Congratulations, Kareza. I mean it. It's an important post and I'm certain that Mexico will benefit greatly from your efforts."

This was not going as he'd planned. He wanted the woman shattered and disillusioned. He didn't want her congratulations. He wanted her tears! Slowly, he took her hand.

"Ah, thank you. This time, Mexico will not be robbed," he declared harshly, desperate to regain control.

"You'll not be spending much time here, then?"

"There is a lot of preparatory work to be done—"

"So this is goodbye?"

"Yes. I meant what I said about the job."

"I know. Good luck, Kareza."

The door closed after him with a soft click. Lauren shook her head and smiled. Poor Kareza. Men can be such fools. Her thoughts turned to another man, definitely not a fool, and her pulse quickened.

* * *

Captain Amanyev switched off the computer, the click of the switch unnaturally loud despite the hiss of air-conditioning and the tremble of machinery beneath the deck. The flat LCD monitor turned dark gray and so did his mood. He stared at the drawn reflection in the screen with detachment. At forty-seven, he did not consider himself old. A touch of frost around the temples, otherwise his thick crop of dark brown hair still had a sheen if he looked hard enough. It was the eyes, he decided, no longer innocent, that betrayed him. They had lived through too much and seen too much.

Wearily, he pushed himself up from the upholstered chair and turned to the porthole. He clasped his hands behind his back and automatically adopted the at-ease position. A soft moist breeze, generated by the easy movement of the cruiser, stirred his hair. He marveled at the deep blue of the glassy sea and the even darker blue of the sky, so different from the gun-metal skies and black waters of the north. This was truly a diverse world from the ice and snow of home. At an easy nine knots the ship barely swayed as it cleaved its way south on the second leg of a triangular holding pattern. Somewhere to port was the Mexican coastline. For most of the crew, this was high adventure and a taste of far travel the navy promised them, but rarely delivered.

Abruptly, he turned to his desk and picked up a black phone.

"Bridge," the officer of the watch replied instantly.

"Captain. Send Commander Grishnakov to my day cabin."

"Aye aye, sir."

He sat down and leaned back to the creak of old leather. Old like his ship, but comfortable. For a moment, he was tempted to put his feet on the desk. That, of course, would not have been consistent with discipline, he mused wryly. Not that Grishnakov would have minded, but Amanyev could not allow himself to be seen as anything other than a stern captain, even before his friend.

There was a sharp knock on the door and the tall, wiry exec walked in.

"You wanted to see me, Captain?"

"Sit down," Amanyev said and pointed at the visitor chairs.

Grishnakov settled himself and waited expectantly.

"Repairs completed?"

"Radiation within the reactor compartments is within limits, but the reactors must not be run over seventy percent. We'll need a dockyard overhaul of the coolant system before I would dare push them harder. Everything else is manageable."

Amanyev nodded with satisfaction. He drove the ship hard, but it hadn't let him down.

"Emergency drills?"

"Improving. Some of the boat davits have seized up—"

"Painted for inspection rather than use," Amanyev growled.

"Yes, sir, but they are in working order now," Grishnakov said woodenly. Strictly speaking, this was a foul-up and his responsibility as executive officer. The captain didn't have to elaborate. Grishnakov already burned with silent shame at having failed in his duty. Of course, the lieutenant in charge of ship's lifeboats was burning with more than silent shame. The bosun in turn would bear the injustice of it all. Such was the order of things.

"Very good. I have read our orders," Amanyev said with a finality that made Grishnakov sit up. "What I am to tell you does not leave this cabin. Understood?"

"Of course, but—"

"No buts, Vanya. Do I have your word?"

"Certainly. It's Comalcalco, isn't it?"

"We are to ready two Granit missiles for firing."

No need to elaborate on the simple statement, or the need for absolute secrecy. If word got out among the crew, some fool might try to contact his family, or worse, the papers. Grishnakov's heavy black eyes were hard when he looked up, Cossack eyes.

"Nuclear?"

"No, thank the mother. If our negotiations with the Americans are not successful, we are to launch once the saucer chamber roof is removed to ensure maximum destruction."

"Why are we doing this?"

"I am a simple seaman, my friend, and I no longer ask such questions."

"The international backlash—"

"We do our duty, Commander," Amanyev said harshly, preferring not to think too much about that. Duty these days meant so many things. Honor and integrity just got in the way. If he was to be sacrificed for the good of the *rodina*, he hoped it wouldn't be a wasted gesture. Too many lives have been wasted already in the name of the masses.

"Captain, the Granit is a good weapon, but even with GLONASS guidance, we cannot guarantee the required level of strike accuracy."

"I know. GLONASS might not be as good as the American GPS, but we allowed for that. Our source on location will supply terminal homing."

"We have a source? Academician Zaminski is our source?"

"Select two missiles for firing and have two more standing by as backup. Use different canisters. I also want you to run two missile firing exercises twice a day and have all firing circuits checked."

"Aye, sir. Captain, if we fire, the Americans will sink us."

"I know."

The Los Angeles 688 hunter-killer submarine shadowing them made no effort to hide its presence, and Amanyev labored under no illusion as to its reason for being there. Two ADCAP Mk 48s would be more than enough to sink his beloved *Pyotr Velikiy*. The ship could probably survive a direct strike against its twenty-centimeter armored hull, but the modern tactic of exploding a torpedo under the keel to create an air bubble into which a ship fell would break the cruiser's back. *Pyotr's* hull would never stand the strain.

"If we have to fire, we'll SCRAM the reactors," he said quietly. A reasonable precaution, one that could avert a major environmental disaster.

"And the crew?" Grishnakov asked.

"They will take to the lifeboats."

"Captain, this is madness."

"My friend, we serve the *rodina*, even when it's mad."

"And the *Kiensan?*"

"What do you think?"

"Probably here for the same reason we are," Grishnakov said and shook his head. "Madness."

# Chapter Seven

Supporting his chin in the palm of his hand, Terr absently tapped his teeth with one hooked finger. The small ship noises hardly intruded into his thoughts. Beside him, Dhar was going through the last of the landing checklist. The darkened command deck a soothing shroud, a momentary escape from the harshness of reality he really didn't want to face right now. Comforting to simply drift, letting his thoughts wander in free association of jumbled and disjointed images. In the end, his mind betrayed him, forcing him to confront the issue he was avoiding. He stretched his arms and pulled them back until the joints creaked. Fixed in the center of the nav bubble above him, he fancied Sol had grown perceptibly, but was probably only his imagination. They were still far out and yet to reach the Oort cloud.

The damned mission haunted him. Data from Sariman's probe only added to his misgivings. The archaeological site was a tactical nightmare, surrounded by thick jungle and accessible only by a single narrow road. A traditional ground assault was out of the question. He did not warm to the idea of hacking his way through dense undergrowth, then breaking through a perimeter fence and the patrolling security force inside who were probably itching to shoot someone. Even if he managed to avoid getting shot, it was highly likely he would be captured, compromising not only the mission, but the Serrll as well, and his orders were not to be noticed. With the site surrounded by sightseers and patrolling military, getting noticed would be almost a certainty. That left the direct approach: drop down in the shuttle, walk into the chamber, place the charges and walk out. Clean, simple and quick. It could work, provided no one looked his way while he was doing it. There were bound to be guards, and that was the rub.

He winced and scratched his scar. Dhar glanced at him.

"Thinking how to penetrate the site?"

Terr chuckled. "You're reading my mind. I'm also thinking that blowing up a ship is an odd occupation for an intelligence sleuth."

"Not exactly what we signed up for, is it?"

"I don't know. This has to be better than boring patrol duty."

"So how do we penetrate the site?"

"How would *you* do it?"

"The same way you would. The site is heavily defended and patrolled. Not good for a land approach. I would keep it simple. Drop the shuttle right beside the wall. In full stealth mode no one will see a thing as we walk in."

"And the two guards posted outside?"

Dhar shot him a look of disgust. "Picky! Before we land, we'll stun anyone who is close enough to be a problem."

"With a needler? Bound to cause speculation."

"How about we just club them?"

Terr chuckled. "I'm being picky, but I don't see any other way of getting in either."

"What if someone is inside?"

"We'll go in late, say two o'clock in the morning. I will wear a full-body suit and headgear. Anyone seeing me will take me for a commando. I figure it shouldn't take more than ten seconds to place the charges. Three seconds after we lift, we set them off and that C-32 will be a very small pile of gray ash."

"You said 'I'," Dhar remarked darkly.

"Privilege of rank," he said with a smile, and Dhar snorted.

"Approaching SMB Surface Command and Control insertion point," the computer announced suddenly. "Initial interrogative verified. All systems nominal for orbital approach."

"State SC&C insertion time," Dhar demanded quietly, only

mildly annoyed that Sankri wanted to take out the C-32 himself. He also knew there was no way Sankri would allow anyone else to take the risk on his behalf.

"SC&C insertion in six minutes. Landing configuration procedure nominal. Ship within acceptable flight parameters."

In the nav bubble display, the Earth-Moon system slightly up along their incoming trajectory. The M-1 still too far for them to see the double world. His thoughts drifting, Terr waited.

"SC&C enabled. Ready to copy."

"Approved."

Terr leaned over the armrest and tapped a comms pad. "Scholar Laraiana? We will be landing shortly. Please get your team ready to disembark."

There wasn't any acknowledgment. Terr frowned and sighed.

His exalted passenger had been in a huff ever since he told her he was commandeering the GS-4 shuttle for the duration of his mission. She quoted him her orders and clearances, which left him unmoved. When she demanded to be allowed at least two flights to Earth before he commenced his operations, he told her she can make as many flights as she wanted, once his mission was done. She turned purple and stomped off, threatening dire consequences from the Bureau of Colonial and Protectorate Affairs.

Right now, he had more serious problems on his hands than Scholar Laraiana's awful temper and soaring blood pressure.

The tactical plot cleared and the stars shifted as SC&C took command of *Sheeva*. At four million talans from the Moon, the ship's distortion field torus depolarized and the ship dropped normal. At maximum secondary boost it took them eight minutes to reach the Moon, the double world system lit in a last quarter phase. SC&C brought the ship over the north pole and down into a valley permanently shielded by towering craggy peaks. The skids extended and the M-1 hovered briefly above the landing pad before settling with a gentle bump. A clang from below as the access tube connected.

Terr pried himself out of the comfortable command couch and swept his eyes over the bleak landscape outside. It *had* been a while. He was a newly promoted Third Scout, first grade, fresh off an M-4, full of drive and unshakeable confidence. They hinted at an executive posting to an M-3 and he felt himself ready for it. When his orders called for him to report to the SMB, he was outraged. Did BuePer regard him as a loser? CAPFLTCOM knew what it was doing and they knew him. Terr had authority. That came with his rank. What he needed to learn was how to exercise command, and as he came to appreciate, the two were not the same thing. Ordering someone and getting them to carry out that order took leadership. In a ship underway, he thought he knew how that worked. Confined within a dreary stationery base, it took motivation to get things done. He learned command and leadership, all right.

"Memories?" Dhar asked.

"Ghosts."

"Look." Dhar jerked his head at the nav bubble. Parked beside them with an access tube attached was the GS-4 shuttle. Although less than half the size of an M-1, it had the same flowing, clean pebble-flat lines.

Terr nodded in appreciation. "So, Sariman kept his word."

The cable-tube hissed open and Laraiana strode through. She glanced out and pinned Terr with frosty eyes.

"Why wasn't I informed that we were about to land?"

"Scholar, you received my comms."

"I expected to be informed personally."

Terr's face hardened. "Scholar, this is a small ship and I have no crew to wait on you."

"You could have assigned Mr. Dharaklin to deliver the message."

"Indeed?"

"Your marked lack of respect has not gone unnoticed, First Scout. Rest assured that your name will figure prominently in my report to the Bureau of Colonial and Protectorate Affairs."

"While you're at it, say hello to my uncle for me," Terr snapped, tired of her posturing. Her eyes widened slightly.

"Commissioner Enllss-rr is your uncle?"

"I can put in a good word for you if you want," he said and watched her turn white with fury. She pursed her lips and stomped out. Terr laughed after her, feeling better.

They took the cable-tube down to the main deck and Dhar cycled the hatch. It hissed as it slid into the bulkhead. Terr didn't loiter and strode down the access tube. At the other end, he tapped a brown sensor pad. It pulsed and the hatch groaned, opening to the SMB's main landing level. He was immediately assaulted by a mixture of scents, some sweetish, others acid and rancid. He sniffed once and made a face. In a closed environment, it was inevitable that certain odors would become prevalent and totally oblivious to the station's personnel.

A very young Deklan officer, his twin hair bands still to form, stood to with a snap, his thumbs pointing down the outer seams of his working grays.

"Third Scout Tembel. May I welcome you to the Serrll Moon Base, sir!"

Terr looked down at him and grinned. "A pleasure, Mr. Tembel."

"Ach! Master Scout Sariman regrets he wasn't able to meet you personally."

"The pressures of command, I'm sure," Terr said smoothly, the subtlety lost on the wide-eyed Deklan.

"I am to escort you and Mr. Dharaklin to his office. If you will follow me, please."

Terr nodded and waved him on. The youngster spun on his heels and marched smartly toward the nearest cable-tube hatch. Terr and Dhar exchanged glances and Dhar shrugged. The boy stopped, pressed a pad located chest-high and the hatch slid open. They walked in and the tube surged up. After a moment the hatch hissed open and the young Deklan marched out, stiff and parade rigid. He stopped before the base commander's door. The door panel retracted and he strode into the spacious office and stood to.

"Diplomatic Branch Mission, sir!" Tembel piped and fled.

Terr grinned after him and walked in. Sariman's impressive matte black desk positioned before a five-katalan-wide floor-to-ceiling window screen that showed the stark perpetual blackness outside. Only the bright profusion of stars relieved the drab Moonscape. The wall on his left held open shelves and paneled cabinets. Vases, holoview cubes and assorted memorabilia cluttered the shelves. Beside him the Wall display station cycled through pooling colors. Several lush potted plants added much-needed color to an otherwise stark interior. The temperature a touch warm for his comfort and the humidity a tad high, but not oppressively so. Apparently, in his office at least, Sariman allowed himself a personal luxury or two.

He nodded to the Karkan. "Agent Terrllss-rr and my associate, Agent Dharaklin."

Sariman tall for a Karkan and his black eyes gave nothing away. He spent a moment sizing Terr up before moving toward a small table surrounded by loose formchairs.

"Make yourselves comfortable," he hissed and sat down. "I was expecting Scholar Laraiana to be with you."

"She didn't want to keep me from my duty, sir," Terr said and Sariman's tongue flickered.

"Yes. A demanding female that. It will be an unpleasant two months having her underfoot," Sariman hissed, obviously not very happy at the prospect. Terr almost felt sorry for him. "Your mission," Sariman went on more briskly. "How much time will you need to execute it?"

"I'll have a better idea once I make my site survey, but I would say not more than two days."

Sariman pursed his lips. "Two days…"

"Is that an issue?"

"No, it is not."

"I gather my mission has somehow upset Scholar La-raiana?"

"The woman wanted me to countermand your order about no overflights for the duration of your operation. She was very forthright in expressing her displeasure when I told her I had no authority to do that. I have no doubt the Diplomatic Branch will be hearing more about this."

"If I may, sir, what is she doing here?"

Sariman looked uncomfortable. "It's compartmented, but you should be able to guess."

Terr stared at the Karkan. There were many reasons why a scientific team would want to poke around Earth, and only one really made sense to him.

"She is a geneticist?"

"Very good, Agent Terr," Sariman said, his smile brittle, "and the less you think about that the better. Now, I know you're bent on doing a visual of the site and I must again advise against it. The on-site probe should have given you enough information."

"It's been invaluable, but there is one thing the probe wasn't able to give me."

"And that is?"

"Situational awareness."

Sariman hissed and sat back. "On your head be it then," he said and stood up. "The shuttle is prepped and ready for you, just as you requested, unless you want to rest first."

"I've rested enough on the way and this will be a short hop," Terr said, gathered Dhar with his eyes and stood up. Sariman tapped his thigh with long fingers.

"In that case, I won't detain you any longer."

In the corridor, Dhar cleared his throat. "Compared to Scholar Laraiana, Sariman was almost pleasant."

"It's probably a temporary aberration only," Terr said and

Dhar grinned.

"Could he be right, about us going down?"

"There is always room for doubt, my brother, but I won't commit to a site unseen."

On the landing level, a harried Mr. Tembel, carrying three bulky carry-cases, gave them a brief nod and a weak smile as he stumbled toward the cable-tube. One of Laraiana's scientists scowled, then jumped aside when it became clear Terr was about to walk through him.

He had no time for Scholar Laraiana or her charges, suddenly impatient to rid himself of the stifling undercurrent of inter-service rivalry and point scoring that seemed to permeate Sariman's every move. The shuttle's hatch already open. He strode through and Dhar closed it behind him. The shuttle had a single deck, carried five passengers and about half a mikan of cargo in the rear compartment. The front part of the curved hull was transparent and acted as the main display for all the heads-up systems. A single simple console on the starboard side served as the pilot station. There wasn't much room in the cramped cabin.

"Take it away," Terr said with a wave and slipped into the left front seat.

"It has been a while since I handled anything like a GS-4," Dhar mused as he squirmed his length into position.

"And I'm trusting my life to an amateur?" Terr stared at him in mock disbelief.

"I'll try not to bend anything…Computer, status?"

"Nominal," the computer responded instantly.

"Secure for lift. Clear with SC&C and file a flight plan for Earth."

"Landing skids retracted and all exterior connections secured. Navigation deflector screen activated."

Inactive pads began to glow soft amber and yellow on the color-reactive panel.

"Surface Command and Control has cleared for lift. System

check complete. Lift sequence enabled." The projected flight plan appeared as a bright green line on the transparent hull and connected with the full-dimensional image of Earth.

"Proceed with lift."

"Recommend engaging full stealth mode before entering line-of-sight with Earth," the computer warned without emotion and Dhar winced.

"Forgot that one…engage full stealth and lift."

"Lift sequence active. Confirm."

"Continue. Quarter boost."

The shuttle lifted quickly, hovered for a moment after it cleared the jagged peaks, then rose straight up and rotated as it lined up on its course. Earth was a fat blue-white streak of color low on the horizon. The shuttle steadied and surged over the gray, cratered surface. At 90 talans per second the Moon swiftly curved and fell away beneath them.

"Half boost," Dhar ordered.

"Boosting to 180 tps," the computer confirmed and accelerated. "Time to destination is thirty minutes."

Dhar scanned the displays and sat back.

"Computer, state local time in Mexico," Terr demanded.

"Eighteen forty-two."

"Perfect. We'll get a chance to observe the site under day and night conditions."

"What do you intend, Sankri?"

Terr brushed the scar above and behind his left eyebrow. "Sariman's last scans showed a lot of activity around the site, like they were getting ready to dig the ship out."

"A logical next step," Dhar said heavily.

"And one that could precipitate a situation," Terr added.

As the shuttle slowed and went into near-Earth orbital insertion, painted by various space-borne and ground defense systems. In stealth mode, its shielding absorbed all impacting electromagnetic radiation, making the shuttle sensor-invisible, but the system went further. Able to distort the local gravitational field allowed it to bend the visible and near-infrared part of the spectrum around the ship to cloak what otherwise would have been a moving black hole.

Earth's night side a darkness filled with flickering lightning flashes. Urban sprawls hugged the American eastern coastline. Glittering phosphorescence smeared the Atlantic waters. The shuttle cut through the upper atmosphere and headed west toward the Gulf of Mexico. Maintaining an altitude of 80,000 katalans the shuttle still transonic when they broke through the terminator into brilliant daylight above Cuba. The brown and black Mexican coastline nudged the emerald Gulf waters. Dhar cut speed and pushed the nose down into a supersonic glide toward Tabasco. Although the shuttle was immune from detection, its heat trail was not. The risk that someone would be pointing an IR array their way was negligible. Given the heightened alert status of Mexican and US military forces, it was still there. Better not be tracked at all than be a topic of suspicious discussion.

At 30,000 katalans altitude and 120 talans from initial point, the shuttle went subsonic. A blue-gray haze obscured the green coastline. Search radar painted them constantly now, the sweeps shown in pale green bands, but it was just air traffic control, not missile batteries. They were also flying through a blanket of radio, television and cellular communications frequencies, displayed on a light blue background. It was rumored that Earth's defensive systems could detect a target as it interrupted these comms signals. If true, the shuttle's stealth systems were vulnerable. Sariman would have warned them if that were the case, wouldn't he?

On the way down they received an ident ping from the probe hovering above Comalcalco. Satisfied with the shuttle's response, it went back to sleep. The coastline opened to innumerable estuaries and tidal inlets. The shuttle glided over the

Comalcalco township and followed the road to the archaeological site. Terr couldn't believe the number of people camped around the exclusion zone. What did they all want? The probe's images did not convey the underlying tension that seemed to hang over the crowd like a palpable blanket. He could now appreciate the need for a heavy military presence.

They slowed to a stop one thousand katalans above Temple I, the largest structure on the site. The restored Temple II an impressive artifact and the uncovered sandstone wall on the side of the mound behind it clearly visible. Long shadows stretched from the eastwest-oriented pyramids. A gauzy haze of humidity hung over the jungle beyond. UN soldiers patrolled the fenced site perimeter. Two surface-to-air missile pods stood in a clearing between the North Plaza Cluster and the Great Acropolis, the white war shot weapons ready to leap off their rails. A gray van was parked near them, the rotating dish on its roof clearly visible. A large white helicopter, its twin rotor sets windmilling, suddenly rose from beside nearby stacked crates and moved silently away, turned and headed west. Four rectangular huts faced the North Plaza. Behind them was a row of tents, presumably housing the troops. Outside the perimeter along the road to the main entrance and the museum, more soldiers and armed vehicles were ready to support the exclusion perimeter. Tents dotted the low hills to the north.

Terr pursed his lips and glanced at Dhar. "I don't like the looks of that crowd. Mobs can get ugly. Move us over the wall and drop to two hundred katalans."

In the fast fading light, the shuttle drifted toward the exposed walls and the earthmoving equipment parked on the north side. The chamber roof partly cleared, but none of the ceiling capstones were removed. Although they could see soldiers wandering between the tents, no one seemed to be guarding the entrance to the chamber itself.

"Audio," Terr ordered and the compartment was flooded with the sharp clatter from the receding helicopter, a clang of tools and background voices. Floodlights suddenly stabbed across the compound and the shadows scattered. In minutes, it became completely dark. Just then two soldiers marched out of the easternmost hut, walked along the western wall, turned the corner and stopped at the chamber entrance. They swung about and strode to the opposite corners, automatic rifles slung on their shoulders, then faced away from the wall and stood to. Terr could see four more strolling casually around the mound and Temple II.

He clicked his tongue and nodded to himself. It wouldn't do to make things too easy.

"Anything from the scans?" he asked and Dhar shook his head.

"There is power flowing through the C-32's hull, but the fusion reactor is cold. They could have activated the computer, however—"

"And are downloading the data."

"I'm afraid so."

Terr frowned and shook his head. Anabb should have ordered Sariman to destroy the C-32 as soon as the BCPA became aware of it instead of wasting precious time to get Terr and Dhar to the site. Everyone playing games...

They waited and watched the guards. After eight minutes the two soldiers looked at each other, swapped sides and assumed their new positions. The action repeated eight minutes later. A man and a young woman appeared out of the second hut. They were deep in conversation as they walked past the guards and disappeared into the chamber.

"When the guards cross again, drop down to ground level," Terr said. Dhar looked at him.

"What if someone wants to come out?"

"We'll get out of the way in a hurry. I need to see the ship."

Dhar shook his head and Terr smiled. This was an unwarranted risk and Dhar disapproved, but wasn't about to say so. Not aloud anyway.

The guards crossed and Dhar brought the shuttle down between them, then rotated the craft horizontally to bring the forward display into line with the entrance. They both craned forward as the chamber opened before them. The C-32 rested on its skids, the interior lit by overhead floodlights. What they could see of it, none of the panels were removed. The chamber cluttered with trailing cables and boxy instruments on benches and trolleys. Terr estimated distances and times. Doable, but the two guards outside worried him.

Dhar cleared his throat and Terr nodded. No use pushing their luck. The shuttle lifted gently so as not to disturb the air with sudden displacement. At two hundred katalans Dhar brought it to a hover.

"The two guards," Terr said flatly. "They could be a problem."

"Make like a commando?"

"If I take them out, they won't be tempted to start making awkward noises."

"What about the awkward noises when their weapons hit the stone floor?"

Terr glared at him. "Let's get out of here before I start making some noises on you!"

"Where to?"

"The American carrier group, then the Russian cruiser."

Dhar looked uncomfortable. "In such a concentration of military assets, my brother, it is possible the shuttle could be tracked."

"I need to see if they're playing casual brinkmanship or are really serious about firing at each other or at Comalcalco."

"If they detect us—"

"We'll know Sariman lied to us, and that would make me very unhappy."

"Mmm." Dhar frowned heavily in disapproval.

"We'll make a single sweep and clear the area before anyone gets excited," Terr assured him. "Okay?"

The shuttle angled up and headed west across the Mexican landscape. At 15,000 katalans they broke through the terminator again and the Pacific glittered silver ahead of them. They found the carrier parked on the ninety-five-degree West line, 120 talans off the coast, which placed them almost exactly 400 talans from Comalcalco. The ranging pings showed the Russian and Chinese vessels some sixty talans farther east. An E-2C Hawkeye tactical warning and surveillance aircraft was doing a lazy track pattern thirty talans east of them. Probably keeping an eye on the Russian and Chinese ships, Terr mused. As the GS-4 lost altitude, different types of search radar illuminated them with increasing signal strength.

Maintaining 5,000 katalans altitude the carrier with its escort of cruisers and destroyers clearly visible from five talans. Two twin-tailed fighters launched off the forward catapults and climbed rapidly to 4,000 katalans. White steam trailed from the catapult tracks. Moving north the ships left creamy wakes trailing behind them. An element of two fighters swung around the carrier and angled down as they lined up into a landing approach. Terr watched with interest as the first trapped in a shower of sparks from its tail hook. The aircraft rolled and swung into a parking slot on the deck to make way for its partner. An impressive business-like operation.

The shuttle dropped to 600 katalans above the glassy smooth water and slowly circled the ships.

"This doesn't look good, Sankri," Dhar said urgently and pointed at the converging scan sweeps on the forward display. "We are getting boxed in a bistatic laser grid, possibly fine enough for a target lock."

"We're supposed to be ladar neutral!"

"Doesn't appear that way."

"Sariman!" Terr sighed and nodded. "Very well, let's clear the datum point."

Even though the search beams radiated by the carrier

group could not directly detect the shuttle, this close, its movement nevertheless left a very faint electronic displacement echo as it interrupted the ladar beams. That faint echo was enough for the Aegis' Advanced Integrated Electronic Warfare System (AIEWS), designed specifically to defeat stealthy targets as part of its countermeasures suite, to track the unknown contact. With Russian and Chinese vessels in the area, maintaining vigil in CIC, the commander of USS *Chosin* did not hesitate.

Three ladar beams crossed each other and blanketed the shuttle. Immediately, gray puffs bloomed from the aft section of the trailing Aegis cruiser as the twin rotary barrels of the Mk 16 Phalanx close-in defense system sent a stream of armor-piercing discarding sabot slugs at 4,500 rounds per minute toward the shuttle in a pattern of parallel lines. Although the GS-4's nav grid was designed to keep out minute space debris, it was not a defensive system and provided no protection at all against the volume of metal that suddenly filled the sky around it. One stream grazed the rear hull plating, shredding the material and the supporting frame members. The shuttle shuddered and sagged to port as the nav shield sparkled in backsurges.

"Lift!" Terr snapped. Dhar did not need urging and sent the shuttle into a shuddering vertical climb.

"Loss of portside hull integrity between frames eleven and thirteen," the computer said coldly and the forward display lit up with warning status indicators. "Stealth mode compromised in the high energy spectrum. Diagnostic systems active."

Another stream ripped through the shuttle's belly and tore away cell arrays that controlled the spinning asymmetric field and ion force lines. With partial loss of vector control the shuttle slued and began horizontal rotation as it dipped down. The computer compensated, but the rate of descent increased rapidly into a powered dive. At two hundred katalans above the slick sea, the shuttle's plunge flattened as the computer struggled to achieve horizontal flight. Although streamlined, the shuttle was not a lifting body and not designed for unassisted flight. Without power, it had all the flying characteristics of a log.

Something tore away beneath them and the shuttle lurched and nosed down.

"Loss of asymmetric field control," the computer stated with infuriating calmness. "Hull charge fluctuations becoming unstable. Unable to sustain controlled flight. Impact in one minute and nine seconds."

"It was that last hit, my brother," Dhar said, his face grim with concentration as his fingers flew over the console.

"Computer, maintain heading one hundred degrees south and open a channel to SC&C."

The dark water an oily blur beneath them as the shuttle's motion became increasingly sluggish.

"Channel open."

Tembel appeared in the display. "Sir, SC&C has monitored your status. Do you wish to declare an emergency?"

Terr stared at the boy. He wanted to rage at him for asking such a stupid question, but refrained. It would just spook the youngster and wouldn't achieve anything.

"We're going to lose the shuttle in about a minute, Mister, and Earth aircraft will undoubtedly be looking for us. Now that we're radar visible, it's likely they'll find us. Retrieval would be good."

Tembel swallowed hard, clearly embarrassed. "Ah, we will have to use your M-1, sir. The M-3 is down for maintenance. If you ditch, the M-1 won't be able to pull out the shuttle. Ach!"

"Is the M-3 flight capable?"

"Yes, sir. But—"

"The shuttle must be retrieved, Mister! We cannot risk it falling into Earth's hands."

"Ah, I will have to clear this with the SMB commander—"

"Then I suggest you do it quickly."

"Acknowledged."

"And Mister, I don't want you coming down on top of me if there are aircraft in the area, understood?"

"Sir, if you're fired upon—"

"Acknowledge your orders!"

"Acknowledged, ach!" the youngster said sullenly and the image cleared.

Everyone wants to be a hero!

"Computer, state distance from the American carrier force," Terr demanded.

"Fifty-six point eight talans."

"Any aircraft approaching our position?"

"Two strike fighters identified as F/A-18Es."

Terrific!

"Ships?"

"Russian unit is fourteen talans east. Chinese destroyer is twenty-three talans southeast."

"Computer, can you maintain hover?"

"Negative. Loss of controlled flight in thirty-four seconds."

"Can you boost us into orbital insertion?"

"Negative. Loss of hull integrity and failure of the asymmetric—"

"Very well. Maintain southerly course and take us down to the surface."

The shuttle arrested its forward motion and settled. Oily swell broke over the front part of the hull and there was a shuddering splash as they hit. The shuttle wallowed, then steadied. Creamy white water surged around the craft.

Terr stared at the advancing swell and ground his teeth.

Rit!

* * *

Flying Combat Air Patrol, CAP, at 9,000 feet, his F/A-18E purring under him, Grazier was happy with the world. The admiral might be antsy over the Chinese tin can and the Russian cruiser creeping about nearby. For Grazier, with his Super Hornet strapped on, life was good. Too bad the Russian heavy didn't have fighters. The three Ka-34 Helixes it carried would be a turkey shoot. He would not have minded mixing it with them, though, just for fun, of course. This 'fox one' and 'fox two' shit was all right for the movies. An Aphid up your tailpipe tended to kind of mess up your day. Maybe they'll get another chance later to jump the Chinese destroyer. More likely get a Croatale in his nose for his trouble. The problem with the Chinese, he figured, they didn't have any sense of humor.

He noted a sudden increase in emissions from the two starboard Aegis pickets as everything lit off: AN/SPY-1, AN/SPS-73, L-band, AN/LPQ-4 ladar, the lot. There was enough loose electromagnetic energy to cook hamburgers. He thumbed his mike button.

"Hey, Spike, what's going on? You detecting anything?"

"We're alone as far as I can see, Chips," Turner responded in his easy drawl. "And there is nothing from the Hawkeye, but something's sure got them dudes spooked. Hey!"

Twin tracks of orange fire leaped low from the trailing *Chosin* into the growing gloom. Almost immediately, less than a mile from the cruiser, the Phalanx sabot rounds struck something. A rippling blue-white discharge like lightning that for a teasing second revealed a fuzzy pebble-shaped outline of something Turner had never seen before. The stream of armor-piercing slugs traversed higher. Another discharge of light, then the firing ceased.

"Shit! Chips, did you see that? What the hell was *Chosin* firing at?"

"You've got me there, Spike. I never saw an aircraft configuration like that before," Grazier said just as CAG's voice came through.

"Strike One from Home Plate. Vector one hundred degrees south and search for a possible bogey."

"Home Plate, state nature of target," Grazier demanded.

"Ah, cannot identify target, Strike One."

"What are we chasing here, CAG?"

"Possible stealth drone. We lost contact when it went below our ladar horizon. The E-2C sentry had something on their scopes for a minute, but it vanished. If it's a drone, it may have ditched. Approach with caution. I don't want you and Spike boring in with your hair on fire. Remember, that big Russian cruiser will not be far off when you hit IP and you might end up looking at a couple of Fort or Osa missiles if you're cute."

"Roger," Grazier said and clicked another button. "Spike, cut to three-fifty knots indicated and follow me down to two thousand." As far as he knew the Russians didn't have surveillance drones, stealthy or otherwise, and what he saw did not look like any drone. The Russians were cagey like that and he would not be surprised by anything. It was an awfully big ocean out there and getting dark rapidly. Their chances of finding a downed object were remote to nil. Still, it beat running a racetrack pattern around the carrier group.

"That's a rog, One."

The two F/A-18Es stood on their port wings and angled down toward a shimmering mercury sea. In the west, the sun was a bloated orange ball ready to dip beneath the waves. It painted the long low clouds with fire and gold. In any other circumstance it would have been a pretty evening. He was simply happy to be flying and happy to leave grand strategy to the brass.

"Chips, what are we after?" Turner asked as the flight steadied.

"CAG tells us to search, we search. When they tell me more, I'll tell you."

"My hero," Turner grunted into the mike and Grazier smiled to himself. There was nothing wrong with Spike a good swift kick in the butt wouldn't straighten out.

The Hornets kept their APG-73 radars and FLIR active. Apart from the prowling *Pyotr Velikiy* eleven miles southeast of them, the sea empty. Although Grazier was well in range of its AK-130 Kashstan, the big ship painted him only with search radar. After a couple of box sweeps, he thumbed the mike button.

"Home Plate, this is Strike One. Negative on bogey within eighty miles and it's getting pretty dark. Do you want us to extend the search?"

"Strike One, that's a negative. Do another pattern, then return to CAP."

"Roger. Spike, the man says to do one more box." An answering click and the Hornets reefed into a three-g turn.

Dusk settled fast and Grazier could clearly see the bright strobe navigation lights on his wingman's Hornet. He checked his displays. Nothing out there, in the air or in the water. If the E-2C Hawkeye couldn't pick up anything, he was wasting his time here.

"Spike, I'm turning in."

"Hold it! I got something on my FLIR. Follow me in."

Grazier clicked his mike. The two Hornets angled down and headed toward the deck. Spike checked his screen as the Hornet bored in. The swell had picked up and it was difficult to make anything out. He cursed softly.

"I can't see anything, Chips. Sorry. Probably a false return."

"Wait!" Grazier snapped. "I've got an intermittent return on my radar as well. Something's down there, all right." He pulled his Hornet into a sweeping turn. The vertical scan line on his screen clearly showed an irregular green blip, the return probably blocked by breaking waves. That meant the bogey had indeed ditched. The western sky almost purple now and the sea turned black.

"Copy contact," Spike said as they skimmed two hundred feet above the water.

"Home Plate, this is Strike One. Have positive lock. Going in for a flyby."

"Copy, Strike One."

The two Hornets overflew the contact point. The FLIR showed an empty sea, but his radar had a nice solid return.

"Spike, do you see anything?"

"Negative on FLIR."

Grazier frowned into his mask. With his FLIR at full gain, he could read a newspaper on a ship's deck in pitch darkness—almost. If this was a downed drone, the damned thing was invisible.

"Home Plate—"

"We see your problem, Strike One," CAG said promptly, monitoring the data link from the Hornets. "You have permission to fire on the radar return."

"Roger." He clicked another button. "Spike, light off a Sparrow."

"Copy that!" Spike hooted with delight and flipped the master arm switch. The F/A-18E turned into its run and steadied up. At three miles the Sparrow's radar seeker head locked on the target and Spike smiled happily when the tone in his helmet changed to a steady warble.

"I've got tone!" Almost caressing the toggle, he squeezed once. "Fox one!"

The missile's motor lit off and the slim body slid smoothly off the rail. Spike squeezed his eyes so he would not be blinded by the rocket's glare. The four delta platform wings shifted and the missile angled down, guided to its target by its RF return. As the missile accelerated, the arming rotor turned, aligned the explosive train and removed the shorting circuit. Spike held his breath. Although an air-to-air weapon the missile bore unerringly toward the RF return. A few seconds later came a bright flash as the missile's eighty-eight pounds high explosive warhead detonated. Spike waited for secondary explosions, but there was nothing. Could the target have disintegrated?

"That's a kill," he said delightedly. A little black star beneath his canopy will look good and will rub it in to the other hot jocks at VFA-151.

Grazier checked his radar. The contact had taken a hit, but it was still there. Whatever the thing, it was built well to take a strike from a Sparrow and survive.

"The bogey is still alive, Spike. I'm going in for a flyby," he said and heard Spike's howl of indignation.

He reefed the Hornet into a shallow turn to bring the FLIR pod to bear and thundered in. The F/A-18E swept over the target. An oval pebble shape wallowed in the swell, the ragged black hole in its stern clearly visible where the missile struck. He estimated the thing to be about eighteen feet long by eight wide. He couldn't see any wings or engine air intakes. Torn off during the crash?

"Home Plate, this is Strike One. Bogey took a hit and is dead in the water."

"Copy, Strike One. Maintain position. We're sending two Seahawks to take a closer look."

\* \* \*

Terr followed the glowing blue-white exhausts of the receding Hornets as they roared by less than half a talan from the shuttle. The noise faded as the two aircraft banked away. The shuttle wallowed in the low glassy swells, the movement hypnotic and soothing. He fancied he could feel the hull settling and looked at Dhar.

"This reminds me of another crash," he mused wryly and Dhar cleared his throat.

"I hate to say it, Sankri, but technically, this is your fault."

"I know. Sariman must be rubbing his hands with glee. Can you believe it? Getting caught in a bistatic search. Why in the pits didn't he warn us we weren't fully stealthy!"

He listened to the lapping water sloshing against the hull. The shuttle unquestionably lower, probably seepage through the rip in the aft compartment and the torn bottom.

"Warning, detecting emissions from two APG-73 attack radars," the computer announced. "One aircraft has established a lock with a radar missile."

Terr winced. "Yep. Definitely reminds me of that other crash."

"We could abandon the shuttle," Dhar suggested.

"If we're fired upon, I wouldn't give much for our chances in open water."

"Here it comes," Dhar said with detached finality. There wasn't anything they could do except hope the shuttle could take it. He glanced at his brother. "Sankri—"

"I know. I'm only sorry I got you into this, Nightwings," Terr said.

They watched the missile bore in, its fiery exhaust bright in the night's blackness. A second later, a thunderous crash in the rear made the shuttle lurch, its stern forced into the water by the force of the explosion. Its natural buoyancy made it rear up before it settled back with a jarring thump. The restraining field gripped them hard. The heads-up display rippled with pulsing orange-white rectangles. Several went solid white, indicating total system failure.

"Status!" Dhar demanded.

"Loss of stealth capability. Loss of lift capability. Rupture of cargo compartment. Total flooding in three minutes. Fluctuation in the power cell containment field. Criticality in eight minutes."

"Well, we won't be able to take another one of those," Terr said, massaging his shoulders. "I just hope the water's warm. Arm auto-destruct and prepare to blow the emergency hatch."

Dhar looked at him, his orange eyes searching, then issued commands to the computer.

"Auto-destruct set."

Terr squinted at him. "It might be a bit late to ask, but you can swim?"

Dhar grinned. "I can float."

"Good enough."

"Warning, two Ka-34 anti-submarine attack helicopters inbound," the computer said. "Intercept in two minutes."

Terr looked disgusted. He only wanted to check the disposition of the American carrier group, not escalate an armed confrontation. What is it with these people!

"The second aircraft is coming in," Dhar said urgently.

"Missile lock?"

"Negative."

"It's a flyby then to check us out."

"Before sending in another missile?"

Terr shook his head. "I doubt it, not with the Russian helicopters so close. The Americans don't know what we are and will not risk escalating things if we turn out to be a Russian drone or something."

"You hope," Dhar said gloomily and Terr grinned at him.

"Then again, the Russians might fire at us on principle if they think we're a *Chinese* drone."

"The thought had occurred to me," Dhar growled dryly.

"And I thought working for Anabb was going to be dull," Terr mused.

They watched the display in silence as the fighter roared overhead, banked, and pulled back. A low wave washed over them and the shuttle settled, sluggish and dead. They could hear the gurgle of water sloshing in the aft compartment.

"Computer, status of Earth aircraft," Terr demanded.

"F/A-18s maintaining a racetrack pattern two talans from the shuttle. The Ka-34s are now in visual range."

The water already halfway up the forward display. Another good wave and they could go down.

"Time to get out of here," Terr said briskly. "Computer, open a channel to SC&C."

Part of the forward display cleared and Sariman's fishy features stared at them. Terr sighed in resignation. It had to be him.

"Our uplink with the shuttle shows you have lost all drive capability and you have activated auto-destruct. I'll be lifting in six minutes. Hold on for ten more minutes—"

"Negative! Your uplink must tell you that the containment field will fail in five minutes. Besides, the shuttle is about to sink from under me and there are hostile fighter aircraft in the area."

"I don't have time to debate this, Mister! Get out now and stand by for retrieval."

"With all the aircraft buzzing us, you'll be seen."

Sariman bared his teeth. "We're beyond that point now, wouldn't you say?" Hiss.

"Sir, you're in violation of procedures!"

"I will have more than violations on my hands if you're taken."

Foam and spray smeared the window and there was a loud clatter overhead.

"Master Scout, I'm out of time. A Russian helicopter is on top of me and I imagine they'll attempt to board. I'm initiating auto-destruct and abandoning the shuttle." With a bum containment field the computer had a hard enough time to stop the power cell *from* brewing.

"You will—"

Terr leaned toward the console and stabbed the comms pad. "Computer, set auto-destruct on a one-minute delay from our egress and enable. Blow the emergency hatch now."

"Auto-destruct now active."

The hatch in the roof blew out with a bang. Water and salty spray poured inside, driven in by the helicopter's deafening downdraft. Terr pointed at the hatch and after a moment's hesitation, Dhar grabbed the lip and pulled himself out. A second later, he leaned over the black opening and extended his arms. Terr reached for them and was lifted up. Warm spray stung his face and he gasped under the force of the downdraft and the raucous clatter of helicopter blades. The night dark, but he could see a rich band of stars covering the sky. A pretty sight, but he didn't have time to admire the view. He pulled Dhar's arm.

"Jump!" he yelled and threw himself into the foaming sea.

Powerful strokes drove him away from the shuttle. When he felt he'd swum far enough, he stopped and treaded water.

"Nightwings!"

"Over here!" Dhar shouted out of the night and Terr felt a flood of relief. He knew the Fleet Academy provided all manner of physical training, including swimming. Dhar's lack of proficiency was one of those silly things that could have had disastrous consequences.

The helicopter churned the water around the shuttle into flying froth. A steep swell swept over the glistening hull. Terr could hear the sharp gurgle as the sea rushed into the open hatchway. A second later, only blackness remained where the shuttle had been. Suddenly the water turned an eerie blue-green and a spurt of steam leaped into the air. A pressure wave squeezed Terr's body as it passed and he grunted. The helicopter rocked wildly and fell away before it recovered.

Dhar brushed Terr's arm and they watched the helicopter move slowly toward them. At first the water felt warm, but the air was crisp and Terr felt the first stirrings of cold coming up his legs. He wondered how long they'd be able to stay afloat. The clatter of helo rotors deafening and flying spray stung his face. He looked up as the ungainly machine hovered above them. A metal ladder dropped down and splashed less than a katalan from his head. He grabbed one of the rungs and pulled the ladder tight.

"Up!" he shouted to Dhar.

"Sankri—"

"I know."

Better to negotiate from a warm and dry helicopter or ship than have some predatory fish taking nibbles off him. The situation shot anyway and way too late to pretend.

Dhar grasped the slim ladder and pulled himself up. The

helicopter barely tilted at the additional weight. Terr waited until Dhar was inside before he started up.

\* \* \*

Grazier checked the FLIR display. Wallowing in the long swell the object had clearly settled, now heavy and sluggish. A wave broke over its smoothly curved back and water sluiced around the jagged hole in its stern where the Sparrow had struck. As he made his pass the FLIR's scanner head rotated to keep the object in view. Spike's Hornet banked in its turn and headed in. By flying reciprocal courses they were able to keep the object under constant surveillance. Flying low and slow consumed a prodigious amount of fuel. In fourteen minutes they would be at bingo state and forced to return unless the carrier directed a 'Texaco' Hornet tanker their way. Anyway, the two Seahwaks should be showing up in a few minutes to take over this babysitting routine.

Flying the racetrack, Grazier was concerned. The Seahawk was an anti-submarine platform, not a rescue helo, although it could act as one. If the admiral wanted the object destroyed, he didn't need a Seahawk for that. Grazier well able to take care of that part himself. What then? Did they suspect the thing was manned? It was certainly large enough to hold a crew. He recalled the sparkling discharge and the ghostly shape that became visible for one tantalizing moment.

What exactly were they dealing with here?

He shrugged and banked into his turn. This was way over his pay grade and the admiral was welcome to it. That's why he wore the two stars, Grazier thought comfortably.

"Strike One, from Home Plate. Be advised that *Pyotr Velikiy's* Ka-34s will be in your area in less than two minutes. You have permission to observe, but do not engage. Repeat, do not engage!"

Great! He now had trigger-happy Russians to worry about

as well.

"Copy, I have them on radar. Home Plate, note that I'll be bingo fuel in twelve minutes."

"Copy, Strike One. Return to Home Plate when bingo."

"Roger." He pressed his mike button. "Spike, you heard that?"

Spike double clicked his mike and the two Hornets continued in their pattern. Grazier's threat receiver quiet, but he could detect the search sweeps from the Ka-34s boring in at nine miles out.

It didn't take long for the Russians to show up. One helicopter stood off about two hundred yards while the other slowly crept toward the downed object. Grazier was coming into his turn when a hatch blew into the air off the object's back.

"Chips—"

"I see it," Grazier said as a figure emerged from the object. So someone *did* man the thing, but was he Russian or was the Ka-34 just being nosy? The figure bent over the opening and lifted up someone smaller. Both dove into the water and started swimming away from the wallowing object. The helicopter remained hovering above the object.

Grazier reefed the Hornet into a tight turn, keeping the nose level. If he wasn't careful, he could be in the drink himself before he knew it and that wouldn't look so hot on his fitness report. He was looking at the HUD and almost missed seeing the green flash and the sudden spurt of steam that reached for the helicopter. For a second, he thought the Russian was going to auger in, but it recovered and moved slowly toward the two figures in the water. It didn't take long to retrieve them and the Ka-34 dipped its nose as it sped off. That was enough for Grazier.

"Home Plate from Strike One. A Ka-34 just picked up two survivors, and both helos are heading for home. The stealth drone seems to have been triggered for self-destruct. Bingo in four minutes."

"Understood, Strike One. You're ordered to orbit out to five miles and observe. Plot shows a large uncorrelated target coming down on top of you."

A large target coming down on top of me?

"Roger, Home Plate. Ah, what's this 'uncorrelated target' stuff?"

"Strike One, I would just shut up and do as I'm told. Copy?"

"Copy," Grazier growled, miffed at getting snubbed like that.

Nothing on his radar. Two minutes later the FLIR screen suddenly filled with something coming down directly over the spot where the drone had sunk. He frowned and twiddled the magnification dial. The view in the screen sprang back and he looked at a fuzzy triangular outline. The thing at least two hundred feet long and fifty high. He couldn't make out any detail of the object itself. It was just a black hole in the night, like it absorbed all radiation—the FLIR making it out only by picking up surrounding heat signatures. He didn't need to see the thing to realize what it was.

His mike clicked.

"Hey, Chips. You seein' this?"

"We've got ourselves a real live ET here, pal."

"And we just shot down one of its buddies."

"Yeah, but the Russians have them now."

* * *

In the helicopter's gloomy interior, smelling of aviation gasoline and hot oil, it was even louder than Terr thought possible. The entire forward bulkhead lit with amber instruments and small display screens. A helmeted operator looked at their dripping forms in open astonishment, the console before him forgotten. A second crewman, dressed in a baggy dark green

201

flight suit, said something into a mike clipped to his head. The helicopter dipped and surged forward. The crewman pulled two blankets from a deck locker and held them out. Terr gratefully wrapped the coarse wool about him. The crewman nodded, then grasped a handle and slid the open hatch home with a clang. The roar of rushing air stopped and it became almost silent. The crewman pointed at the rear bulkhead and motioned with both hands that Terr should sit down.

Terr leaned against the metal wall and allowed himself to slide to the deck. Dhar gave him a weak smile. Water oozed from his long hair.

"You okay?" Terr asked.

"I swallowed some water." Dhar groaned and made a face.

The crewman leaned over them and shouted something. Terr shook his head, not understanding. "We not far from ship," the crewman repeated slowly in English. "You understand? Then you be safe."

"Thank you for fishing us out," Terr said. The man bobbed his head, smiled and sat next to the other crewman. Terr looked at Dhar.

"We're apparently being taken to the Russian cruiser."

"Great. What will Sariman do, I wonder?" Dhar asked.

"I am more concerned about what the Russians will do."

"Shot down has seriously compromised our mission, my brother, not to mention violating our orders about getting detected."

"Yeah." Terr sighed and chewed his lip, his day ruined for certain. As for revealing themselves, he didn't even want to think about that. Caught by the Russians could unmask Serrll's presence on Earth at a level that might not be deniable, compromising Captal's policy regarding the protectorate. There would be crap to pay no matter which way he sliced it. He could not blame Sariman either. Stealth-capable or not, Terr shouldn't have been poking around those naval units at all. *Great job, my boy.* He feared he bungled badly.

Rit!

Would Sariman break regulations and come after them?

Terr spent the next few minutes listening to the clatter of rotors and the whine of machinery around him. Opposite him the two crewmen sat on thin metal seats monitoring a bank of instruments and screens. He felt the helicopter slow and the sound of turbines changed as the machine assumed a hover. The helicopter descended, paused, and with a bump, it landed. The turbines immediately began to spool down.

The side hatch jerked open and harsh white light bathed the helicopter's interior. Terr and Dhar stood up. The figure outside gaped at them, then motioned them to come out. Terr grasped the hatch opening and looked out. The air filled with a steady whine of ship machinery and the hiss of roiling foam from the stern. He turned as another helicopter approached the ship's side, hovered, and slowly slid toward the open deck. Two sailors rushed under the machine and secured it to the gently swaying deck. The ship's superstructure towered above the yawning helicopter hangar. Radar dishes turned rapidly on tall masts. One large flat monster swung around ponderously, dwarfing its companions. Twin turrets of a powerful gun pointed horizontally into the night sky. Terr looked down at the metal steps and climbed to the deck.

It wasn't the kind of welcome to Earth he dreamed of.

Four helmeted men stood beside the helicopter, their automatic rifles held at port arms. Their eyes flickered with undisguised curiosity as the two aliens climbed to the deck. Gawking sailors clustered near them to watch the strange proceedings. Clearly, the ship had been warned to expect unusual visitors. Two senior officers pushed through the crowd and stopped before the standing aliens. One of them snapped to attention and saluted.

"I am informed that you speak English. Please allow me to introduce myself. I am Captain Rashin Amanyev, and it is with the greatest pleasure that I welcome you aboard the Russian

Federation cruiser, *Pyotr Velikiy*, gentlemen."

Terr grimaced and nodded. This is going to be very awkward.

"My thanks to your crew for getting us out of the water, Captain."

"It is nothing," Amanyev said with a shrug, staring avidly at the two aliens. "May I introduce my first officer, Commander Grishnakov."

"Captain—"

"You must be uncomfortable in those wet clothes. Allow me—"

A sharp *whoop…whoop* blared from the single midship-mounted stack's siren. The twin Osa-MA and Kashstan close-in defense mounts swiveled up ready to unleash their deadly missiles into the air. Amanyev's head instinctively jerked up. The stern gun tubes whined and pointed into the night. An officer ran toward them, gawked at the aliens, then spoke rapidly. Amanyev gave a curt order and the officer hurried away. Amanyev regarded Terr and gave a tight smile.

"It looks like your countrymen, if that is the right expression, have come looking for you."

Terr followed the captain's gaze over the port side. The gloomy shape of the M-3 loomed out of darkness and settled above the black sea, paralleling the ship at some three hundred katalans. He felt a prickling rush of emotion wash over him at the sight of the elegantly contoured sweeper. Sariman may have violated procedures by revealing the M-3, Terr was happy to face that problem later. Happier than facing inquisitive Earthmen with possibly dubious intentions.

He looked at Amanyev's expressionless face and wondered if he was being premature. Would the Russian commander fight the sweeper to keep his two visitors? The man would be foolish if he did. However, the engagement might not necessarily be so one-sided. The M-3's shield grid not directly designed to prevent penetration by solid matter, as his attack on Tanard's ship by survival blisters had demonstrated all too clearly, and the sweeper was too close for its nav deflector grid to be fully effective. The M-3 could be severely damaged if the cruiser opened with a salvo of missiles and gun tube rounds. Sariman must have been aware of the danger, for the projector dome beneath the hull began to glow a dull orange. A faint yellow sheen of its primary grid enveloped the sweeper.

Amanyev turned to him, his expression quizzical.

"May I ask what your ship is doing?"

"It raised a defensive energy screen and readied its offensive systems," Terr said simply and waited.

"I see." Amanyev looked deep into the alien's gray eyes. They were hard eyes, but kindly. That told him a lot. The aliens had obviously gotten themselves into trouble nosing near the *Constellation* group, but the appearance of this larger ship sent a clear message. The aliens would not stand still for any further interference. There were any number of things he could do, and all of them might be wrong. Moscow may not agree with his choice, but this was his call and trying to hold onto the two aliens just wasn't a realistic option, no matter how much he personally wanted to test himself and his ship against the alien craft. There was another consideration. He could not afford to forget he had a mission here. Engaging in a firefight with an alien spaceship could seriously undermine his ability to execute that mission. He didn't want an encounter anyway.

There were also longer term objectives to keep in mind. These aliens were not new to Earth. They might be secretive now, but one day when they chose to reveal themselves publicly, Russia could use this incident to demonstrate to them its good will. That reminder could count for a lot. He turned to Grishnakov and snapped an order. Grishnakov nodded and hurried forward. Amanyev smiled at Terr.

"An armed spaceship is a persuasive argument, sir. As much as I would relish the prospect of extending my hospitality to you and your friend, for now at least, I'll have to deny myself that pleasure."

Terr felt relieved to hear that. "Believe me, Captain, neither of us wants the alternative."

"And I beg you to excuse the automatic readiness reaction of my ship. You would never have been harmed."

"No need for apologies, sir."

Terr breathed more easily when he saw the gun mounts swivel back and the missile launchers made safe.

After what seemed an eternity where everyone stood frozen, the M-3 dropped its shields and slowly approached the ship. It slipped sidewise and settled, its hull almost touching the port rail. An access tube extended silently from the featureless hull. Several armed sailors appeared out of the helicopter bay and rushed for the railing. Amanyev shouted something and they stood back.

"Captain Amanyev," Terr said. "With your permission, sir…"

Amanyev tore his eyes away from the hovering spaceship. "Another time, then," he said gravely and saluted. "Russia will welcome you as a friend," he added.

Terr nodded, gathered Dhar with his eyes and walked deliberately toward the access tube, conscious of armed sailors behind him. He didn't relax until he stepped inside. The open hatch at the other end a welcome sight.

"I did not understand what went on back there," Dhar said looking bemused, "but I can guess."

"Unfortunately, I didn't have to guess," Terr snapped.

On the main deck, a rating stood to and touched a contact pad as the two of them came through. The hatch hissed shut, closing one incident, and opened another bound to be equally unpleasant.

"If you will please wait here," the rating said and marched off.

Terr clutched the blanket to him, leaned against the warm bulkhead and his shoulders sagged. He felt a hollow fluttering in his stomach and tensed.

"Nightwings, next time I want to overfly an Earth ship, please give me a kick."

Dhar chuckled. "The gods have smiled on us today, my brother."

"Yeah, but I think they were smiles of gleeful anticipation."

On cue, the cable-tube opened and Sariman walked in, flanked by two ratings. Terr straightened and the blanket dropped to the deck. Sariman extended a long finger at Terr and nodded to the two ratings.

"Place these officers under arrest!"

"Stand to!" Terr roared.

Faced with authority the two ratings instinctively obeyed.

Sariman's lips curled back. "You heard my order!"

"Master Scout, you have no authority over me. Before this gets out of hand, do you mind explaining what's going on here?"

"With pleasure!" Sariman hissed and shoved his head into Terr's face. "Disregarding a superior officer, dereliction of duty, loss of Fleet property, conduct unbecoming, and I can now add insubordination. I'll think of a few more things later. Your little excursion over the American carrier force has landed you in quite a mess. Mister, you may consider yourself some kind of hotshot, but to me, you're a below average officer and it will give me great personal satisfaction to run you out of the Fleet!"

"Rit! I *am* out of the Fleet!"

"Not while you wear that uniform. Draw your weapons!" Sariman hissed at the ratings. "If they move, shoot them!"

The ratings glanced at each other and reached for their needlers. Terr stepped back and shot out his right arm, his face an expressionless mask. Wet, uncomfortable and cold, he did not want to face Sariman's tirades. Small blue sparks danced silently between his fingers.

"Freeze!"

Dhar instantly stepped aside and raised his right hand,

ready to support his brother.

Faced with Death, the two ratings blanched and their hands dropped.

Sariman's face took on a deep green hue and his tongue showed as a flickering blur.

"A Discipline adept," he muttered in a strangled whisper. "You would use force against a superior officer?"

Terr ignored him, his eyes fixed on the ratings. "You two…" He jerked his head in the direction of the cable-tube.

The ratings were caught in a dilemma and looked at Sariman. After a tense moment, he nodded and they did a grateful fade. Trouble in upper ranks always meant even more trouble for those who happened to get caught in the middle of it, no matter how innocently.

"If I had a weapon, I would shoot you on the spot. Both of you!" Sariman hissed. "How dare you—"

"Master Scout," Terr said more calmly and dropped his arm, but the power inside him raged for release. He trembled to control his emotions. "If it's the shuttle, the Diplomatic Branch will cover all replacement costs—"

"I don't give a worm's ass about the shuttle! You disregarded my order not to go down, and you've now compromised not only yourself and your mission, but the Serrll's presence in this system!"

"Perhaps I have jeopardized the mission, and that's my problem. However, I don't see how we're compromised."

"Oh? What about the aircraft and the helicopters, not to mention getting you off that warship? I suppose everyone just imagined you and this sweeper?"

"Officially, no. There hasn't been any public exposure and I don't believe the Russians nor the Americans will want to make one."

"As the mission commander, you were automatically responsible—"

"Agreed! And I will accept the consequences. If you don't

like the way I have conducted myself, Master Scout, you're free to file a protest with the Diplomatic Branch."

"I'll file more than just a protest. This isn't the end of it, Mister!"

Terr believed him. "And I'll be filing a protest of my own—with CAPFLTCOM."

"CAPFLTCOM?"

"You violated procedure by revealing the M-3."

"You had to be picked up! It was a command decision."

"As was mine to overfly the carrier group. None of this would have happened if you'd warned us about Earth's ladar bistatic capability. I asked you about that, remember?"

Sariman glared at Terr, his black eyes full of impotent fire. He badly wanted to wipe that look of confident arrogance off the youngster's face. It was insufferable to have his authority snubbed like this. To be threatened in his own command! What galled him, the little worm turd was right. Shielded by the Diplomatic Branch, he couldn't touch him. Sariman clenched his fists. He might not be able to punish the insufferable snot, but the Diplomatic Branch Director certainly could, and he would hear about this incident and Terr's behavior in detail.

"Mister, you've been one monumental headache ever since I learned of your miserable existence!"

"I have only carried out my duty, Master Scout," Terr said, feeling weary and not really giving a damn. "If you want to make an issue of it, go right ahead."

Sariman's lips trembled as he fought for control. "Pits, man! Do you know the position you've put me in? Scholar Laraiana was in SC&C and saw everything. When the shuttle went down, you'd have thought I just killed her baby. Her program totally compromised, and she's stuck here until COMROLOPS can send another GS-4. A negative report from her will ruin me!"

Terr blinked and almost laughed. Sariman more worried about covering his butt than doing his job, and he was a fool if he thought sucking up to Laraiana by punishing Terr would placate her. The woman was a control freak.

"I regret if losing the shuttle has complicated her work schedule, but that's hardly your fault," Terr said, his tone neutral.

"Unfortunately, she doesn't see it that way. This has complicated your schedule as well. What do you intend doing now?"

"I'll use an Assault Battle Penetrator," Terr said with resolve.

The little attack craft was designed to carry a six-man assault team, attach itself against a target ship, burn its way through the hull and board it. Heavily armored to withstand limited bursts from an M-4, the little ships could penetrate a vessel's secondary and primary shield grids, making them particularly deadly in any close-quarter encounter. It wasn't an ideal substitute for a GS-4, but that's all he had.

Sariman stared at him. "An ABP isn't stealthy, you know."

"It will be once I have it modified."

"After everything that's happened, you're still determined to carry on?"

"I haven't received any orders to the contrary."

"You're insane! Comalcalco will be alerted and this action could precipitate the very escalation your mission was designed to prevent."

"Then I better get this done quickly, wouldn't you agree?"

Sariman bit his lip, his frustration all too evident. He didn't need the Diplomatic Branch meddling in his command. This was a Fleet job!

"Pits! Prima Scout Anabb Karr didn't have to send you!" he lashed out. "I could have done the job myself and avoided this mess. That's why I'm here, or doesn't he trust me?"

Terr was genuinely taken aback by the outburst and some things fell into place. Was the Karkan really so insecure?

"It has nothing to do with you. It was *me*."

"You?"

"Anabb wanted to see if *I* was up to the job."

"That risked a lot on an incompetent fool like you!" Sariman snarled and stomped off.

Terr's mouth twitched, but he wasn't amused. All this over Scholar Laraiana and a bruised ego? His original assessment was right. An SMB posting *was* for losers. Why else would the Fleet dump an otherwise valuable officer into what was really a First Scout billet. Well, as long as Sariman did not attempt any more lame arrests, happy to keep out of his damned way.

Dhar watched the retreating figure, then turned to Terr.

"Would you have used your aspect against those ratings?"

"No, they didn't deserve my wrath, but I would have given them a fright."

"It is a dangerous thing you do, my brother, playing a god."

Terr nodded. "I know, and you better get used to it, Nightwings."

# Chapter Eight

"Kari, good to see you again!" Harford said with a broad smile and extended his hand at the couch. "Make yourself comfortable."

"Thank you, Mr. President." The Russian ambassador looked grave as they shook hands. He nodded to Morris, already seated.

"Coffee?"

"Thank you, sir. I will have a cup. It's a bit chilly out there."

"You, a steppe Russian, are telling me it's chilly?"

"I'm afraid Washington has made me soft, sir," Karijan said, allowing himself a tight smile.

Morris poured him a cup and sat back. A thin man, Karijan Miroslavski, had gaunt, strained features. He carried a cane, mostly for effect, as there was nothing wrong with him—apart from being a Russian. Kari's sad expression excited sympathy, which quickly turned to concern when confronted by his startlingly clear blue eyes. They were cold, emotionless and forever wary. It was hard not to look into those eyes and feel Kari dissected everything he saw, filing it away for later analysis. Of average height, his assured bearing made him appear much taller. A new generation of diplomats from the post-Putin era, Kari seldom smiled, said little and listened a lot. His heart a piece of Siberian permafrost, and when Morris first met him, he had the impression if Kari didn't particularly like what the US administration had to tell him, ICBMs would be coming over the horizon. The Russian was polished and smooth and played the game by his rules, which unfortunately, most of the time did not coincide with those of the US.

Harford took a sip and placed down his cup with a soft

click.

"Kari, every day I get up gives me something new to worry about. Today, I am worried about you."

"Me, sir?"

"You. Tell me what's going on off Mexico, and no more stonewalling."

Karijan took a slow sip of the excellent rich coffee. He would miss this luxury when recalled to Moscow. Must stock up, he reminded himself. Reluctantly, he looked up and searched the American's face. Harford maintained steady eye contact. Karijan allowed the silence to build for half a minute. Control, he must maintain control.

"The Russian Federation has not shifted its position, Mr. President. *Pyotr Velikiy* is on station to provide whatever support Mexico or the UN may deem necessary."

"I see. You are there to protect Mexico from the US Pacific Fleet, is that it?"

"Or the Chinese destroyer, sir."

"Ah, the Chinese destroyer, I almost forgot. What's it carrying? SS-N-26s, isn't it? Now, why would the Chinese put one of their capital ships within cruise missile range of Comalcalco? Curious, don't you think?"

Karijan's mouth barely twitched and he kept his face inscrutable, but he enjoyed Harford's levity. The American obviously well briefed and was toying with him. And why not? The president spoke from overwhelming strength and they both knew it. In the fourteen years since the turn of the millennium, American credit had done much to modernize selected areas of Russia's dilapidated industrial infrastructure and smooth the paths of international trade. America wasn't altruistic and would not hesitate to slam those doors shut should its own interests become compromised; especially after the global financial crisis a bare six years ago. Russia desperately needed those doors kept open. He needed to be very careful here.

"Mr. President, I cannot speak for our Chinese friends, but

does the United States object to the presence of a lone Russian warship in international waters?"

Harford regarded the ambassador with a measure of fondness. After two years, they now knew one another well enough and understood the other's fenced-off areas as far as possible, given their respective positions. Karijan represented an emerging breed of business diplomats who now fought with the dollar rather than a Kalashnikov. Both were equally dangerous. Russia had largely shaken itself down after a hesitant embrace of a more market-driven economy—he hesitated to call it capitalism—and managed to rid itself of rampant corruption that plagued its formative years. The country avoided a general meltdown solely due to its staggering abundance of natural resources and the stoic acceptance and patience of its citizens. He did not consider Karijan a friend, but he respected the Russian. That didn't mean he was not prepared to expel his butt should Russia contemplate something dumb, and sending in that cruiser was dumb.

"Object, Mr. Ambassador? The United States doesn't object. As you pointed out, the ship is in international waters. My worry for the day, Kari, is that *Pyotr Velikiy* is a warship. They make me nervous. Its augmented Granit missiles can easily reach Comalcalco. That also makes me nervous. The Chinese destroyer makes me nervous. My carrier groups make me nervous. My doctor advises me to relax more and take up stress management before I burst a vessel. Ha! He means well, but he doesn't have to sit in the Oval Office. If I were to suddenly keel over with a heart attack or something, I'm sure the event would raise one or two approving smiles, but I'm not dead yet. Until I am, the United States will continue to be nervous while *Pyotr Velikiy* and that Chinese tub are engaged in a tropical cruise. It would help my nerves a lot, Kari, if you pulled that ship out and parked it someplace else—as a gesture of good will?"

If Harford looked nervous, he hid it well, Karijan thought. So far, everything the president said he anticipated, if somewhat late. Karijan expected America to be fulminating at the UN over the missile cruiser's presence, but it had been a token gesture only. That, more than anything else, concerned him. He admired the image of a quiet cowboy, not saying much, but when provoked, shot for the heart. He needed to find out if Harford was ready to shoot.

"If I may tell you something, Mr. President. The United States is powerful and rich and fears no one. The dollar is the de facto world currency and you dominate international trade. Compare that with the situation in my country. The find at Comalcalco changed all that, or has the potential to do so. Russia wants to make sure we share equitably in that potential."

"Are you worried we would *steal* the ship?"

"More likely the knowledge it contains, sir."

Harford's eyes blazed. "Kari, the Geneva team has everything we have. They're online with the site, for Chrissake!"

"That is not enough, Mr. President," Karijan said softly,

After a moment, Harford slowly nodded. Kari was right. Having the knowledge only wasn't enough, not when Russia was powerless to exploit it. They had their research centers and some respectable industrial complexes, but its infrastructure could not compare or compete with the West, not when some of its finest minds have flown to Europe and America. How could they hope to keep their elite on 2,000 rubles a month when the US paid 20,000 in dollars.

"Okay. So what are you going to do? Blow up the saucer and deny it to everyone?"

"That is a rhetorical question, Mr. President."

"Perhaps not. If you wanted our help, why didn't you simply ask! This posturing is a dangerous thing for everyone, my friend, and does nothing to make me extend you a helping hand."

Karijan gave a sad little smile. "Russia is suspicious of American altruism, sir. Look at the Siberian natural gas pipeline."

Harford chuckled, but it wasn't with amusement. A consortium of US oil companies had won a contract to refurbish Russia's leaking pipelines and extend the system to supply natural gas to China. The deal went sour after they made the Russian holding company hostage to exorbitant pricing of spares and support. In retaliation, Russia threatened to nationalize the pipelines, but it was a hollow gesture. Any move toward centralized control would have driven away badly needed international investment. Court action and political pressure from Washington finally convinced the consortium that such rapacious tactics were counterproductive to everyone's long-term business interests.

"Not our finest hour, I admit. Kari, you know I can pick up a phone and order the *Pyotr* sunk."

"You can, sir." Both of them knew it for the empty threat it was. Sinking the Russian cruiser without provocation would raise a storm of international indignation. Harford could go on TV and make his explanations, but who would believe him? And if Russia were to retaliate? Karijan knew it wouldn't. It could not afford to risk the delicate web of economic aid merely to salve its pride. How far they have sunk…

"Mr. Ambassador, I am not about to apologize for the way America conducts its business. It's a tough world out there, as you know. Europe hates our guts and the Japanese bow and smile and keep their markets locked while expecting an open-door policy from us. China is flexing its economic muscle and is sore at us over Taiwan. They're still amateurs in the international arena, but they're learning fast. I only have to look at what they're doing to us with currency manipulation. Despite everything, the US has no choice but to deal with all of them. With Russia, I do have a choice. Tell me why I have to deal with you?"

Karijan's smile was genuine. Harford did not attempt to dress things up or go all moralistic and he liked that.

"Because we can do business, Mr. President."

"What business?"

"Oil, sir."

Harford grunted like he'd been punched. Kari didn't have to explain. Much of America's foreign policy was colored by the need to pacify the Arabs, even when those countries openly harbored and financed international terrorist groups bent on destroying America and its interests. He only had to look at the last Iraqi war. The US was forced to swallow a lot of world criticism for the sake of its economy and the need to keep the people warm in winter. Having a secure independent supply would give his administration enormous freedom in what the US could do.

"I am listening."

"Russia has considerable reserves, sir. Reserves that could be developed to our mutual profit, while sidestepping, shall we say, delicate and intractable problems with your Arab sources. What we don't have is the necessary technology and infrastructure to exploit those reserves to their full potential. The Federation is prepared to supply you oil and natural gas at a considerable discount in exchange for joint and full cooperation with American corporations to develop new industries that will undoubtedly arise from the Comalcalco ship. The move may irritate OPEC and alarm the Europeans, but it would also unshackle American foreign policy, sir."

Harford kept his face impassive, but his heart raced. After Saudi Arabia, Russia held the largest oil and gas reserves on earth. For him to secure supplies that were not tied up in a web of political concessions would be a major coup. He doubted it would be enough for the Democrats to win the next election, but he felt comfortable with that. This was in America's interest, no matter who sat in the Oval Office.

"What about Mexico? They will squawk."

"May I suggest, sir, despite their brave rhetoric, they will soon find themselves in a similar position, forced to seek joint ventures with America. Politically, that might be sour grapes, as they would prefer to deal with someone else, like Europe, but you are a powerful neighbor whom they cannot ignore. They will deal with you. You can see where this is going, Mr. President. America will be in an overwhelming position to exploit the saucer while the rest of the world scrambles to catch up, hating you all the way."

"I can live with that."

"And if someone hates you enough to retaliate?"

"I can live with that too." Harford chewed his lip. "How would you get the oil to us?"

"Through Alaska, sir, under the Bering Strait. It wouldn't take much to extend the Siberian pipeline and drive it to Alaska where you can connect it to your existing infrastructure."

"Are you serious?"

"I am perfectly serious, sir."

Harford glanced at Morris, who shrugged.

"It could be done, Mr. President," the chief of staff said. "Of course, there will be a raft of technical and environmental problems to sort out, but nothing we can't handle."

Harford stood up and offered his hand. "Kari, you've given me something new to worry about, but I'm still nervous. If *Pyotr* does something stupid, it will find itself on the bottom, as will your fine country. As for your offer, please extend my warmest greetings to President Melnikov and tell him…tell him the United States will be happy to pool its resources for the peaceful exploitation of the Comalcalco saucer."

"As always, it has been a pleasure, Mr. President," Karijan said guardedly.

Morris escorted him out, then came back and poured himself another cup.

"It's an enticing proposal, Mr. President," he said without sitting down.

"Crafty little bastard," Harford murmured. "Why the hell didn't we think of this Alaska option ourselves?"

"Sand in our heads, sir."

"Yeah. He's right about Russia needing our help with the saucer." Harford shook his head in disgust. "See why I'm nervous? As God is in heaven, sooner or later someone is going to do something dumb and we'll end up shooting at each other. I almost wish the damned thing was never found."

Morris looked directly at his friend. "Mr. President, I think it's time we faced up to a fundamental truth. The Comalcalco saucer is no longer a question of maximizing our national competitive advantage. We've gone beyond that. What you decide in this room right now will determine how we treat the underprivileged of the world. Sure, the UN is seen to be running things at Comalcalco and the information is shared. Like Karijan said, it's all bullshit when they cannot do anything with it. It's like giving Congo a box full of plans for a nuclear reactor, then tell them their power problems have been solved. India is leading the charge, sir, but the others are not far behind. Africa and South America are already grumbling that they're sidelined, while the world's powerbrokers split the benefits among themselves. And they're right.

"For decades the world's major economies have been feeding a growing imbalance between the rich and the needy, generating powerful resentment along the way. That resentment is even more bitter this time because those countries know they're powerless to do anything about it. Mr. President, America was built on the backs of the poor and the unwanted of the world with one single idea in mind, personal freedom and an opportunity to make a better life for themselves. Somewhere along the line we've forgotten that, while the multinationals the world over have become ever more vocal in dictating not only our economic and foreign policies, but seek to shape the very fabric of our society, and not necessarily for the benefit of consumers they claim to represent."

"Quite a speech, Morris," Harford said after a time. "I agree with much of what you said, and under different circumstances, I would applaud your sentiment, but I have to deal with reality, not idealism."

"I would call it vision, sir."

"So? We may decry the predatory practices of some of the multinationals, but those same bastards also give Joe Smith his two-door garage, his TV and food on the table. They also give us one of the highest standards of living in the world."

"And we make everybody else pay for it, Mr. President. We rape third-world countries off their resources, then force them into a manufacturing and agricultural pattern of products and services useless to them, ensuring their servitude. While eating our fries and Big Macs, we shake our heads at the starving children in Ethiopia. To salve our conscience and because we're rich and great humanitarians, we send the poor bastards bags of wheat, proudly labeled 'Product of USA'! What that thirty-second sound bite fails to show, Mr. President, the reason why those children are starving is because the IMF forced their government to grow coffee in order to repay loans for a dam they didn't need in the first place!"

"We cannot hold everybody's hand!" Harford snarled. "If we let our guard down once, those European and Jap bastards will screw us into the ground! We *have* to play hardball—"

"With *them*, Mr. President! We don't have to do it with the likes of Ethiopia."

"You think the average voter out there gives a shit?"

"Perhaps it's time we all did, sir."

"Half the people in this country wouldn't even know where Ethiopia is."

"Doesn't say much for our education system, but we cannot have it both ways. We parade our military might around the world and rule Pax Americana. We cannot walk away from what we helped create. The values that mean so much to us don't stop at our borders. Democracy must be pushed along."

"With hard dollars, right? Morris, you cannot be this naïve. All right, let us pretend for a minute things are that simple—"

"Sometimes, that's the only way to get things done, sir.

We've allowed far too many issues to fester because we deluded ourselves that they're intractable, allowing the diplomatic process to bury us."

"Humph! All right. How would *you* handle it?"

"We just made a deal with Russia, Mr. President."

"More deals, eh?"

"The Chinese Ambassador—"

"Lieu Ching Hu is a little shit," Harford grated, and Morris smiled.

"He may be, but he'll be in this office tomorrow at ten a.m. What will you tell him, Mr. President?"

Harford groaned. "I don't know. And you're a shit as well for rubbing my nose in it."

"The buck stops with you, sir."

"Yeah. Okay, since I'm already worried, what else have you got?"

"Mr. President. We need to talk about the *Chosin* firing incident."

Harford scowled. "Nothing from the Serrll Moon Base?"

"No, sir."

"Bastards! That little scooter of theirs had no business messing near the *Constellation* battle group. Anyway, the damage is done now. What's our exposure?"

"Directly? Only the two F/A-18E pilots. For everyone else the contacts were merely blips on screens."

"Come on, Morris! What about the patrolling E-2C Hawkeye and the *Constellation's* CIC crews?"

"They saw nothing, Mr. President. And the two pilots saw nothing."

"What about the Russians?"

"Karijan would have said something if they wanted to play the publicity card."

Harford stared at his chief of staff, then smiled. "I bet that Russian captain peed himself when the Serrll ship came down on top of him. I'd have loved to see that."

Morris chuckled, then his face turned wooden. "Mr. President, the Serrll obviously know about the Comalcalco saucer."

"The question is, what are they going to do about it, right?"

"I know what *I* would do," Morris said softly.

"Yeah. Call the UN and get them to beef up site security."

\* \* \*

"No!" the aged Sargon Pro-Consul roared and with a sharp crack, slammed the palm of his hand against the black-veined stone desk. His wrinkled jowls were flushed and his long goatee trembled with emotion. He might be old, but he was still a powerful and commanding figure, used to intimidating his opponents by the sheer force of his presence and the unstated threat of physical violence his bulk exuded.

Ed-Kani not intimidated in any way, either by the Pro-Consul's imposing figure or the power the old man wielded in Sargon's Dumas Conclave parliament. Frankly, the old fossil had started to become a liability for the AUP Provisional Committee, becoming increasingly conservative and cautious, reactionary rather than visionary. Ed-Kani had another detail he could not allow himself to forget. The Pro-Consul was one of the figures who sought to have him removed from the General Assembly two years ago. That he was still here testified to his skill as a political operative. After handling Executive Council representatives, with the Pro-Consul, he wouldn't even have to spit out the bones.

Alone in the conference room, he waited as the holoview images around him stirred, their faces impassive, stamped with power and years of authority. Regrettably, that didn't mean they were exempt from acting like children. Was he the only one to see that the Committee had descended into complacency, becoming just another bureaucracy-driven club? He regretted that only two of their number were purged; an opportunity missed to bring in fresh blood and ideas. Perhaps it wasn't too late to remedy the oversight.

The full-dimensional Wall images made it appear like the others were all in the same room. He would have preferred the Committee met as a body, but hardly practical given the distances involved, and in his view, the current issue too important to be delayed by organizing a physical meeting. With BueCult security sniffing for them, bringing the members together would also be an invitation to exposure.

The room window screens were opaque and the walls glowed dull beige. A handcrafted tapestry adorned part of one wall, depicting the Battle of Anantor where the Sargon fleet met and routed Sofam's forces. A proud moment in their history and was the only decoration Ed-Kani allowed himself. He would see that pride returned if only the fools here could be stirred out of their comfortable complacency. Alone at the end of the long table, he drummed his fingers.

"Would the member care to explain himself?" he said tightly and the Pro-Consul glared back.

"Gladly! The Provisional Committee's goal will be pursued and will be achieved, but not like this! Lemos taught us the folly of hasty action—"

"Which you endorsed!"

"With grave reservations, if you recall!"

"They were not grave to you at the time!"

A withered, shrunken Palean Congressman banged his gavel and frowned in disapproval.

"Order! This is a free forum, but there are limits. Let's stick to the issue at hand. If you will, friend Pro-Consul."

"Thank you, Mr. Chairman," the Sargon member huffed. "The Dumas needs time to reorganize and consolidate, as does this Committee. I claim that we're not in a position to embrace another half-baked scheme simply because it holds superficial appeal. Have we forgotten already the price we all paid because of Lemos, and are still paying?"

"What I have forgotten when I look at you, Pro-Consul,"

Ed-Kani growled in disgust, "is Sargon turned moody and introspective, afraid of its own shadow. Where is your pride, old man? The problem with you, trade and profits now color your thinking and you have forgotten Sargon's heritage of independence and conquest. Paravan is not our enemy. It is soft, indulgent living that will conquer us all."

Outraged, the Pro-Consul rose and placed clenched fists on his desk.

"You…you dare talk to me of Sargon's heritage and soft living, Director? Where do you think bread and meat comes from to feed our people, if not from the profits you find so abhorrent? Climb down off your lofty Captal perch and see how your constituents subsist, then talk to me of soft living!" Without looking away, he pointed at the hanging tapestry. "That image is false history, a delusion. The days when our conquests were bought with the blood of our warriors and the steel of our ships are gone, and you're a fool to think of bringing them back. We use different tools now. This very Committee is a vivid example of the application of such a tool. Could it be, Mr. Director, that your objection is not with me, but with the possibility that failure to consummate the Sargon/Palean merger within the term of your office will rob you of a crowning career achievement?" The Pro-Consul's eyes blazed as he sat down to a ripple of murmuring and nodding of heads.

*Oh, you sly bastard*, Ed-Kani fumed.

He shifted and the formchair squirmed about him. The stone faces around the table were fixed on him and he could feel the rise in tension. The remark perceptive and hit too close to the truth. After a lifetime of commitment to Sargon, what was wrong with leaving a legacy of achievement? To have Greater Sargon a reality was worth striving for, worth some sacrifice and risk. If a little glory should happen to come his way because of it, why not? Great things were always realized by singular individuals who were willing to embrace the challenge.

It's not like he wanted more power or riches. A little recognition would do fine. He looked steadily at the Pro-Consul without allowing the turmoil of his emotions to betray him.

"We all have our individual ambitions to pursue, otherwise we wouldn't have reached for power," he said with quiet force. "I for one am not afraid to pursue my ambitions if they will further the Committee's cause, and I make no excuses for that. Granted, we've had a costly setback with Pizgor and Lemos, for which two of our members paid with their lives," he said and glanced pointedly at Ti Inai. "That, however, does not invalidate the merits of my proposal to you now. If we deliver the Fleet base to Rolan, I believe they will secede. The Committee will have its five systems and it won't cost us anything. I really don't understand your objection."

"The move can all too easily be misinterpreted. That's my objection," the Pro-Consul said stiffly. "If the Palean Congress was a unified block that fully supported the merger, I would say, let's go for it. But it's not. Your proposal, Director, could drive swinging Congressmen into Tao Karam's pro-Revisionist faction, which would set back our program for years. The cost to the Committee may be incalculable. It could mean the abandonment of a dream."

"With Italan lost, the cost to the Committee is already incalculable, Pro-Consul," Ed-Kani snapped. "If we're going to be candid, why shouldn't Sargon take advantage of an opportunity to secure a second Executive Council seat for itself? If some Palean Congressman's commitment to the merger is so shallow, and he feels outraged by this to cross the floor into Tao Karam's faction, then I don't want him anyway. We should be rallying the common Palean citizen to our banner, not just the politicians. Without genuine grass-roots support, we won't win and the Alikan Union Party *will* remain only a hollow dream. If the Committee cannot see this, then perhaps it's time we reconsidered our objectives."

Ti Inai squinted his large black eyes and regarded Ed-Kani

with a mixture of admiration and revulsion. He still smarted from the censure the Committee had passed against him, but it could have turned out much worse—terminally worse. Membership in the Committee was a life commitment, as two of them discovered. It could have been him marched out at gunpoint if he'd stayed on Captal. Italan was a debacle without doubt, but it had also been a calculated risk. Had Kai Tanard's raid against the Unified Independent Front delegates worked, instead of being chastised, he would now be hailed as a daring tactician. His long fingers twined in agitation. Such were the fates.

He cleared his throat.

"Friend Ed-Kani, no one here is questioning your commitment or dedication to the Provisional Committee or the merger," he piped smoothly and nodded around the table, gauging the effect of his words. "It is your tactics and perceived haste to achieve results that are in question. In that, the Pro-Consul has made a valid point. You have to understand that in the current climate, Congress is understandably wary of entanglements—speaking from personal experience," he said dryly, which raised a ripple of appreciative chuckles. "Like Sargon, we also need time to regroup." A murmur of agreement came from the Palean members. "Friend Pro-Consul's concerns are valid and the Committee should be cautious in how we handle Rolan. I don't speak for the Palean Union, but in principle, I approve your proposal. Rolan would remove the need for the Committee to seek the necessary systems from other potentially more difficult sources such as Kaleen, saving the Committee considerable time, expense and organizational effort currently being expended elsewhere, effort that can be spent neutralizing Tao Karam's faction." Effort he spent with loyal Alikan Union Party cells in pressuring outlying Kaleen systems to cede to the Palean Union. It wouldn't do to mention that here, not after what happened to Italan.

"However, the transaction will need to be handled carefully

to allay Palean fears that we're sidelined. The Committee's existence and its ability to function is based on equal partnership. Rolan has the potential to tip that balance too far in Sargon's favor and polarize not only the Committee, but to alienate the otherwise sympathetic Palean population as well. It might only be an issue of perception, but I don't think we would survive the ensuing backlash without adequate preconditioning of the populace. At the risk of stating the obvious, we are more than merely Palean and Sargon members sitting together. We're a nascent Alikan Union parliament-in-waiting. Do we want to jeopardize that by pursuing Rolan now, no matter how advantageous the short-term outcome? I submit that Rolan should be treated like any other option and the Committee not be rushed into hasty action that's driven by the Fleet's agenda."

Ed-Kani stared thoughtfully at Ti Inai, impressed with the Palean's sharp, incisive analysis, even if he didn't agree with it. He swept his gaze over the faces, allowing it to linger momentarily on the Pro-Consul before looking at Ti Inai again.

"That was well said. Another cautious, calculated approach, but misguided and an opportunity missed. However, I am not unreasonable. To remove any possibility of simmering resentment by the Palean Congress, I propose that Sargon make the Rolan Executive seat a revolving one, held by the Paleans after every other electoral session."

"Satisfactory," someone added, and there was an assenting nod of heads.

"That will contravene the Articles of Association," another voice pointed out. "One political block cannot hold or vote another's Executive seat."

"I meant once we are merged," Ed-Kani hissed with evident irritation at the other's obtuseness.

"There will not be any Sargon or a Palean Union then, only the Alikan Union," the same voice asked.

"What do you want to do?" Ed-Kani exploded. "Hold back simply because the Palean Union isn't ready to consummate the merger? We take our advantages as they're offered."

Ti Inai bobbed his head. Ed-Kani, always so impatient. One more thing needed to be said.

"Since this is at the core of our discussion, may I remind the Provisional Committee that the Palean Congress also tendered for the Fleet base."

"Pits! Why did you want to do that?" Ed-Kani demanded, clearly frustrated by the whole process.

Ti Inai's hands twined. "The Committee's existence has been revealed, friend Ed-Kani, and BueCult has a program to penetrate our organization. They will not be successful. Even if they are, the Committee's executive arm is untouchable and beyond prosecution. However, Captal's sensitivity to our activities, and particularly those of the more militant factions within the Alikan Union Party who BueCult feels carried out the attack on the Unified Independent Front's delegates, has alarmed the Security Council. The Bureau of Defense wants an increased Fleet presence in the Palean Union—"

"Set up a Fleet base just to send a message to the AUP?" Ed-Kani looked incredulous, furious at Illeran for not mentioning this development. Was this another one of Karkan's subtle byplays? Damn Illeran and all Karkans! And damn all Paleans!

"It is more than a message, friend Ed-Kani," Ti Inai piped, hands twining. "BueDef regards a militant AUP as a direct threat to Serrll stability. Of course, Congress is opposed to this and views it as illegal intervention into Palean internal affairs—"

"If a new base is going to be built, Congress wants it done on its terms, right?" Ed-Kani's cold eyes probed the Palean for several long seconds.

Ti Inai smiled urbanely, ignoring the penetrating stare. "A simple strategic initiative, driven by Tao Karam's faction."

"And your faction didn't have the numbers to defeat it," Ed-Kani growled in disgust.

"The Committee can accommodate this," Ti Inai said

sharply.

"I beg to differ. With Rolan in its hand, the Committee has an opportunity to secure another Executive seat. The Palean tender delivers nothing," Ed-Kani said stubbornly.

"The tender may be counterproductive for the Committee, friend Ed-Kani, but a new Fleet base will hold as much economic value for the Palean Union as it would for Sargon. If you truly see us as a united partner, it shouldn't *matter* where the base is located," he said smoothly, his oily smile designed to intimidate. The Palean Union may be going through a crisis, but that didn't mean we're ready to knuckle under to Sargon's demands.

"Have I lost the plot somewhere?" Ed-Kani queried, wearing a look of mock bewilderment. "We're here to secure Rolan's five systems, and with it, another Executive Council seat. Something I naively thought would be to our mutual advantage, and something that would aid our merger. The only way to achieve that advantage is to site the base in Rolan. The Palean Congress can give assurances to Captal that it will curb the militant arms of the AUP. We can exert some pressure there as well. Locating the base in the Palean Union on the basis of a possible AUP threat sometime in the future is unwarranted and does *nothing* for the Committee, as I said. An opportunity to seize an Executive seat doesn't come around every day and we should not squander this one with unnecessary posturing." He took a deep breath and glared at Ti Inai. The little worm shit should have been liquidated, not reprimanded!

"Let's table that argument for a moment and look at Rolan," the Chairman suggested. "How sure are we that Rolan is willing to give up its independence and secede?"

"What independence?" Ed-Kani demanded. "They maintain a comfortable fiction while going, begging bowl in hand to Sofam, bowing and scraping for the dubious privilege of accessing Sofam's markets. Access that's subject to crippling restrictions and punitive tariffs, while the Paravan Trading Association exercises open monopolies in Rolan's systems that stifle local industries. For what? So Rolan can pay exorbitant rates to Paravan for carrying their goods to the rest of the Serrll? They've been living that lie for too long."

"What about the other independents?" the Pro-Consul asked. "By ceding to Sargon, they could be perceived as abandoning the cause."

"Cause? Has any independent offered Rolan favorable trade concessions? They're all struggling to make ends meet just like Rolan."

"Well, I don't know," the Pro-Consul mused. "Orgomy and Kaleen have always been good and fair trade partners."

"In the past, yes. Can Rolan afford to count on that? Once they merge into the Unified Independent Front, they'll be too busy consolidating themselves to worry about Rolan."

"The Unified Independent Front, bah!" someone remarked. "A pest we should swat!"

A murmur of agreement rippled around the table.

"Order! Rolan will seek assurances before agreeing to any deal," the Chairman insisted.

"Of course. I would be disappointed if they don't," Ed-Kani said.

"Are we prepared to honor those assurances?" a cloaked Palean demanded to another ripple of murmuring.

"Why not? Even if Rolan demands autonomous status, the price will be worth it."

"I concur," the Pro-Consul said with an assurance that brooked no argument. He may bear personal animosity against Ed-Kani, but he could see advantages for Sargon in the deal.

"What of Rolan's assurances to us?" someone else asked. "We hand the base to Rolan, or the approval committee does, what's to stop Rolan from reneging on the deal?"

"If we win the bid," Ed-Kani said, "the articles of agreement must demand that Rolan formally announces its secession in the General Assembly. If they fail to comply, Sargon will reserve the right to occupy them by force. To defuse the likelihood of any intervention by the Assembly or by Sofam, we should seek to ratify the articles by the Executive Council. Once that's done, Rolan will find it very difficult to break the agreement."

"They can always declare themselves independent again," a voice echoed everyone's unspoken thoughts. The Pro-Consul grinned, his sharp little teeth glistening.

"The Committee needs to be reminded that Sargon has never lost a system through secession. Rolan, I am sure, will be equally aware of that fact."

"It's naïve of us to expect that any discussions between Sargon and Rolan will remain closed. The Committee must consider fallback positions should Sofam become involved. For all we know, they may have approached Rolan with the same offer."

"Why would they do that?"

Ed-Kani's grin was cold. "To stop Sargon from getting another Executive seat? What do you think?"

The Chairman regarded Ed-Kani, then nodded. He was still not convinced the Committee should pursue Rolan, but he was willing to keep the discussion open—for now. When the conversation died, he looked at the expectant faces and banged his gavel.

"I move that the AUP Provisional Committee advances discussions with Rolan for the secession. Seconds?"

Ed-Kani raised his hand.

Bang!

"Carried!"

* * *

Dawn was a pearly display of soft sunlight, hanging mist, clear skies and a promise of another fine day. A distinct odor

231

of frying bacon, eggs, hash browns, and other breakfast smells filled the compound. Tendrils of white smoke drifted into the still air from colorful campsites that dotted the low hills to the north. A quiet time of day before the soldiers started moving about and the protesters began their endless chants. Some of them made half-hearted attempts to breach the exclusion perimeter. So far, no one had yet mounted a determined effort to test the military's resolve.

Looking past the accommodation huts, the sagging tents, the parked helicopters, trucks and stacked supply crates, Lauren imagined the place empty again, covered by unspoiled lawns and the quiet majesty of the temples holding a silent vigil over this magical land. An odd group of tourists brandishing cameras and camcorders would gawk and marvel at the monuments, while their guide filled their imaginations with tales of glory, riches and enchantment. A grand vision, but false. She pressed her lips and the image faded, leaving behind a drab reality. More than anyone, she knew that blood and tears had colored this land, and conquest and suffering was the lot of its people, not glory and riches.

A metal door clanged shut behind her and she turned her head. Martin beamed at her and nodded.

"A glorious morning, doc," he said brightly and stopped beside her. He placed both hands on his chest and inhaled deeply. "If we could bottle this air and sell it to uptown New York, we'd make a fortune."

Lauren smiled. Taking a deep breath herself, she agreed the air had a crispness and freshness to it that invigorated.

Bill emerged from the mess tent and waved. "A great day, isn't it?" he said as he joined them.

Lauren beamed at his infectious enthusiasm. His eyes softened when he looked at her and something passed between them—an understanding and an acceptance. Last night's moment of brief intimacy had been disturbing, thrilling and disquieting. She didn't sleep well, her mind filled with doubts and questions. Was it simple flirtation, hormones gone into over-drive? She'd had relationships, but they were fleeting, transitory things that satisfied her immediate needs and didn't touch her core as Bill's melting eyes did. She recalled the feel of his firm lips on hers, the prickly scrape of his stubble, and a shiver ran through her.

Looking into the green depths of his eyes, she suspected his night had also been a restless one.

"You guys going to the ship?" Bill asked, wanting to reach out and draw her against him. His hunger must have been transparent, for her lips parted in silent amusement.

"We need to get some work done before the rest of you take over," she said.

"Like what we're doing isn't important, right?"

"Toys for boys."

"Ha! I know what toy I would like in my Christmas stocking."

Lauren's eyebrows arched. "Why, Dr. Faroway! I do believe you're flirting with me."

"Absolutely, Dr. Hopking," he growled and glared at the bemused Martin. "Take her away and don't let her touch any buttons."

"You got it, doc," Martin said. He watched Dr. Faroway disappear into his hut and turned to Lauren, who raised a finger.

"Don't even think it!" she warned and walked easily toward the chamber entrance. Her trim form filled her Levi's in all the right places and Martin admired the view until she turned the corner, then gave a resigned sigh and followed.

Inside, the doc was pouring herself a cup of coffee and fielding a sassy remark from Zaminski. Yesterday, the Russian looked gloomy and moody, but the bright morning seemed to have lifted his spirits. Having a natural skepticism of all governments, Martin had a morbid curiosity at the workings of bureaucracies and often wondered what it would be like to be a fly on the wall when Zaminski and Chee had their daily satellite link with their respective masters. Of course, he saw plots and conspiracies in everything, and he firmly believed some of them might even be true.

"Ah, Martin!" Zaminski boomed. "Have a cup of this excellent Mexican coffee and try to explain to the lovely doctor here that figuring out what makes this amazing craft fly is equally important as finding out where it came from. After all, if we could build a pitch drive, we could go and return this museum piece to the aliens. Heh heh."

Martin couldn't help himself and chuckled. He liked being around the burly Russian—mostly. When Zaminski assumed his professional persona the joviality vanished and in its place stood a prominent world scientist. The Russian's bulk hid a lot, Martin decided.

"I'm afraid explanations wouldn't do us much good, Doctor," he said, looking sad. "Once the lady makes up her mind the best thing to do is hang on and enjoy the ride."

Zaminski's heavy laugh reverberated through the chamber and Lauren glared.

"Martin Teller! It's the corner for you!"

Still chuckling, Zaminski wiped his eyes and gave Martin a hearty slap on the back. Martin staggered and winced.

"Forget archaeology, my boy! It's a waste of time, a waste of time. If you switch to plasma physics, I will see to it that you graduate with honors from Moscow University."

"If I lived through the winter."

"Bah! It is nothing. A Russian winter puts backbone into a man!"

"Yeah, I heard. It's called ice."

Zaminski laughed again. "That was good. I like it. You would make a good Russian, Martin, and you have the required sense of humor to survive my country."

Babich walked in with Sheppard in tow. The two had become inseparable and were always arguing about something. A clash of brilliant minds, which Faroway as a general synthesist, did nothing to dampen. Hiro and Chee trailed in after them and the chamber suddenly became a loud and crowded place. Martin stepped away from the fast-depleting urn and quietly sipped his coffee. It really was good. He glanced at Lauren, but the doc did not seem to be in a hurry to get to work, which suited him just fine. Listening to the scientists was an education beyond price.

"Rubbish!" Zaminski boomed and prodded Babich in the chest. "The problem, my dear colleague, the computer is assuming a level of basic knowledge we simply don't have. It was designed to explain processes, as Dr. Hiro succinctly pointed out, not the underlying theoretical concepts."

"If you stick that thing at me again, I'll bite it off," Babich growled.

"My apologies," Zaminski said, not looking at all apologetic, and slowly withdrew his finger.

"The other problem we have is that all the displays are three-dimensional, and we can only record them in two," Kopan lamented.

"We could remove some of the panels and start examining the fusion torus," Sheppard suggested hopefully. Kopan immediately shook his head.

"I cannot agree to that, Doctor. The cranes and the flatbed will be here this afternoon. Tomorrow, we start removing the roof capstones. It would be foolish to expose the saucer's interior to needless contamination. Besides, we don't have the equipment to properly study the drive assemblies. Once we're at the Villahermosa facility—"

"Just a thought," Sheppard remarked, clearly disappointed.

"We must contain ourselves and concentrate our efforts on what is achievable now," Zaminski said, then grinned wickedly. "It would be fun to start pulling the thing apart, no?"

"If the computer lets you," Lauren said quietly and heads

turned in astonishment. "Has anyone noticed that since we activated the computer, it has never been down? How do we shut it off?"

"Order it," Hiro said and Lauren shrugged.

"Perhaps."

"All the more reason not to do anything hasty before we know what we're doing," Kopan commented.

"My dear Doctor, we want to pull the thing apart because we *don't* know what we're doing," Sheppard said with a weary smile.

"My man!" Zaminski boomed and gave him a hug.

Martin felt a pull on his arm and turned. Lauren jerked her head toward the saucer and strode off. He drained the last of his coffee and placed the cup next to the empty urn.

"Excuse me," he mumbled and squeezed himself past Chee and Babich. He walked slowly around the saucer and absently reached up to run his fingers along the raspy surface. When he signed up for this dig, he expected to do lots of shoveling, sifting and boring cataloging. He'd certainly had his share of that, but he never imagined events would lead him to this fantastic discovery, not in a million years. Did the doc suspect the saucer was here all the time? Dr. Hopking was many things, but foremost, she was a hard-nosed professional whose feet were firmly planted in the scientific method. Still, he had fun speculating.

He climbed the steps and looked about, amazed yet again at what he was seeing. The functional simplicity of the flight deck belayed the awesome sophistication of the underlying technology that produced this ship and the culture that supported it. After five thousand years, what were the aliens like now?

"Good morning, Martin," the computer said pleasantly.

"Hi. How's things?"

"Everything is functioning smoothly, thank you."

"Careful of the cameras," Lauren warned him from the right seat.

Facing the center display screen were two video cameras mounted on tripods. He gingerly craned his head past one of them and peered at the screen, which slowly scrolled through 3-D schematics of the ship's systems. The UN photo gofer had set up the equipment last night and presumably, someone changed memory cartridges. His camera and stand waited near the steps.

"What's the program, doc?"

"Martin, have you started your thesis paper?"

"I have an outline," he said defensively, thrown off stride by her question. Lauren looked at him without expression. "Really! I have over 12,000 words and stacks of notes, but I want to change the subject."

"Oh?"

"I want to write about this ship—"

"Forget it!"

"But—"

"I said, forget it. This ship isn't archaeology, Martin, and you're an archaeology major. Stick to your original research. That's all solid and recognized work. You don't want to upset the accreditation committee. Not now. You're aiming for a bachelor's degree, not a Pulitzer."

The accreditation committee being Dr. Hopking, the message loud and clear.

"I'll give you the outline," he said stiffly.

Lauren sighed, stood up and placed her hands on his shoulders. Her eyes were large and captivating and her scent shot a hormone rush through his body.

"Martin, listen to me. You're a most promising student, but you must remain focused, or that scholarship will evaporate. Nothing must stand in your way of getting that PhD. Without a PhD, you might as well resign yourself to being a glorified gravedigger, while someone else less talented grabs the glory. You can write about the ship for your master's, by coursework."

Coursework was usually by invitation only and meant publishing papers. He could have his degree in twelve months—on the course advisor's recommendation, of course.

Stunned, he stared at her. "I...I don't know what to say, doc."

She patted his shoulder and stepped back. "I look after my best. While you're working on your bachelor's, we can collaborate on a couple of papers so you can get the hang of it."

His name with the doc's? He could have kissed her then. It must have shown, for she grinned at him.

"I'm sorry as hell, doc, for thinking you were shutting me out."

"Idiot! Let's get to work."

# Chapter Nine

"Mr. President, the People's Republic of China Ambassador, Dr. Lieu Ching Hu," the White House chief of staff announced solemnly and extended his hand through the open doorway.

Ching nodded to Morris and strode briskly into the Oval Office. He stood on the great seal and extended his hand. Taller than most Chinese, plump, dressed tastefully in a very fine and delicate dark-gray gabardine suit that could have come straight out of London. Relatively young for his post, only fifty-two, he looked younger. But then, as with the Japanese, the Chinese looked young for a long time before they were suddenly worn out and old.

"Welcome to the White House, Mr. Ambassador," Harford said as they shook hands. "Make yourself comfortable. Tea?"

"Your summons could not be ignored, Mr. President," Ching said smoothly as he sat down. He waited politely as Morris poured him a cup of green tea from an excellent Chinese porcelain pot. Probably a gift from some past dignitary.

As a relative newcomer to Washington, having replaced a long-standing incumbent, he was still learning how to navigate through the labyrinthine corridors of Congress and the White House machinery. He might be naïve in the finer nuances of Western etiquette, but he understood very well the rules of realpolitik as the game was played on the international stage. He did not love or hate America. To him, the US was merely a powerful player his country had to deal with. His attitude would have shocked his superiors, but that didn't prevent him from enjoying himself while carefully having built important relationships with several select Congressmen from both sides of the House and the Senate. He took the long view when dealing with

America.

Harford settled himself and regarded his visitor with undisguised interest. He knew Ching as a progressive thinker, as far as allowed within the Chinese Communist Party, and had powerful backers within the Central Military Commission and a number of influential PLA generals. He rode the wave of reform brought on by internal economic pressure and expanding world interests, which finally forced the Communist Party to embrace elements of a free market economy—the Chinese have always been pragmatists. That did not mean they have embraced capitalism. Ideological isolationism was all very well, but did nothing to feed a growing population, birth control notwithstanding. Keeping the masses happy also kept the ruling clique in power. The same principle applied in America, Harford reflected. Only the methods differed. Looking at his visitor, he found it hard to read emotion in that clay face. He decided Ching played the faceless man well.

"We have a potentially unsettling situation off Mexico, Mr. Ambassador," Harford said without any preamble or pretense, although a gross breach of protocol. "I am again asking the People's Republic to withdraw its destroyer. Its presence is provocative and is a source of needless international tension, which cast a dark shadow over the cooperative and otherwise successful effort at Comalcalco."

Ching's face remained expressionless and he hoped his discomfort wasn't showing, although shocked by the president's blunt approach. It confirmed again that he dealt with uncultured barbarians—albeit dangerous ones. Secretly, he agreed with the president, but Beijing's instructions were clear.

"Mr. President, my government is aware of your meeting with Ambassador Miroslavski. Of course, we don't know the substance of your discussions, but we can guess easily enough. The Russian Federation is not the Soviet Union and no longer commands the respect it once held, or economic influence. Mr.

President, the People's Republic of China is a growing and influential power on the world's stage. Any move to limit our freedom in expressing ourselves politically or economically is viewed with disagreeable concern."

"Mr. Ambassador, as I told Ambassador Miroslavski, I will tell you *my* concern. Every country in the world has unfettered access to information gathered at Comalcalco. Once the craft is permanently housed at Villahermosa, with proper equipment and research facilities the possibilities for everyone can only be seen as exciting. The presence of one of your country's warships suggests to me that your government is questioning the integrity of the UN investigation, one that you approved! If you have specific concerns, I would advise you to raise them with the UN."

Ching admired Harford's approach. The problem was that Beijing *couldn't* fault the UN effort. Reports sent in by Dr. Zuang Kui Chee were thorough as they were damning. Time to lay the issue on the table.

"Mr. President, the People's Republic has nothing but praise for the efforts made by the UN teams in Comalcalco and Geneva. Our concern is—"

"What you perceive as the unfair technological advantage the US enjoys in its capability to exploit that information," Harford said with a wintry smile. China may be feeling its political and economic muscle, but they still face many of the same problems that held Russia embroiled in a mess largely of its own making. Despite China's proud rhetoric the two were not all that different.

Only sheer effort of will prevented Ching from biting his lip. Well, he wanted the issue on the table and the American would not be deceived. He understood enough to realize this was simply business. Helping China to expand its technological base, develop new industries and expand its world markets would harm America's global trading interests. Ideologies aside, one did not help a competitor.

"To use one of your quaint colloquialisms, Mr. President, what will it take?"

Harford smiled. "The United States is prepared to enter into a full and cooperative venture with the People's Republic in the peaceful development of the Comalcalco saucer—"

"Provided—"

"China acknowledges Taiwan as an independent and sovereign state, and that it relinquishes all territorial claims to the island," Harford said bluntly and raised his hand. "Before you say anything, Mr. Ambassador, let's have a reality check. Taiwan may be an ideological thorn in the side of your leadership, and I'm not discounting the historical importance of their position, but in practical terms it's a non-issue. China has already established an open trade relationship with Taiwan, and movement between the two countries is practically unrestricted. Build on that. A shift in your position will result in immediate and tangible benefits, economic as well as political. It costs me a lot of money to keep the Seventh Fleet loitering in your backyard, and frankly, Mr. Ambassador, the United States is getting tired of it. More importantly, the gesture will signal to the world that China has at last shed its narrow parochial position and is ready to join the community of nations as a mature power. Urge President Janse Leong to withdraw the ship."

"You speak eloquently, Mr. President, but there is, of course, a corollary."

Harford nodded and his face grew hard. "To avoid any possibility of a misunderstanding, sir, I will be direct. Should your destroyer take hostile action against Comalcalco, it will be sunk without warning. Moreover, the US will immediately revoke China's most favored trading nation status and I'll invoke unilateral economic sanctions. My UN ambassador will also be calling for general worldwide sanctions. The IMF and the World Bank will freeze your international assets. Your accounts here will be seized. While the destroyer remains on station, any attempt to move funds from those institutions will be blocked.

Should the People's Republic decide to deploy a nuclear weapon against Comalcalco, a state of war will exist between our two countries. Is all that clear to you, Mr. Ambassador?"

Ching listened hard to every word as Harford talked, looking for hidden meanings, but the language had been altogether clear, if shockingly blunt. He relished this aspect of the American character, so far removed from the silken nuances and veiled plots and hidden counterplots that colored so much of Chinese approach to politics. Nevertheless, his skin crawled and he found the atmosphere in the room decidedly chilly. He did not doubt at all that America would do exactly what Harford had said, but would his superiors be as convinced? Well, he came to find out the extent of American commitment, and he certainly got that.

He stood up, not having touched his tea.

"Mr. President, I fully appreciate the frankness and gravity of your words, which I shall convey to my government."

"When you're conveying, convey this as well. At eleven a.m. today, the United States will make an announcement to the General Assembly, deploring the posture adopted by the Russian Federation and your country. The announcement will include our reaction to any hostile act committed by either power. Good day to you, sir."

Morris escorted Ching out and closed the heavy white door after him.

"Maybe I was a bit hard on him, but I enjoyed wiping that smug superior expression off his face," Harford growled, glanced at the teapot and winced. He leaned across his desk and pressed the intercom button to his personal aide.

"Yes, Mr. President?"

"Rachel, bring me a fresh cup of coffee."

"Yes, sir."

"I wouldn't worry too much about grasshopper—" Morris began.

"Grasshopper?"

"Kung Fu, Mr. President."

"Ah."

"Ching's forays into Western humor, sir. At any rate, he doesn't have any feelings. He is hardboiled as they come."

"Bastard! I won't have these standover tactics. I tell you, if they let off a popgun, I'll fry their ass. Advise Space Command that we could have trouble and place Brilliant Mirror on ready alert."

"That will not stop an SS-N-26 if *Kiensan* squirts one off," Morris pointed out quietly.

Just then, the door opened and Rachel walked in with a steaming cup of coffee.

"Thanks, and you can take that stuff away," Harford said, indicating the tea set.

Rachel smiled, picked up the tray and hurried out.

"I hate tea," Harford growled and took a sip. "Give me good old American coffee—"

"Brazilian actually, Mr. President."

"Whatever. Anyway, if the Chinese light off a cruise missile, we're screwed. I know that. Let's hope the bastards are smart enough not to make it nuclear, for as God is in heaven, I'll level them."

"They've waited too long, Mr. President, and made a tactical error. If they planned to do so, they should have fired at the saucer as soon as *Kiensan* came into range. Now, it's too late. We already have enough technical data to start some very interesting research. The fact they *haven't* fired—"

"Shows they realize the consequences. I hope to God you're right, Morris."

* * *

Holding the warm coffee mug between her hands, Lauren watched with mixed feelings as two self-propelled cranes lumbered into the compound. She winced as the caterpillar tracks left horrible wounds in the lawn. After everyone left, the site would need a major makeover before again fit for tourists. With trucks, jeeps and cars coming and going the place looked like a used car lot. A burly sergeant windmilled his left arm and pointed angrily at Temple I. The leading crane driver waved and brought the unwieldy machine to a clanking stop at the base of the temple. The second crane parked itself beside it.

Bill paused, saw Lauren outlined against the sunset's orange glow and marveled at her poise. Remarkable that someone so young should have such a commanding presence. This was one formidable lady. He walked to her and stood beside her.

"Our little hideaway has been invaded," he said softly.

"It couldn't last," she murmured wistfully without looking at him, then pointed at the low hills. "I do wish they would go away."

"A lot of them already have."

She turned. "And who is left? The troublemakers?"

"Or extremists. It's a long way to Villahermosa, and there is always some nut out there willing to blow himself up for a cause. I would hate to be the man responsible for transporting the saucer."

"Yes." She took a sip of coffee. "Why don't they simply fly it out? By a lift helicopter, I mean."

"Too heavy, I'd guess. I'm sure somebody must have looked into it."

"Don't count on it," Lauren said darkly and watched as the two crane drivers climbed down and began an argument with the irate sergeant. "An order is given and brains are switched off."

He chuckled. "You could be right. Anyway, it's out of our hands."

"Like that speech we made to the UN this morning? God, I feel so helpless. I expect a cruise missile to come whistling in at any moment and blast us to dust."

"No one is going to be that stupid, Lauren."

"No? The Russian and Chinese ships are here on a summer tour, right?"

"My, Dr. Hopking, your cynical streak is showing."

She smiled and punched him on the shoulder. "Idiot!"

"So, how is the research going?" he asked, massaging the tender bicep. The lady had a hard fist.

"We only made a scratch. With everyone trying to cram a month's work into one day, it gets pretty crowded in the ship, but I did get some tantalizing glimpses. As an archaeologist, astronomy was the last thing on my mind, but I'm getting the hang of it. The main problem is to establish a common frame of reference with the computer. When it mentioned some place called Salina, I couldn't tell whether it was talking about a star or a planet."

"And which is it?"

"Salina? It's a planet. Actually it's fairly close, about forty-six light-years."

"You call that close?"

"Bill, I haven't got it all yet. What we have here are one hundred and thirty-four inhabited systems spread over eight hundred light-years, two hundred and eighty-six planets, and hundreds of occupied moons and asteroids. If I read the data right, one of them is our Moon."

He gave a low whistle.

"You have to remember, this was the setup five thousand years ago," she reminded him. "Probably nothing there now."

"You got all that from just reading navigational data?"

"Yes, but don't you realize what it means?"

"That we're dealing with a very advanced and organized culture."

"More organized than you might think. Martin asked the computer about different languages, something one would expect if we're talking about coexisting species. But there is only one language. What does that tell you?"

"Well…" He frowned and his brow knitted. "Either all

those systems are occupied by a single race, unlikely, but not impossible, or—"

"We're talking about a level of socio-political integration among a number of species who have agreed to use a single common working language. Logical when you think about it. It also suggests a society that's relatively stable and probably peaceful, at least peaceful enough for the concept to work."

"A shaky conclusion to draw on such scant data, Lauren," he said and she smiled. Her name sounded so much nicer when he said it.

"I'm just starting, smarty. Lots more work needs to be done before I would dare publish even a tentative analysis."

"You're not doing too badly now, but have you considered this one? If five thousand years ago the aliens had a social structure such as the one you propose—"

"What are they like now? Believe me, I have thought about it. All those stories of flying saucers and alien abductions suddenly take on a new meaning. There is an even more important question. What were the aliens doing on Earth then?"

"Molding man's fragile humanity?" he offered and she snorted.

"A romantic notion, but hardly scientific."

"Sometimes you have to reach beyond science," he murmured and reached for her, her back against him, his hands across her belly.

The afternoon sun still bright, but the harsh glare had faded and the sky looked softer, darker blue. Thin streamers of cloud hung low in the south, bathed in yellows and reds. Bright lines of silver colored their edges. She stared at the sky and the clouds and was at peace. She felt Bill's hand rest lightly on hers and drew comfort from his touch.

"Lauren, we need to talk," he said softly.

Was it only last night that he'd kissed her? She felt a flush spread through her body and turned to face him. His eyes glinted deep green and she lifted her head. Still holding her hand, he wrapped it behind her back and pulled her against him. The coffee mug fell from her nerveless fingers. She closed her eyes and waited. His breath smelled of cheese and pickles as his mouth covered her lips in a fleeting touch. Teasingly, he pulled away, then their lips met again. His mouth firm without being hard, she squirmed when his tongue coaxed her mouth open. The velvety embrace made her moan. She fancied she heard someone whistle. After an eternity of wild sensations, he pulled away and she stared into his eyes. She saw tenderness and desire and love in those eyes, and smiled.

"Doesn't this say it all?" she purred teasingly.

"You know what I mean," he said gruffly.

"Bill, don't be so right now. We'll talk, later. Let's join the party before Zaminski eats everything in sight. It's our last night together as a group and I want to savor it. Let's not rush what we started."

He frowned, then gave in. She was right. They have made a tentative beginning and Lauren was not a woman to be pushed around. He'll have to be careful not to start taking her for granted, not that he ever would, being far too independent to allow herself to be manipulated. He'd already learned that beneath her lovely exterior lay a core of steely determination. It will be interesting to see how far he would manage to bend it.

"What are you smirking at?" she demanded.

"Savoring the thought of putting you across my knees and spanking you."

"I wouldn't advise it," she said frostily. "I bite."

"No doubt. And other things besides."

"Guaranteed, Dr. Faroway."

He gave a throaty laugh and pulled her arm. "Let's join the others, then."

Only some hundred feet to the mess tent, but neither of them was in any hurry to get there, even if it was everybody's last night here. Tomorrow, the saucer would be moved to Vil-lahermosa and they would lose that closeness of spirit built over the last few days. He stole a sidewise glance at her, admiring her tall, slim form, appreciating the effort she made with her attire for the evening.

Her hair piled high and held in place by a slender pearl in-laid clip. The rich cream of her dress, bunched around the shoulders, plunged to a ruffled V above her breasts. He wanted to reach with his fingers and feel their secret swell and softness. A single pearl on a thin black choker decorated her delicate throat. She looked elegant and ladylike in light brown two-inch heeled shoes with slender black straps that held her feet.

He gently squeezed her hand.

He enjoyed holding her hand. He enjoyed the feel of her delicate, yet strong, fingers entwined with his. It gave him a sense of intimacy and closeness far more electric than he expected from a simple touch. He and Dheera had never touched, at least not like this. On reflection, that relationship now seemed shallow and stilted, a mere physical encounter. The feel of Lauren's hand filled spaces he never knew were empty.

His little squeeze conveyed a wealth of emotion to Lauren. A tiny doubt worked its way through her mind. Would Bill still feel the same way about her once their intimacy progressed to the next level? That they would make love was the inevitable next step, the thought of which sent tiny prickles of anticipation racing across her skin. Careful dearie, men only want one thing, a tiny voice of pessimism whispered to her. Once their desire was satisfied, their eyes turned to other conquests. That was unfair, she knew, but she couldn't banish the demon of doubt. Was she that insecure?

Bill wouldn't do that to her, or she'd break his balls! The image left an impish smile on her face.

They reached the tent and, judging by the noise inside, everyone seemed to be enjoying themselves. Bill pulled back the flap and stood back to allow her to get in. She gave him a small curtsy.

"Thank you, kind sir."

"My lady," he said stiffly and offered his bent arm.

Before she could react, Zaminski spotted them and beamed.

"Lauren! I was starting to worry—"

"About me?"

"No! Dr. Faroway!" he boomed and his ample belly heaved as he laughed. "Come on in," he said and reached for her hand. "You look radiant in that dress, my dear."

She preened and gave Bill a helpless shrug as Zaminski led her away.

Babich pressed a glass of pale Mexican wine into her hand. He glared and shook a finger at Zaminski.

"You behave yourself now."

"I've been a perfect gentleman," Zaminski lamented with a hurt look. "Haven't I, Dr. Hopking?"

"He's been a lamb."

"There!"

"I would watch him anyway," Babich said darkly.

"Not much chance of missing him," she said and patted Zaminski's generous belly, which caused Babich's eyes to sparkle.

"It's a pity, Lauren, that you American women are all so skinny, otherwise you would make a fine Russian wife," Zaminski said, looking wistful.

"Our winters are not as long or as demanding, Doctor," Bill said and flashed Lauren a possessive smile.

"I bet you could keep me warm," she said teasingly and bumped Zaminski with her hip.

"Ah, you're flirting with me again, but beware the bear's claws, my dear."

The UN steward announced that dinner was served and everyone made their way toward the long table. It was only natural that the officers and scientists tended to cluster in their own groups. The only observed protocol was to seat the colonel commanding the UN detachment—a mean looking thin-lipped little German—and Babich as head of the investigative team, at opposite ends of the table.

Dinner turned into a lively affair. Living in tight cramped quarters for a week, the team members had learned to tolerate each other's idiosyncrasies and built a bond cemented by a common purpose. Discussions were free and hot, and even Chee managed several fleeting grins between composing rejoinders to Sheppard's probing verbal thrusts. He didn't mind the mild ribbing, but the evening weighed heavily on him.

He stared absently at his plate, then looked up with a start. "Excuse me?"

"I was saying, Dr. Chee," Sheppard said with an indulgent smile, "I will feel a whole lot better once the saucer is out of here."

"I agree. Villahermosa—" Kopan began with an enthusiastic nod, but Chee didn't hear him.

"And why is that?" he asked softly, knowing the answer. Suddenly, it became very quiet around the table, and faces turned to Sheppard. Unfazed, he plowed on.

"We will no longer be a target."

"My country—"

"Is misguided, my friend," Sheppard said to a supportive ripple of agreement. Zaminski knew exactly what Chee was going through and glared.

"We are scientists, Dr. Sheppard. Our governments may behave like children, but that isn't an excuse that we should."

"Besides, if someone decided to do something foolish, Villahermosa will be just as vulnerable," Bill added.

"I disagree, Dr. Faroway," the German colonel said from his end of the table. "Villahermosa is a city with a considerable population. Russia and China may seek to destroy the saucer for their own ends, but to strike at a foreign city would be tantamount to a declaration of war."

"As a military man, Colonel Kessler, when would *you* do it? Speaking hypothetically, of course," Bill said.

"I would strike while the saucer is still here. Speaking hypothetically, of course."

"That would still mean a declaration of war, Colonel," Kopan said darkly.

Babich gave his wine goblet a sharp rap.

"We're supposed to be celebrating, not holding a council of battle." He picked up his glass and nodded to Chee. "To a successful mission, Doctor."

Chee was grateful for those words and smiled warmly as he raised his glass.

"And to an even more rewarding one once we're all at Villahermosa."

Babich chuckled, then glared at the others. "Well?"

Everyone hastily picked up their glass and Sheppard grinned ruefully.

"I apologize for my lack of tact, Dr. Chee. I didn't mean to scratch any sores."

"It isn't important," Chee said. His cell phone went off and he plunged a hand into his pocket.

"Throw the damn thing away," Sheppard growled. "We're supposed to be enjoying ourselves."

"Excuse me," Chee mumbled and pressed the phone to his ear. His face expressionless, but his lips tightened as he switched off the phone.

"Bad news?" Sheppard asked.

"I'll be back in a moment," Chee said and hurried out.

"Now what the devil was all that about?" Babich demanded, staring after the figure.

Outside, Chee sagged and his legs trembled. Taking a deep breath, he walked briskly toward the mound. The guards hardly glanced at him as he went into the chamber. Inside, he paused and looked at the alien ship for one last time. Without thinking, he placed his palm against the hull, savoring the warmth of its skin.

He walked to the instrument bench and pulled out the

Nokia cell phone. He stood there for a moment and stared at it. He had no choice, never had, the two words of his controller still ringing loud in his ears. *Dragon fire*, that was all. It was enough. Chee detected uncharacteristic tension in the other's voice. After listening to the American announcement at the UN, easily accounted for.

He entered the five nines and pressed the hash key. The small color screen cleared and displayed the standard menu. He locked the keypad and placed the phone beside the mass spectrograph. On the table, the phone looked innocent, not at all the harbinger of death it now was. When the SS-N-26 went into its terminal phase, it would send out a signal and the cell phone would activate, guiding the missile unerringly to its target. Not religious, he gave a silent prayer for sanity and restraint. Perhaps his superiors were right and the world would be better off without the saucer. What would happen to his country when the Americans retaliated? He was absolutely certain they would. Feeling a thousand years old, he turned and walked slowly out of the chamber.

The dinner concluded in a cheerful atmosphere. Afterward, everyone broke into little groups, waving cigars and brandy balloons. As the only woman there, Lauren came in for more than her share of attention, but she handled male-dominated groups before and knew how to divert unwanted advances. When the atmosphere began to get a bit thick and a little too boisterous, she broke away and went outside. The air crisp and smelled sweet, unlike her dress, which reeked of cigar smoke. Her nose wrinkled at the powerful stink. High in the east the fat quarter Moon buttery yellow, waxed into full bloom. Bright enough to cast thick black shadows over the ground. She spent a moment looking at it.

There was a soft crunch of gravel behind her and she tensed expectantly. His footsteps stopped and she felt his hand reach for hers. They stood in silence, content to enjoy each other's company, content to feel each other's touch. His close-ness made her feel safe and protected, and she savored the feel-ing. It wasn't protection from physical danger; she'd been on some rough field trips and could take care of herself. Something else, something deeper and instinctive. His hand soft, warm and comforting, and the moon had paled as it climbed into a star-studded sky. A rich sky, not the washed out imitation seen from her New York apartment.

Then she understood. Bill wasn't demanding anything. He didn't attempt to take over her life or launch into a male macho display of dominance. He was quietly happy for her to sort things out for herself, not sure whether to be flattered or an-noyed at his perceptiveness, and almost smiled. Instead, she squeezed his hand and tugged his arm.

She sat down in the loom of Temple I's side and patted the brick step beside her. Bill grinned and sat down. The mess tent glowed pearly white and shadowy figures moved inside. The conversation loud, but muffled.

"You've decided to stay with the team," he said, making it a statement.

"I'm flying back to New York tomorrow, but I'll be back—"

"Even if you have to face Imatlan?" he said teasingly.

"I won't even notice him. I need to tie up a few things with Boulcher for the second semester. Three or four days at most, and the best thing about it, the UN will be paying for every-thing," she said brightly and gave a delighted laugh. "The Uni-versity was very happy to learn they won't be footing the bill for my flights. And I kind of like the idea of globetrotting first-class. I could get used to it."

He grinned at her enthusiasm, then turned to look at her directly.

"I'm glad you decided to stay, Lauren. You've become a disturbing influence in my life, and I hardly did any work today because of you. Last night the thought of you walking away sent me into a wild panic."

"You'll have to watch those hormones, Doctor," she told him sternly. It wasn't exactly a standard romantic line, pleased he didn't see her as just another fleeting amour.

"Damn the hormones. It's you I want," he growled and gathered her into his arms.

The kiss progressed from passionate urgency to a lingering and warm embrace. He pulled away and took a deep breath.

"Phew! I didn't realize archaeology could be such hot work."

She giggled and brushed his lips with hers. "And I always thought atom smashing was the exciting part."

"We haven't tried that yet," he said candidly and she giggled again.

"Why, Dr. Faroway, I believe you're taking advantage of me."

"No, Dr. Hopking. I think I am in love with you."

She pulled back and looked into his eyes, but his face lay in shadow. "I like the sound of that," she whispered and he kissed her again.

Resting her head against his shoulder, she could hear the rumble of his heart and felt the rise and fall of his chest as he breathed. His hand brushed away a lock of hair off her face and a shudder ran through her.

"You've become somewhat of a problem for me as well, Dr. Faroway," she murmured dreamily.

"Well, I'm certainly relieved to hear *that*!"

She smiled into the night. "But you're in San Francisco and I'm in New York—"

"You can always move," he said.

She sat up and glared at him. "Just like that, eh? A typical male—"

"Down, girl. Aren't you getting ahead of yourself here? It's likely Villahermosa will keep both of us busy for quite a while. It'll take time to sift through the mountain of information that will continue to flood us, let alone work out parameters for any practical applications. Being part of the UN team hasn't hurt our reputations either."

"Such a selfish attitude from a dedicated and noble scientist," she chided him.

"Damn right, and a necessary one, I'm afraid, as you no doubt know."

"Unfortunately, I do."

Bill was right. She was making plans for a future simply too fluid. One step at a time, Dr. Hopking.

Crickets chirped nearby and her mind drifted. Hidden floodlights bathed the Palace temples and the Great Acropolis with a pale glow and she wondered what it was like to have alien beings walk through these grounds. The thought made her shudder.

"Cold?" Bill asked.

"No, just thinking, trying to picture this place with a living community, markets, priests and warriors, families—"

"And aliens?"

"Imagine it, Bill. A craft lands in the square and two aliens climb down and ask for a basket of potatoes. Seems almost ridiculous."

"And probably is. Whatever they were doing down here, I doubt very much they'd have been mixing it with the local population."

"Spoilsport! Where is your sense of grandeur?"

"Back in my lab at Livermore. When you're trying to find out what the universe is made of, now *that's* grandeur."

She hadn't thought of it that way. It was only natural Bill would see his world from the atomic to the infinite, a world that must have a fascination all its own to captivate a mind like his.

"Don't you wonder even for just a teensy bit what they were like and what they were doing here?"

"Sure I do, all the time, but I am far more fascinated by

their technology."

"You don't have any poetry in your heart, Dr. Faroway. I guess that's where we're different."

"Oh, I don't know. There are one or two other differences," he murmured and blanched, shocked to have said that. He never dared talk to Dheera like that.

She giggled and punched him on the shoulder. "You're crude!"

"Just another randy man under that polished exterior," he blurted, throwing caution to the winds.

"I'll say."

Zaminski emerged from the mess tent, his left arm draped comfortably across Kessler's shoulders. The Russian roared a booming good night and slapped the German on the back. Kessler staggered and shook his head at the lumbering figure retreating toward the accommodation huts. Lauren smiled and glanced at her wristwatch: 1:40 a.m. The green hour dots glowed steadily at her.

"I want to check something in the ship before turning in. Do you mind?"

"Like saying goodbye to the computer?"

She reached up with her free hand and brushed his face with her fingers. "You don't think I'm being silly, do you?"

"Not at all, Lauren. It's only a machine, but it does respond to you better than to any of us."

Hand in hand, they walked beside the exposed wall of Temple II and rounded the corner as the two guards crossed over. One of them nodded, but said nothing as they entered the lit chamber. Inside, Lauren paused. Tomorrow or the next day, the chamber would be empty and cold. Only ghosts from an ancient past would prowl its bare stones. With the saucer gone, what then? Will they turn this place into a shrine, a pilgrimage for UFO believers? The thought made her skin crawl as she realized she would never see Comalcalco again. It felt like a door closing on a part of her life.

She walked around the ship and climbed the steps. Pushed against the display screens, cine cameras and camcorders silently recorded the changing images. Martin's camera was taking down a translation of the alien language. She wanted a voiceprint, but that would have to wait until they were at Villahermosa where the technicians hoped to rig an audio-visual interface between the computer and a mass-storage device. In a sense, what the scientists were doing here was totally unnecessary. The activity purely a political exercise, Bill told her once, designed to placate prickly international pride. He said real work would start once they had the saucer disassembled. That might have been true, if cynical, but she didn't like the idea of seeing this magnificent machine reduced to a pile of stacked plating and circuit boards. The others may only be scratching the surface, but her language data had already caused ripples of consternation around the world, given its similarity to some Semitic root elements, contrary to all expectations that the alien language would have formed the basis of Mayan text. Just one of those mysteries she hoped to tease open after further and more exhaustive interrogation of the computer.

A thought popped into her head and her eyes widened.

"Bill! The computer said it had communication protocols. Has anyone actually tried the radio, or whatever the thing uses?"

"You mean, ask it to contact base?"

"Why not?"

"Base could be at least forty-six light-years away."

"This isn't an interstellar craft, all of you agree on that. Why would they need to communicate with Salina?"

"I can think of lots of reasons, but you mean the Moon, don't you? An interesting notion. What makes you think that after all this time the aliens are still there?"

"What you're telling me is no one tried it, right?"

"Lauren, we only gained access to the computer last night, remember? We haven't exactly been sitting on our hands."

She bit her lip and brushed his arm, suddenly contrite. "I'm sorry—"

"Should have thought of it myself," he mused and smiled. "Computer?"

"State your command, Dr. Faroway."

"Bill, should we be doing this now?" Lauren said in alarm as the possibilities flashed through her mind, all of them bad. The idea of someone actually answering was suddenly unnerving.

"They can only shoot us," he said comfortably. "Computer, do you have active communication capability?"

"Inter-system comms enabled."

"Open a channel to Moon base," he said and winked at Lauren.

"Link established with Surface Command and Control. Interrogative pending."

"Shit! Someone *is* up there. Jesus," Bill marveled. "Computer, what is Surface Command and Control?"

"Flight management system. Contact terminated by SC&C."

"Bill, I'm not sure we should have done that," Lauren said, looking concerned. "What if they come here?"

"Then we'll know, won't we?"

"I'm serious," she hissed impatiently and stomped her foot.

"Lauren, if the aliens *are* on the Moon and were hostile, don't you think we would have known about it by now? SC&C could be an automated station—"

"Then why cut contact?"

She heard a muffled clang and both of them turned toward the hatch.

"What was that?" Lauren asked.

"Someone is outside," he said.

Another clang. A few seconds later another one.

"Wait here," he said and started for the hatch as a black-suited hooded figure appeared in front of the steps. They stared at each other for a second, then the figure raised what looked like a gun, except Bill couldn't see any hole in the stubby barrel.

"Rit!" the figure said in disgust.

# Chapter Ten

Clearly exasperated the elderly electronics technician stabbed the glowing pads with a stiff finger. He looked at Terr and shook his head.

"Eighty-nine percent, that's all you're going to get."

"Mr. Dharaklin!" Terr bellowed without turning his head.

Dhar appeared a moment later in the hatchway and peered into the ABP.

"How does it look?" Terr demanded.

"There is perceptible fuzziness and a flowing ripple effect running stem to stern," Dhar said gravely. "In the dark the distortion should not be noticeable and the guards won't be looking at the chamber entrance until they cross. The ABP will be above them by then."

Terr ground his teeth. They spent a better part of four hours calibrating the local field effect and everyone was getting increasingly frustrated. The Assault Battle Penetrator wasn't designed to be stealthy. The drive's field lines were unable to maintain the necessary smooth gradients around the stumpy ends needed to prevent distortion, and no amount of fiddling and fine tuning would change that.

No operation he had ever been on turned out as planned, and this one would most definitely not be setting any records. Sariman had cooperated, albeit grudgingly, and his men worked hard to get the ABP ready. There were the inevitable glitches, which made everyone irritable and snappy, but Terr could not fault their commitment. The fact that Scholar Laraiana also saw a use for a stealthy craft, although not a GS-4, was probably a motivating factor for Sariman. As long as the thing was done, Terr didn't care who did the prodding.

The one thing he did not do was contact Anabb. The way he figured it, Anabb wanted results, not listen to his whining about problems. Given what happened, it was a thin argument to hang himself on, he admitted grudgingly. Anabb had not relieved him, and until he did so, as far as Terr was concerned, he still had a mission to execute. He didn't know whether Sariman had carried out his threat to lodge a complaint, and frankly, at this late stage, he hardly gave a damn.

"If eighty-nine percent is all we're going to get, it'll have to do," he said with more confidence than he felt. There is always a point of diminishing returns and he reached his. He nodded to the technician and slapped him on the back. "Good work, Chief, and thanks."

"No problem, sir. The ABP is a cantankerous bitch at the best of times," he growled, stood up and walked out after giving Dhar a jerky nod.

Dhar stepped into the ABP and sat down. "Sankri, have you considered that the mission has now become marginal?"

Terr gave a sour chuckle. "This mission became marginal ever since that picket cruiser opened fire on us."

"We're still going ahead?"

"I haven't heard that someone has blown up the C-32."

Dhar grinned, showing even brown teeth. He learned many things about his alien brother, and one of them was that Sankri never gave up. He would take the M-1 and blast the thing in broad daylight, if that's what it took and damn the consequences.

"Then we better get ready," Dhar said simply and stood up. "I will check the plasma charges."

"Good. I'll be in SC&C. Computer, state local time in Mexico."

"Eleven twenty-five p.m."

Terr pursed his lips. "We'll push off at two a.m. Mexico time, that's in slightly over two hours SMB time."

In SC&C, Tembel monitored the site probe's live feed. Terr

stopped behind him and touched his shoulder. The youngster jerked and looked up.

"Didn't mean to startle you," Terr said with a smile.

"Everything is quiet down there, sir," the boy said earnestly. "With the exception of the two entrance guards, only one person entered the chamber since dusk, and he has since departed. There hasn't been anyone else. Ach!"

"Good." Terr leaned forward and looked at the display plate. Two cranes were positioned near Temple I's eastern face. He could see a large tent and figures moving inside. "A party?"

"The evening meal is unusually long, sir," Tembel ventured.

"Mmm." Looking at the exposed capstones, preparations were clearly under way to move the C-32, perhaps even tomorrow. The long meal could be a celebration, then. It could also mean someone might be wandering through the chamber even at two a.m. "Report any movement in and out of the chamber. When I get there, I want to make sure it's empty."

"Ach! I won't let you down, sir!"

"I know you won't. Remember, Mister, no comms of any kind once I am in position. Clear?"

"Aye, sir."

"On mission completion, instruct the probe to take a parking orbit for retrieval."

"Already programmed."

"Good man," Terr said and patted him on the back. When he turned, Sariman stood in the open doorway.

"You're ready to proceed?" Sariman demanded.

"In two hours, sir."

"I'm told the ABP isn't one hundred percent stealthy."

"It'll do."

"I admire your enthusiasm, Mister, if not your judgment."

Terr too tired to argue and too tired of Sariman's defeatist attitude.

"It's my responsibility."

"It is," Sariman said and walked out.

*Bastard!* Terr's day had already been long and he just wanted to end it. Fifteen, twenty minutes tops, was all the mission should take if everything clicked, and he would happily take himself out of Sariman's face. Even the prospect of calling Anabb didn't faze him.

Tembel sat unmoving, rigidly watching the display plate as though nothing had happened. Terr grinned and strode toward the door.

He went to his quarters, flopped on his bed and attempted to sleep, but rest eluded him. He was simply too keyed up to rest. Nevertheless, he forced himself to stay immobile, his mind churning over the possibilities, endlessly running through mission scenarios. It was a long two hours.

Suited up in his black marauder outfit, which attracted more than one curious stare from the base personnel, he walked into the cavernous main hangar. When he approached the stubby ABP, he wasn't surprised to find Dhar already at the pilot station prepping the machine. Dhar looked him up and down and grinned.

"You would make a terrific raider, my brother."

"I'll keep that in mind if this doesn't work out," Terr said with a scowl and stepped inside. The hatch promptly slid shut behind him.

"We are in all respects ready," Dhar said easily, but there was no mistaking the automatic formality and precise movements as he carried out a systems status check.

"Let's get it done, then," Terr said, impatient to finish it.

"Computer, enable preset flight plan Mission One and open hangar doors," Dhar commanded.

In the repeater plate, the interior hangar lighting faded and two massive doors slid away from each other. Terr could see the faint orange shimmer of the entrance force field that did away with the need to laboriously depressurize the vast space. The ABP lifted, drifted out and the doors immediately closed behind them.

Terr glanced at Dhar and nodded.

"Engage full stealth mode and proceed at half boost," Dhar said. At its full boost of 1,700 talans per second the ABP could traverse the distance between the Moon and Earth is less than three minutes, a bit urgent even for Terr's taste. Six minutes at an easy half boost would do fine.

The ABP rose straight up, swung a bit, then surged toward Earth's blue crescent. Terr crossed the narrow deck and picked one of the three plasma charge casings—a dish-sized flattened sphere—from the empty seat. The charge amazingly heavy for its small size. He turned it over and peered at a small display. The indicator a solid green—inactive. He touched one of the control pads under the plate and the display turned a pulsing brown. Without hurrying, he activated the other two charges.

"Check arming circuit," he ordered and Dhar nodded.

"Armed."

"Enable five-second delayed pulse."

"Enabled."

"Ready firing sequence."

Dhar touched a pad on his console. It turned a solid brown. "Charges ready for manual trigger."

Terr nodded and sat down. The ABP smelled of oiled equipment, old pressure suits, stale sweat, fear and anxiety and death. Perfect for the job. He realized he was getting morbid when he should be focused on the mission. Forcing himself to concentrate, he ran through the sequence of placing the charges, but his mind kept drifting.

Rit!

"For a simple exercise this mission has certainly had its twists," Dhar remarked, conscious of Sankri's pensive mood.

"It's not the mission, Nightwings, it's all the add-ons," Terr said darkly and Dhar chuckled.

They were biting through the upper atmosphere when Dhar slowed their downward plunge. At 40,000 katalans the

ABP went subsonic as it steered itself for the IP. High above the horizon, a hint of smudgy yellow remained where the moon had faded. The night dark and comforting, and that was good. With reduced stealth capability the less light the better. There would be enough floodlights throughout the site.

Late campfires dotted the northern hills and the road leading to the site, otherwise everything was quiet. The temples were lit an eerie yellow and black shadows lay thick between them. The ABP barely crept as Dhar brought it into position two hundred katalans above the chamber entrance. Although the place seemed deserted, the radar dish on the van's roof faithfully sweeping the skies and a shaft of white light streamed from the van's window. The two guards at either side of the chamber wall turned and crossed over.

"Drop down when they cross again. I want to make sure they're still on an eight-minute schedule," Terr said softly and reached for the console.

"SC&C, this is Mission One. We're in position and ready to commence operations. Confirm the chamber is clear."

"Affirmative."

"Comms blackout in effect…now!"

"Acknowledged."

Terr nodded and stood up. He pulled the black mask over his head and patted the bulge in his pocket. He didn't expect to have to use the needler, but it was just one small ingredient at being prepared. He cradled two of the charges against his chest and held the remaining one in his hand.

"Right. Lights, hatch, and adjust gravity."

The interior immediately plunged into darkness. Only the steady glow of the main display plate and color-reactive pads kept the ghostly shadows at bay. The outer hatch opened, and crisp, fragrant air rushed into the cabin. After the SMB's pre-processed fumes, this was refreshing.

The minutes dragged on. At last the ABP began to sink and Terr tensed. When it reached the ground, he calmly stepped down on the stone floor and walked into the chamber. He turned his head, but the ABP had already risen.

The first part had gone well enough. He hoped that getting out would be just as easy.

He had eight minutes before Dhar dropped down. Dhar wanted him to place the charges while the ABP waited, exposed to the glare streaming from the chamber entrance and the surrounding floodlights. Although unlikely, one of the guards could get restless and look about, or start a chat with his partner and make out the slight shimmer of distorted air around the ABP. It would take perhaps ten seconds to place the charges and be out, but Terr had time and didn't want to rush it. The downside, of course, some restless fool could come in while he waited with his thumbs up his ass.

He slowly looked around the chamber. The C-32 slightly larger than a GS-4 and he admired its clean lines. A piece of outmoded junk, but it looked pretty sitting on its skids. He marveled that anyone would actually entrust his life to the crate. He took a step and stumbled as his foot caught a trailing cable, almost dropping the charges. He looked down and cursed. The floor a jungle of tangled cables attached to various parts of the hull and ran to instruments mounted on trolleys and benches. He would have broken his neck if he tried running through the mess to make the ten seconds mark.

He counted out five minutes: one Sariman, two Sarimans…then added a few more just to give the canal worm his due. With exaggerated care, he stepped over the bunched cables and reached up with one of the charges. The casing squirmed in his hand as the sensitized surface fought to mate with the hull. Even though he slid the charge against the plating, it still made a dull clang, the sound shockingly loud.

Rit!

He held his breath and waited. No one came rushing in.

He should have experimented placing the charges. It never occurred to him the damned thing would make so much bloody noise. Always the little things that scuttled a mission.

He walked a third of the way around the ship, stopped and gently pressed the charge against the hull, but the casing still made a muffled clang. There was no help for it. He hurried around and placed the last charge.

He then heard a clear female voice.

Someone was inside the ship!

How in the pits was that possible? The chamber should have been deserted. Young Tembel had goofed off and not seen someone walk into the chamber. *May the canal worm crap on his ancestors!* Standing there, he considered his options. He knew the best thing to do was get out now and wait until the occupants left before setting off the charges. What if someone discovered the charges? What if the occupant or occupants didn't leave? Damn the boy!

He dragged out his needler and made a small adjustment. If he needed to fire, the beam would interrupt all neural electrical pathways, effectively stunning whoever happened to be unlucky enough to be standing at the other end of it.

He padded around the curved hull and stopped when he saw the lowered steps. Slowly, he walked toward the hatch.

"Wait here," he heard a solid man's voice say in English as he peered inside.

He stood rooted as he looked at the man. The other young and perhaps 178 tetalans tall—Terr's height. Behind him stood a very attractive woman, her yellow-streaked brown hair piled high over her head. Her one-piece cream dress clung comfortably, revealing a supple form. Her breasts were firm and not overly large. He tore his eyes away from the female and raised the needler.

"Rit!"

Company or not, high time he withdrew from here. He motioned with the needler.

"Out, both of you," he hissed in English. "And no noise." He stepped away from the hatch to allow them to climb down.

Bill regarded the black figure. The stranger's accent sounded cultured, New England perhaps. This was no wild-eyed terrorist then. Some foreign government seeking to level the playing field? American even, judging by the other's accent? He reached for Lauren's hand and she pressed herself against him. Outside, Bill looked about, but they were alone. If this was a terrorist attack, it appeared the hooded man wasn't out to kill anyone, something he appreciated.

The clangs!

The man came here to destroy the saucer!

Unconsciously, he glanced under the curved belly of the ship, but couldn't see anything. When he looked up, the weapon was pointed at his chest.

Terr pursed his lips. The man was smart and dangerous, but he probably still thought of Terr as a native terrorist, and he wanted him to keep thinking that.

"I am not here to harm you," he said calmly, "but if you make a sound, I will not hesitate to shoot you. Do you understand?"

"I understand," Bill said woodenly. With Lauren beside him, he would be a fool to try anything and the stranger carried himself too confidently to be an amateur. The saucer wasn't worth Lauren's life, or his. He reached for her hand and gave her a reassuring squeeze.

"When I exit, wait four seconds then run out," Terr said. "You don't want to be in here after that." If the two kept their heads everything could still work out all right. Slipping the needler into his pocket, he hurried toward the entrance and stopped. He peered out and saw the welcoming gloom of the ABP's interior.

About to step inside, the comms alert beeped and his heart froze. He saw Dhar's shadowy hand flash for the pad, but it was already far too late.

\* \* \*

Long glassy swells gently rocked the heavy Chinese destroyer as it plowed through the waves at a leisurely nine knots. Phosphorescent blue-green froth creamed from its sharp bow. Bright water sparkled and hissed along the hull, only to be churned into roiling foam in the propeller wake. A band of stars stretched from horizon to horizon, impossibly bright and thick. The night completely dark, the moon having set, but the stars made the blackness seem comforting, almost friendly.

At four bells in the middle watch the officer of the deck rang for a course change. The *Kiensan* leaned its 153-meter length into the swell and headed south. He verified that the new course would not take him anywhere near the Russian heavy cruiser, checked the surface and air search radar screens, then settled himself for the two-hour-long leg that would take him to the end of his watch and sleep. Four on and eight off; it could have been worse, he thought comfortably.

At the same time, a nervous rating shook the communications officer out of his sleep. As in all navies, ratings existed to be shouted at, and it was no different in the PLA-N. Before the lieutenant could yell at him, the rating hastily explained he had an encrypted flash message from the South Sea Fleet headquarters at Zhanjiang. Grumbling, the comms officer climbed out of bed, pulled on his pants and followed the rating to the communications center. He wondered what Zhanjiang could want in the middle of the night until he remembered the time difference: only 4:00 p.m. back there.

At 2:05 a.m. the captain, still wooly from lack of sleep, read the yellow flimsy and his eyes lit up. It had two words only: dragon fire. Command had finally decided to stand up to the American imperialists. Without looking at the lieutenant, he dragged on his pants and shirt, and strode out of the cabin. On the bridge, the duty petty officer announced his presence and the deck officer quickly straightened and twitched his jacket into place.

# A Whisper from Shadow

"Sound action stations," the captain ordered, "and ask sonar to give me an update on the American 688."

The claxon blared and the 250 officers and men readied to fight the ship, most of them rudely roused from a sound sleep. This could be an exercise, but the order still had to be obeyed. The executive officer arrived on the bridge in time to hear sonar's reply.

"Comrade Captain, the 688 is approximately 4,000 meters off our port side, running at a depth of ninety meters," CIC, Combat Information Center, reported.

The 688 Los Angeles-class attack submarine mounted aging technology, but still a deadly weapons platform. The captain felt confident *Kiensan* could defeat any attack made against him. The advanced type 52C *Luhai*-class multi-role destroyer carried the latest in Russian and French technologies, including retro-engineered sensor suites acquired clandestinely from American sources. Not that he expected to be attacked. Despite American fulmination at the UN, Zhanjiang's political commissar convinced the US wouldn't dare retaliate for fear of compromising its business interests in China and risk destabilizing their precious dollar. The next few minutes would prove one of them right.

"Very well. Ring for twenty-four knots and open the range. Ready ASW countermeasures, but do not deploy. Launch the Helix and position it over the American submarine. If the 688 attempts to launch a torpedo or a Harpoon, order it to sink the American! When the Helix has acquired, prepare to fire two Yakhonts on preprogrammed bearings."

The executive officer frowned. The Russian Ka-34 Helix helicopter, armed with electric homing torpedoes, an excellent anti-submarine hunter, but he doubted its chances against the American's AA missiles launched from vertical tubes. Nevertheless, he approved the move.

He approached the captain and whispered, "Sir, shouldn't we drag a torpedo decoy just in case? If the American launches,

271

there might not be enough time to deploy."

The captain stared at him and sneered. "Are you question-ing our ability to defeat the American?" he demanded loudly. Heads turned toward them. The exec blinked and stood his ground.

"It's a standard precautionary measure, Captain."

"I'll not hear of it! Back to your station!"

Faced with a direct order the exec nodded and withdrew, thankful darkness prevented the captain from seeing his look of professional disapproval. He didn't share his captain's distain of the 688's capabilities.

The destroyer trembled under increased power and the stern dug deeper as the two gas turbines spooled up. Roiling foam frothed behind the ship. On the stern hangar deck the pilot and weapons operator ran toward the waiting Helix. Sec-onds later the twin Klimov turboshafts began to whine and the contra-rotating blades started spinning. The ground crew re-moved the restraining chocks and the Helix clattered into the night.

It took only a few minutes for the Helix to reach the 688's reported position. The helicopter went into a hover and low-ered its dipping sonar and MAD detector head. The character-istic *whoosh…whoosh* of the 688's turning blade made the weapon's operator smile as he lifted his thumb to the pilot. The pilot nodded and ordered two torpedoes spun up.

On the *Kiensan* the exec lowered the phone receiver. "Com-rade Captain, CIC reports the Helix has acquired the American submarine and it's ready to launch torpedoes."

"Very well. Fire the Yakhonts."

Stored in its pre-launch portside container ready for use, the modified SS-N-26 Yakhont's solid propellant booster ig-nited and hurled the 8.9-meter missile into the moist Pacific night. A fiery plume momentarily lit the weather decks and black billowing smoke obscured the superstructure before trail-ing in the ship's wake. Four seconds later a second missile launched from the starboard container. On liftoff the missile's wings deployed and it went into its acceleration and ascent mode, following the programmed high-low flight path. Within five seconds it reached Mach 3.6 as it climbed toward its 14,000-meter altitude cruise phase. On booster burnout the liquid propellant ramjet cut in and the missile's seeker head activated and went into target acquisition. In a straightforward supersonic ballistic trajectory against a fixed target, which this was, flight time from the *Kiensan* to Comalcalco would be approximately five-and-a-half minutes. Armed with a 250-kilogram conventional warhead, the two missiles were immune from any available countermeasure USS *Constellation* or any other American warship could bring to bear in the time available.

Nine seconds after launch, a Mark 85 SLAAM, Submarine Launched Anti Aircraft Missile, broke surface 1,600 meters east of Helix's position and bore unerringly toward the helicopter in a supersonic surge. The pilot blanched in shock when he saw the rocket exhaust, realizing he was dead. The American had fooled him and he hovered over a decoy! Before he could react, the SLAAM crashed into the exhaust nozzle and exploded, immediately igniting the onboard fuel, torpedo and depth charge weapons load, which ripped the helicopter and the two occupants to shreds. The rotor blades were blasted clear as the Helix disappeared in a ball of orange flame. A shower of glowing debris rained into a black sea.

On *Kiensan's* bridge the captain saw the fiery bloom and a few seconds later, heard the dull boom of the explosion. It appeared the political commissar had erred in his assessment. The exec suddenly turned to the captain, his face pale.

"Sonar has detected high-speed propellers! We have torpedoes in the water!" *And we aren't streaming a decoy*, the exec mumbled to himself in disgust.

"Engage air masking and ring up thirty-two knots!" the captain shouted, ignoring the exec's lack of respect. Time to redress that later, if they lived.

The engine room enunciator clanged in acknowledgment and the deck trembled beneath his feet. Even with turbines, it would take precious seconds to accelerate the 8,600-tonne ship to flank speed and he suspected a futile gesture. The torpedoes were simply too close, but he would not give in to the imperialists.

Jets of air bubbles surged into the water from emitter belts located around the underwater girth of the ship. The bubbles created an impedance between the surrounding water and the hull, reducing transmission of machinery noises. Unfortunately, the system could not protect a ship from a magnetic anomaly detector-capable torpedo, which the American Mk 48 Mod 7 ADCAP weapon was, but the captain had to try it, and they had run out of time to deploy a towed decoy. He should have listened to the exec and deployed the infernal thing before going into action. Stupid, and his error might cost them their lives.

Traveling at 64 knots the two torpedoes came in on the *Kiensan's* port side. On active homing, both units acquired the target and went into terminal phase. Four meters below the *Kiensan*, the proximity sensor detected the steel hull and the 300-kg Torpex warheads detonated within one second of each other. The blast instantly vaporized 360 cubic meters of seawater directly beneath the turbine room and sent a foamy plume over one hundred meters into the air around the stricken ship. The force of the blast initially lifted the ship clear off the surface before it smashed into the hole left by the explosion. Already weakened by the detonation, the keel instantly snapped and *Kiensan* folded in on itself with a wounded screech of torn metal.

As the deck lifted, the acceleration instantly broke both of the captain's legs and of those around him. Blinding pain shot through his spine and he screamed. Bulkheads were ripped apart and screens exploded, sending lethal shards scything through the crew. The agony of tearing metal drowned out the cries of his men. Thrown against the deck, he stared in horror as the entire forward bridge bulkhead reared over him. As the ship folded, the instrument panel crashed down and smeared him against the crumpled deck.

The twin shafts were still spinning furiously as the two halves of the ship went down, taking its crew with it.

There were no survivors.

* * *

"Who's there?" one of the guards demanded nervously and raised his rifle. "Show yourself!" At the other end of the wall his partner stared at him in surprise.

Terr didn't wait and stepped out.

The guard saw a strange black figure walk out of the chamber and immediately fired. His partner at the other end of the wall instinctively hit dirt.

The three-round burst ripped past Terr, shockingly loud. He gasped as something kicked into his left side and burned with an intensity that seared his mind. The pain flashed through him in waves and he moaned through clenched teeth. A round chipped the stone entrance above his head and whined into the night. He clamped his hand against the wound and felt warm blood trickle between his fingers. He willed his legs to move, but they refused and he stood there staring helplessly into the ABP. His side already numb and a spasm shook him. He saw Dhar stand up and clutch his side just as another burst tore the night apart. Fiery agony lanced through Terr's right thigh and the leg collapsed under him. He gave a muffled cry as broken rib ends grated against each other. Darkness took him as the stone floor slammed into him.

Bill reacted on instinct. He didn't relish the idea of some nervous soldier poking his weapon into the chamber and spraying the interior.

"Hold your fire!" he yelled and rushed for the entrance—

and skidded to a stop. Instead of darkness, he looked at a round hatchway into a dim interior of…something. He got another shock when he saw a yellow-skinned, orange-haired giant emerge out of the gloom.

Dhar paled and his chest clamped tight when he saw Sankri fall. His own side and right leg burned with fire and he knew where Sankri was shot. The thought of his brother hurt momentarily clouded his mind. Someone yelled inside the chamber and he shook off his daze. With a strangled grunt, he pushed back his pain and reached the hatch in two long strides when a figure walked into the entrance. He barely glanced at the gaping man as he scooped Sankri's prone body with one hand and pulled him inside. His hand came away bloody. He flinched when another three-round burst whined past the hatch to the sound of shouts from the camp, the crack of M-16 rifle fire painfully sharp. The situation was deteriorating rapidly.

Traveling at 2,400 feet per second, the .56" round ricocheted off the entrance stone and ripped into Lauren's right breast, tearing through the pectoral muscle and ligaments. It carried with it fragments of dress and bra material as it exited through the shoulder blade, shattering the thin bone in the process. She gasped and staggered under the impact and her arm sagged. Then the burning came, a blazing lance that cut through her shoulder. Pain exploded in her head and flung her into a bright light.

Bill felt Lauren's hand jerk. He turned and stared in shock at the blood spattered against her chest, glistening wet as it seeped down her dress. An icy vice gripped his heart at the thought of his life suddenly empty without her.

"Lauren!"

Torn in a split second of indecision, Dhar could really do only one thing. He reached with his arm and literally flung the man into the ABP. It took him an instant to gather the woman's limp form and place her on the deck. His hands and working grays were soaked with red blood.

"Lift!" he commanded and the ABP surged up. "Secure the hatch and set course for the SMB; full boost in fifteen seconds. Open a channel to SC&C," he ordered and bent over Sankri's body as the hatch cycled shut, mercifully cutting out the sounds of shouting and gunfire. He checked the pulse and found it still strong. He picked him up and laid him gently on the narrow bench that ran the length of the starboard side. Blood dripped from Sankri's leg and side onto the deck.

"Mission One!" It was Sariman. "Be advised the Chinese destroyer launched two missiles. Warhead type unknown, but could be nuclear. Clear the datum point!"

Dhar growled as the mission fell apart around him. He reached for the console and touched two pads. The interior instantly lit with harsh light and he blinked. He stared at the main display plate still focused on the site below, now rapidly falling away. A spear of blue-white light lanced from the chamber entrance. A second later the chamber ceiling dissolved as the ravening plasma sphere devoured everything. Abruptly the reaction stopped. The sphere turned dull red, then splotchy brown and disappeared.

"Computer, assume hover."

"Mission One, respond!"

Dhar wearily tapped the comms pad. "SC&C, the C-32 is destroyed, but I have critical casualties. Agent Terr and a human female."

"Mission One," Sariman's hiss unmistakable. "Are you bringing her here?"

"Affirmative."

"Negative! You are ordered—"

Dhar touched another pad and cut him off. Sariman's protests were irrelevant. The facts were simple. The female seriously wounded, perhaps fatally. If she is to live, she needed the best medical attention possible. Leaving her behind to the mercy of Comalcalco's primitive resources would mean her certain death. It wasn't even an option. Bringing the man will be harder to explain. He could have been shot by the anxious guards, Dhar told himself. A flimsy excuse, but it would have to do. Besides, judging how the human reacted, it was clear the woman meant something to him. Leaving him behind would have been emotional torture.

He bent over her and gently pushed the man away. The woman's whole upper chest was covered with blood. The man grabbed his arm, said something urgently and pointed at her. His words were gibberish and Dhar ignored him. He understood what the problem was without the man's gabbling. He grasped the man's hand, indicated that he open his palm, then firmly placed the hand over the woman's oozing wound.

His hand smeared with Lauren's warm and sticky blood, Bill looked at the alien and slowly nodded. Things had gone horribly wrong for everyone, that much was clear. The tall alien had shown compassion, or was it merely a move to remove evidence from the scene to mask the destruction of the saucer? Whatever the reason, she needed desperate attention and he hoped the alien realized that. Besides, if the alien meant to simply dump them, he needn't have bothered bringing them on board.

He leaned over Lauren's waxy face and brushed away a strand of hair. His mouth twitched with emotion and he swallowed hard to clear the lump in his throat. Her skin was cold to the touch and her pulse irregular. The pressure of his hand slowed the bleeding, but blood still oozed from the exit wound in her back. It looked bad. His eyes stung and he bit his lower lip to stop himself from crying.

Even though his insides were churning with anxiety, the scientist in him could not help looking around. He was inside a small craft, utilitarian and clearly military. The benches along the port and starboard sides were probably designed to hold a contingent of troops. So, these aliens were not as peaceful as Lauren surmised. Lauren…

"Nightwings…" Terr's strained voice jerked Dhar around

and he knelt beside the bench, wincing slightly at the pain in his side and leg. So, it was true that linked with his brother meant more than merely a merging of personalities. Something to explore with his master later. He gently pulled off the black mask and his heart tightened at the sight of Sankri's contorted face.

"Don't talk, my brother," he said softly, his voice a rumbling emotional tremble.

"The C-32—"

"Destroyed."

"That's something at least…" Terr trailed off when he saw the two humans. "Rit! Sariman will be pissed."

"I dare say."

"He mentioned missiles…" Then his eyes closed and his head slumped back. He was unconscious.

Dhar could do nothing for him, for any of them, not in the time available, and he had to do something about the missiles. He turned to the console and sat down.

"Tactical!" he commanded and the main display plate showed a full-dimensional image of the immediate area. The two missiles were only one hundred and twenty talans from Comalcalco and already in their descent phase, boring in at 1,050 katalans per second. He had about one and a half minutes to divert them.

"Computer, designate missiles as targets one and two. Climb to 4,000 katalans, extend shield grid to one talan and engage targets in sequence. Effective boost is 2,000 kps."

The Assault Battle Penetrator surged into the sky, a soundless yellow-white streak.

The ABP was a troop transport, not a weapons platform, and ramming the missiles with his shield grid was not Dhar's first choice, but the only way he knew how to stop them. If the missiles were armed with nuclear charges and they cooked off, the ABP would be vaporized, but the people at the Comalcalco site would be safe. He could not even use his aspect, as Death's lightning discharge would go right through the ABP's hull—

which wouldn't be good either. It was possible to loose Death's wrath at a distance, but he had only undergone his first trial and did not have that ability. He briefly considered blowing through the missiles ballistic trajectory, effectively nudging the weapons off their course with his shields, but the problems with that option were obvious; the weapons could re-acquire their target or crash on a populated area as they tumbled out of control.

At a combined closure rate of 3,050 kps, he made intercept less than forty talans from Comalcalco. The first missile slammed into the ABP's shield grid that sent a searing back-surge of blue arcs along the grid force lines and the warhead exploded in a flash of white brilliance. Most of the blast deflected back by the shield into an enormous plume clearly seen from the archaeological site. The ABP staggered under the impact of the blast wave and the restraining field gripped the occupants inside and kept them immobile. Pads flickered in warning on the small console. Before the ABP could recover, the second missile hit, but the warhead did not detonate. A hail of supersonic shards penetrated the shield and debris peppered the ABP's hull. The enormously tough polymer construct easily kept the stuff out. The shield grid went into cyclic fluctuation before it stabilized. The missile's fuel was a writhing yellow-orange conflagration. Burning remains fell in a cascade of glowing rain to the jungle below.

Under control again the ABP arced up and accelerated.

Muted thunder rolled over the dark landscape.

Startled when the restraining field snapped, Bill gasped as the ship lurched under a sudden impact. The sound of the explosion a long, booming crash. Despite the restraint, he winced when a second explosion sent the little ship corkscrewing. When the field released him, he glanced at the alien, but the giant stared intently at the display screen, talking softly to what he presumed was the craft's computer. He looked down at Lauren. Her breathing shallow and her face had turned deathly white. Pink foam tinged her mouth and he gently wiped it away.

About to ask where they were going, that Lauren was dying, then closed his mouth. The black-clad alien on the bench barely breathing and brown blood dripped to the deck from his side. A lot of blood smeared the deck, red and brown. He realized that more than one person here needed urgent attention.

Looming large in the display plate, the Moon obscured the stars. Under SC&C command the ABP slowed from its max boost as it approached the dark mountain range that hid the Serrll base. It stopped, then dropped swiftly. The hangar doors retracted and the ABP drifted in. The comms alert beeped.

"Mission One. You are clear to disembark."

Weary, Dhar wiped his face. "Acknowledged. Computer, adjust gravity and open the hatch."

Bill felt a small lurch and realized they had landed, but landed where? They could not have gotten very far in the few minutes of flight. The armored hatch barely slid away when an astonishing alien rushed in. Clad in a gray uniform, perhaps five-foot ten tall, fishy black eyes looked at him from horizontal slits hidden by a thin ridge of dark green scales. His first really alien-looking extraterrestrial, Bill's senses were taking a beating. The alien inclined his slightly flattened head with a precise twist of a long slender neck and knelt beside Lauren.

"What are you doing?" Bill demanded as the alien pressed a flattened silver tube against her neck and immediately motioned to two attendants who brought in a stretcher. The alien looked up and a long greenish tongue flickered from his mouth.

"Don't be alarmed," he hissed. "The woman will be safe."

"You speak English!" Relief flooded through Bill.

"Are you injured?"

"What? No, I'm fine."

"Stand back."

One of the attendants slipped on the bloody deck and muttered something. The green alien stood up as they laid Lauren on the stretcher and carried her away. Bill lunged after them, but the alien was stronger than he looked and held him back.

"She is badly wounded and you'll not help matters by getting in the way. Do you understand?"

Bill nodded and sank back on the bench, weary and drained. He felt no change in gravity when they landed. Could he be still on Earth somewhere? He shuddered and lowered his head into his hands, too distraught to think. What will they do to Lauren? What will they do to *him*!

The Karkan stepped back as his attendants took Terr away. He saw Dhar slumped against the console and gave him an anxious look.

"Are you all right?"

"I am not hurt," Dhar said.

The medic hissed and shook his head. He fiddled with another cylinder and pressed it against Dhar's shoulder.

"Something to counteract shock and reaction stimulus."

"Agent Terr—"

"His condition is serious, but he'll be fine. We'll pump him full of nanobods and the genotherapy sequencers should be able to repair the damage. It's simple tissue trauma and looks worse than it is," the Karkan said absently. Dhar recalled the blood and the pain contorting Sankri's face and he did not consider any of it simple.

"The female?"

"It's bad and she might die. We have a batch of experimental nanobods developed by Scholar Laraiana and her team a while back, which should work. The priority will be to stabilize her before we can attempt genotherapy. Given the SMB's remoteness, our facilities are more than adequate. I am hopeful."

"And him?" Dhar nodded at the man. The medic looked at the bewildered and lost figure on the bench.

"An awkward case, that. I don't really know what to do with him."

"You could give him reassurance!" Dhar snapped. "His partner might die and he is in an alien environment."

"Second Scout, I am not insensitive, you know," the medic said and his tongue flickered out.

"I apologize. I should not—"

"Forget it. I'll talk to him," the Karkan said and turned to the human. There was a rapid exchange and the man appeared to calm down. The Karkan showed him the cylinder, said something and pressed it against the man's shoulder.

The human stood up and some color returned to his face. He looked at Dhar and extended his hand.

"He wants to shake your hand," the medic said. "A local custom. It's a sign of friendship and greeting. Right now, I think it's one of thanks for bringing Lauren, the woman, with you."

Dhar wiped off some of the crusted blood and extended his hand. The human grasped it and shook it once, then smiled. Dhar nodded.

Sariman appeared in the hatchway, took in the human and Dhar's bloody working grays and hissed, his tongue flickering. The medic cleared his throat, said something to the human and led him away. Sariman placed his hands on his hips and nodded slowly.

"This operation will go down as unique in the annals of the SMB," he grated with obvious relish. "Second Scout, you have violated a number of directives and it'll be my pleasure to bring charges against you. Shielding behind the Diplomatic Branch will not help you this time." Hiss.

Dhar brought his two point-three katalan form to its full height and glared at the Karkan.

"Don't talk to me of charges...sir, or I might be tempted to bring a few charges against you."

"Me?"

"You have tried to disrupt this mission and discredit First Scout Terrllss-rr ever since we got here. First, denying us information about Earth's bistatic ladar lock capability, which cost us the GS-4. The chain of events that followed, culminating in our detention by the Russian cruiser, were inevitable. What you did now could have cost us our lives, not to mention allowing the ABP to fall into Earth's hands."

"What are you talking about?"

"Were you present in SC&C when Terr ordered that no comms of any sort be sent once we were in position?"

The Karkan lost some of his arrogance and his tongue flicked in a blur.

"He may have mentioned something to that effect."

"If there is any doubt…sir, the SC&C logs will bear me out."

"So what. Your action—"

"A direct result of a comms alert sent while we were already engaged!"

Sariman involuntarily pulled back under the booming voice, but recovered quickly.

"Not that I have to explain myself to you, Second Scout, but you needed to be warned about the missile attack!"

"Not with the mission already underway! I had sensors."

"It was my decision! You only had minutes to react. There is something else. The C-32's computer attempted to open a channel. Someone had to be in the ship to order the uplink."

"How could someone be in the ship with the chamber supposedly under constant observation? Since someone *was* inside, why weren't we warned beforehand? This is another matter that will bear close scrutiny, Master Scout. Whatever your motivation, when you sent out that comms signal the sound alerted the chamber guards. You *knew* they would retaliate. You wanted the mission to fail."

"Wild speculation."

"Perhaps. In the meantime, I'm seizing all SC&C logs pending an open inquiry."

"You don't have that authority, Mister!"

"With Agent Terr temporarily incapacitated, and I sincerely hope it *is* only temporary, I automatically became Head of Mission. You will find, Master Scout, that I have all the authority I need to send you to Cantor."

"If anyone is sent to Cantor, Mister, it will be you!" Sariman hissed. "You deliberately interfered with Earth's affairs when you destroyed the Chinese missiles!"

"I did what was necessary to prevent loss of life and I am prepared to testify accordingly before any hearing CAPFLTCOM or BueCult care to convene. You cannot have it both ways." Without a backward glance, Dhar strode out of the ABP, totally disgusted.

His brother was right. An SMB posting *was* for losers.

\* \* \*

TERRORISTS BLOW UP THE EZEKIEL SAUCER!

MEXICAN GOVERNMENT BLAMES UN FOR LOSS OF SAUCER!

CHINA TO RETALIATE FOR SINKING OF THEIR DESTROYER!

WORLD HOLDS BREATH WHILE WAR LOOMS!

"Jack Willison reporting from the CNN center in New York. KH-11 Keyhole satellites positioned over China have detected increased readiness of missile sites across the country. In response, the United States has brought its forces to Defcon-2, the highest such alert since the 1962 Cuban missile crisis. While China bitterly castigated the US for what it claims an unprovoked attack on its destroyer in international waters, the world is waiting expectantly, wondering whether this is a first step toward a full-blown nuclear exchange. Behind the scenes, the Security Council is holding frantic meetings in an effort to avert global Armageddon.

"Although the scientific community is openly lamenting the loss of the alien artifact, world leaders are secretly relieved. Technology contained inside the Comalcalco saucer may have expanded Earth's sciences, it also brought it to the brink of self-annihilation. Clearly, we're not ready to deal rationally with such a gift from the gods."

\* \* \*

"Waking up this morning, only to learn the Comalcalco saucer was purportedly destroyed by an unknown terrorist group, the Leave Earth Alone Society protesters could do nothing but pack up their tents and withdraw from the site. The Friends of Aliens took the loss less calmly, accusing the United States in destroying the priceless artifact by a black ops team. Enraged, they trashed everything remaining around the archaeological site.

"Extending his sympathy for the two missing scientists at Comalcalco, it is said that Archbishop Waller gave thanks for destruction of a dangerously destabilizing influence on the Church. Nevertheless, Vatican is still to deal with the wealth of information gained from the alien craft that forced many theologians to review the origins of Earth's major religions. This is Mark Rown for NBC news."

\* \* \*

"Circle around," the National Science Advisor ordered and craned his neck as the pilot shifted the cyclic control and the Bell 430 tilted. He had seen the photos and the video footage, but he wasn't prepared emotionally to take in the majestic grandeur of the archaeological site. Temple I towered into the still morning sky, shredding the last of the mist, which swirled about it in silent protection. Metal huts, tents and crates of stacked supplies filled most of the open space between the temple and the Great Acropolis, but did nothing to diminish the sense of history that reeked from the site. The partially restored Palace structures provided a touch of rustic, unfinished flavor to the place.

He glanced at the nearby hills and the dotted tents, smeared with writhing gray smoke from breakfast fires, and grinned sardonically. It would be a hell of a day for sightseers when they find the saucer gone. A hell of a day for everybody. For him, it started badly very early.

The helicopter came around and he peered eagerly at the vaporized remains of the saucer chamber. He could not see any scorch marks or signs of fire. Some of the still standing capstones showed part of a perfect circle burned through the stone. Much of the roof had fallen in when the metal support beams were melted. Dark shadows hid the interior and he knew without doubt the chamber was now empty.

"Okay, you can take it down now."

The pilot nodded and the helo headed for the white circle marked in the lawn below. Three waiting figures looked up as the helicopter flared into a landing. A slight bump and they were down.

A Secret Service agent opened the left door and jumped down. Vlad unclipped his seatbelt and followed him. The blades whooshed over his head to the whine of a spooling turbine. The military man saluted and offered his hand as Vlad stepped forward.

"Welcome to Comalcalco, Mr. Gorkanin," Kessler said with barely an accent.

"Thank you, Colonel."

They shook hands and Kessler turned to the civilians beside him.

"May I introduce Dr. Babich, head of the UN investigation team, and Dr. Kopan from Juarez University."

"I am pleased to meet you, Dr. Kopan," Vlad said and shook hands. "I've heard a lot about you."

"We hadn't expected President Harford's National Science Advisor to come jetting in," Kopan said lightly, but his eyes were probing. Vlad chuckled.

"Believe me, Doctor, neither did he. Manfred, how are

you?"

"I've had better days," Babich said dryly.

"Hah! Still plenty of time for things to go wrong."

"Nothing would have gone wrong if our security had been on the ball!" Kopan snapped and glared at Kessler.

Kessler's brows came together and he scowled. "If you are implying—"

"Please!" Vlad raised his arms, palms open. "Later, okay? Now, can I see the chamber?"

"This way, sir," Kessler said stiffly and strode toward Temple II.

The other scientists stood clustered near the mess tent, talking quietly as the four figures walked briskly toward the wall between Temple II and the adjoining mound. Looking at Kessler's stiff back, Vlad felt slightly sorry for the man. Not his fault, of course, but someone would have to be sacrificed, and Kessler would probably be the likely lamb. Too bad, but one career was worth it to keep the truth from getting told.

Truth, such a fickle mistress when she wasn't a bitch.

And she'd certainly been a bitch last night.

He was asleep when the call came from the Chief of Naval Operations himself. As the Administration's point man for the Comalcalco mission, it was his job to keep Harford advised. What the CNO said hadn't made his day: the saucer blown up in a commando raid and a Chinese destroyer sunk. He didn't ask how a commando team managed to penetrate the site or why the Chinese were firing at the same time. Two separate and unrelated operations? Those questions would come later. Fully awake, he had just enough time to make the 3:30 a.m. Oval Office meeting from his Georgetown apartment. Harford mainly listened during a brief and very unpleasant session, then turned livid when told about the Chinese missiles. He wanted the Chinese ambassador *now* when Vlad left to board a Gulfstream GV jet at Andrews for Villahermosa. What the *hell* were the Chinese thinking!

# A Whisper from Shadow

Vlad noted that no one stood guard along the entrance wall and gave a wry smile. At first glance, nothing suggested that anything was amiss, until he looked up. Part of the sandstone totally vaporized, but the entrance was intact, probably because the blast had vented itself through the opening. An elliptical scorch mark remained on the ground directly in line with the doorway to indicate that something had happened.

Kessler stood beside the entrance and Vlad peered in. Where the fireball had touched, the stone was vitrified, turned glassy from the intense heat. He looked up and clicked his tongue. The melted ceiling capstone edges had a slightly curved, inward-sloping polished surface. Vlad could picture all too vividly a sphere of intense radiance leaving such a trace after devouring everything in its path. Silvery metal beams sagged into the chamber, bent and deformed when the unsupported capstones tumbled down. The chamber floor littered with broken slabs, but they were unable to hide a concave outline of melted stone. Only puddles of gray metal remained to show where the saucer once stood.

"Amazing," he said in wonder.

"It wasn't nuclear, we know that," Babich said and sucked on his pipe. A cloud of white aromatic smoke swirled around his head. "We checked. No radiation."

"You wouldn't be here now if the thing was nuclear," Vlad remarked gruffly. "Your theory?"

"We think it was some kind of a forced plasma reaction device, but I couldn't tell you how you would power one. A conventional explosion powerful enough to destroy the saucer would have left debris and an enormous blast crater. The whole site would have been leveled. As you can see, the event was local. This took some very advanced technology, my friend."

"Well, it certainly wasn't the Russians, and you know what happened to the Chinese," Vlad said with a wan smile. If the saucer was destroyed by a plasma reaction, the bomb or whatever it was, didn't come from Earth.

But he knew that already.

"Dr. Faroway and Dr. Hopking—"

"They never came out of the chamber," Babich said soberly. The loss had hit everyone hard. One thing to lose the saucer, but this senseless loss of life was a tragedy. Dr. Chee took it particularly hard and understandably so. Not the man's fault, but the rest of the team avoided him, and some talked of having him withdrawn. Poor bastard.

Vlad turned to Kessler. "Last night, has anyone else entered the chamber?"

"Not that I know of, Mr. Gorkanin. Pardon me…Doctor."

Babich frowned. "Dr. Chee—"

"The Chinese metallurgist? He was inside?"

"I don't know. We were having dinner. He received a cell phone call and went out of the tent in a hurry."

"So you didn't actually see him go into the chamber?"

"No."

"I will check with the guards," Kessler said. "Is it important?"

"I don't know, probably not. Not now. Colonel, about the two guards who survived the incident, I'll want to talk to them."

"I don't see how their story will help you; firing on a black figure who disappears into thin air? Both swear they saw someone drag Drs. Faroway and Hopking out of the chamber into *something*! It doesn't make any sense."

"Perhaps, but I want to talk to them anyway."

"As you wish, sir."

"The loss of data," Kopan muttered and sighed. "Terrible. We had recorders going in there. All lost."

"Colonel…Dr. Kopan, can I have a moment alone with Dr. Babich?"

"Of course, sir." Kessler nodded stiffly and walked off. Kopan frowned, then turned and followed him.

Babich grabbed Vlad's arm and spun him around. "You know what happened here, don't you?"

"Have you talked to the two guards, Manfred?"

"Of course. But—"

"Then you also know what happened," Vlad said quietly.

Babich stared at him, then puffed furiously on his pipe. "Are you telling me this was done by aliens?" he demanded with a sweep of his hand. "Preposterous!"

"I'm not telling you anything, Manfred, but you tell me. Do *you* believe what the guards said?"

"I prefer to believe in a commando raid, that's what I prefer. The alternative would cause me to jump from a high building."

Vlad chuckled. Whatever his friend may think privately, Babich was prepared to tow the official line. After all, he had a successful career to protect, which any wild talk of aliens might put at grave risk. No fool, Babich knew how the world wagged.

"That's a very sound position to take," Vlad said approvingly and Babich brightened.

"I wouldn't mind listening to *your* speculative ramblings, Doctor," Babich said with a sly smile, confirming Vlad's suspicions.

"Okay, some speculative fantasy for you, then. Suppression of knowledge," he said simply and waited.

Babich chewed on the stem of his pipe for a while, then nodded. "Yes, it makes sense. The saucer was a mine of information, but also a dangerous and destabilizing influence. Maybe that's what the Chinese thought and were willing to risk America's wrath to remove."

"Perhaps."

Babich clamped his mouth on the pipe and grinned broadly. "But they didn't get it all."

"You mean the data we already collected? You're right, and we will have to live with that heritage."

Babich peered at him, then prodded him with the stem of his pipe. "You know more than you're telling, Vlad."

"Believe me, Manfred, it's better that way."

# Chapter Eleven

Terr smelled antiseptic and slowly opened his eyes. The ceiling glowed creamy blue and he heard a soft hum of background machinery. He felt warm and comfortable and spent a moment savoring the feeling, but it didn't last and the memories flooded back. He remembered the rifle fire and the searing pain and Dhar hovering over him. He gingerly moved his right leg. His thigh a little stiff, but otherwise the leg seemed to work fine. He also remembered a hole in his side and prodded the area with his fingers. Tender and slightly sore, but the damage was repaired. In one piece, and that was good enough.

One nice thing about recuperating, he told himself. He was not facing Sariman, and that couldn't be all bad.

Cautiously, he raised his head. Two empty utility beds lay hard against the opposite wall. Blank sensor panels hung above them. A bright green safety strip bordered a dark gray floor. An open doorway led into another part of the medical complex.

The entrance panel slid away and a Karkan medic hurried in.

"Awake, eh? Good." He stopped beside the bed and glanced at the active sensor panel above Terr's head. Apparently satisfied, he nodded to himself. "You can stop wasting valuable space and get out of that bed," he hissed.

Terr was about to tell him to shove it when Dhar came in. He broke into a huge smile.

"Nightwings!"

"About time you were stirring," Dhar said, snagged a small formchair and slid it beside the bed.

"How long have I been malingering?"

"Thirty-four hours," the Karkan said as Dhar sat down.

"You'll be somewhat stiff and sore for about three days, but you're well enough to be released and your leg needs the exercise."

"What about the female?"

"She is in isolation next to you. I was about to wake her."

"How is she?"

"The female has recovered sufficiently that I can discharge her. The nanobods will be completely absorbed within a day or so and her natural regenerative processes will complete the healing. Scholar Laraiana has been surprisingly helpful at treating her."

"Scholar Laraiana?"

"Of course, you don't know. Scholar Laraiana is a leading Captal geneticist and an authority on Earthmen," the Karkan beamed. "A privilege to work with her."

"Probably running an experiment," Terr said uncharitably. "Is the woman conscious?"

"No."

"Then she doesn't know where she is? I want to be there when you wake her."

"I don't have any objection to that, but you may want to get dressed first. For what it might be worth, Master Scout Sariman—"

"Is the least of my problems right now," Terr told him.

"—urged me to return her—both of them—to Earth as quickly as possible. However, I would advise against it. The woman needs at least a day of observation."

"Thanks for mentioning it," Terr said. "Both of them are my responsibility now."

"Don't say I didn't warn you. I'll be back in a couple of minutes," the Karkan said and walked out. The door panel clicked shut after him.

"You are well, Sankri?" Dhar asked softly and placed the palm of his hand on Terr's chest. Terr reached for the hand and clasped it with desperate emotion.

"I am well now, my brother."

"As always, my spirit glows in your shadow, Sankri."

"Thank you for getting me out of there, Nightwings."

They reveled in the peace of each other's presence. Terr cleared his throat and slid his legs out of the bed.

"What's the aftermath?"

"After the Americans sank the Chinese destroyer that fired the missiles, they went to Defcon-2 and for a while it looked like China would retaliate. They made threatening noises at the UN, but the tension has eased somewhat."

"No talk of aliens?"

"The Russians haven't said anything. Whatever the Americans may know, they're not talking either."

"Well, that's something. We may have bent the directive a bit about not revealing ourselves, but at least we haven't fractured it."

"Not completely, at any rate," was Dhar's only comment. "There is a set of working grays in the wall cabinet."

Terr grinned at him without humor. "I'm not off the hook yet, I know."

"Sankri, you should know that Sariman is under investigation for sabotaging our mission."

"The comms call?"

"Third Scout Tembel saw the two humans enter the chamber—"

"And Sariman ordered him not to report it?"

"It appears that way."

"Fool! We could all have been killed or captured."

"It looks like he will pay for his foolishness."

"Serves the canal worm right," Terr murmured and climbed off the bed.

He dressed quickly and flexed his leg. The medic was right. All it needed was exercise. He could not imagine living under Earth's primitive conditions without genotherapy or other modern medical conveniences.

The medic walked in, glanced at Terr and strode through the open doorway.

"Wait here," Terr told Dhar and hurried after the medic, wincing at the protesting muscles in his leg and side.

The intensive care room small, brightly lit, and held two beds. A display station took up one whole wall, showing a soothing beach scene: blue seas, white sands, palms and circling gulls. The woman lay on her back, the blanket just covering the swell of her breasts. Her hair made a splash of tangled gold and brown on the black pillow. The sensor panel above her alive with wiggly lines and full-dimensional graphical data. The Karkan pressed a cylinder against her neck and looked hard at the sensor panel.

"She will be awake in a few seconds," he said. "If she becomes alarmed, call me right away."

"Thanks," Terr said after the retreating figure. He pulled a formchair next to the bed, sat down and waited.

The woman gave a stifled moan, stirred and her eyes fluttered open. She looked about her with undisguised curiosity, stopping to stare at the Wall. Terr stirred and she gasped when she saw him and instinctively clutched the blanket to her chin.

"How are you feeling?" he said cautiously, hoping she wouldn't go all hysterical on him.

"Where...where am I?" she whispered, her eyes alive with interest.

"That's a bit complicated—"

"I remember being shot...You're the masked man!"

"Yes, I am," he said, surprised at her quick perceptiveness.

"Where is Bill?"

"Your partner? He is safe."

"Partner?" She looked at him and a strange expression crossed her face.

"Husband?" Terr offered.

She smiled and looked very pretty. "Bill is not my husband—"

"Ah, boyfriend."

"Yes..." she started, then trailed off as she took in the room. "This doesn't look like any hospital I know, although it smells like one," she said and her nose wrinkled. Terr grinned at her reaction, mirroring as it did his own earlier on. "That image..." she nodded at the Wall.

"You are in the Serrll Moon Base infirmary," he said carefully and watched her go pale.

"O my gosh! Then...you're not human?" she whispered, not in fear, but wonder.

"No, I am not an Earthman," he amended. She digested that for a moment.

"The ship's computer said you had a base on the Moon. Shouldn't I feel lighter or something?"

He smiled. This was one sharp lady. "We're in a controlled gravity environment."

"I see." She regarded him with wide eyes. "It's true, then."

"What is?"

"That you've been here all this time, watching us?"

"Ah, how do you feel?" he asked, sidestepping an awkward issue. She frowned, lifted the blanket and peered down. Holding the blanket to her, she sat up, moved her right shoulder and winced.

"Pain?"

"It's a little stiff," she admitted and adjusted the blanket around her. "No scars. How long have I been here? That wound must have taken weeks to heal."

"Just under three of your days," he said. "Accelerated regeneration. Our medicine—"

"Is obviously more advanced. Thank you. You probably saved my life."

Terr frowned and his face turned hard. "You'll have to thank my brother for that. He saved both of us," he said harshly and saw her flinch. "Sorry. I didn't mean to alarm you, but you must know not everything went according to plan."

"The saucer. You were sent to destroy it?"

There was no need for him to say anything. Her large brown eyes were clear and intelligent as they swept over him, answering her own questions. Then they softened and he suddenly became very much aware of her as an extremely attractive woman.

Conscious of his scrutiny, Lauren blushed.

"You speak English very well, ah…"

"Terrllss-rr," he said and grinned. "But you can call me Terr."

"I'm Lauren. Will I see your brother…Terr? I really must thank him for what he did."

He bit his lip, wondering how to tell her. "Lauren, this base is crewed by—"

"Different alien species? I figured that. Oh! You didn't want me to freak out when I see a genuine extraterrestrial, right?"

"You're very perceptive," he said at length. This Bill of hers was one lucky guy.

Dhar stood in the open doorway, his imposing form filling the entrance. He nodded and slowly walked in. Lauren gave a strangled little gasp and her knuckles turned white.

"Lauren, I want you to meet my brother Dharaklin."

Her eyes grew round in shock. "*He* is your brother?"

"It's a long story."

She cleared her throat as her eyes traveled up to Dhar's face.

"Sir, Terr tells me you were the one who saved my life. Mere words are inadequate to express my thanks."

Terr translated for her and Dhar gave a small bow.

Then she saw another figure and her lips quivered with relief.

"Bill!"

Dressed in a set of plain working grays, he hurried to her bed, bent over her and gathered her in his arms.

"Ow!" she protested and he immediately let her go.

"Sorry. Still hurts?"

"A little sore," she said, her fingers splayed across her chest.

"Oh, Lauren," he murmured. "I was so worried about you."

She turned up her face and kissed him, her eyes glistening with happy tears.

"I was in a bad way?"

"You were a mess. Wired up like a surround theater system."

She sniffed and giggled and gave him a quick hug. Then she pulled back and fondled the gray material of his tunic. It had a density that made it look heavy, but it felt light and warm.

"After I showered, I found this," he explained the uniform, then turned to Terr. "Ah, excuse me...Terr?" Bill asked diffidently. "What will happen to us? No one told me anything and you seem to be an important official..."

"Sariman had him in what amounted to isolation," Dhar said quickly and Terr frowned. He understood why it was done, but it couldn't have been comfortable for the man, and Sariman wouldn't have gone out of his way to make things easy. Locked up in an alien base, not knowing what would happen to him or Lauren, Bill must have been going quietly mad.

"You flatter me, sir—"

"Please! Just Bill."

"Nothing sinister will happen to either of you. Now that Lauren has recovered sufficiently to be moved, both of you will be returned to Earth."

"Just like that?"

"Bill, don't start believing your own fiction. No one here will harm you."

Bill wasn't so sure about that. His quarters were comfortable enough, but a guard stood outside to make sure he did not wander about. He didn't resent the security really. Having him and Lauren underfoot was probably very awkward for the aliens as well.

"And our knowledge of you and this place?"

Terr shrugged. "An unfortunate byproduct of our encounter. How you use that knowledge will be up to you."

"I guess it won't do me any good asking those million questions, then?" Bill said hopefully, wearing a rueful smile.

"I'm afraid not. You already know more than is good for you."

"You mean, more than is good for *you*!"

"You're more correct than you know."

Lauren looked concerned. "Are you in some kind of trouble for bringing us here?"

"You needed help," he said simply. Dhar shifted his feet.

"Sankri, although I did not understand what Bill said, I can guess. *Sheeva* is prepped and ready for lift. I can take them down now if you want."

"She needs observation."

"Sariman—"

"Isn't the one who is hurt. What's the local time on Earth, America?"

"Just after midnight," Dhar said at once.

"That settles it. We'll take them down in the morning their time."

"Do you feel up to it?"

"It's a short hop. What can happen?" he said and they grinned at each other. "Besides, before I fly off anywhere, I need something to eat. I'm starved."

"It's now, isn't it? You're taking us down now?" Lauren asked timidly, looking from Terr to Dhar.

"In about eight of your hours," Terr said and Bill automatically glanced at his wristwatch. "I regret I cannot give you that grand tour," Terr added. "It's best that you be returned as quickly as possible. Remember Lauren, don't exert yourself for a day or so. You still need rest. Now, are you hungry?"

Lauren suddenly became aware of a gnawing emptiness inside her.

"I'm ravenous!"

"Excellent. I will have meals brought in and leave you two alone. Feel free to eat anything and you'll find the food interesting." He walked around Lauren's bed and opened a drawer. A black ribbon choker with a single pearl lay folded neatly over a set of working grays.

"It appears your clothing didn't survive the encounter, but this did," he said and lifted the thin ribbon.

"My choker! Thank you," Lauren cooed and clipped the thing around her throat.

"There is a standard working uniform here that should suffice. Sorry, no cosmetics, I'm afraid. If you need a bathroom, I'll call an attendant to help you."

Lauren grinned impishly. "Is flushing a toilet so different?"

Terr smiled. "We wouldn't want you to have an embarrassing accident. If you need anything, touch this pad," Terr said and pointed at a pulsing brown pad below the sensor console. "If you prefer, you can get dressed and wait with Bill in his quarters. I fear you'll not be allowed to wander unescorted…"

"I wouldn't mind getting out of here—"

"I don't like hospitals either," Terr assured her and turned to Bill. "When you're settled in, use the comms pad and your meals will be brought to you. Call me if you need anything."

He gathered Dhar with his eyes and they walked out.

Lauren watched the retreating aliens, sighed and sank back against the pillows. Things were going too fast and she needed a moment to put all the pieces into place. Bill took her right hand and stroked it. She turned her head and her eyes softened.

"Love you," he whispered.

"What happens now?" she said. "When we get back, I mean."

"I don't know," he admitted. "With the saucer gone—"

"Everyone thinks we're dead."

"That will take some explaining, but you know what? I don't care. You're safe and that's all that matters. For a while there, I was going out of my mind not knowing whether you would live or not."

"I was really that bad?"

"If Dharaklin hadn't brought us here, you would have been dead."

She shuddered. She remembered the pain and the blackness, then nothing. The totality of that nothing that troubled her. If that was death, it was not like anything she'd been told. What frightened her how fragile the moment that separated life from darkness.

"Bill, they must know an awful lot about human physiology to have treated me."

"They had five thousand years or more to learn," he said seriously.

She wasn't sure she liked the sound of that. Bill patted her hand.

"Let's not worry about it. You want to get out of here?"

"Yes! Let me get dressed." When he made no move to leave, she grinned at him. "Out, thank you!" she said primly.

He shrugged, stood up, leaned over her and gave her a quick peck on the cheek.

"I'll be next door…"

Alone, Lauren smiled and snuggled back into the pillows. She still found everything so incredible. This very room was incredible. Terr…If it weren't for Bill…*Stop being a fool*, she told herself. The alien merely friendly toward a canoe-pedaling savage, but she felt a connection, or simply imagining things? Still, if the alien ever offered to take her sightseeing, she did not think she would say no.

Finally, she took a deep breath and swept back the blanket. The movement sent a painful twinge through her right shoulder and she winced. The floor looked like ceramic tile, but warm. She pulled open the bed drawer and dragged out the one-piece gray coverall. She could not see any undergarments, socks or shoes. Frowning, she opened the lower drawer: gray panties and soft brown shoes—no socks or bra. She pulled on the panties and climbed into the coverall. The thing clung to her and molded itself to support her breasts, automatically sealing itself at the front. She instinctively ran her hands down her sides, marveling at the sensuous feel of the fabric. Her hair a mess and she wanted a shower. Hopefully, she would be able to get one in Bill's quarters.

Satisfied, she walked out of the room. Bill looked her up and down and nodded.

"On you, that isn't a bad outfit."

"Come on!" she said and fisted him on the arm.

* * *

"Thunderation, boy!" Anabb bellowed. His chiseled narrow, olive face livid, and the blue-veined burn on his left cheek turned a lively blotched red; not a good sign. "A GS-4 shuttle lost and you revealed yourself against express orders not to! And to the Earth's military, no less! Then you brought two humans to the SMB. What was *not* screwed up, tell me that?"

Terr winced under the onslaught. Anabb was clearly pissed and he fervently hoped not terminally so for him.

Rit!

Anyway, what's such a big deal about herding an oiler on the Cantor run?

Standing rigidly at attention in Sariman's office, he wondered whether he was a tad optimistic about getting even that. He also managed to piss off Scholar Laraiana—again. When she found he planned to return the two humans to Earth, she overloaded all her safeties. How *dare* he interfere with her work! The humans were none of his business! There was more along those lines. He could ignore Laraiana's wrath, but Anabb's bite was something else.

"Sir, I am prepared to accept the consequences of my actions," he said stiffly. Perhaps he could ship out as a merchant pilot. The thought made him squirm.

Anabb stewed as he studied the boy. He had been livid ever since Scholar Laraiana's first vitriolic call after being picked up from Salina. The gall of the woman! Just because her father happened to be a Pro-Consul in the Sargon Dumas did not entitle her to any special treatment. Secretly, he approved of Terr's action. The boy had a mission to carry out and pandering to a bunch of deadheads wasn't part of the program. When Enllss himself called, offering gratuitous advice about political etiquette, that had burned it and he told the Commissioner to make his complaint through channels, knowing that nothing would happen. Then there were all those reports from Sariman, damning in their detail. Did Terr really use his aspect to threaten the churlish Master Scout? He would have loved to see that. Well, he wanted to find out how the boy handled bureaucrats and he certainly did that. What really sent him over the edge, Terr had not seen fit to report any of it. He knew why the boy had not called, of course. Terr didn't want his hand held, but that did not make it any easier to swallow. No respect for the due process at all, Anabb mused. He should have him shot!

Then the boy went and brought two humans to the SMB! That had really blown it with Enllss.

"I should bust Dharaklin to crewman third—"

"I bear the full responsibility—"

"You don't interrupt me!" Anabb snarled and crashed his fist against the desk. "And I should bust *you* for violating orders! I *told* you not to get discovered, for reasons that should have been obvious, but apparently not to you. Albeit it wasn't a public exposure or a different conversation we'd be having right now. As it is, it would have been better had you taken your M-1 and blasted the damned thing!"

Terr admitted the thought had not occurred to him. In hindsight, it would have caused far less grief.

"I shall keep that suggestion in mind for next time, sir," he said woodenly. What the hell, he was screwed anyway.

Anabb's face turned purple and Terr thought the old bastard would implode. Was there a twinkle of amusement in those gold-flecked brown eyes? Wishful thinking on his part.

"If you're insubordinate, boy, I'll shoot you myself!"

Terr didn't say anything and waited for the axe to fall. It was fun while it lasted. He could always go crawling, cap in hand to Enllss. The BCPA might have an opening for an ex-Fleet officer.

Anabb cleared his throat and appeared to search for something on his desk. He fought hard to keep from bursting into laughter. The boy was a scamp with no trace of respect for his superiors.

"Hrumph! At ease, son. I won't shoot you, at least not yet."

Terr relaxed a tiny bit and allowed himself a cautious exhale. It looked like his sins were not terminal after all and old Anabb may have been using him to vent some of his frustration. Whatever the reason, he wasn't about to complain.

"I know that bringing those two humans to the SMB brought the house down," Anabb went on. "Commissioner Enllss went on a rampage. I appreciate why you did it, but Captal bureaucrats are less compassionate and less forgiving." Anabb could not stop himself from grinning. "Still, it did my soul good to see those deadbeats squirm." Then his features hardened and he scowled. "Given the circumstances, I approve your action and I'll endorse your report to that effect."

Terr opened his mouth, but nothing came out. His shoulders sagged slightly with relief. He had always known bringing Bill and Lauren to the SMB could blow up in his face. Had Nightwings suffered because of that, he was ready to resign not only from the Diplomatic Branch, but from the Fleet as well. Sometimes a man has to be prepared to lay it on the line and still be able to look himself in the face.

"Thank you, sir."

"Confronting those naval warships showed your lack of judgment. You had no business being there. Nonetheless, you were on the spot and I wasn't," Anabb said grudgingly. In fact, he was pleased with the way the boy conducted himself, and also pleased that Terr made no attempt to make excuses, not that there could be any. That told him a lot. The boy had shown rare determination and resourcefulness in a difficult situation, and had not run whining for help when the mission went into a meltdown. The other things would come with experience and maturity. Despite the setbacks, it had not been a bad first effort and Enllss would eventually get over his pique. Earth may hold some significance for the BCPA, but in the larger scheme of things, the place was irrelevant. What counted, the C-32 was destroyed.

"You should know that Master Scout Sariman will be relieved and placed under open arrest. They're sending a new SMB commander from Salina. Second Scout Dharaklin did well to commandeer those logs." Always regrettable to see an officer buckle under the strain and best to weed out such individuals fast. The fact that Sariman's actions largely contributed to the subsequent chain of events weighed heavily in Terr's favor.

"I understand you were wounded."

"Still a little stiff, sir, but otherwise it's all working."

"Hah! You're ready to lift?"

"I need to return the two humans, sir."

"Very well. When you've done that, I want you on Taltair for a full debrief." Anabb studied the boy for several seconds. "A satisfactory performance, First Scout," he said gruffly and cut contact.

Terr stared at the pooling color patterns in the Wall, then grinned broadly.

*Yes!*

Relieved, he snapped his fingers. So, old Anabb really did have a heart buried somewhere under that crusty exterior.

Outside, Dhar looked anxious. No matter how correct

one's actions, it was not a guarantee that superiors would always view such actions with approval. Seeing his brother's smiling face, some of the tension went out of him.

"It went well? I heard shouting."

"We are still alive, Nightwings. What's more, Sariman's got the chop, except he doesn't know it yet. I wouldn't mind hanging around just to see his sour fish face when he gets the bad news."

"That could be a dangerous indulgence, my brother."

"Oh, well. I guess I'll simply have to live with the disappointment. Let's collect our charges and get out of here."

"We're off, then?"

"Back to Taltair for a debrief."

"I don't mind. *Sheeva* is ready."

Bill was also ready and glad to be going. They waited in the corridor while Lauren attended to last-minute women things.

Terr gave Bill a speculative look. "You were one of the scientists at the site?"

"Trying to figure out what made the thing go, yes. You wouldn't care to give me a hint or a quick layman's rundown, would you?"

"Me? I just push the buttons."

"Right."

"Bill, I'm sorry you and Lauren got caught up in my little operation—"

"I wouldn't have missed it for the world. I know why it was done…"

"But?"

Bill stared hard at the alien. "I am disappointed the Serrll thought Earth couldn't be trusted to exploit the knowledge peacefully."

Terr pursed his lips and nodded. "I don't have a simple answer for you and the complicated one would take more time than we have. But ask yourself this, Bill. What were all those warships doing off Mexico's coast?"

"*Touché*. The way you healed Lauren…" Bill said softly, afraid to voice a suspicion bubbling inside him. "Have you been experimenting on us, Mr. Terrllss-rr?"

Terr didn't say anything, but he did not break eye contact either. What could he say? The man would have to figure it out for himself.

Then the door hissed open and Lauren walked out. Her hair neatly combed and rolled up into a bun. The working grays clung to her figure and she carried herself with elegance and confidence. She smiled brightly at them, looking chipper and eager.

"Ready?"

"This way," Terr said and led the way to the cable-tube. He could feel Bill's eyes boring into his back. It took only a moment to get to the landing level. He ignored the light twinge in his leg and side as he walked to the access tube.

Bill and Lauren looked about them with wondrous enthusiasm as they entered *Sheeva's* main deck. The stylish, yet practical simplicity of its design quantum levels ahead of the Comalcalco saucer. For Lauren the awesome power of this kind of technology also somewhat overwhelming and not a little intimidating.

On the command deck, Dhar sat in the center couch and started giving last-minute flight instructions to the computer. When Lauren looked around the interior, it hardly bore any resemblance to her saucer, but she would have been astonished if it did. What she looked at was a product of more than 3,000 years of technical evolution. She glanced up at the transparent nav bubble and tugged at Bill's arm. She couldn't see much of the alien base, shrouded as it was in the shadow of towering black peaks. It was exciting just to to see out. The profusion of stars was overwhelming and her eyes skidded from one wonder to another.

Terr pointed at the right seat. "Lauren, if you please…Computer, extend right side supplementary couch,"

Terr ordered. A panel in the deck slid away and another couch pushed up. "Bill…"

Lauren sat down and almost jumped when the chair began to contour itself about her. She had forgotten.

"No seatbelts?" she asked when the seat stopped squirming.

"The ship obviously cancels out the effects of inertia," Bill murmured, "but that would mean—"

"We are cleared for lift, Sankri," Dhar said and Terr nodded.

"Computer, proceed with lift. Quarter boost, and raise primary shield grid," Dhar said. The shield won't give them full stealth capability, but they would render them immune to all electromagnetic detection.

"Lift sequence active. Confirm."

"Continue."

Lauren jumped a little when she heard the strange, hauntingly familiar voice and realized it was the ship's computer. For a fleeting moment, she imagined herself back at Comalcalco in her saucer. It brought a lump of nostalgia to her throat, all the more painful as she knew her saucer was now gone.

Only a machine, she told herself.

*Sheeva* rose, steadied and surged up. The mountains fell away and the thin blue thread of Earth appeared on the horizon. The M-1 tilted and Lauren gasped and clutched the armrests. The ship accelerated and Bill's heart raced as he watched Earth grow visibly larger. He looked at Terr.

"About three and a half of your minutes," Terr said with a smile.

"Jesus!"

Bill couldn't hear anything. No scream of engines or the rattle of plating. The glowing pads on the sloping consoles blinked occasionally, but otherwise everything was quiet. Well, he wanted to see a reactionless drive vehicle in action and he was certainly seeing one now. He had a lot to discuss with Babich and Zaminski.

"Any particular place you want to land?" Terr asked.

"The White House," Bill said promptly. Lauren glared at him, rolled her eyes and shook her head.

Terr grinned. Under different circumstances, he would have enjoyed talking to Bill. As it was, he and Dhar had already violated a raft of Bureau of Colonial and Protectorate Affairs regulations. If the BCPA wanted to discipline them, he suspected the Diplomatic Branch umbrella would probably turn out to be a leaky sieve. To hell with the bureaucrats. Dhar had done the correct thing and Terr was determined to stick by his brother through any ensuing fallout, unlikely now that Anabb had given his approval.

Earth grew large alarmingly quickly and filled the forward part of the nav bubble. The M-1 crossed the terminator and broke into dazzling sunlight, the curve of the Earth a sharp line against the black backdrop. Lauren stared in awe at the blue of the oceans, the brown landscapes and smears of green. Long streamers of brilliant clouds stretched all the way from eastern Canada down to Alabama. A breathtaking, yet fragile sight.

In seconds they were plunging through thick, gray fog. There was no sense of motion and Lauren was startled to see wooded hills and valleys shrouded in heavy gray mist. Tall spruce and birch rose around them as the ship settled. A gentle bump and they were down. It took her a moment to realize they had landed in the middle of a road.

She pushed herself out of the seat as emotions chased each other in a confused dance. Even in swirling fog, being back on Earth was like returning to her apartment after a lengthy field trip. It felt good and comforting, a point of stability. She turned to Bill and he gave her a reassuring smile.

Terr stood up and walked to the cable-tube hatch. "I hate to dump you like this and run—"

"But we might get run over by a truck, I know," Bill said.

"And the natives might not be friendly."

"Where are we?" Lauren asked, always practical.

"In the north-western part of West Virginia," Terr said simply as the hatch slid open. "As close to the White House as I could manage."

Bill and Lauren thanked Dhar again and piled into the tube.

On the main deck the landing ramp was already down. Lauren shivered as a gust of frigid air swirled around her, cutting through the thin uniform. The garment may have been satisfactory and comfortable in the controlled warmth of the Serrll's Moon base, but totally inadequate for February in West Virginia. Terr noted her discomfort, strode to the bulkhead, opened a cabinet and pulled out two bulky jackets.

"These should help."

"Thanks!" she said with feeling and pulled hers on. A winter parka about two sizes too big, she gratefully wrapped her arms about herself.

"Something we, ah, borrowed from the locals," Terr said with a smile.

Bill gave him a sidewise glance. "I see."

"Goodbye Lauren…Bill."

Lauren stared at the alien for several long seconds, a quizzical smile fixed on her face. He looked so human. Dressed in ordinary clothes, he would not excite any comment. Yet a gulf existed between them that was literally five thousand years old and hundreds of light-years wide. Alien he may be, but they still shared love and pain and compassion. Beneath the exterior superficiality, perhaps they were not all that different after all. She approached him slowly, hesitated, then gently touched his cheek.

"The Serrll must be an enchanting place," she murmured softly.

"As is Earth," Terr said.

Bill offered his hand and Terr clasped it warmly. "Don't give up on that drive."

"Earth may surprise you yet, Mr. Terrllss-rr of the Serrll Combine."

"Believe me, Bill, it already has."

Bill put his arm around Lauren's waist and together they walked down the ramp. The fog clung to them, cold and clammy. At the edge, they hesitated, stepped off the ramp and turned. The ramp swung up and the landing skids retracted. Bill felt his skin go all prickly as a charge of electricity shot through him and his hair stood on end. Lauren gave a little squeal and clamped both hands over her head to stop her hair peeling off her scalp. The ship lifted slightly and Bill felt he could just make out a faint orange shimmer surrounding the pebble hull. Then it surged up, a silent ghost quickly swallowed by the clouds. He stared hard into the spot where the ship had vanished. Thinking about the effects when it took off, he was convinced that while in the atmosphere, the alien ship employed some advanced type of electrogravitic propulsion.

He glanced at Lauren and she gave him a small smile.

"This isn't a dream, is it? We are really home?"

"Home all right, and cold."

He looked at the rising road disappearing into the mist, then down the slope. The soft ship's boots they wore were very comfortable, but he suspected not designed for hiking.

"Do you want to start walking up or down?" he asked, knowing exactly how she would vote.

"Down," she said promptly.

# Chapter Twelve

"Was he cute?" the First Lady asked with a conspiratorial twinkle in her pale blue eyes as she regarded the young woman.

Lauren grinned, remembering Terr's strong features, aquiline nose with a hint of a cleft in his chin. A determined face with character used to command. His gray, penetrating eyes captivated her. They hinted at an inner strength, a power that transcended will. It would have been very easy to fall under his spell. She could also tell Terr wasn't married. It was a feminine intuitive thing. He wasn't awkward or anything, but there was a reserve and a formality that marked an inexperienced man. With Bill…

She caught the First Lady smiling at her and blushed.

"Yes, he was cute, but I wouldn't trade him for Bill."

"My dear, there is nothing wrong with checking before you buy. It keeps the men from taking us for granted," the First Lady said comfortably and touched Lauren's shoulder in an intimate gesture. "Marriage needs to be one long courtship if it's to work best, and you always need to keep in mind that men are physical creatures and make allowances accordingly."

"We always come to that, don't we," Lauren said and her mouth drooped. The First Lady chuckled.

"We're still very crude beings, my dear. We better go down before they send the Secret Service after us."

Lauren stood up and looked critically at herself in the large vanity mirror. She and the First Lady—she could not quite bring herself to call her Heather—were almost the same height, and although the First Lady no longer a trim beauty, she was still a very striking woman. Lauren ran her hands down navy blue slacks and gravely eyed the white cashmere sweater that curled around her neck. She wore very comfortable black high-heeled pumps, and probably very expensive, she reminded herself. She was moving in a rarefied circle and felt out of place, but could learn to get used to it. Her hair washed and combed to a satisfactory luster, with one long, thick braid that tastefully covered her left breast.

It would do.

"You have poise, my dear," the First Lady said approvingly as she led them out of the bedroom.

"Thank you, but when dealing with Professor Boulcher, a club is far more useful."

The First Lady laughed. "What an adventurous life you've led. I envy you. The only thing I have ever known is politics, and even though I enjoy its successes and the trappings of power, I can tell you it can get a little trying."

Looking at the visible trappings of power around her, Lauren found that hard to believe.

They took the private elevator down from the residence, the Secret Service agent grim and watchful. Lauren very conscious of her intimidating presence, but the First Lady didn't even seem to notice her. A gilded cage, Lauren thought.

The West Wing was a bustle of hurrying, harassed people, jangling phones, loud conversations, shouting; a government in action. It all looked chaotic, but the First Lady took it in her stride. The president's personal aide stood up hastily when they appeared.

"The President is expecting you, ma'am," she said and hurried to open the door to the Oval Office.

"Thank you," the First Lady said and they walked in.

Heads turned and everyone stood up. Lauren knew all of them only as faces on TV, but meeting them like this, and in the Oval Office, a little overwhelming. She willed her heart to stop hammering.

"Dr. Hopking, I'm so glad you could join us," Harford said warmly and apparently meant it. "Please, sit down."

"Thank you, Mr. President," Lauren said a little breathlessly as Harford steered her to a chair next to him.

"You know everyone here: Dr. Garkonin, my National Science Advisor—you already spoke to him; Carl Mansky, my National Security Advisor, and of course, Morris Paddington, my Chief of Staff."

"Gentlemen…"

"Morris, pour the Doctor some coffee." Harford said, then glanced at his wife and a silent communication passed between them.

"Come and see me later, my dear," the First Lady said with a conspiratorial wink and walked out.

The atmosphere informal, Lauren soon felt at ease, although more than a little excited by her surroundings. After all, one doesn't have coffee with the president of the United States every day. Sitting on a couch opposite her, Bill gave her a reassuring smile.

"The doctors tell me you're almost fully recovered," Harford said musingly. "Remarkable. Dr. Hopking—"

"Just Lauren, sir, if you don't mind."

Harford nodded and smiled. "Of course. Bill was telling us how you two were brought back. I wish I could have shared that flight with you. It must have been an extraordinary experience."

"It almost made up for the loss of the Comalcalco saucer, sir," she said and the president smiled knowingly.

"Wearing those coverall uniforms, I imagine you received more than one curious stare waiting at that roadside diner," Morris added with a broad grin.

"Not as curious as the ones we got when the President's Marine helicopter landed on the road," she said dryly and everyone had a good chuckle.

It was all a bit overpowering, and the ride back to Washington no less intimidating. On landing, the Secret Service bustled her and Bill into the president's residence where both were given a quick, thorough checkup. Someone mentioned placing them in quarantine, and the First Lady put her foot down. If they carried any contamination from the alien base, it was far too late to do anything about it now.

"You and Dr. Faroway will be my guests today," Harford said. "I promise you there will be no grilling."

"Not much, anyway," Vlad said woodenly and everyone smiled politely.

"I need to get back to New York, Mr. President," Lauren said at once. She needed to pick up the threads for the next semester.

"Yes, your commitments at Columbia U. Bill told us. This is where I have a problem—"

"Excuse me, sir, I don't see it that way," Lauren said firmly and Morris looked at her with keen interest. This lady knew what she wanted and wasn't afraid to say so, even to a president.

"With the saucer destroyed, the UN project is effectively derailed and I cannot now pretend to have an ongoing role."

Harford took the interruption in stride. "Not quite accurate, my dear. Although it's true that with the loss of the saucer, Mexico suffered a major bargaining setback, as has the UN, but the project is far from derailed. Comalcalco has yielded a lot of useful information that will take us years to analyze. Your contribution, although not technical, has been invaluable and you're still our ranking authority on the Serrll."

Bill looked sharply at Harford and Lauren's mind whirled. *The Administration was already aware of the Serrll and the Moon base!* She saw Morris go a little pale as he glanced at the president, and her heart skipped a beat.

They did know! This was unbelievable.

"Mr. President—" Morris started after a tense pause, but Harford silenced him with a raised hand.

"The damage is done and these are perceptive people. Dr. Hopking, Dr. Faroway, the United States—"

"Mr. President! You can't do this!" Carl shouted and

jumped up.

"—government has been aware of the Serrll Combine and their base on our Moon for some time." He regarded Carl with cold disdain. "Sit down before you embarrass yourself."

Carl shot Lauren and Bill a threatening look, then bit his lip and sat down.

Lauren's head reeled. "I have always wondered why we haven't returned to the Moon since the Apollo program. Was that because of the aliens?"

Harford shifted in his seat and cleared his throat. "Lauren, I'm not going to tell either of you any lies. At the same time, I am not at liberty to tell you the truth," Harford went on unperturbed. "I can say the Serrll Combine is in the main a benevolent neighbor. In many respects, your find at Comalcalco is a huge relief to us…and to others. The realization that alien beings have visited our planet in the past did not cause mass hysteria and social dislocation as predicted by some. This encourages us to think that the next step, formal contact, may be equally benign—and beneficial. However, we also cannot forget that the Serrll is a power who could do us untold harm should they be so disposed."

Lauren understood his concern, but her experience on the Moon and how they cared for her, confirmed her firm impression of Serrll's benevolence.

"Mr. President, you have experts to advise you, but speaking as a scientist, there is a gulf of difference between a saucer that's thousands of years out of our past and the idea that we're observed, and perhaps even visited by aliens whose technology is the stuff of science fiction. May I suggest, sir, Comalcalco has given you a unique opportunity to extend a formal hand in friendship to the Serrll and trust that mankind will accept them."

Vlad nodded vigorously. "I've been telling him that."

Harford sighed and leaned toward her. "Lauren, your sentiments are to be applauded, but I'm afraid our veneer of civilized thought and behavior is alarmingly thin. There is a lot more social conditioning required before we can contemplate that next step. Formal contact with the Serrll will not be anytime soon. I only have to look at what the Chinese tried to do."

"The Chinese, sir?"

"Of course, you and Bill had no way of knowing. While the Serrll were busy extricating you and themselves out of Comalcalco, a Chinese destroyer fired two cruise missiles at the site. Both missiles detonated under mysterious circumstances some forty kilometers from the site. You can both guess how that was done. That single act by the Serrll saved a lot of lives and prevented what could have escalated into a major international confrontation. As it is, the Chinese have paid a very stiff penalty for their misguided act. You can get the details from Morris later. Much as I deplore what they have done, I would like to think I understand why it was done. This is where you come in."

"I?"

"Isn't it obvious? Although we're aware of the Serrll and have communicated with them, we know precious little about them. To them, we are very much a backward civilization. The information you obtained from the saucer, albeit it's 3,000 years old, has given us our first real glimpse into their social, political and economic structure. That and what you saw on the Moon—"

"From a hospital bed!"

"That might be, but it's more than anyone else managed to do, and you may have remembered things you're probably not even aware of. I'm not discounting the value of likely technological breakthroughs that may eventually flow on from the Comalcalco saucer, but we need to understand the Serrll a whole lot better than we do now if we ever hope to make that first formal contact a peaceful and lasting one. Your work will help us to achieve that."

Continue researching the Serrll? Lauren found the prospect irresistible. A whole new field and it would be all hers. That would certainly be worth permanent tenure to Columbia—if she hinted it was her condition for staying there. Chair of Applied Serrll Studies, it sounded good to her. She would have autonomy and the work would attract the brightest minds from every field. Martin…she needed to make sure he would be part of it. She pictured Boulcher's consternation at being eclipsed by her. A very pleasant thought and a fitting revenge.

"What did you have in mind, Mr. President?"

Harford smiled. "The thought appeals to you, good. As much as I would like to grind the Chinese into the ground, I don't have the luxury to allow myself that indulgence. There is too much at stake here for everybody. However, that doesn't mean I am prepared to let them off the hook right away. Let the bastards stew for a while. Sooner or later, though, world opinion will shift and everyone will start to feel sorry for them. Because of that, and because it's in America's interest to do so, it's vital that the UN initiative be maintained. You haven't seen the latest papers. There is already an undercurrent of international tension regarding what some see as our unfair economic and technical advantage in exploiting information gathered from the saucer. The United States undertook certain agreements, which should ease these tensions. The UN's efforts must also be seen to be working for everyone else. I don't know where the research will be based, but I want you on the team heading the social sciences," Harford said and glanced at Bill. "I am sure Livermore will spare you for a few months, Doctor; in case you two want to compare notes."

Lauren grinned, then smiled broadly. "This is blackmail, Mr. President."

"No, Dr. Hopking. It's reality."

"Okay. How are you going to explain our disappearance for four days?"

"We don't have to explain anything, Dr. Hopking," Morris

said flatly. "The media release simply stated the saucer was destroyed in a terrorist attack by an unknown party. Several extremist organizations have already claimed responsibility, which has obviously helped our cause. You and Dr. Faroway were simply reported as missing—"

"But the other team members—"

"Will keep their mouths shut," Harford said coldly. "So, you two, what will it be?"

Looking at him, Lauren understood that this man could make her and Bill disappear for real without anyone raising an eyebrow. After all, everybody already *knew* they were dead.

She was thankful America didn't work that way; at least not this administration. She glanced at Bill and knew what she would say.

# Epilogue

A cool breeze ruffled his long faded hair and Leoichan grasped the fine red llama blanket closer to his thin body. His gnarled hand trembled and his breathing labored. Gold thread woven into the blanket glinted in the afternoon's dying light. Dying like him. The prospect of death did not trouble him. He had lived a long and full life, and in the nine years since the gods returned, his people prospered again and spread into new lands in the west where Qatzeltal, the new god protector, held law. He carried out the will of the gods and was content. One last thing to be done.

Leoichan's palanquin was placed on the knoll so he could see the star nest below. The retainers stood back respectfully. His sons waited in silence. The King had sent the Oracle to attend him, the shrew not pleased at the honor done to her. The woman too interested in the trappings of her position than the exercise of her duties to the gods and the people. He was thankful he wouldn't have to deal with that problem. The High Priest and his attendants softly chanted the litanies of observance.

A coppery glow smeared the setting sun and painted the thin streamers of high cloud red. He knew this would be his last sunset. Unperturbed, Leoichan waited. The gods had promised, but would Kukll and Oryana come? It was always dangerous to presume on the will of the gods. Not that Kukll had been harsh, and the laws were just, even if the people did not always obey. He so desperately wanted to see the god again before Kukll and Oryana returned from wherever the gods came. A glint of light high in the sky brightened and he squinted. His eyes were not as they used to be, but he felt a prickle of anticipation race through him. Kukll had returned his faith.

Shrouded in a shimmering yellow cocoon the thick gray disk descended silently toward the stone landing pad of the star nest. The Oracle reluctantly began her chant. The heavenly bird grew in size, paused above the pad and extended its landing skids. The yellow light faded around the ship and steps dropped down from its side. An air chariot raced toward the waiting ship from the maintenance hangar at the edge of the landing pad. Two figures emerged from the ship and Leoichan's breath caught in his throat. There was no mistaking Kukll's red uniform and Oryana's blue coverall. The two gods climbed into the waiting air chariot and the machine sped toward the gathered crowd on the hill.

A respectful hush fell as the air chariot slowed and stopped beside Leoichan's palanquin. Kukll stepped down, cast his eyes over the assembly, then smiled as he strode to the palanquin. Everyone bowed low. Leoichan struggled to rise, but Kukll gently pushed him back.

"My lord," Leoichan husked, "it is not seemly that I lie in your presence."

"My faithful servant," Kukll said warmly. "We are past such foolishness, you and I."

Oryana stopped beside Kukll and her tender smile lit Leoichan's soul.

"My Lady…"

"Leoichan, this day you shall sleep with the gods," she said in a trembling voice.

"Then my life will have been fulfilled, goddess," he breathed. The gods were powerful, but even they could not stay the hand of Death.

What happened next shocked him. Kukll bent over him and gathered him into his arms.

"Lord!"

"Rest easy, my friend," Kukll whispered.

The Oracle and the High Priest gaped as the god carried

Leoichan to the air chariot and sat down. Oryana took the controls and the chariot turned and sped toward the star nest.

Kukll hardly felt any weight in his arms. Leoichan was a frail sack of wrinkled skin and bone with little life left in him. Kukll climbed the steps into the scoutship and placed his servant on the reclined formchair. Oryana came up behind him and sat in the command couch. The nav bubble cleared and Leoichan marveled at this wondrous vehicle. Once before, long ago, he had the privilege to sit inside a heavenly bird, but what he saw now overwhelmed him. The hatch cycled shut and he felt a change in pressure.

"It will not be long now," Kukll said beside him.

The ship hovered, then surged into the sky. Leoichan gasped when the sky lost its softness and he could see the stars.

"Lord…"

"Wait."

The stars spun and Leoichan saw the sharp curve of a blue world laid below him like a distant shore. And the world was like an island in a black lake, and the clouds were mists that painted the waters. He could almost embrace it. Was this really where his people lived? His labored breathing eased and he felt a quiet warmth steel through his body. He envied the gods their heaven. Were they here to take him there?

"Lord, I have tried to be a faithful servant."

Oryana knelt beside him and brushed his forehead. "You have been more than that," she whispered and smiled, her eyes glistening bright. "You were a friend."

"I don't mind dying then," he tried to say, but the words would not come. He stared at the blue world even as life left him.

The fires of death burned high in the temple that night.

# About the author

Stefan Vučak has written twenty-one novels, which include eight SF books in the Shadow Gods Saga. His *Cry of Eagles* won the coveted Readers' Favorite silver medal award, and his *All the Evils* was the prestigious Eric Hoffer contest finalist and Readers' Favorite silver medal winner. *Strike for Honor* won the gold medal.

Stefan leveraged a successful career in the Information Technology industry, which took him to the Middle East working on cellphone systems. Writing has been a road of discovery, helping him broaden his horizons. He also spends time as an editor and book reviewer. Stefan lives in Melbourne, Australia.

To learn more about Stefan Vučak, visit his:
Website: www.stefanvucak.com
Facebook: www.facebook.com/StefanVucakAuthor
Twitter: @stefanvucak

# More Books by Stefan Vučak

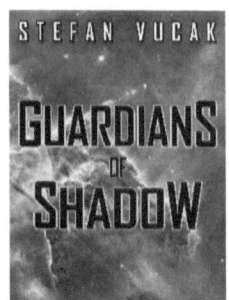